**The very idea of being intimate with
a stranger, with this stranger—**

"I hope it all fits." He thrust toward her a gray flannel gown, a chemise and a petticoat, and a pair of shoes. She clasped them to her breast, bewildered.

Once the carriage was again in motion, he tugged his shirttails from his breeches. *Oh, no.* Daphne bit into her lower lip, fixated, as he wrenched his shirt over his head. Shadows and light played on his damp skin. Daphne inhaled sharply, shocked, her mouth gone instantly dry. But she didn't look away.

She'd never seen anything like him, nothing *real* and in the flesh. He hooked his thumbs inside at the hips and—

She must have emitted some sound, because he looked up suddenly.

He flashed a grin, one that made her heart turn over inside her chest.

If her mother knew—Lord, *anything* about tonight— she'd never recover. It was just another secret of this night that she would forever be forced to keep from everyone....

ACCLAIM FOR
NEVER DESIRE A DUKE

"Dalton's Regency debut resonates with genuine feeling...
Unlike some one-note tortured heroes, Vane is sincere and
appealing. Sophia's pain is very real, and every interaction
is fraught with honest emotion. As they struggle to recapture their romance, readers will feel deep sympathy with
both characters and hope for them to find happiness."
—*Publishers Weekly* (**starred review**)

"4½ stars! The first in Dalton's One Scandalous Season
series grabs the reader's emotions in an intensely passionate love story, filled with misunderstandings, past
indiscretions, trust, and forgiveness. But, for all the intensity, this gifted storyteller also deftly lightens the mood in
a very well-written and satisfying read by adding a few
zany characters bent on mischief and mayhem."
—*RT Book Reviews*

"*Never Desire a Duke* is a terrific debut novel—it reminded me of Lisa Kleypas' most memorable novels with
a to-die-for hero and a lovely but heartbroken heroine. It's
an intensely beautiful, moving story (but it does have its
funny moments) and you won't be able to help yourself—
you'll be rooting for them to get back together."
—**EverAfter.com.au**

Never Entice an Earl

Also by Lily Dalton

Never Desire a Duke

Never Entice an Earl

LILY DALTON

FOREVER

NEW YORK   BOSTON

Forever
Hachette Book Group
237 Park Avenue
New York, NY 10017

www.HachetteBookGroup.com

Printed in the United States of America

First Edition: April 2014
10 9 8 7 6 5 4 3 2 1

OPM

Forever is an imprint of Grand Central Publishing.
The Forever name and logo are trademarks of Hachette Book Group, Inc.

The Hachette Speakers Bureau provides a wide range of authors for speaking events. To find out more, go to www.hachettespeakersbureau.com or call (866) 376-6591.

The publisher is not responsible for websites (or their content) that are not owned by the publisher.

ATTENTION CORPORATIONS AND ORGANIZATIONS:

Most Hachette Book Group books are available at quantity discounts with bulk purchase for educational, business, or sales promotional use. For information, please call or write:

Special Markets Department, Hachette Book Group
237 Park Avenue, New York, NY 10017
Telephone: 1-800-222-6747 Fax: 1-800-477-5925

For Mom and Dad,
who raised me to believe I could do anything.
I love you both!

Acknowledgments

With each new book comes the challenge to write a better book than the one before. As I endeavored to do that, there are so many people that I thanked my lucky stars for every day, and who deserve mention here.

Such as my husband, who is my real-life romantic hero and anchor every day. And my two beautiful kids, who never complain when it's hot dog night. Again. I also want to thank my writer friends who are a constant source of laughter and encouragement: Cindy Miles, Shana Galen, Sophie Jordan, Vicky Dreiling, Mary Lindsey, Kimberly Frost, Tera Lynn Childs, Nicole Flockton, Lark Howard, and all the members of WHRWA. Thank you for your friendship and your constant support.

There is also my agent, Kim Lionetti, who continues to wholeheartedly support my penchant for tormented heroes. And my editor, Michele Bidelspach, who I feel also should have her name on the front of the book for not only her perfect suggestions but all the coaxing and emotional excavating she does in bringing these characters to life. Special thank-yous also to Julie Paulauski and Megha Parekh.

Prologue

Somerset

At the first glimpse of stonework through the trees, Cormack Northmore exhaled at least *half* of the breath he'd been holding.

"There she is, as lovely as ever," he softly announced, smiling and easing away from the window. From the opposite bench, his three dark-haired traveling companions—his two mastiffs, Hugin and Munin, and his newly hired footman, Jackson—studied him, bracing themselves against the cushion as the carriage bounced and rattled over the country road.

Relieved, he rubbed a hand across his face. The gesture, combined with the perspiration that had gathered there, caused his upper lip to sting like the Devil, his skin still being tender from yesterday's visit to a London barber and his first proper English shave in months.

He added, "Bellefrost has not collapsed into a pile of rubble, as I had feared. All is well, just as I hoped it would be."

All *was* well. Of course it was!

And the disturbingly realistic nightmares he'd suffered in the five months since setting sail on his return journey from Bengal had been only that—nightmares inspired by the smothering heat and endless rise and fall of the sailing vessel as it crossed the ocean to bring him home.

Home. He was almost home. He'd been away so very long, but now excitement welled up inside him in an effervescent rush.

Again he addressed his fellow travelers. "You, more than anyone, must know how worried I've been." At that very moment the house appeared again through a break in the trees. Prideful warmth swelled within his chest. "But look there, the ancestral home still stands. I have not stayed away too long."

And yet...there was still the other half of that breath, hovering at the back of his throat.

Lord, he prayed he'd not stayed away too long.

Again, he shifted to the edge of the carriage seat, feeling as though an army of beetles marched through his veins.

"I shouldn't worry so...it's just that the most recent letters I received from my mother and father, and likewise from my sister, Miss Northmore, are months old, delayed as all letters are when one has taken residence on the far side of the earth. So much could have happened. I realize that lives change and events occur, but my family has suffered enough hardship. Certainly when I cross the threshold of Bellefrost, I will find everyone well."

But did he truly believe that? Nearly suffocated by impatience, he pushed open the window, granting entrance to a brisk northern wind, and at long last simply breathed. Hugin and Munin joined him at the window, whining and drooling. They were dogs, after all, his protectors and companions for the last six years. The conveyance rumbled down the familiar rutted road, lined on both sides by towering black pines. No matter where he had wandered, *this* had always been home.

"How I've craved that smell," he said. One formed of *earth* and *rain* and *all things rich and green*.

"It is delightful indeed, sir," said Jackson, straight shouldered and proper in his uniform. Not whining or drooling.

Cormack had taken an instant liking to the young man, and when he'd grown bored of the ride and of talking to the dogs, he'd insisted Jackson travel inside with him rather than the perch on the back of the carriage, which seemed more designed to rearrange a fellow's bones than to provide him with a comfortable means of travel. He would have invited the driver as well, but unfortunately someone had to mind the reins.

Jackson continued on, "It's been a long time since I've smelled anything but the soot and stench of London."

"I myself have always preferred the country." Cormack returned to the window and inhaled again.

But there, in the farthest reaches of his nostrils, or perhaps only in his mind, hung the stench of saltpeter, proof his experiences in Bengal had stained him to his very soul. But Bengal—and the fetid fields that he'd worked and cultivated until his soul bled—had made him rich. That was because his efforts had resulted in mountains of saltpeter, an ingredient necessary for the production of gunpowder, for which England's war machine had an unquenchable thirst.

Without question he would do it all again and suffer

those hardships just to be able to give his family the gift he was about to bestow upon them: an absolute peace of mind—and the means by which to regain possession of ancestral lands that seven centuries of Northmores had married and warred and died to keep. The very same properties his dreamer of a father had been forced to sell nearly ten years ago after a series of calamitous investments in the fanciful electric and mechanical inventions that had always so intrigued him.

"Miss Northmore, sir, will she be here to welcome you as well?"

"Unfortunately, no," he answered, remembering his sister as she'd seen him off that day, with tears in her eyes and sharp words on her tongue that he alone should bear the burden of correcting their father's mistakes. Of course, the moment Cormack had disembarked from England, she had secured employment for herself, determined to contribute. "She is a governess in the neighboring county, for a family by the name of Deavall, in charge of their three boys. According to her letters, they love to fish and climb and play mischievous tricks—which makes her a perfect companion for them, because she is adept in all of those activities as well. But they will have to make do without her now."

It would give him such pleasure to travel there tomorrow and inform her that she could give her notice. Though like him, Laura had passed beyond the first blush of youth, she was still young. With the very generous marriage settlement he could now bestow upon her, she could marry well and have the family of which she'd always dreamed. But he had not worried about Laura as much as he had his parents. His father had grown frail over the years, burdened by the toll his dreams of fancy had taken on those he loved.

But Cormack had never loved him less. How could anyone despise a dreamer? And his mother, of course, loved his father to distraction, so the elder Northmore's pain—and shame—had been hers as well. He could not wait to see them, to let them know the dark days they had endured were now over.

Cormack tugged the leather cuff of his glove. "It will only be a moment now."

All at once, Jackson jerked and sat straighter.

"Curse me for a fool!" he muttered.

He rapped his gloved knuckles on the roof.

"What is it?" Cormack asked, as the carriage slowed.

Jackson grinned. "It won't do for you to arrive sitting in a carriage in the company of your footman. We've got to give you a proper entrance."

When the conveyance slowed his manservant leapt out, leaving Cormack alone with the dogs, who did their best to follow, butting their heads at the closed door and *woof*ing in complaint. Moments later, the carriage again jostled to a halt and Jackson held the door as he descended the iron step.

"Welcome home, sir." He winked, standing with his chest puffed out.

Hugin and Munin, penned inside, whined from the window as he left them behind. With each step toward the door, happiness welled higher inside him, a bubbling, elated fountain of love and affection and memories, both joyous and painful. There had been days when he'd doubted this moment would ever come. Interestingly, a horse and wagon already occupied the drive, likely only the vicar, come round for his obligatory monthly visit. The house had thronged with visitors once, but everything had changed with the collapse of their fortune. Invitations from the local landed gentry had become rare, and social callers had simply ceased to call.

Soon all that would change. While today the gardens were overgrown and fractured slate shingles marred the expanse of the roof, tomorrow he would hire men from the village to undertake all the necessary repairs, and of course a full staff to tend to the house, much of which had simply been closed off in recent years and gone unused. In no time, Bellefrost would be returned to every bit of her former splendor—*splendor* being a relative term, of course, as the Northmore estate could truly only be considered modestly splendorous when compared to the great country estates of the titled wealthy. Such as the home of his father's second cousin the Marquess Champdeer, who in the Northmores' time of need had refused them all assistance and taken every opportunity since to chide them over the loss of their fortune and lands.

On the top step, Cormack took a moment to pause and glance over his shoulder.

Perhaps he wasn't a nobleman like Champdeer—but by God, he looked like one. He could not imagine that under any circumstances the Almighty would consider the pride he felt in this moment a sin. In London he'd chosen every glorious, ostentatious detail with care, from his boots to his coat and hat, to his magnificent equipage, intending to convey his wonderful surprise without words. Piled high on top of the vehicle were chests and boxes, packed with luxuries brought with him from Bengal and Bond Street. Perhaps even now, his father looked out from the window of his study and wondered what illustrious visitor paid him a call.

With those fine thoughts foremost in his mind, he rapped on the door and waited . . . yet his knock brought no answer.

Anxiety tripped along his spine, but no . . . he felt certain that their elderly butler, old Jessup, who had remained with the family even after their decline into poverty, had simply not heard the knock. Perhaps even time had claimed the old fellow, a sad but very real possibility.

After the third attempt, Cormack opened the door himself and peered into the darkness of an unlit house with all its curtains drawn. The scent of damp and soot met his nostrils, the result of chimneys and carpets and plaster gone too long without the daily attentions of a skilled staff. For a moment he feared the place had been abandoned. But then, from out of the darkness shambled a familiar figure.

"Jessup!" Cormack laughed, immensely relieved, and strode forward to greet the old man.

Jessup wore a rumpled suit of clothes and an off-center cravat. Wiry gray hair encircled his bald pate. He froze upon seeing Cormack, his gaze rheumy and wet behind rectangular spectacles.

"Oh, sir." He lifted shaking hands toward Cormack, and then turned toward the interior of the house, gesturing. "You must hurry. The doctor says there isn't much time."

It took a moment for the words to filter through, and as they did, the smile faded from Cormack's lips. *The doctor? Not much time?*

His father.

Everything inside him, every nerve and muscle and cell, seized in instantaneous grief. Let his father be alive and lucid. Let there be enough time, at least, to tell him he had done as he had promised, that they could at last buy the family lands back from their neighbor, Sir Snaith, and that the good name and the pride of the Northmore family had been restored.

He rushed past Jessup, his heart already half-consumed by grief.

"Laura has come home to be with my mother?" he asked of the old man as he passed. He would not want his mother to have been alone at a time like this.

Jessup nodded, his lips turned downward in sadness. "Upstairs."

On the landing Cormack gripped the banister and launched himself up, two at a time, and traveled the dark corridor until he arrived at the doors of his father's room. He pushed inside, expecting to see Laura there beside their father's bed, his mother and the physician—

But the room was dark and empty, and the bed neatly made.

"No, sir," said Jessup, who lumbered behind him, breath wheezing from his lips. He pointed down the hall.

Down the hall to—

Realization trickled like shattered ice along Cormack's spine.

In that moment, Jessup appeared to age another ten years, as his mouth sagged and his shoulders slumped. "I thought you understood, that you must have heard some-how—"

No, God, please. No.

As if bound by a terrible dream, he continued to the end of the hall, to Laura's room, across the corridor's thread-bare carpet from the one he had occupied as a boy. There, instead of his sister's familiar lilac scent, the sharp tincture of camphor weighted the air.

At the door there stood a thin, kind-eyed woman dressed in the apron and cap of a nurse. Her gaze met his, wide with regret, and then she blinked and looked away. Inside, two small lamps provided light. Dr. Graham, who had tended them when they were children, stared out the window, arms crossed over his chest. Cormack's mother sat in a chair beside the bed, in a dark gown, her eyes closed and her hands clasped, whispering prayers. In the six years since he had last seen her, her hair had turned from brown to completely gray. His father stood beside her, narrow and gaunt and impossibly old, his hand on his wife's shoulder.

Laura lay in the shadows of her curtained bed, small and thin beneath a neatly turned blanket, her face turned to the wall. Her long, brunette hair streamed across the pillow, so much darker than his own.

"Laura?" He'd intended to speak in a tone of reassurance, but his voice broke under the weight of his emotion.

His sister did not turn her head—she did not move—but his father jerked toward him and his mother stood, her Bible thunking to the floor.

"*Cormack*," they cried, together all at once, and rushed toward him.

He pressed a kiss to each of their faces, and glanced into their stricken eyes, but broke free of their embrace. Somehow he forced one foot in front of the other, over the dark green carpet. His heart pounded so hard that he could scarcely breathe. He wanted nothing more than to see Laura's smile and to hear her voice, the one he'd heard so clearly in his mind when reading her letters for the past six years, always charming and convivial, so like her. Yet at the same time, his heart demanded that he turn and run out of this room and out of this house, because seeing her would make the tragedy real.

The doctor says there isn't much time.

Most certainly he had misunderstood. Laura was too young, and too healthy. Always the picture of springtime and life. Laura *wasn't* going to die—he wouldn't allow it.

He rounded the bed, and for one confused moment didn't recognize the woman lying there. Though similar of appearance, here unquestionably lay an imposter, with bloodless lips and dark hollows beneath her eyes and cheeks. But in the same moment his mind acknowledged the truth his heart did not wish to believe.

"Laura?" He leaned over her, taking her limp hands in his. "It is Cormack. I've come home."

Her eyes fluttered, and she whispered, *"Mack."*

Her countenance blurred, because now he saw her through tears. "What has happened to you, my darling? How can I make you better?"

His father made a sound of wordless grief. His mother sobbed quietly. Because, he realized, nothing could be done.

He'd never felt so helpless. The hardships of the past six years...all the finery parked outside the house...it all seemed so stupid and pointless now. He should never have left. He should have stayed here, and kept everything together, kept everyone safe.

Laura's lips moved, producing a whisper of a sound. She said something, a word or a name, he could not make out.

"Sweetheart, what did you say?" He lowered himself closer, nearer to her face.

"For...*Michael*." The linen at her throat rose and fell. Tears beaded against her lower lashes.

He sensed metal pressed against his palm, and he glanced down to see something gold and circular clenched within Laura's hand, which with a sigh, she released into his. A medallion he had never seen before, with a blank-eyed Medusa embossed at its center.

"Laura, did you say 'Michael'? Who is Michael?"

But she only closed her eyes and her breathing slowed.

"Oh, Cormack—" his mother whispered, clutching a hand to her mouth.

His father closed his eyes and bent his head.

Cormack looked to his parents, and then to the physician, but no one said anything.

"What has happened to her?" he demanded in sudden desperation. "Would someone please explain?"

Beside him, Dr. Graham spoke quietly, offering a clinical recitation of words that included *perforation* and *toxic* and *peritonitis*.

His mind could not process them, nor assign them any true meaning. Why did Dr. Graham not look into his eyes?

"She shouldn't have waited so long to come to us," choked his mother. "We would never have turned her away."

His father grasped her shoulders, pulling her into an embrace. "She wanted to protect us."

"Protect you from what? Her...illness?" Cormack stared at his sister.

"No, my dear boy." His mother stared at him through swollen eyes. "From—from—" Her voice broke into a sob.

His father pressed a hand to his eyes, and whispered, "The scandal."

"Scandal?" Cormack repeated. "What sort of scandal?"

The doctor straightened from where he'd bent over

Laura, his features grimmer even than before. "I'm sorry. I'm afraid she's gone."

Cormack stared at the man's lips, not believing. Laura, gone? She couldn't be.

"Laura?" he demanded, taking hold of her hands.

Just then a sound came from somewhere in the house, a wailing cry that filled the room and chilled his blood and made him want to cover his ears. The nurse disappeared from the doorway to rush down the corridor, but the sound only continued, increasing in intensity and volume until he feared he could bear it no longer.

That sound. What sort of creature made such a sound?

But then, Cormack realized...

He knew.

Chapter One

London, in April
Two years later

I think it all sounds perfectly horrid," Daphne Beving-ton declared, glancing toward the door of the conservatory to be certain that no one had overheard any part of her and her two sisters' conversation—most especially their mother, Lady Harwick, who would no doubt be horrified by the scandalous topic of discussion.

Only when she'd confirmed they remained unobserved did she look back to her older sister, Sophia, the Duchess of Claxton, and urge with a sly smile, "But don't let that stop you from telling us more."

Clarissa, the youngest of them, bit into the corner of her bottom lip and toyed with a tendril of her hair. "It also sounds vexingly strenuous. And *sweaty*. Is it . . . very sweaty?"

Their rattan chairs creaked in unison as they both leaned forward, eager for whatever bit of forbidden knowledge Sophia would share next. In a large gilt cage in the corner, two lovebirds fussed and flitted about.

Sophia laughed, her eyes sparkling. "Sweaty. Hmm, well, it certainly can be." She took after their dark-haired mother, while Daphne and Clarissa were both sunshine-and-fair like their father, the late viscount. Sophia had married the Duke of Claxton two summers ago. "But only when it's especially good."

The three of them fell into another round of stifled giggles. They could have shut the door, but knew from collective experience that nothing would draw their mother's suspicion more quickly than that. They sat around a narrow table, surrounded by lists and envelopes and various tea accoutrements, addressing engraved invitations to Daphne's debut ball, to be held in two weeks' time.

Utterly flustered, Daphne scrutinized her portion of the list. The *N*s. Wasn't that where she'd left off? She attempted to compare the names on her list against those she'd already written out, to be certain no one had been omitted, but her mind couldn't seem to make sense of things. Sophia's wicked revelations had scrambled her thoughts!

"No wonder mothers wait until the morning before the wedding to have *the talk*," Clarissa said, with a dramatic wave of her ostrich quill. Yesterday, while out shopping on Bond Street, they'd each purchased one, dyed in a luxurious shade of emerald, peacock, and, in Clarissa's instance, scarlet, certain such decadent writing implements would make the dreaded task of writing five hundred invitations pass all the more quickly. "If we all realized our fate, none of us would ever agree to a season. Daphne, can you imagine granting such liberties to your Lord Rackmorton—"

Daphne grimaced at the mention of the named gentleman, who of late always presented himself at her side and remained there as if he owned her, glowering at any other man who approached. He had sent her roses the day before, and the day before that, which made her exceedingly uncomfortable despite her mother's assurances that she would receive flowers from many gentlemen this season.

"He is not *my* Lord Rackmorton." She rocked the blotter across the envelope she'd just addressed. "I have not encouraged him in the least, and do not intend to do so."

"Good, because I don't like him," said Sophia, placing another envelope on the stack, flap open. On Friday, two of the footmen would finish them all with the earl's distinctive green wax seal. "Not one little bit. He has cold eyes, and I swear I caught him staring at your bosoms more than once."

"I thought I was the only one who noticed," Clarissa sniffed. "I also overheard him being rather cruel to one of Lord Bignall's footmen at the end of the evening when his hat and coat were returned. Can you believe he accused him of holding the hat too tightly and smudging its brim? Why, he threatened to speak to Bignall and have the poor fellow dismissed, and I do believe he would have followed through, except...well, let's just say that Daphne entered the foyer, and that the footman has her bosoms, and the distraction they provided, to thank for his continued employment."

Daphne sighed heavily. "I just *knew* he was a cretin."

For any young woman tasked with finding a match, the challenge of distinguishing a potential husband from a terrible mistake could be disconcerting. What a relief she had no intention of ever marrying.

She'd even gone so far as to officially inform her family,

because everyone knew the London season was above all a marriage mart, and her conscience wouldn't allow her to proceed under false pretenses. Her grandfather and mother had told her not to be rash and to keep her mind open to possibilities—and most of all, to enjoy her debut season. Her sisters just pretended as if she'd never said the words, and they looked amused whenever she reinforced her decision.

None of them had taken her seriously, of course, and they thought she was just being skittish about standing upon the precipice of womanhood. But eventually they *would* come to accept the finality of her decision, the same way she had. They just needed time to understand the person she'd become. Not wanting to hurt their feelings or worry them, she'd done as they encouraged her to do—and yes, she'd gotten caught up in the excitement, which truly made her very happy, because in the end how could she disappoint Clarissa?

Since their days in the nursery, they had dreamed of a season together and delightedly planned every last detail a thousand times over. It would break her sister's heart if they didn't partake in all the festivities together. Not only that, but Lady Margaretta had privately begged for Daphne's assistance in watching over the wildly romantic Clarissa, who she feared would lose her heart to the first determined scoundrel who paid her court. London abounded with them, men consumed with personal ambition—Rackmorton being a prime example, more eager to wed to increase his wealth and political connections than for any care of a young woman's heart. But Clarissa saw right through him, which gave Daphne renewed hope for her sister's future.

Sophia reached for another card. "Clarissa and I weren't the only ones who noticed Lord Rackmorton ogling you, Daphne. Claxton was prepared to call His Lordship out over it last night, but I calmed him, saying any uproar would only embarrass you, rather than the culprit. I hope I wasn't wrong to intervene."

"No, you weren't. I'd have told His Grace the same." Daphne sighed, still pleased to hear of the duke's concern. "Claxton is such a dear."

Indeed, Claxton treated their sister like a queen, and spoiled her and Clarissa with the sweetest of brotherly affections. To think they'd all been two seconds from murdering him just last year. Which made the whole subject of men even more confusing, because if Claxton had undergone such a transformation, couldn't others? Still, she didn't believe Lord Rackmorton was at all salvageable. She certainly wouldn't choose him for Clarissa.

"Claxton is indeed a dear," Clarissa agreed. "But Lord Rackmorton is a toad. And yet by the opinion makers of the *ton* he is considered to be a highly prized catch. I think we all know why." Her eyes narrowed in discernment.

"He *is* very rich," murmured Sophia, dipping her blue quill into the indigo. "And connected."

"Handsome is as handsome *has*," Daphne declared wryly.

The youngest Bevington *harrumphed*. "How many times have we heard that ridiculous statement, as if all that matters is a man's title and fortune?" She chuckled. "Those awful Aimsley sisters are clearly in agreement. Every time Lord Rackmorton speaks to you, Daphne, they both turn crocodile green and grow sharp pointy teeth to match. But do you think they would want him so badly if they knew about the rest?"

Daphne lifted her teacup. "All young ladies certainly understand that intimacies will be expected when they marry."

The thought of being touched by Rackmorton in the way Sophia had described just moments ago made her queasy.

Clarissa poked her sleeve with the fluffy end of her quill. "But no one talks about the details, and that might make quite a bit of difference to some if they knew beforehand what to expect. Why, it's wrong for us to be kept in the dark. If not for Sophia thinking it proper to share with us, we'd have no idea of the wild passions that may very well ensue during those private times...the heat and nakedness, and all the touching and squeezing and the...the..."

Her mouth worked to produce another word.

"Turgidity?" Sophia calmly supplied, her green eyes bright with mischief. She, too, glanced toward the door.

"Tur—tur—GIDity!" Daphne sputtered, half-choking.

Her sisters must have conjured much the same images, because their faces contorted with mirth.

"Yes! The *turgidity*!" exclaimed Clarissa, the flush on her cheeks darkening from pink to scarlet. "Why, I had no idea."

"I'm still trying to comprehend that particular phenomenon," Daphne blurted. She had seen nude male statues, of course, but none that depicted such an inflamed state.

Clarissa gasped for breath. "If it's true that male bodies transform so bizarrely—"

"Oh, it's true!" Sophia interjected, eyebrows raised.

"Well, then, it's no wonder they don't tell us anything more." Clarissa hovered on the edge of hilarity, lips trembling and eyes watering. "Why, if word got out, there would be anarchy in the drawing rooms of Mayfair and Belgravia." She threw her arms wide.

At the thought of London's well-bred debutante population unanimously declaring revolt, Daphne's throat closed on another sudden rush of laughter. She coughed, and coughed again, before reaching for her teacup, which she lifted to her lips.

Sophia leaned forward in her chair, her countenance aglow. "It would be the end of civilization as we know it. Can you imagine? The streets would be jammed with curricles full of young ladies fleeing town for the safety and seclusion of the country, never to return for another assembly or musicale or ball."

At the idea of scores of young ladies vacating London in a wild jumble of pastel ribbons and flowered hats, Daphne gave a little yelp. Only she'd just taken that sip—

Everything *stung*, from her nose to her brain.

"Ow! I think tea came out my nose!" She planted her teacup onto its saucer, where it clattered.

"It did," Sophia gasped, nearly sobbing. "I saw it, you spurted. Watch out, the invitations!"

She thrust a napkin at her, which Daphne seized to her nose.

They all laughed until they could laugh no more.

Clarissa collapsed back against the cushioned rattan headrest. "Sophia, now that you've shared these secrets from the marital boudoir, how will we ever be able to look our suitors in the eye?"

"All I intended was a nice sisterly talk." Sophia dabbed

tears of laughter from her eyes. "How did things turn so...so...so prurient? It's because the two of you urged me on, and coaxed me into saying things I ought never to have said."

"Such as the detail about you actually enjoying it?" Daphne gave her sister a wicked wink.

"Yes!" the duchess exclaimed, wide-eyed. "*That*. I should never have told you." She pressed both hands to her cheeks.

"Claxton, that rascal, has turned you into a wanton." Daphne sighed, then added in a quiet voice, "I can't imagine ever actually *wanting* it to happen."

Yet her sister appeared deliriously happy. What would it be like to wake up each day in love with one's husband? Daphne found a number of male acquaintances attractive and interesting, but no one made her feel warm and jittery and anticipatory inside. No one inspired dreams of forever. *All for the best*, she thought. Not everyone was meant to experience a grand love affair, or else such love affairs wouldn't be grand at all, but common.

"Oh, but you will," assured Sophia, once again proving she did not accept Daphne's self-recusal from the state of marriage. But...how could Daphne be angry when she knew Sophia only wished for her happiness?

With a blissful sigh, Sophia eased back in her chair, looking drowsy and flush cheeked. She rested her hand on the barely visible swell of her stomach. Prurient? No, not prurient at all, because as a result of all the marital love and passion described by Sophia, in three months there would be a sweet new baby for them all to adore and spoil. "But as I said, only if you marry someone that you respect and love—"

Daphne wouldn't, though. She didn't intend to ever fall in love. To one day lose a beloved spouse or a cherished child? Thank you very much, but no. She would not accept an invitation to that painful future. She had lost quite enough loved ones in her life already with the death of her brother at sea, and then her father two years later to an equine accident...one that should never have happened. Instead she would devote herself completely to her widowed mother and her elderly grandfather, for as long as life allowed, and become a favorite aunt to her sisters' children. Truly, she wanted nothing more.

"Of course," Sophia concluded. "It also helps to find whomever you marry to be immensely attractive."

"We can't all marry someone as handsome as His Grace," said Clarissa, but her eyes were full of hope that she would.

Their elder sister shook her head, her expression earnest. "I didn't say 'handsome.' I said 'attractive,' which means something very different for all of us. You'll see. You will. That's what I've been trying to tell you. Wait for something special to happen, because it will. And it's worth it." Sophia smiled and exhaled. "Oh, my dear sisters, is it ever so worth it."

"I'm very happy for you." Daphne reached for her sister's hand and squeezed. "That you and Claxton worked through your difficulties."

At that moment, their mother, Margaretta, Lady Harwick, appeared in the archway of the conservatory door, dressed in a meadow-green morning dress. Her eyes widened in dismay. "Daphne and Clarissa, why are you still here when I told you to watch the time? I know each of you has a perfectly accurate timepiece, because Aunt

Vivian gave them to you as gifts for your last birthdays. Up, up! We leave for Lady Buckinghamshire's in one hour."

Clarissa's shoulders slumped. "Can't we miss just one party, Mother? There will only be the same people there who we saw yesterday...and the day before."

Daphne knew the real reason why Clarissa wasn't interested in attending. The night before, a certain Mr. Christopher Donelan had informed her that he had other obligations and would not be in attendance. The handsome and well-connected Mr. Donelan was Clarissa's latest fascination—since Tuesday evening, to be precise. Before then she'd been completely enamored of the dashing Captain Musgrave, who on Tuesday afternoon had sadly lost her love when he'd bent to kiss her gloved hand with an unfortunate glob of clotted cream nestled in his tawny mustache.

Daphne had witnessed the whole tragic incident. It didn't matter that the poor fellow hadn't realized his unintended faux pas. By then it was too late. The moment Musgrave's back was turned, Clarissa had discreetly pulled a change of gloves from her beaded reticule, and after brief soliloquy of regret shared only with Daphne, released him from her heart.

They could be friends. Of course they could. Always! But anything more was now impossible.

While her sister was exceedingly romantic, she also had highly idealized expectations of what an amour should be. Unfortunately for Captain Musgrave, when he had smeared Clarissa's glove with the remnants of his tea plate, he had disqualified himself from that category forever. It wasn't that Clarissa was shallow, not at all. Quite the opposite. It was as if she felt so intensely and too quickly, hoping to find true love, that the slightest crack in the mirror of perfection could shatter her perceptions completely. It was why their mother, and Daphne as well, feared that the wrong man could win her quickly and later, when it was too late to turn back the clock, break her heart.

But in this moment Clarissa did speak the truth. At Lady Buckinghamshire's Venetian breakfast—which of course wasn't to be a breakfast at all, but an afternoon party—they would see all the same people they had seen the day before. Thus far the season had been a blur of activity, and wouldn't it be nice to spend an afternoon at home, and to be done with the invitations, once and for all?

Hoping to support Clarissa's cause, Daphne added, "And Sophia and Claxton have only just returned from Belgium. We've barely visited with her, with all the coming and going."

Margaretta tilted her head and spoke with gentle authority. "Of course you can't miss the party. Lady Buckinghamshire has taken a special interest in seeing the both of you successfully matched and wed, which I don't have to tell either of you is quite an honor."

Daphne exhaled, biting her tongue, for this was just another indication no one took her declaration never to marry seriously.

A potted red amaryllis stood on a small three-footed table beside her. Lady Margaretta plucked off a wilted bloom and dropped it into a rubbish receptacle near her feet. "It would be ill-mannered to miss her breakfast. It's all she's talked about for weeks. Sophia, you will stay here and recover from your travels. Mother's orders."

"And husband's orders," said a male voice behind her.

Claxton appeared, dwarfing their delicate mother. He had spent the morning with their grandfather, escorting Wolverton to breakfast with Lord Liverpool and elsewhere about town. Dark-haired and tall, his cool blue gaze found his wife and, in an instant, warmed with adoration. Just like that, a snap of electricity came into the air. The heat of their attraction took Daphne's breath away.

"As if you give me orders," Sophia retorted softly, yet she reached for him.

The duke strode past them to take her hand. Bending low, he pressed a kiss to her lips.

"I shall delight in continuing to try," he murmured in an intimate tone.

Clarissa sighed audibly, her attention fixed on the couple. Only then did Daphne realize she, too, stared, enraptured.

Biting her lower lip, she glanced downward to the invitation list, a blur of paper and ink. It wouldn't do to pine for a similar passion when she'd already resolved not to have it.

"Out now, the both of you," the viscountess ordered suddenly, a telling blush on her cheeks. "There is no time for delay. I will see you in the foyer in one hour. Don't forget your parasols."

Daphne accompanied Clarissa up the marble staircase, where they separated to go to their own rooms. She couldn't wait to share all the *turgid* details with Kate—

Oh, fig! Kate wasn't in residence today!

Kate Fickett, her lady's maid, and truly, her dearest friend in the world who wasn't a sister and obligated to love her. For the last three years, Kate had awakened her with breakfast every morning, except for her day off, which was Monday. Only this morning, Hannah the upstairs maid had awakened Daphne, saying Kate hadn't slept in her bed the night before.

She'd told herself not to worry, that Kate had likely stayed another night to assist with all the work at the Fickett family's new haberdashery shop. After all, with the season in full swing, the store would be teeming with customers and orders and bespoke work to be done.

Still, Daphne did worry and would continue to do so until she knew all was well.

She found her door ajar and stepped inside to hear the rustle of brocade as the draperies were drawn back from her window.

"There you are, Miss Bevington. I was about to come for you." A pretty oval face, made even prettier by a sprinkle of freckles across the nose, peered back at her.

Kate, her auburn-haired lady's maid, pulled back the remainder of the curtain.

"Kate." Relief bubbled up inside Daphne. "You're here. I was worried about you."

"Just a bit of trouble at the shop, but it's all resolved now." She set off to bustle about Daphne's gold-and-cream-papered room, which her grandfather had commissioned to be redecorated in honor of her debut season. He'd done the same for Clarissa, who of course had chosen her favorite color, pink.

Oddly, Kate didn't look her in the eye, and her voice seemed artificially light in tone. Daphne knew Kate. Something wasn't right. Intuition told Daphne that whatever sort of trouble there had been at the shop, everything wasn't completely resolved.

Daphne said, "You needn't have rushed back, if there were matters requiring attention. You should have just sent word, and taken the entire day—"

"The day?" repeated Kate incredulously. "All day?"

Daphne's heart twisted at that. She felt such an enormous affection for Kate. Every morning Kate—like all of Wolverton's servants—woke up and devoted herself to the service of the family, not necessarily by choice, but because of the circumstances of birth and their absolute need to earn a living, not only for themselves but their families. They all took such pride in their employment, and made everything look so effortless, but Daphne understood the hardships that went with the work. The long hours and the time spent away from family. She admired them all so much.

"Fickett, you have never, ever asked for so much as an extra day off, or three, or ten, and you know very well, if you should ever need to, the request would be granted. Hannah can always step in. I'm certain your mother and father would appreciate the help, being that this is the busiest time of the year at their shop."

"What, and miss out on all of this?" Kate laughed, her expression vivid, but her eyes...suspiciously damp. With a flutter of her lashes, she quickly turned away, her voice hushed and thick as if she were trying to keep her emotions in check. "Even if it's not my season, it's all very exciting and I don't want to miss out on a single moment. And besides, someone has to dress you properly for Lady Buckinghamshire's Venetian breakfast, and it won't be Hannah, not again."

Daphne watched in silence, even more certain something wasn't right. Her friend was upset about something.

After a brief pause, in which Kate straightened her shoulders and cleared her throat, she briskly took up Daphne's petticoat and dress from the chair, where Hannah had neatly abandoned them the night before. "Dear girl, she does her best, but she ought not to have allowed you to wear the blue silk last night. Now your entire wardrobe is thrown out of sequence. The blue had been set aside specifically for the Vauxhall Gala next week. Each dress is clearly labeled, so I don't understand how this happened—"

"It isn't Hannah's fault," Daphne asserted quietly, twining an arm around the bedpost, and leaning against it. "The lace on that atrocious green dress itched under my arms, and I rather insisted on the change."

Kate disappeared into the dressing room, only to emerge again moments later with a different dress, this one delicate yellow with puffed sleeves and four inches of pleated ivory lace at the hem.

"I did not doubt that for one moment," Kate responded with her customary pluck. "Which is why it's best I've returned to attend to you. Your *insistence* means absolutely nothing to me." Her gaze then settled on Daphne's head and her lips thinned with disapproval. "I see Hannah used the frizzler on your hair. I suppose you talked her into that as well?"

Daphne raised a hand to touch her hair.

"I wanted something different," she answered, only mildly exasperated. "Everyone else frizzles."

With a roll of her eyes, Kate continued past the bed. "All those tiny curls, so inelegant and impossible to smooth out the next day. Your hair is far too delicate for such torment."

Kate was jabbering, and still avoiding eye contact.

She crossed the carpet to stand behind Kate, who stood at the window. Kate held the dress to the light, allowing the sunshine to filter through the muslin.

Kate grumbled, "I'm of a mind to make you wear the blue again to the gala, even with the lemonade stain on the sleeve. Hannah ought to have treated the spot last night, immediately upon your return. Now I fear I'll never get it out—"

"Fuss, fuss, fuss," Daphne chided softly.

"Things ought to be done right, or not at all," Kate retorted.

"I don't know why I suffer your continual impertinence," she teased. It was a continuing jest between them, because they both delighted in impertinence.

Kate laughed. "After three years, I'm afraid you've no other choice."

Yet on the last word, her voice faltered again. Her head dipped and she dashed her fingertips against her eyes.

Daphne touched a hand to her back. "Kate?"

Kate turned, tears spilling over her cheeks. "Oh, *Daphne*."

She fell into Daphne's open arms and sobbed into her shoulder.

"Kate, what is it? What is wrong?"

The girl's shoulders heaved between sobs and gasps. Daphne squeezed her tight. Kate never cried. She never lost her composure.

"Everything, Daphne. Everything is terribly wrong."

Chapter Two

$\mathscr{D}$aphne pulled away, just enough to look Kate in the eyes and see tears streaming down her cheeks. "Tell me."

"My father, he...he...he borrowed a lot of money to invest in the new shop, hoping to attract more customers of a wealthier class. Fine carpets, rich draperies and furnishings, and also a large and expensive inventory."

"A smart investment," Daphne declared softly. "He is a good businessman."

"Always before, yes, but unbeknownst to me or my mother, he borrowed the money from the most unsavory man—" She flinched, her face paling a shade more.

"And now what has happened?" Daphne pulled a handkerchief from her skirt pocket and dabbed at her friend's eyes.

"The term of the loan was to be two years, but of course, there was a tiny notation in the contract that it might change at any time at the lender's discretion, and suddenly he has demanded that my father repay the entirety of the loan with all its interest. Immediately." Kate's bottom lip trembled, and tears spilled over her cheeks. "It's just all very upsetting. Mother has sold her heirloom silver, and Grandmother offered up her pension monies from when she served at the palace. But worst of all, Robert may have to come home from school."

Daphne's heart broke at hearing that. Kate referred of course to Robert, her younger brother, who at just nine years old already boasted advanced scientific and mathematical honors at the exclusive Mr. Gibbs Academy. They were all so very proud of him, and they'd had such high hopes for his future.

Daphne recalled all too vividly the dark days when grief had devastated the Wolverton household. Daphne'd had her grandfather, mother, and two sisters for comfort, but understandably they'd all been consumed by their own private grief. And she in particular, who after the death of her father had suffered the most terrible guilt. It had been Kate, then newly hired, who had been her rock.

Now Kate found herself faced by a terrible difficulty. Shouldn't she be there for Kate just as unwaveringly as Kate had been there for her?

Daphne reached for Kate's hand. "Let me help in some way. You know I love everything in the shop, as do my mother and sisters. If we all went shopping there this afternoon—"

"No, no, Daphne." Her face pallid and drawn, Kate shook her head. "Thank you, but...I'm afraid the amount of the debt quite exceeds that sort of simple solution."

Daphne nodded, feeling spoiled and sheltered from the dreadful financial realities of life that so many suffered. Most of all, she felt helpless. She lived such a life of privilege, but had no money of her own. Just pin money, and accounts at several shops that her grandfather's accountants paid, as long as the expenditures remained within reason.

"Kate, how much?"

"I can't even say it." Her hand curled on Daphne's sleeve. "I'll become ill, right here on the carpet."

"Go right ahead," Daphne urged. "I don't give a fig about the carpet. I want to know."

"I'm not going to tell you," Kate replied, her eyes tightly closed. "So don't press me."

Daphne's frustration only grew.

"There has to be something I can do." She worked her bottom lip, trying to conjure a solution, but already Kate was shaking her head and scowling at her.

"Don't say that." Kate took the handkerchief from her hand and dabbed her own eyes. "It only makes me feel worse that you'd feel the need to intervene, and besides, that's not why I told you. You've helped me just by listening. Everything will be fine, and we'll get through it." She nodded and smiled bravely, and nodded again. "We *will*. This hardship will only make the family stronger, and bring us closer together."

That much Daphne knew to be true. Her own family had become immeasurably closer in the dark days after her brother's and father's deaths. But now she needed to concentrate on Kate's well-being, not on her own tragic memories. Kate stared over her shoulder at nothing, seemingly a thousand miles away.

Daphne inquired softly, "You are certain everything will be all right?"

Kate blinked, appearing to break free from whatever

spell that held her. "Yes, Daphne. Of course it will, without a doubt. Thank you for being such a friend."

With a glance to the clock, her tearstained eyes widened.

"Look at the time. Come along now," she said. "To the dressing room with you. I have less than an hour in which to transform you into the *ne plus ultra* everyone expects you to be. When you return I want to hear so many compliments about your appearance today that even I become morbidly conceited!"

Kate's enthusiasm eased her concerns just a little, but Daphne wouldn't forget. They would revisit the matter soon, and she would press for more details, just to be certain the Ficketts' difficulties resolved completely. Still, what a relief to return to the easy banter that usually transpired between them. They always had such fun together.

"Kate, just wait until I tell you what Sophia just told Clarissa and me, downstairs, when we were in the conservatory." Daphne sat on the tufted stool at her dressing table.

Kate peered over her shoulder, and their gazes met in the mirror. "I can't wait to hear."

"It's very wicked," she warned.

"All the better!"

* * *

Only three hours later, Daphne and Clarissa stood at the entrance to the female servants' quarters, having just returned with Lady Margaretta from Lady Buckinghamshire's Venetian breakfast. Though the afternoon was young and there was the Heseldon ball to attend, a note from Daphne's grandfather, Lord Wolverton, had summoned them home with word that a number of the staff had been stricken by an undetermincd malady. From the distant end of the corridor came the sounds of someone suffering from the most wretched effects of illness.

"Oh, my, I do believe that was a lung," Daphne fretted, curling her fingers into the straw summer bonnet she held at the front of her skirt.

A door opened and Lady Margaretta emerged, accompanied by the housekeeper, Mrs. Brightmore. They both wore frowns of concern.

"They are very ill, then?" inquired Clarissa.

That was rather obvious, Daphne thought, given the sounds of misery still emanating from behind the row of doors.

A housemaid moved briskly past, carrying a stack of fresh linens and several tin buckets on her arm. With a knock, she disappeared into the first of the rooms.

"I'm afraid so," answered Lady Harwick.

"What of Miss Fickett?" Daphne asked, having been told Kate was onc of those who had fallen ill.

It had taken every bit of Daphne's will to remain in the corridor as her mother had insisted, rather than barging inside to assess her condition herself. Hadn't Kate suffered enough from the shocking news of her family's financial predicament?

"Unfortunately the dear girl is in no condition to assist you for the Heseldons', and Hannah has been stricken as well, but there is sufficient time for Clarissa's maid to dress your hair."

"Oh, indeed, Miss Randolph is exceedingly efficient," agreed Mrs. Brightmore. "I will speak to her and make her aware of this temporary arrangement."

"I don't care a fig about the ball or my hair," Daphne retorted, stung by the superficial bent of the conversation. "I care about Miss Fickett!"

How was it that those closest to her sometimes seemed to understand her the least? She couldn't go to a ball and smile and dance and charm while her dearest friend lay confined to her bed. For a moment, her fears got the better of her. What if the illness was of a serious nature? She'd already lost too many loved ones. She couldn't lose Kate, too.

Clarissa put an arm around her shoulder. "I care about Miss Fickett, too, and I hope she and the others feel much better soon."

"We all do," added the viscountess. "But there is nothing to do now but await the arrival of the physician. Depending on what he tells us, we may need to make changes in the household to protect His Lordship from exposure."

The aging Lord Wolverton had largely recovered from the infirmity that had left him an invalid throughout the winter, though his aged muscles and weakened limbs still necessitated the use of a bath chair. Lady Margaretta and his granddaughters, not to mention his valet and other devoted staff, remained in constant vigilance with regard to his health, which at times led to his complaints of being treated like a child.

"By Heaven, I pray it's not the influenza," murmured Mrs. Brightmore, a hand pressed over her heart.

As if Mrs. Brightmore had voiced Lady Margaretta's exact fears aloud, Daphne's mother extended a hand in the opposite direction. "Come now, let us all return upstairs. There is nothing more we can do here at present."

Her voice bordered along urgency, as if removing her daughters from the corridor would protect them from all threat of illness and danger, though they all knew Providence would selfishly do as it wished, as it had done with her eldest son and her husband. Out of consideration for her mother, Daphne accompanied Lady Margaretta and spent the next two hours writing out the remainder of the invitations with Clarissa's help. Lord Wolverton sat nearby, reading aloud any details of note or amusement from the morning newspapers.

Eventually it was time to prepare for the Heseldon ball, and Daphne abandoned her inkwell and pen. Yet while Clarissa ascended the staircase, Daphne quietly slipped away and returned to the servants' hall. Peering down the corridor to be certain she would remain unobserved, she knocked on Kate's door.

"Come in," came a feeble reply.

As a lady's maid, just a notch in the household hierarchy below the housekeeper, Kate enjoyed the privacy of her own room. To Daphne's surprise, however, Kate wasn't in bed. She stood, pallid and gaunt, struggling to don her cloak. "Kate Fickett, where do you think you are going?" Daphne rushed inside, reaching a hand to steady her.

"Daphne, please leave," Kate answered, her voice weak. She wobbled, unsteady on her feet, as if she might topple over at the slightest draft. "Her Ladyship would not approve of your being here, not with everyone else being so ill."

"Everyone *else* being so ill? Including *you*, do you mean? Kate, you look dreadful."

"It is nothing, I assure you," she insisted faintly, listing to the left. "The others have it much worse than I." Kate's hair had slipped from its usual neat knot, and most of it now hung limp around her face. For someone who always took such pride in their appearance, her dishevelment told a different story.

"I don't believe you, not for a minute."

"Truly, I have only the mildest of stomach pains, with none of the other symptoms." Kate let out a sudden gasp. Bending at the waist, she moaned. Perspiration dappled her forehead and upper lip.

"Ah, do you see?" Daphne said, guiding her by the arm into a wooden chair. "You really should be in bed."

"But I must go," Kate protested. As soon as she was seated, she stood from the chair again but teetered, lacking balance. "I'll rest later. If you could please just hand me my hat."

Shadows, almost as deep as bruises, darkened the skin beneath her eyes.

Daphne scowled at her friend's continued obstinacy. "I forbid you to go. You can't even stand up straight, let alone walk down the street." With a gentle push to Kate's shoulders, Daphne urged her down again.

"You don't understand," Kate declared, throwing a glance at the door and looking trapped. "I can't remain here. I've a certain obligation to which I *must* attend."

"Yes, I understand, your family. You feel as if you need to return home. If my family were suffering, I'd want to go home as well. Allow me to send word that you are ill and being cared for here."

"Not *that* obligation," Kate whispered with desperate intensity. She twisted in the chair, refusing to meet Daphne's gaze. "Not exactly."

"Then what?"

The young woman balled her hands into fists, looking

miserable, and lifted them to her temples. "Please, Daphne, I beg you not to press me."

Seeing Kate so anguished caused Daphne no small measure of alarm. Clearly there was more at issue here than getting home.

"How can I help you if you don't confide in me?"

"It is a distressingly private matter," whispered Kate.

"I have the feeling you didn't tell me everything. The situation is worse than you led me to believe. Fickett, you don't think I'll understand?" She rested a hand on Kate's arm.

With a sudden jerk, Kate wrenched her arm free. She glared at Daphne, eyes wild and feverish. "You couldn't possibly understand. You've not a care in the world. Everything is so easy for you going from party to ball, your only responsibility to look pretty and marry well—or not. Whatever you decide, because you are wealthy and have that freedom."

Daphne froze, as if she'd been struck.

Certainly their lives were different. They'd been born into disparate circumstances. But to think that Kate had felt this way about her all along when Daphne had actually dared to believe them close friends. Kate was wrong, of course. No amount of money could buy the one thing Daphne's heart desired most. Neither wealth nor influence could turn back time and allow her to repair her life's greatest regret.

"Oh, no." Kate's face crumpled and she sank to the bed, her hands covering her face. "I didn't mean what I said. You have been nothing but constant and understanding, my dearest friend. Please forgive me."

Daphne sighed, relieved to hear the words, but at the same time she knew Kate did hold that opinion of her in some way. Otherwise, she wouldn't have said it. And why should her feelings be so bruised, when just a few hours earlier she'd thought the same thing, that she was a spoiled girl compared to Kate, who'd had to work in some form or fashion since the age of twelve?

"Forgive you for what? It's already forgotten," she replied, hoping to soothe her, and to show she did indeed understand. But of course she hadn't forgotten. "I can only imagine you have taken another position at night for extra earnings to pay off your father's debt. Is that it?"

Was it possible that Kate turned a shade greener? Daphne grabbed up the empty bucket from the floor and handed it to her.

"Of a sort," the young woman whispered, grasping the edges and staring inside.

"While I hate that you'd exhaust yourself that way, you mustn't fear that you'd endanger your position here. And surely this employer, whoever they are, will understand. You're ill. They wouldn't want you present for duty in this condition."

"They won't understand." Kate closed her eyes, but even so, tears spilled down her cheeks. "*He* won't understand. Don't you see? I *must* go."

There was so much pain in Kate's face, Daphne's heart nearly broke with the magnitude of it.

"Kate, what aren't you telling me?" Daphne squeezed Kate's shoulders. "Have you gotten yourself into some sort of trouble?"

"Oh, yes, Daphne, of a terrible sort—" Kate hiccupped, shoulders hunched.

"Everything will be all right."

"No it won't." She shook her head morosely. "My father is indebted to the most *horrible man*." Her words spilled out in a rush, accompanied by tears. "He has threatened to see my family turned out from our home, and committed to the debtor's prison if we do not comply with his demands. My father, my mother, and my grandmother—who as you know is already frail. And the *children*! He showed us a signed order from the magistrate, who is his brother-in-law, and said he can use it at any time."

"Kate, no." Daphne's temper caught flame. It wasn't fair that any person could prey upon weaker souls, by wrongly and falsely enforcing the word and power of the law, but it happened all the time against those who did not have sufficient fortune to protect and defend themselves.

"How much is owed? You must tell me."

The number Kate whispered made Daphne's head spin. Kate had been correct earlier that afternoon in saying there was no way Daphne herself could produce the required funds.

"Your family can't pay off the debt as quickly as he demands!" she exclaimed. "Certainly some sort of an arrangement can be made to pay off the monies over time, on a schedule."

Kate cried, "Oh, yes, there is an arrangement indeed. My parents don't know, but last week I sought him out, Daphne, and he has *very kindly*"—she gritted the words out—"allowed me to work off the remainder of the debt, which is why I really must go." Suddenly she rocked forward in her chair, and her hands tightened on the bucket. She grimaced in pain.

"Work off the debt?" Daphne didn't like the sound of that. Not at all! Her eyes narrowed. "Doing what?"

"I can't tell you." Kate shook her head vehemently. "It's too mortifying."

Daphne's concern increased tenfold. Now *she* felt ill as well. "Fickett, please tell me you haven't—"

"No, not *that*. I—I haven't prostituted myself, though he...he certainly extended the opportunity, saying the outstanding amount would be satisfied more quickly if I were willing to do so, starting with him as my first client." Her lip curled in revulsion.

"Then what, Kate?" Daphne exclaimed, relieved but still alarmed. "You are going to tell me every mortifying detail, so that we can solve this problem."

"It's not your problem to fix Daphne," Kate whispered, looking dazed and rubbing a hand over her face. Perspiration shone on her forehead, and her upper lip. She moaned, appearing one inch away from being insensible. "It is mine, and I must be there by midnight, else he'll send those men to my home—"

A knock sounded on the door, and the housekeeper stepped in. "The doctor is here to see Miss Fickett. May we come in?"

At that, Kate buried her face in the bucket and retched.

*   *   *

"I hope you have a marvelous time," Daphne urged, perhaps a little too enthusiastically, as she walked Clarissa toward the vestibule from the conservatory, where they'd chosen a fragrant gardenia for her sister's hair.

She had to get Clarissa and their mother out of the house as quickly as possible.

"I still wish you were coming." Clarissa pouted.

She looked like a princess in blush-pink silk, a color Daphne would never choose to wear as long as she lived. She'd developed an aversion for the color in her youth, when Lady Harwick had oftentimes insisted on dressing her and her sisters in matching pink dresses. Daphne shivered at the memory but reminded herself not to lose focus.

"But you understand how fond I am of Miss Fickett."

"Of course I do, and I pray her health improves. You're such a dear to offer to stay and nurse her and the others." Concern warmed her blue eyes. "At least it's nothing contagious. Tainted sausages on the servants' midafternoon tea sideboard!"

Indeed, it was the only reason her mother had agreed to allow her to remain behind at all. Daphne had further persuaded the viscountess with the argument that once she was in charge of her own household she might need to tend to ill servants, and this was the perfect opportunity for practice.

"Poor Kate. She ought to have chosen the mutton." Daphne forced an easy laugh. "Why, did you see Cook when he left to confront the butcher? I thought I saw smoke coming out from his ears. Thankfully no authorities were called—"

"Like last time?" Her sister giggled. "When he threatened to burn down the butcher's shop and Wolverton had to travel all the way across town to intercede on his behalf."

"I remember," Daphne said, but inside her mind raced and her heart pounded, so hard and rapidly she could scarcely breathe.

She'd told Kate not to worry, that she'd take care of everything, and poor Kate had been too depleted by her illness to do anything but collapse into an exhausted sleep. She simply had to do something. Daphne could no more allow the Ficketts to be turned out into the streets or sent to a debtor's prison or workhouse than she could allow the same misfortune to befall her own family.

Clarissa said something about Lady Grant's charming nephew, and hoping she would meet him tonight, but all Daphne heard was the thunderous *ticktock* of the clock inside her head as the moments passed.

"Er...what about Mr. Donelan?" Daphne asked distractedly, peering hopefully up the stairs. Lady Margaretta, always prompt to a fault, was nowhere to be seen. She considered sending one of the maids to let the viscountess know they were waiting.

"Mr. Donelan has turned out to be a terrible disappointment." She sighed. "Why don't we sit, and I'll tell you everything while we wait?"

She gestured in the direction of a large potted palm, behind which a bench was situated.

"No!" Daphne blurted, catching her hand and drawing her back toward the center of the room. "Ah, I'm certain Mother will be right down. I heard Lady Heseldon has arranged for wandering minstrels and pantomimes. You won't want to miss a moment of the fun, so the moment Her Ladyship arrives you had best hurry her posthaste into the carriage."

She prayed Clarissa did not discern the urgency in her voice—an urgency she would be unable to explain. Kate, having sworn her to secrecy, rightfully feared losing her position if it became known that she had spent her nights this past week in the seediest district of London, working as a dancer in a bawdy house. Clarissa had always been terrible at keeping secrets. Not intentionally, of course, but she was unfailingly honest—and, as a result, dreadfully inept at concealment, especially where their mother was concerned.

"Promise me you'll look after Mother. I don't want her to spend all evening in a corner chair worrying about me." *Or coming home early. Heavens, no.* "Now tell me all about Mr. Donelan."

Clarissa adjusted the folds of her glove at her elbow. "In all the excitement this afternoon I forgot to tell you that I have heard a very reliable rumor that he is swimming, up to his aristocratic nose, in gambling debts, which of course puts the motive for his interest in me in question—"

"Tell me that's not true." Daphne frowned, seeing the depth of disappointment in her sister's eyes.

"Oh, it's true all right," a man's voice drawled from nowhere, echoing through the rotunda.

Startled, they both whirled round to see a pair of legs, clad in dark trousers and gleaming ankle boots, extend from behind the same potted palm where Clarissa had only moments before attempted to lead her. Two steps in that direction revealed a man they had only just met the year before, a man their grandfather's investigators had informed them was very likely a cousin, Mr. Kincraig. He sat, half-sprawled on the bench, red-eyed and rakishly disheveled. He always looked like that, libertine that he was. After the deaths of their brother and father, Mr. Kincraig had become their grandfather's solitary heir and the reason Wolverton and their mother wanted Clarissa and Daphne to marry well, so their futures would not be dependent on his whim.

"It's ill-mannered to eavesdrop on a private conversation," said Clarissa, her voice elevated.

Daphne crossed her arms at her waist. "Any proper gentleman would have announced himself."

"When have I ever claimed to be that?" he muttered, scowling.

Daphne could not disagree with him on that point. There was no love lost between her family and the man standing before them. He had been a disappointment in every respect, to say the least, not only for the scandals in which he involved himself, but his general air of unreliability. He was also rumored to have won and lost fortunes several times over.

"Besides, I wasn't eavesdropping on your little"—he waved a hand in the air—"female *conversation*. I nodded off while waiting for you ladies to appear. Where is Lady Harwick? Are the three of you always so vexingly late?"

"Late for what?" Clarissa demanded, faintly alarmed. Certainly, like Daphne, she already knew the answer: he was here to be their escort for the evening. Suffice it to say, they would have preferred to go alone. Sometimes, Mr. Kincraig behaved like the perfect gentlemen. Other times, he did not. There was just no predicting. At least tonight he did not smell atrociously of perfume and drink.

"The Heseldon ball," he confirmed, nostrils flared in arrogance as he stood to glower down on them both. With his dark, longish hair brushing his jaw and sliding over his eyes, and his devilishly pointed mustache and beard, he looked like a pirate. "Wolverton requested—" He raised a finger. "No, let me reword that—he rather *commanded* that I present myself to escort the three of you this evening."

Wolverton did that on occasion, more recently of late, hoping that Mr. Kincraig would abandon the life of a rogue and rise to the family's expectations. The earl had explained more than once it was in all their best interests to bring him into the fold so that after the earl was gone, the transition would not be so difficult. The knowledge loomed over them always! At any moment, Mr. Kincraig might become master of their lives, though Wolverton had made arrangements, as well as he could, that none of them would be destitute if Kincraig drank and gambled their family fortune away.

"That's just prime," Clarissa muttered. "The least you could do is dress properly."

"What do you mean?" he scowled, glancing downward over his attire.

Daphne gestured in the general direction of his throat. "Your cravat, sir, is an abomination." She did have to admit, the rest of him looked very fine.

His eyes flashed in response and the muscle along his jaw tightened. He touched his hands to the named item of clothing. "Well, then, since you have both been so kind as to point out the flaw, I would be much appreciative if one of you would repair it."

They both stood motionless, staring at him.

"*Please*," he gritted through clenched teeth.

Clarissa broke ranks first. "Oh, very well." She reached for the tangle of linen and efficiently set about its rearrangement. "So tell me, how would you know anything about Mr. Donelan's situation?"

At that, his scowl transformed into a rakish grin. "To whom do you suppose it is that Mr. Donelan is indebted?"

"Why am I not surprised?" Daphne muttered.

Could this night be any worse? She felt like screaming out in impatience.

Clarissa froze, her hands falling away. "Mr. Kincraig, is that a bruise around your eye?"

"Ah—" His gaze shifted to the stairs. "Lady Harwick."

There! At last, their mother appeared at the top of the stairs, a vision in a vibrant yellow gown that they'd had to convince her to purchase. For a moment, Daphne forgot all about Mr. Kincraig, Kate's situation, and the time.

Though the viscountess had ceased wearing the colors of a widow before Christmas, she'd continued to choose muted shades, evidence of her continued grief over the deaths of the viscount and her son. But tonight her mother looked radiant. Beautiful, even.

"Oh, dear, you're all staring." Lady Margaretta blushed. "Do I look like a canary? I'm still doubting my decision, both about this dress and about letting Daphne remain behind this evening."

"The dress is lovely," Daphne effused. "*You* are lovely."

Her sister nodded approvingly, her eyes damp and shining. "Just as we said at the dressmaker's shop, canary is your color."

Even Mr. Kincraig appeared affected. "Indeed it is, my lady," he said, rushing with uncustomary gallantry to assist her down the final stairs.

"Mr. Kincraig." Her mother greeted him with a smile, albeit a reserved one, no doubt wishing in that moment that it was her husband or her son who greeted her. Mr. Kincraig and Vinson would have been much the same age, but were of course nothing at all alike. Mr. Kincraig was

NEVER ENTICE AN EARL 47

more akin to a pirate than a gentleman in his complete unwillingness—or perhaps a genuine inability—to submit to any social expectation or practice of manners.

With a start, Daphne remembered the matter at hand, and the time. "You had all best be on your way. You don't want to be late."

The footmen reached for the doors, opening them for the party's anticipated passage.

Clarissa waved a gloved hand. "I'll tell you all the on-dits tonight when we return—what everyone wore and who asked me to dance."

"As will I," Mr. Kincraig added drolly, pressing a hand over his heart, which inspired a dramatic roll of her sister's eyes. Yet Daphne did not miss the little twitch of a smile on Clarissa's lips—one that mirrored her own. Even the viscountess smiled.

In that moment her heart softened just a degree toward the man who had, through no fault of his own, taken her father and her brother's rightful place. Perhaps... perhaps they could all one day accept Mr. Kincraig as a true member of the family.

"Tomorrow at breakfast," Daphne responded. "Most likely I'll be asleep when you return." Balls always ran late, and it would be two or three o'clock before they arrived home. At least that was her hope.

At last, in a shimmer of pearls and diamonds, her sister and mother were gone, in the company of a man who remained so much a stranger to them. Daphne breathed a sigh of relief.

Finally—time to help Kate! Thank heavens Wolverton had decided to make an early evening of it and take dinner in his room. She'd glimpsed O'Connell, his valet, descending the servants' staircase some thirty minutes before, having already been dismissed for the night.

"Hurry, hurry, hurry," she whispered to herself, as she rushed down the stairs, returning again to the servants' corridor.

She'd already considered every option. For her, simply paying off Kate's debt wasn't possible; despite her privileged life, she had no access to money of her own, not of the magnitude required. She couldn't sell her dresses or her jewels. Anything of value that went missing would be noted immediately either by her mother or the keen-eyed Mrs. Brightmore, and the loss construed as theft. The servants would be questioned, and she would be forced to step forward and declare herself the guilty party in stealing from... well, from her own self. A strange predicament, indeed.

If only she could go to her grandfather or her mother and simply ask for the money, but she knew from experience her grandfather, no matter how generous he might be, would soundly reject the lending of money to a servant. The problem had presented itself before, and she had heard his reasoning. What he did for one, he must do for all. There would be no loans granted, only fair wages earned, and never in advance.

She could only imagine the earl's explosive reaction, as well as her mother's dismay, if they learned that she'd involved herself in the financial affairs of a servant. Likely by opening her mouth she would only find herself on the receiving end of a lecture about proper boundaries between herself and the staff—and Kate in search of a new position.

She couldn't even go to Sophia, who very well might take pity on Kate's plight. The Duke and Duchess of Claxton had departed that afternoon for a week at their estate outside of Lacenfleet, where Sophia could rest and be doted on by Mrs. Kettle, the elderly caretaker's wife, while His Grace approved recent renovations to the manor house, necessary after a fire had destroyed much of the main hall just before Christmas.

Daphne hadn't felt this helpless since the day her father died. She'd been powerless to change the course of that tragedy. Now, having knowledge of the danger Kate's family faced, she had no choice but to act.

Hurriedly, she spoke to the nurse who had been brought in to tend to the stricken. Afterward, she visited each of the female servants, fluffing pillows and coaxing spoonfuls of weak beef broth through pale and unwilling lips. All the while, her brain churned out one useless idea after another before returning to the only one that made sense. At last she again arrived at Kate's door. Inside, thankfully, Kate was sleeping, her face pallid against the linen pillowcase.

Hands shaking, she took up Kate's reticule from the table and searched inside until she found what she wanted— a scrap of paper upon which all the necessary particulars had been neatly inscribed in her friend's familiar handwriting.

* * *

Cormack stared at the doorway from across the road, the scent of rubbish filling his nostrils. Had he, indeed, found the Blue Swan? By all appearances, he stood outside an abandoned warehouse. Just then, a hackney clattered down the pavestones and slowed in front of him, only to speed off again. But there, in the shadows, he caught just the barest glimpse of a man who rapped his fist on the door two times. The sound echoed outward. After a moment, he rapped two times more.

He observed movement, but not so much as a glimmer of light. Men's voices sounded, a quiet rumble in the night, and the newly arrived visitor disappeared inside.

Crossing the road, he replicated the knock against the door.

A panel slid open, behind which he perceived the shadowed features of a very large man, who stooped to peer out at him. "Say th' word, govna."

Hmmm. Entrance, it appeared, required more than a special knock, but he'd come prepared for that possibility.

"The precise word slips my mind." From his coat pocket, he produced a heavy pouch, and on his open palm, he presented it to the man. "Might you be able to give me a hint?"

The bully quickly took possession of the offered bribe and, behind the door, appeared to weigh the pouch in his hand.

With a squint, he muttered, "The word is slippin' me own mind at the moment—I'm tryin' me best to remember—"

Another pouch, and the door swung open to darkness. "Enjoy your evenin', sir."

Cormack walked with outstretched hand until he touched a heavy velvet curtain, which he pushed aside, only to be met with more darkness and a second curtain, but also sounds—voices and female laughter. He swept aside another drape and entered the Blue Swan.

"Cheatin' nob!"

Cormack intercepted the fist that drunkenly hurtled toward his face. Grabbing the red-nosed fellow by his shoulders, he spun him round and shoved him in the direction of his intended opponent.

Lord, he despised bawdy houses. If only vengeance had not commanded him here tonight.

Tobacco smoke clouded the air, dimming his view of the men who crowded around the faro tables, gentlemen in evening dress intermingled with tradesmen in dark suits and rough-hewn men off the wharves. Gilt-framed mirrors cluttered the walls, and lopsided chandeliers hung from the ceilings, trappings of faux luxury. A ramshackle quartet was assembled in the distant corner. The establishment had the feel of transience, as if every fixture, table, and drape could be snatched up at any moment, thrown in the back of a wagon, and installed elsewhere for the same effect. Understandable, as Cormack's source had warned him the club changed locations often so as to avoid discovery by the constables. Predators with painted lips and rouged cheeks circled him, already taking note of the newcomer in their midst.

"Looking for a bit o' company t'night, good sir?" inquired a redhead, boldly assessing him with kohl-lined eyes.

"Two is company. Three is a party." The brunette sidled closer, offering Cormack an unrestricted view of her breasts, only barely constrained by a bodice of sheer muslin. "You look like the sort of man who requires more than just one."

Hmmm…perhaps. But his tastes were far more refined than what he would find here.

As far as London brothels went, the Blue Swan was the seediest he'd visited thus far. But he wasn't here to drink, gamble, or to whore. He was here to find the man he had sworn to destroy. If only he knew who the hell he was looking for.

His hand passed over his coat pocket, confirming the existence of the hard lump within—the gold amulet he'd accepted from Laura's hand in the moments before her death, one bearing a severed Medusa's head and the Latin word *Invisibilis*.

Two years had passed, but in many ways time had stood still. His parents remained mired in grief for the death of their beloved daughter, still unable to fathom the mysterious circumstances in which she met her end— circumstances that Cormack now felt compelled to avenge.

From what his parents had told him, he knew that Laura arrived at Bellefrost on the back of a farmer's wagon, in rags and with no possessions of which to speak, already in the throes of childbirth labor. This had come as a shock, as they'd believed her to be contentedly serving as a governess at the Deavalls'. Her letters had come with all regularity, never giving the slightest hint of distress. Their questions had brought no answers—only tears from his sister. In shock, they'd called for the doctor. Within hours of what had seemed to be a normal birth, her health suddenly failed. She died, never revealing the name of the man who had left her to give birth alone to a pale-haired little boy. Was it because she wished to keep her seducer's identity a secret, or because she hadn't expected to die?

Left with no answers and his sister's honor to defend, Cormack had asked questions of his own. Against the wishes of his parents, who wanted only to grieve and raise Michael with as much dignity as possible, he had traveled to the Deavall estate, only to be informed by the housekeeper that Laura had abruptly left her employment some five months before her death. It did not take long for him to discover she had spent the first week after leaving holed away at an inn in the neighboring village before moving to another, this one much shabbier than the first. Before long, she had simply...disappeared.

He wasn't a fool. He knew she'd gone into hiding to conceal her condition from the world. From her own family. But Laura had always been so smart, and so strong and self-disciplined. She wasn't *that* woman. How had this happened to her? The questions atc him up inside. Who was the child's father, and why, in the end, had Laura suffered such a shocking dishonor alone, and left her child to suffer the lifelong stain of illegitimacy?

Of course, his suspicions had immediately fallen to the Deavall estate, but a chance encounter with a local tavern girl—very pretty, except for the shadows in her eyes—had provided a more startling answer when she glimpsed the medallion in his hand. She shared of her harrowing experience with a group of aristocratic young hell-raisers at the Duke of Rathcrispin's hunting lodge, which lay adjacent to the Dcavall estate. For two weeks the libertines had gambled, drank, and done their best to debauch every woman within a ten-mile radius of the place, including herself, which was why she now had a little girl of her own and no husband.

Desperately accepting the coins Cormack pressed into her hand, she'd told him she knew from intimate experience that several of the men had worn a medallion identical to the one in his possession. She believed them dangerous and powerful enough for her to warn him against showing the medallion freely. Perhaps, like her, Laura had been momentarily dazzled and seduced, she'd said. But she would not exclude a more sinister explanation, had his sister been unwilling. The men exuded entitlement and a lifetime of privilege. They had no qualms about taking what they wanted.

Truly, it was all the answer he needed, save for a name.

Simmering with rage, not only for the wrong done to his sister but to the girl as well, he had gone to the hunting lodge, even though the men were no longer in residence. He had been seeking answers. Seeking names. The place teemed with guests, a house party, yet in his attempt to make inquiries he hadn't made it past the door. Though he had been raised as gentry and possessed a fortune from his time in Bengal, he was no aristocrat. He might as well have been a street beggar in rags in the haughty eyes of those he sought to question. He had been rebuffed like so much rubbish.

So for two years he'd tended to his parents and little Michael, ostracized by their neighbors now not for their poverty, but because of scandal, so much so that even their neighbor, Sir Snaith, had declined to honor his gentleman's agreement to sell their lands back to them. Yet winter had delivered to him an unexpected gift—the key to obtain the answers and, yes, the vengeance he sought. An unexpected series of deaths had made his father the new Marquess of Champdeer and him an earl. At last Cormack had the necessary entrée to step behind the high wall of aristocratic protection that had held him back for so long.

For that reason he had come to London for the season when twelve men who remained unnamed—and one who remained unpunished—would in all likelihood converge from all corners of England, like the others of their kind.

Having arrived one week ago, he found himself woefully without connections, but at night he frequented their favorite gaming halls and discreetly asked questions, not of those men of privilege with whom he rubbed elbows, but of those who found themselves trampled beneath their well-polished heels, who in common whispered one word, but only after glancing fearfully over their shoulder: Invisibilis. At last, he felt…close.

His hatred renewed, Cormack made his selection carefully and caught her wrist as she moved past, a woman in an ill-fitted, jade green gown. Older than the others, with a faded complexion and dull hair, perhaps she would be more eager than her competitors to earn a bit of coin in exchange for a whispered, forbidden secret.

"'Ay!" The harridan's eyes widened in outrage but, upon assessing him, softened into heavy-lidded seduction. "Well, 'ow do you do, 'andsome?" she breathed. "'Aven't seen you 'ere before. I'm Nellie. What are y' lookin' for tonight?"

"I'm looking for you, Nellie." He took care to remain in the deepest of shadows. Though few would recognize him in London, he expected that might change, depending on how long this business of retribution kept him here.

In the crush of the crowd, she pressed against him, curling her hands into his lapels. "I've a room upstairs, nice and cozy. Wot do you say? I'll get us a bottle, just for ourselves."

"Actually, I've become separated from friends, and would like to rejoin them. I was hoping that perhaps you know them?"

"Friends?" Her eyes narrowed. "Wot sort of friends?"

He pressed a crown into her palm.

After a quick glance to assess the coin's worth, a smile eased onto her lips. "Per'aps I do know them. I've known everyone 'ere, at one time or another, it seems. Tell me about them."

He spoke near her ear. "They follow this club from place to place, but keep to themselves, perhaps in a back room, rarely if ever mingling with the other customers."

Her face went slack, but she said nothing.

He continued, "Each of them wears a gold medallion depicting—"

"A woman," she murmured. "With snakes for hair."

The beat of his heart increased. He nodded, keeping his face expressionless so as to not reveal the depth of his excitement. "Those would be the same gentlemen. The Invisibilis."

"You're not one of 'em, 'at much I know. And I very much suspect they aren't your friends." She chuckled wryly. "A mysterious lot, they are. Don't come 'ere for the entertainments, for the most part, though when they do, they pay the girls well, though some of them can be a bit...rough."

"Can you provide their names? Even the name of an associate or lackey?"

She glanced over her shoulder before whispering, "Never actually seen their faces. They wear 'oods, fashioned of black silk, y' see, but gentlemen they be, all of them, with fancy clothes and carriages. They've not yet arrived, but soon, I think. Keep an eye over there, beside the stage. If they're 'ere tonight, they'll come through the back."

"Thank you, Nellie." He stepped away, and her hands fell from his coat.

"Wot, that's all?" She pouted, a saucy smile tilting her carmine lips. "You paid for better than just a bit of chitchat."

"If anyone comes asking later, forget about me. That's all I ask."

"Beshrew me, forget 'at 'andsome face?" Her gaze traveled over him longingly. Regretfully. She sighed. "Don't think 'at's possible, but Nellie don't tell tales on her favorites." She came near, her voice lowered. "But be careful w' those ones. They're dangerous men."

"How do you know I'm not the same?"

She answered softly. "You still have a soul. I can see it in your eyes."

Cormack wasn't so sure about that.

Chapter Three

I don't really care wot your name is, just as long as yoov got two of *those*—" Mr. Bynum's bloodshot gaze dropped to her bosoms. "And one of *these*."

He grabbed her by the shoulders and spun her around, and with an open hand smacked her bottom. Daphne yelped and whirled back around, her hands raised to strike, but he shoved a bundle into them and roughly herded her toward the corner, where a burlap curtain had been hung crosswise on twine.

"There's no time to waste," Mr. Bynum lectured coldly, his eyes touching her everywhere in a way that made her shiver in disgust. "You're late. Don't be late again. We have a schedule here, and you will do well to keep it, strict as law, else your friend Miss Fickett will pay the consequences."

Daphne held the bundle tight to her breast, her gaze moving to two ladies who moved past in gowns only half there, their faces powdered white and brightly painted.

They stared at her with dull-eyed curiosity, smirking unkindly before passing through a doorway to a room that seemed to quake with laughter and inharmonious music.

For what had to be the thousandth time, Daphne conceded that perhaps it had been unwise to take Kate's place after all. Not that Kate even knew she was here, of course. She would never have allowed Daphne to walk out the door if she'd realized her intentions. Unwise decision or no, she wouldn't change a thing. Given the urgency of the situation, taking Kate's place had been the only alternative. As a true friend, she'd had no other choice. She had no doubt Kate would have done the same for her.

Praying she didn't look as terrified as she felt, Daphne stood straighter and forced her shoulders back, assuming a nonchalant pose.

"Pay the consequences how?" she demanded, more forcefully than she'd intended, in her effort to force the breathlessness from her voice.

Call her foolish, but she'd imagined the Blue Swan to be a slightly more elegant venue. Instead she felt as if she'd been yanked from the clean and comfortable world she knew and dropped into hell, or at least purgatory, overcrowded with wretched creatures and smelling of rubbish and cheap perfume. While it was all keenly interesting, and her curious mind took in every mortifying detail—including the man and woman shamelessly groping one another against the far wall—she understood the very real peril in which she'd placed herself. She couldn't imagine Kate in this place. If she survived the night with her life, neither of them were ever coming back.

"By forfeiting her earnings thus far." He smiled, flashing yellow teeth. "I won't 'esitate to throw her kin out on the streets and seize every last one of their belongings, including the contents of that shop, do y' understand, gel? I know people. Powerful men, and that makes me powerful as well."

She didn't like Mr. Bynum or his threatening words, but she knew better than to give him the dressing down that exploded on her tongue. He was a dangerous man, and she was very much at a disadvantage should things go wrong.

"I said do y' understand?" he repeated lecherously.

"Yes," she answered through clenched teeth.

He grunted in response and, with a nod, said, "I'll return to give you your stage instruction." He paused and touched a hand to her hair...and then her cheek. Daphne flinched and twisted away. "You're very pretty, you know." He chuckled, low in his throat. "With hair like that, you and I could make a lot of money together. You like money, don't you?"

She understood what he suggested. Her eyes flew wide in outrage and her face burned. "I—I don't—"

A man rushed into view. "Mr. Bynum, please come. One of the patrons has hit a dealer over the head with his walking stick, and the dealer is now quite senseless."

"Well, get another dealer to take his place. I can't have a table out of service."

"I tried, but Charles is nowhere to be found. I think he's gone upstairs with one of the gels—"

"Damn it, man, must I tend to everything myself?" Bynum shoved past him, but pivoted on his heel to point at Daphne. "You. Five minutes. Be dressed in your costume."

Daphne grabbed hold of the burlap and yanked it closed, concealing herself as well as she could, though when released the drape sagged several inches from the wall. Still, she exhaled in relief, thankful for a moment in which to collect herself, to gasp for breath and tremble in private. Foremost, she considered escape. She'd paid a kind-eyed, elderly hackney driver to wait for her...but running away wouldn't help Kate or her family. She couldn't take the chance. It was too late for any other resolution. She had to carry through.

Fearful that Mr. Bynum would return when she was only half dressed, she frantically changed into the garments, balancing on one foot and pinning the curtain against the wall with her toe as she struggled to don the close-fitting costume.

"Dearie, are you ready?" shouted a female voice through the curtain.

With shaking hands, Daphne tied the black satin bow at her waist.

"I...ah...am ready. You may pass the rest of the costume through the curtain whenever you are ready."

In a dingy flash, a woman's hand shoved the burlap partition back to reveal a powdered face and painted lips drawn back in laughter. Three girls stared back at her, each dressed like her, in flesh-colored, near-transparent pantaloons and matching corsets.

"Wot rest of the costume?" said a cat-eyed, black-haired girl with kohl-lined eyes that reminded Daphne of Cleopatra.

"'Ere, let me tighten yer stays," said the closest, a brown-haired beauty, moving to stand behind her. "We want those lovely bosoms up high, as close to your chin as we can manage wi'out them poppin' off and blacking some poor bloke's eye."

A sudden jerk of the ties left Daphne gasping for breath.

The third, a redhead who wore a mouse-hair beauty mark affixed to her cheek, appeared with powder and rouge, which she set about applying to Daphne's face.

"Wot happened to the gel from last night?" asked the Beauty, before inflicting another squeeze. Indeed, Daphne felt her breasts had never been quite so near her chin! She pressed a hand to the wall for support, but then thought better of touching anything in this place, and snatched her hand away.

"She's ill, so I'm taking her place."

"Don't she talk funny?" The redhead laughed, holding a kohl pencil high.

Didn't *she* talk funny? She could barely understand what any of them were saying.

Cleo—as Daphne silently called her—sidled closer, eyes narrowed. "Why *do* you talk so funny? Just like that girl last night?" She leaned close, so that her nose was two inches from Daphne's. "Good thing she didn't come back, else I was going t' have t' cut her." In a flash, she produced a narrow blade from the center of her corset. "Thought she was better than the rest of us. You don't think you're better than the rest of us, do y', girly?"

Daphne didn't cower or break away. She hadn't done anything to provoke such a threat, and she found Cleo's manner and words offensive. The only experience she had with brawling were a few angry, hair-pulling tussles with her sisters when their governess wasn't looking, but that had been years ago. Still, the girl wasn't all that large, and if matters took a turn for the worse, she thought she just might be able to take her.

But Beauty wedged between them and shoved Cleo away.

"Don't mind Cat." Ah, so her name was Cat. Beauty continued, "Ain't a one of us that 'aven't been cut by 'er at one time or another, and we've all lived to see another day." She pointed to a narrow scar near her shoulder.

Daphne looked toward Cat, who flashed a dangerous smile and winked. Just then, a crash sounded from the room next door, sounding something like a table overturned. Voices shouted curses and laughter.

The redhead reappeared with a bottle in her hand. "We're all good friends 'ere and look out for each other. You'll see!" Her grin revealed a rotten tooth, the only flaw in an otherwise pretty face. "Care for a nip o' gin?"

Daphne stared at the offered bottle for a moment before answering, "Why yes, I think I would."

* * *

Cormack stepped back as another insensible man was carried past, in the direction of the street.

Just then, the musicians struck up a tune. Beside them, curtains jerked apart on ropes to reveal a makeshift stage made out of wooden shipping crates, a common sight on the nearby quay. On each of the four corners stood a young lady, frozen in a dramatic pose. Elaborate gold Carnival masks, studded with paste jewels and feathers, concealed their faces above their painted lips. Close-fitting, flesh-toned costumes conveyed the illusion of nudity. Those men not otherwise engaged at the gaming tables surged forward to jostle for position along the edges of the stage, shouting out expressions of vulgar admiration. The stage rocked and several of the girls wavered from their poses.

A bulldog-faced man in an ill-fitted great coat and top hat strutted to the center of the stage and bellowed, "Gentlemen, gentlemen. Do control yourselves!"

Hands held high for quiet, he waited for the clamor to subside.

"We have assembled here, for your personal erudition and viewing pleasure, four of the foremost actresses of Drury Lane presenting the finest in *tableaux vivant*." He gestured toward the young women. "For your eyes only they will enact the most memorable scenes of the classics, the first being the story of Electra and the grievous murder of her father, the king Agamemnon."

Cormack chuckled. Actresses, indeed. Though he could not claim to be an expert on strumpets, these four were clearly of a higher quality than the others who crowded the room. Young and pretty, at least from this distance, they had bodies to match with high breasts, pinched waists, and flared hips. Having studied the classics, he could not discern what any of the poses had to do with Electra or Agamemnon, but he supposed that wasn't the point.

His attention lingered on one of the dancers in particular, one with starlight-blonde hair and luminous skin. Something about her commanded his attention. Perhaps it was the blue flash of temper in her eyes, or the quarrelsome set of her pretty mouth. He felt as if he'd caught sight of an angel masquerading amongst lesser mortals, who'd become entangled in mankind's sin and was now helpless to escape.

Apparently he wasn't the only one who noticed her, for suddenly the young woman yelped and smacked the hand of the patron closest to her, a man who, after being so rebuffed, snatched his hand away from the girl's well-turned ankle. The collective thunder of male laughter shook the floor beneath Cormack's boots.

Cormack did not laugh. Instead, he maneuvered closer to the stage, fixated. Inexplicably smitten. A bright flush moved up the girl's throat, into her cheeks, to disappear beneath her mask. She resumed her pose, and yet...her hands trembled.

He realized instantly that she didn't belong in this place.

With each step forward, a tangle of memories and regrets welled up inside him along with a sudden impulse to protect her, to make right whatever had gone wrong. Something he'd been helpless to do for Laura.

So distracted was he by the girl that he almost...*almost*...missed the man ducking down the back corridor, dressed in the clothes of a gentleman, his top hat tilted so as to conceal his silk-obscured face.

* * *

Daphne glared at the filthy creature who had grabbed her leg, and resumed her pose. Was it only her imagination, or did her skin now *itch* where he had touched her? *Ugh.* A shiver of revulsion rippled through her.

But being on the stage meant her time at the Blue Swan was almost done. In just a matter of moments, she'd be in the carriage on her way home.

She kept telling herself that, but another, increasingly hysterical voice continued to break in, emphatically demanding: *What have you done?*

It had been easy to imagine doing "the right thing," but it was completely different now that she was here on the stage, surrounded by a hundred men with lust in their eyes. The peril of her situation closed in on her like a thick fog until she found it difficult to breathe.

Stop it! It was too late for fear. Hysterics would only draw attention and increase her danger. She had to push through, not only for herself but for Kate. According to Mr. Bynum, that foul-mouthed bully of a stage master, they would perform their rotations on the stage ten times before taking their leave of the stage. Only then would Kate's debt be satisfied, at least for the night. Given a day or two, Daphne was certain she could come up with some other solution for satisfying the remainder of the Fickett family's debt.

She simply had to be home tonight by the time Clarissa and her mother returned from the Heseldons', else her intricate tangle of not-necessarily untruths would fall to pieces. If Lady Harwick ever learned the truth of this night, Daphne feared the viscountess would expire on the spot.

"Pirouette."

Mr. Bynum's command jerked Daphne into the present. She mimicked the movements of the young woman on the stage beside her, and twirled like a ballerina. More like a *drunken* ballerina. Her throat still burned from that single gulp of gin. While spirits no doubt took the edge off her present humiliation, she hadn't anticipated its strength. To her good fortune, no one seemed concerned about talent or proper form, only that they prance around under the pretense of being actresses, wearing unseemly costumes for the illicit pleasure of the men salivating at their feet. Coming to a stop, she sashayed to the next corner and took the place of the girl who had just vacated the spot.

Mr. Bynum shouted a French command. *"Parader!"*

Truly, he had the most appalling accent. Yet she complied and executed a different "classical" pose, her arms thrown wide.

He blathered on, this time about Helen and the Spartans. In that moment, she desperately tried to forget where she was at the moment and mentally transport herself a thousand miles away. She imagined herself as Helen, the face that had launched a thousand ships. She had always had a flair for the dramatic. She and her sisters had always put on productions for the family, and in secret she had dreamed of a life onstage, of a life of adventure. In some ways, tonight's daring excursion had been exceedingly exciting, and she might actually enjoy herself if not—

If not for the fact that she, Daphne Bevington, the Earl of Wolverton's granddaughter, was at this moment standing on a stage in London's most notorious bawdy house, half foxed, half naked, and making a naughty spectacle of her jiggly bits for the entertainment of strangers.

Daphne bit down a gasp. *Not all strangers*, for *there*, having just come through the back doorway, was—oh, of all people—Lord Rackmorton. She'd sensed he was a rat. Now, at the earliest opportunity she could rebuff him without the slightest guilty conscience. Look how he laughed, with a salacious turn of his lips, and greeted the ladies, all the while appearing so at ease.

A sudden terror struck her. What if, even though her face was half-concealed by the mask, he saw her and recognized her? For the first time, a different terror struck her—the realization that not only her family might discover her secret, but the entire *ton* as well.

Yet in a blink, two women plastered themselves to His

Lordship's side and escorted him off, laughing, into the shadows, past *another* gentleman who, strangely, had concealed his face with a dark hood—

"Pirouette!"

Just then, a big hand smacked her buttocks, latched there, and *squeezed*.

Daphne squawked and jumped. A glance over her shoulder confirmed her assailant to be the same cretin as before, looking rather pleased at getting such a solid handful of her. Indeed, in the next moment, with the help of a friend's knee, he hurled himself half on the stage, reaching for her, his tongue hanging out of his mouth like a hound on the street. "Come on, sweet, how about a little ballum-rankum? Just tell me how much?"

Lunging away, she somehow managed to twirl with one leg raised—

Only to crash into Cleopatra the Cat. The room erupted in laughter. In her discomposure, she'd gone the wrong way. The girl shouted a vulgarity a lady ought not to even know, and gave Daphne a shove in the opposite direction—

Just in time for her to see the most *attractive* gentleman plant his fist in the face of the man who had affronted her.

Looking up, he glared at her, rather ferociously, something that ought to have frightened her but instead inspired everything inside her to tingling. In that moment, everything inside her arrested completely, and the churning crowd seemed to disappear, leaving just the two of them for one crystalline moment in time. He looked so very fine with his cravat so perfectly tied, and his dark blond hair so neatly cut, somewhere between short and longish, the ideal frame for his broad cheekbones and astonishing gray eyes.

"Thank you," she shouted, though she knew he couldn't hear her for the din of the room.

The gleam in his gray eyes intensified, but with a different sort of appreciation than what she saw in the eyes of the degenerates crowded at her feet, one that didn't send revulsion down her spine, but instead something...wonderful.

"You're welcome." Or at least that's what his mouth appeared to say. She couldn't hear him, either.

A large crash sounded from the direction of the entrance. A woman screamed. The music trailed off into a discordant snarl. An enormous man in a black suit and top hat appeared on the threshold. Patrons scrambled away from him, pushing and shoving.

Bracing his legs wide, he bellowed, "Under His Majesty's authority, this bawdy house is hereby closed for the crimes of lewdness and common nuisance." Lifting both hands high he displayed what appeared to be a constable's blazon and a piece of paper that could only be a warrant. "You are all under arrest."

A swarm of men rushed in behind him, wielding batons.

Daphne stood paralyzed for a long moment. She? Daphne Bevington, under arrest?

Like everyone else, she dashed for the door.

Pulse racing, she leapt from the stage into a tumult of shoulders, hats, and feathers. After that, she had no choice in the path of her escape. The crowd *pushed...jostled...* and carried her to the street where a frigid rain pounded onto her skin and soaked her costume through. All she could think was that she'd left her cloak inside, but behind her came shouts and screams and glimpses of batons raised. She couldn't go back. She ran for the hackney, praying the driver still waited, as she'd paid him handsomely to do.

There, at the corner. He had waited. Thank God. His pale face peered over the roof from where he stood on his driver's perch, wide-eyed and dismayed at the scene unfolding before him. She ran toward him, arms flailing, wanting nothing more than to be inside, safe and far away from this terrible place. She'd been such a fool! She would go to her grandfather tomorrow and beg on her knees for the money to pay Kate's debt, and pretend that this night had never happened. She should never have come.

"Hurry, girl." The driver reached his hand to assist her up.

"Thank you, sir," she cried, almost in tears—

A fierce tug pulled her backward, out of his grasp. *Splash*. Her teeth clicked at the sudden jolt of her buttocks against the cold pavement. It took a moment for her mind and vision to clear, to realize what had happened.

Mr. Bynum, Cat, and the redhead crowded into the hackney. The vehicle swayed and creaked beneath their sudden weight.

"You get out," bellowed the old man, his hands raised to force them out. The horse, startled, danced in its harness and the vehicle rolled forward a few feet.

"That's my hackney." Daphne leapt to her feet, and grasped the handle. "You can't leave me here."

"Oh, let her in," insisted the redhead.

"There's no more room," Cat screeched, giving her a shove. The jewels on her mask sparkled darkly. The dark red rouge on her lips had smudged across her cheek. With another hard shove, she broke Daphne's grip. A gun appeared in Mr. Bynum's hand, and he pointed it at the old man's head.

"Drive," he bellowed.

"Oh, miss," shouted the driver. "Forgive me. I've eight grandchildren to feed—"

The vehicle clattered into the darkness. Mr. Bynum's laughter echoed against the walls of the warehouse buildings.

"Selfish cowards," Daphne shouted after them, meaning Mr. Bynum and the girls, of course, not the poor driver. Whistles sounded shrilly. Footsteps pounded past, patrons running toward the side streets, with constables in pursuit. Panic electrified her blood. She'd been abandoned to the city's roughest streets, without as much as a cloak for protection. Now what? How would she get home?

A flash of movement in the corner of her eye, and suddenly she could not breathe, because two large hands constricted her throat. She flailed and twisted, her feet dragging against the pavement, unable to see her assailant.

"'Ay, sweet, so I see you're waitin' for me," murmured a gravelly voice beside her ear. The stench of liquor and foul breath crowded her nose.

"He—help—" she gasped, seeking to draw the attention of the very constables she'd striven to escape just moments ago.

The man dragged her toward the shadows, his arm winched against her throat. Her heart sank in a downward spiral into utter hopelessness.

* * *

In the ensuing madness, Cormack took an elbow to his side and a boot heel to his toe. Irritated at allowing himself to be so distracted by the chit on the stage that he'd lost sight of his prey, he endeavored to do a lot more pushing and shoving himself. Within moments, he'd made his way to the maze of ramshackle rooms behind the stage, which were of course, *bloody damn hell*, a wild crush of people, none of them the distinctively elegant, masked men he sought.

He half-turned, intending to escape with all the others to the street, but a sudden flare of intuition made him turn back, and press in the opposite direction until he found himself alone. He heard the faint bark of men's voices. Following the sounds of wood scraping on the floor and a slamming door, he found a large room adorned far more elegantly than the rest, with a large table at its center, cluttered by a jumble of chairs, crystal liquor decanters, and more than one article of woman's clothing.

A door, cut into the opposite wall, bounced ajar and he raced forward, delving inside to find himself in a narrow, pitch-dark passageway. But in the distance there were voices, and an intermittent flash of light. Taking a corner, he saw them, illuminated in the golden light of a lantern held high: men in hoods, with several bare-shouldered ladies among them.

The last in line glanced over his shoulder and, catching sight of him, shouted, "*Hurry!*"

They pushed and shoved and the ladies screamed. Cormack reached them just as the door swung closed—

He reached through, grabbing the man's shoulder, but the man twisted, and several more threw their weight against the door. Cormack bellowed in pain, but his fingertips grazed silk and he *pulled*, enjoying the subsequent sound of head thudding against wood. Hands shoved and pummeled his arm, but he fisted his hand in the silk—

A tearing sound rent the air, and he fell back a step, the hood in hand—

The door slammed. He reached, but heard a frantic scrabbling against metal and a turn of the lock. He yanked, but the door held fast. Cursing, he turned on his heel and retraced his steps down the passageway and into the room. He had to get outside before they got away.

In the corridor, he joined others still making their escape, some holding chairs or paintings or whatever else they could carry. Near the door, he came face-to-face with a constable. Cormack curled his fists, and leveled a blistering look on the man, having no time for this nonsense. The officer, appearing overwhelmed by the selection of miscreants with which to take into custody, took one long glance at Cormack, all six foot four of him, and determined him to be too troublesome.

He bellowed, "Get out of me way, then."

With a wave of his baton, he lunged toward less sizable quarry.

Moments slipped past. Cormack prayed there was still time to catch them outside, men he'd glimpsed only in shadows. All he needed was the identity of one, and then he could track the rest. To have come this close, only to have the Invisibilis slip away like ghosts in the night, fueled within him a desperate fury.

Cormack hurtled into the alleyway, splashing into an ankle-deep torrent. At some point the sky had opened. Thunder and lightning crashed. Rain hammered the cobblestones. Beside him a driver shouted and lowered his whip. Carriage wheels spun and vehicles clattered into the darkness, even as constables carried off countless fellows, kicking and cursing, to a box wagon. More constables rounded the corner, having emptied out the brothel.

Cormack cursed as well, rounding the corner—almost

to be plowed over by a magnificent town carriage speeding past, its window crowded with silk-hooded faces staring out at him with blank holes for eyes. A dark cloth had been draped over the door so as to obscure the familial crest.

Too late. He was too goddamn late. For a long moment he stood in the midst of the melee, allowing the cold rain to hit his face, to soak his clothing, wishing in that moment he could drown in his hate. Instead, he cut down a side alley and abandoned the Blue Swan.

Just then a golden mask floated past, carried by rainwater, its jewels dully reflecting the dark night sky.

The muscles along his shoulders rippled, and drew tight.

He paused, searching the darkness. Listening. A scream found his ears. Up ahead, a flash of pale skin lured him deeper into the shadows. It was *her*, the angel, kicking and flailing as she was being dragged by the fellow he'd pounded in the face for having touched her earlier. He followed, rounding a brick corner, to see the bastard on top of her, tearing at her clothes.

In a flash, Cormack's rage exploded.

Everything after came in a blur, until she screamed again, this time in his ear, her hands yanking at his coat sleeve.

"Don't kill him!" she exclaimed.

He stared down into a bloodied face, then up into hers. Rain trickled over her pale skin, plastering sodden curls against her cheek.

"Please. Not because of me." Wide, dark-lashed blue eyes pled with him.

All he could think was that while the mask had been alluring, and the stuff of fantasies, it was nothing compared to the face beneath.

"Damned lecher." Cormack stood, stepping back from the crumpled heap. "Come with me."

He extended his hand.

She backed away, shaking her head, her eyes bright with terror and tears.

She was a small thing, and he towered over her. Her muslin costume clung slick and transparent against her skin. The young woman crossed her arms over her chest, doing her best to cover her nakedness. God curse him for looking. He could not help himself. Cormack prayed the darkness concealed the magnitude of his hunger, his physical reaction.

Of course, she would expect the same thing of him as of the man who lay motionless at his feet: that like an animal, he would victimize and shame her.

With a curse, he tore off his coat and held the weighty garment out as an offering. "You don't belong in that place. I understand that. I won't hurt you. Let me see you home safely."

She did not move. She only shivered.

"Do you have a home?" he demanded.

Did she have a lover? A protector? A husband? Those were the questions he wanted to ask, but he did not. If she did have someone, the bastard wasn't good enough for her, wasn't worthy. She ought not to be out on this mean street, unprotected. Ought never to have stepped foot inside the Blue Swan.

"Of course I have a home," she retorted, her pronunciations polished, not those of a woman of the street.

"Then let us go," he ordered, glaring at her now, for being so obstinate when they ought to be off and away. Rain pattered down around them. "I've a carriage waiting not far from here."

She stepped closer, her face stark and beautiful, peering into his eyes as if she could gauge his true intentions within them. At last, she appeared to come to some decision.

"Very well. Thank you." She nodded curtly. "But don't you dare touch me, do you understand?"

She snatched the coat from his hand, but the rainwater made the wool unwieldy. Reclaiming it, he shook the garment out, intending to drape it over her shoulders, but a sudden blast of male voices echoed down the alley. The light of lanterns bobbed, signaling the approach of what could only be the constables, searching side streets.

"Oh, no," she gasped, eyes wide. "I can't be arrested."

Every protective instinct within him roared to life. There was no way to escape the alley without being seen. Forgetting the coat, he seized her by the wrist and urged her into the archway of a crumbling stoop.

She went rigid, her lips parted on a complaint—

"Just cooperate," he ordered, his hands going to her waist to guide her more urgently into the corner.

They were face-to-face. Her hands came against his chest, pressed flat against his wet shirt, and her breasts rose and fell with her ragged intake of breath. He caged her within the deepest of shadows, shielding her body with his. It wasn't that he feared discovery. He felt quite capable of handling himself on the street or in the gaol, but the idea of the angel spending even one night in a filthy cell with the dregs of London offended him beyond bearing.

"They are coming—" she whispered, curling her hands in the front of his shirt.

"Quiet," he hissed near her cheek, savoring the feel of her forehead against his jaw, the softness of her body pressed so intimately against his.

The light of a lantern swept over the bricks above their heads. Footsteps splashed on the wet cobblestones, coming nearer, just behind his back.

"This fellow's beat all t' bloody hell."

"Ay, but 'e's alive. Let's get 'im on 'is feet."

Cormack did not breathe. The girl trembled against him, her breasts pressed soft and full against his chest, something no man alive would fail to notice. He pulled her closer and she cleaved even more tightly to him, her hands clenching his arms. The threat of discovery only heightened the unintended sensuality of the moment. Shuffling, wet sounds, and groans from the injured man, and then silence, at last indicated their departure.

"Come. Hurry." Vacating the stoop, he quickly settled his coat onto her shoulders and led her in the opposite direction. Together they distanced themselves from the Blue Swan, their feet splashing on the cobblestones. The girl kept pace with him without complaint. The rain subsided, but a frigid chill remained. Two streets more, and Cormack found Jackson waiting exactly where they'd arranged to meet, sitting atop the carriage. True to form, the young man was smiling down at three girls gathered beside his perch, his mouth slanted with roguish mischief. Here, streetlamps illuminated the night. Wagons and conveyances crowded the street. "We'll cross here."

Yet the young woman held back, reaching down to rub her foot, her expression one of pain and desperation. "A moment, please."

Only then did he realize the slippers she'd been wearing had disintegrated into little more than ribbons.

"I've got you."

This time she did not protest, and he lifted her in his

arms as if she were a child. She pressed her face to his neck, twisting her hand in his collar and shunning the curious gazes of passersby. The animal in his chest growled with satisfaction that she should cling to him so trustingly. Seeing their approach, Jackson waved his admirers away and leapt down to open the door, his gaze keenly fixed on the figure in his employer's arms. Inside, enveloped by shadows, Cormack deposited the girl on the bench. Bloody hell, it was good to be back in his own domain, if only just his carriage.

He lowered himself beside her, the opposite bench being presently removed for repair. His two black devils, Hugin and Munin, had gleefully ripped the upholstery to pieces as he spent his night in an inn that had refused them entrance. Needless to say, the following day he had found new lodgings, one amenable to canine traveling companions.

Only now…returned to safety, the magnitude of his failure reverberated through him. Who knew how long it would be before the Blue Swan opened again elsewhere, or before the Invisibilis congregated in such a fashion again? Weeks? Months? Perhaps bloody never, depending on who appeared on the pillory in the coming days. They had slipped through his grasp. He had no other leads to follow. Unless, by chance, the girl could offer some helpful bit of information.

"Instructions?" Jackson inquired, peering inside.

Crowded into the corner, the girl appeared to assess all avenues of possible escape, color gathering high on her cheeks, more distressed at being alone in a carriage with him than she had been on a bawdy-house stage.

He didn't want to frighten her, so sought to ease her fears. "Miss, you may call me Cormack, and this is Jackson. Jackson, please make the acquaintance of Miss—" Ah, her name. At last he would have it.

She blinked, and her pretty mouth opened. For a moment there was only silence, then she whispered, "Ah...Kate. My name is...Kate."

Did she tell the truth? Probably not. He supposed it did not matter.

"Mademoiselle Kate, you may tell Jackson your address or wherever else it pleases you to go."

She did so, leaning forward to murmur instructions to the young man, holding his coat closed over her breasts.

Jackson nodded, and under raised eyebrows threw Cormack a dazed look, silently professing his bewitchment. "Yes, Miss Kate."

With that, she withdrew into the deeper shadows of the corner, shivering. Cormack's gaze fell on her bare calves, and her ankles, visible beneath the hem of his coat. She was slender without being thin, with luscious curves and creamy skin. Deep in his chest, the primitive male animal inside him growled in pleasure. His carriage. His coat. *His woman.* Yet with a twitch of her hand, she concealed her legs, drawing them up beneath her on the seat, and watched him warily.

"Jackson, stop on Houndsditch if you will, near the clothing stalls. Kate needs a dress and some shoes."

"Of course." Jackson then secured the door, throwing the cab into darkness.

She exhaled loudly. "I don't need clothes. I just want to—to—"

"To escape me, as soon as possible?" He grinned. "Now you're hurting my feelings. After everything we've been through together tonight?"

She stared at him in silence, her eyes not frightened, but flashing and accusatory.

He feared he'd offended her with his teasing, when all he wanted to do was earn her trust. Perhaps she could help him find the proprietor of the Blue Swan.

He softened his voice. "Wherever you're going, you can't make an entrance in that insufficient costume or wearing a strange man's coat."

After a long moment, in which a thousand emotions played across her face, to include a flash of impatience, she nodded. "I suppose that's right."

"We'll stop for only a moment and then be on our way again."

"Very well," she whispered. Shadows painted the hollows beneath her cheekbones.

Lord, she was pretty.

"So," he said, his gaze descending slowly along the column of her lovely throat, down to the upper swell of her breast, barely visible within the shadow of his coat. "Home is Hamilton Place, the exclusive domain of the *ton*'s rich and powerful. I knew you didn't belong on that stage. Care to tell me who you really are?"

Chapter Four

I...I work as a maid at a private residence there," Daphne lied, nearly breathless to find herself in the company of the man she'd connected with so powerfully from the stage, a man who had very nearly beaten someone else to death in order to save her. The violence he'd exacted both horrified...and pleased her.

A sudden chill rippled through her. The night was cold, and she wanted nothing more than to be warm. Her savior—Cormack—relaxed not a foot away from her, as soaked through as she, yet he didn't appear the least bit chilled. Robust and ruddy cheeked, he might as well have been dressed in flannel and slippers, and sipping brandy beside a roaring fire.

Only he wasn't. Blood stained the cuffs of his sleeves and, she realized, likely the coat she wore as well, though she could not perceive its presence for the dark wool and shadows.

"You've gainful employment, then." His gaze moved

over her with such heated interest she shivered from it, more so than from the cold. "So why were you at the Blue Swan?"

As the carriage proceeded along the road, intermittent flashes of light from the streetlamps illuminated the interior. Other carriages crowded close at times, and the loud voices of nighttime revelers could be heard.

He raised his hands—fine hands, with long, square-knuckled fingers—to his cravat and deftly worked the knot. Her attention fell to where his linen shirt clung damply to his skin, revealing with his every flex of muscle the indentations that defined his chest and abdomen, and her mouth went dry. With a lift of his chin he removed the cloth from his neck and abandoned the sodden linen to the bench beside him.

She did not answer him. She only stared at the place where his shirt had parted to reveal his throat, and wondered what it might be like to kiss a man there. Not any man, but Cormack.

"Kate, why were you there tonight?" he pressed, his voice quiet and assured.

"I'd rather not say," she responded abruptly. The less he knew about her, the better.

"Oh?" His brow went up. He dragged his fingertip across his lips—and a faint smile that after a moment, broadened a degree more.

Amused. She amused him—which vexed her, of course, because if she were honest with herself, she would prefer that a mysterious and intriguing man like Cormack find *her* mysterious and intriguing, not entertaining, like some precocious child.

"So that's it. Because you helped me I'm now obligated

to confide in you my most private matters, despite your being a complete stranger?"

His smile faded. "No, of course not, Kate. It's just obvious that you didn't belong at the Blue Swan. I can't help but be curious over how you came to be on that stage."

Daphne stared into his eyes, mesmerized by the blaze of heat she saw in them, heat apparently inspired by her. Instinct told her she could trust him. He had saved her virtue and very likely her life.

"If you must know—" she began.

He raised a hand, and shook his head. "Please, you don't have to—"

"Your carriage smells like dog."

He smiled. "That's because I have two very stinky dogs."

"I like dogs. But not smelly ones."

"I suppose I should endeavor to have them bathed." He chuckled.

Oh, dear. She liked Cormack very much. It seemed only seemed proper that she offer him some explanation, even if the details weren't precisely true.

"I am paying off a debt."

"A debt, you say." He glanced away, lifting the curtain to look out the window.

The movement provided her with an unexpected thrill, his face in profile, and the muscle that corded the length of his neck. She was quite the expert on noses, having enjoyed sketching faces in her youth, and his was distinctly Roman, prominent and regal, but it was his lips that made her think of—

She closed her mind to the thought.

Only she didn't. Not successfully, anyway.

His lips made her think of *kissing*, rather desperately, even though of course, she didn't want to kiss him. Not a stranger. Because that would be wrong. And impetuous! And not just a little unseemly.

"To whom do you owe money?" he asked. "The owner of the Blue Swan, I presume?"

"Yes, but it's not me. It is my father's debt."

Her conscience complained about speaking the words. Untruths! It was Kate's story to tell, not hers. Yet still the well-intentioned lies spilled from her lips, because she knew not what else to say.

His eyes narrowed. "Your father could not repay the debt himself because he is...?"

She whispered, "Unable to do so immediately, under the terms imposed. He doesn't know, you see, that I have made alternate arrangements to satisfy the balance. He would never allow it, but something had to be done, else my family would find themselves on the streets..."

Her voice trailed away.

"I see." He frowned, clearly disliking her answer. "How much remains to be paid?"

More questions! Without a doubt, she regretted having taken this path. She ought not to have said anything at all. But his eyes commanded her to speak.

Daphne bit into her lower lip. "Too much."

"So you'll have to return to the stage, once there's a stage to return to?"

"I don't know what will happen now."

"It won't be long until you find out. People like that don't just forgive debts when things become inconvenient."

"No, I suppose they don't."

The heat in his gaze intensified. He leaned toward her,

his handsome face commanding her full attention. "So tell me, Kate, in addition to being a dancer to pay off this debt, and not a very talented one at that, did you also entertain patrons?"

"Entertain?" She blinked, flustered by his proximity, and his overwhelming maleness. Had he truly said she was not a good dancer? And wait…he had said *patrons*. She frowned. "I beg your pardon?"

Certainly he did not believe…well, she supposed he *might*, given the sordid circumstances in which he'd found her.

One dark eyebrow lifted. "The Blue Swan *is* a brothel."

"Never," she blurted, heat rising to scald her cheeks. "This was my first night ever to go to that place, and it was not at all what I'd expected." She spoke the truth now. Not all her words were lies. "All I had was the address on a scrap of paper, and instructions that I would be a model in the *tableaux*."

A sudden fear came over her, a dreadful worry that in her naïveté she'd misjudged the stranger beside her, that he wasn't a gentleman but instead just like the others who had crowded against the stage, mindless with lust. He could easily overpower her and satisfy whatever male urges he wished.

But he did not. He instead eased back into the seat until shadows obscured his countenance, all but his sensual lips, which pursed and frowned. She sighed with relief.

"Good." He nodded. Below his breath, he muttered, "Yes, good…I suppose."

He conveyed a mixed message, one of approval but also disappointment. What if she'd answered yes? Would he have sought to make use of her services? All the wicked things Sophia had described came to her in a vivid rush. Her mind entertained a fleeting fantasy, one of tangled sheets, muscled limbs, and bare skin.

The very idea of being intimate with a stranger, with *this* stranger—

She exhaled, bemused.

—was not as appalling as it ought to be.

Perhaps it was the graveness in his eyes, above lips that she suspected always carried some semblance of a smile, that made her heart contract and her blood run hot.

He really was nonpareil. No man in her social circle compared, but that was because he obviously wasn't a nobleman. No nobleman would travel about London in a shabby, half-destroyed carriage nor converse on such familiar terms with his driver.

"Who are you, Cormack?" she asked.

"Just . . . a man."

"Are you a newspaperman? A store owner, or a sea captain? Please tell me—I want to know."

"I'm . . . er, a merchant, actually. Saltpeter."

That answered her question. After tonight, she most certainly would never see him again. A merchant would never be allowed into the ballrooms of the *haute ton*. Even if he was deliriously rich, which he obviously wasn't, given the condition of his equipage, the upper echelon of the beau monde, to which she had been born, simply did not intermingle with men of trade.

Her adventurous nature awakened. No, she didn't intend to ever marry, but . . . what would be wrong with kissing a handsome, intriguing stranger she'd never see again?

Everything inside her soared and spiraled and exploded into sparkly stars at wondering. Again, her gaze settled on his mouth, which slowly, as if it read her mind, turned up at the corners, making her catch her breath.

At that moment, the carriage executed a sudden turn and tilted steeply, as if on two wheels. Daphne toppled, the whole of her weight crushing into Cormack. His arms came round her, seizing her and holding her in place against his chest. The carriage bounced down again and continued on, to the sound of Jackson cursing at another driver, but Cormack didn't release her. How she wished she wasn't wearing the coat, which smelled of damp wool. He, on the other hand, smelled delicious, like rainwater and soap.

"How unexpected," he murmured, his mouth so close his breath feathered across her lips. "But not unwelcome."

"No," she whispered. "Not…unwelcome."

Just then the carriage jerked to a stop and a hard rap sounded against the roof.

A low growl emitted from Cormack's throat. "What a pity."

Gently, he released her to push aside the window curtain.

"I'll be just a moment." He slid from the bench, a vision of crouched male splendor and shining boots. With a turn of the handle, he disappeared onto the street.

Unwilling to release him from her sight, Daphne scrambled across the bench and lifted the curtain. Just a few feet away, Cormack stood like a giant in the midst of a street stall crowded with clothing, hats, and shoes. He gestured to the shop owner, clearly attempting to describe her. Apparently she had breasts. Daphne covered her mouth, smothering a smile. Very nice breasts, based upon Cormack's raised eyebrows and sideways grin. The shop owner chuckled and set about searching his collection.

Within moments, Cormack returned.

"I hope it all fits." He thrust toward her a gray flannel gown, a chemise and a petticoat, and a pair of shoes. She clasped them to her breast, bewildered.

He had purchased several items for himself as well. Once the carriage was again in motion, he tugged his shirt-tails from his breeches. *Oh, no.* Daphne bit into her lower lip, fixated, as he wrenched his shirt over his head. Shadows and light played on his damp skin. Daphne inhaled sharply, shocked, her mouth gone instantly dry. But she didn't look away.

She'd never seen anything like him, nothing *real* and in the flesh. He could have served as a model for the Achilles statue she'd seen last week in the vestibule of the British Gallery. The only items missing were a helmet, battle ax, and sword. Oh, and he was still wearing those breeches.

Not for long apparently. Dropping the sodden shirt to the floor, he unfastened the placket at his crotch. Fascinated, she glimpsed a dark spiral of hair on his lower abdomen that disappeared beneath the buff wool of his garment. He hooked his thumbs inside at the hips and—

She must have emitted some sound, because he looked up suddenly.

He flashed a grin, one that made her heart turn over inside her chest.

"Don't be ridiculous," he said. "Put the clothes on. They aren't perfectly dry, being that I bought them off the street, but they are far drier and warmer than what you've got on. But first, mind giving my boot a tug?"

He presented her with the flat of his foot.

After a moment's hesitation, she grasped the leather by the heel, and tugged it free. She'd never assisted a man with such a familiar task, and her mind buzzed with unexpected exhilaration of doing something so forbidden. If her mother knew—Lord, *anything* about tonight—she'd never recover. It was just another secret of this night that she would forever be forced to keep from everyone, including Kate.

After doing the same with the second boot, she averted her gaze while he changed his breeches for a pair of loose trousers, catching only the flash of bare skin out of the corner of her eye. And perhaps one stolen glance of a well-muscled hip and chiseled torso.

Daphne closed her eyes tight, knowing she would never forget this terrifying and thrilling night. That while she regretted placing herself in such danger, and had never before been so frightened in her life...she would forever hold these moments close. And when she was an old maid, living a life filled with nieces and nephews and quiet evenings in her room alone, she would fashion fantasies from these memories.

"Kate?"

She started, realizing he spoke to her, and opened her eyes to find him studying her with amusement.

"You won't put on those clothes as long as I'm in this carriage, will you?"

"Of course not."

Again, he smiled, and everything inside her melted because she knew he would do the right thing. Indeed, he rapped a fist against the roof. Immediately, the carriage swayed, changing directions and decreasing speed. Cormack perched at the edge of the bench, as if prepared to exit. But then—

He moved toward her, a shadow in the night, until he

half-crouched, half-knelt with his hands planted on either side of her legs. Her heart raced, and she breathed him in, savoring his scent and his heat. Gray eyes stared straight into hers.

Her pulse jumped wildly, taken over by a dark and pleasurable desire for a stranger. Against all good sense she liked him this close, with his attention fixed so intently on her.

"Cormack," she whispered.

He kissed her suddenly, catching her mouth slightly open. Before she realized, she'd leaned into him, kissing him back with fervent eagerness. His tongue slipped inside her mouth, something that ought to have shocked her but instead felt completely natural. She sighed, and touched her tongue to his, too. Oh, how sweet and warm he was, inside and out. Who needed dry clothes and a fire, when there was kissing?

He chuckled low in his throat.

She froze. Why did he laugh? Had she done something wrong?

She very well might have, because she'd never kissed a man, unless one counted young David Waddington from the neighboring estate, when they'd both been just twelve. It had been a hurried, sloppy affair with neither of them knowing what they were doing. Her brother, Vinson, had caught them behind the hedge and given David a fat nose, but refused even under intense interrogation to tell their father, the viscount, why.

On the contrary, Cormack clearly knew his way around a kiss. With a slant of his head, he kissed her more deeply, easing her backward into the cushions and thrilling her with the confident glide of his tongue over her upper teeth.

With each brush of his lips, each warm breath into her mouth, the invisible velvet cord that ran along the center of her body tightened and quivered. Her toes curled into the cushion.

He exhaled and murmured near her ear, "Sorry—I couldn't help myself."

And apparently she couldn't, either, but something told her to keep that to herself. The same something held her silent, preventing her from begging for more. Her upraising, she knew, and the expectation of her family and society that she would always behave as a lady.

His face hovered near her cheek, but he did not kiss her. He gave her an opportunity, she realized, to reject him, to protest. The moment lasted only that long—a moment—before he bent a few inches more and nuzzled the side of her neck, just below her ear—

"All right, then. You haven't screamed...or poked out my eyes."

He pressed his lips to the sensitive skin there. Her fingers curled in his shirt.

"Tell me if you're opposed," he murmured against her skin. "Tell me if I should stop."

She couldn't say *anything*. He couldn't possibly understand why, and she wasn't about to tell him. But his breath tantalized and tickled. With a sigh, she clasped his head there, and he found her earlobe. They sank into the corner, the shadow of his body closing over hers, a delicious blanket of heat and weight, his mouth again claiming her lips.

"Cormack—" she whispered against him, inhaling his breath. Kissing him back. "Yes."

Beneath the coat, his hand found her bare skin, and smoothed up her thigh.

The carriage jerked to a stop.

He groaned, kissing her hard, and breaking away to stare at her through glazed eyes.

"Fortuitous timing." He dragged a thumb across her toes and smiled. "I shall leave you to change into your new old clothes."

He exited the carriage, leaving her to darkness and silence and the overwhelming realization she'd likely just had the most thrilling moment of her life. She'd been rescued and kissed senseless by a handsome stranger.

Now the moment was almost over. Why did she feel so dissatisfied, when she ought to feel relieved? Male voices sounded above her. The carriage started, nearly jolting her from her seat. In reality, they could be abducting her away to the country or taking her to the wharves to sell her off to a harem. She and her sisters read such sordid stories in the papers all the time, and thanked God for their protected lives. Yet her heart couldn't summon the slightest impulse of alarm. She only felt exceedingly morose that in mere moments she would have to say good-bye to Cormack and his delightful kisses.

After dressing, in garments that fit her surprisingly well, she folded Cormack's coat on the opposite end of the bench. A glimmer caught her eye, followed by a dull *thunk*, something fallen from its pocket. Bending, she retrieved the object, a medallion covered with the raised image of Medusa. Tilting its face toward the window, she made out the word embossed along the bottom: *Invisibilis*.

A memory danced along the back of her mind, teasing and elusive. She had seen the image somewhere, with the Latin word for "invisible." But where? She returned the object to his pocket, and settled to wait.

Some time later, after countless turns, the conveyance rolled to stop. Outside, the strike of boots sounded against the pavement. Cormack himself opened the door, his face hidden by shadows, and extended his hand to assist her down. Just seeing him again made everything inside her feel light and excited. Behind him stood the familiar stone walls of the earl's mews.

She'd been right to trust him. She was just steps away from being returned to her real life.

"Nice dress." His gaze moved over her hotly, and he bit his lower lip in appreciation. "I'll walk you to the door."

"To the door?" she blurted, horrified. "Oh, no. It's far too late for that."

Though the lane was deserted, the sounds of music and voices traveled over the walls. Though nearly three o'clock, many balls were still underway. They proceeded toward the house. Thankfully, it was very dark.

"Even for the servants?"

"I'm a lady's maid," she explained. "Not a scullery maid, and there are certain expectations with regard to my behavior. There would be questions, and my mistress would most certainly dismiss me. I cannot simply come and go, and keep company with strange men."

He paused at the center of the lane, catching her arm, and then—her hand. "And yet, this strange man wishes to see you again." She stared down, knowing she ought to break his touch. "Somewhere pleasant, apart from the madness of this night."

His words were like magic to her ears. If only she could see him again. But that was what made this moment so excruciatingly painful. So beautiful. Once she crossed the threshold of her grandfather's house, she wouldn't be

"Kate" anymore. She was the granddaughter of one of England's most influential earls. She simply couldn't, under any circumstances, consort with men off the street. Commoners, or merchants. But she couldn't tell him the truth, even if she wished it. To do so would be to place her family's reputation in terrible peril.

She removed her hand from his. "I'm afraid that's not possible."

His nostrils flared in a sudden display of displeasure. "Because you don't like me or because—no, wait." He breathed though his nose. Then, with a tilt of his head and a smile, he winked at her. "I know you like me. The way you kissed me back in the carriage quite gives you away."

Her cheeks warmed, because he was right. "You are a conceited fellow, aren't you?"

"Not at all. A man can tell." He threw her a devilish look. "In fact, you want me to kiss you again."

"That's not true!" she exclaimed in mortification, though she could not help but laugh because he looked so mischievous saying it. "Even if it were—"

But it was. She wanted to kiss him, with a desperation that astounded her. But that would be sending the wrong message, which wasn't fair to him, not when she liked him so much.

"It's just that I can't see you again," she said, with a firm shake of her head.

"There is someone else, then."

Someone else. Oh, yes. A whole gaggle of them. Her mother, her grandfather, her sisters, not to mention all of London society. All with expectations of her, very high ones.

"Yes," she answered simply.

He exhaled sharply through his nose. "Very well. That is that, I suppose. I shouldn't have taken the liberty of kissing you without all the necessary vetting and permissions and I should apologize, both to you and to *whoever he is*." The last three words dripped with disdain and derision. "But forgive me if I don't, not to him. Because he's a bastard and he doesn't deserve you. If he did you wouldn't have been at the Blue Swan tonight. He would have died before allowing you to go."

His sudden ferocity stunned her, and she could do nothing but stare at him in silence, her thoughts in disarray.

Part of her unwisely and against all good sense wanted to take it back, to assure him there was no one else. To run back to his carriage and let the night and its adventure play out until dawn. She felt so much curiosity about the world that she'd never been allowed to see firsthand. What other young lady of her acquaintance had ever been inside the walls of a low-end gaming hall, and seen the life the less fortunate half of London lived? It had been ugly and dangerous and a mistake for her to go alone, but she felt grateful for having expanded her understanding, and Cormack made her feel safe.

But she had to let go. To do so, she forced herself to face the reality she'd chosen to ignore: that he'd been at the Blue Swan, which meant he'd been looking to drink, gamble, or find a woman. Yes, the night had been exciting and he had kissed her and seen her safely home, but it was time to say good-bye.

"It's time for me to go," she said.

Scowling, he turned to consider the back façade of her grandfather's town house. Lamps would be lit in the entrance hall, in expectation of her mother and sister's return from the Heseldon ball, but the back of the house, where her grandfather's bookroom and the conservatory were located, was dark.

"If you aren't going to the door, how do you propose to get inside without being seen?"

"I left a window unlocked on the ground floor, behind some shrubberies."

"Of course you did."

His manner, more acerbic now in tone, stung, and she bristled. It seemed clear that now that he couldn't have what he wanted, he couldn't wait to be rid of her. In silence, they walked together toward the back of the house, making their way through the small garden.

She couldn't help it. She wanted to hear it from him. "Why were you at the Blue Swan tonight, Cormack? Are you a gambler, or was it a woman you wanted—or both?"

She hoped he'd be shockingly honest with her, and destroy every heroic idea she had about him.

His boots crunched on the gravel. "I've been looking for someone for a very long time. A man." His mouth twisted with displeasure. "I thought that tonight at last I'd found him."

It was not the response she'd expected.

"I see." Why did it relieve her so immeasurably to know he'd not been at the Blue Swan for gaming or women, but to find a man?

"A friend of yours, or a business associate?" Daphne led the way down a narrow gravel path that led between the house and a row of tall shrubberies, every nerve in her body drawn tight, knowing that Cormack followed close behind.

"Most certainly not," he growled.

"An enemy, then." She glanced behind, so that she might see his expression. Yet he towered above her, an inscrutable shadow.

"He wronged someone very important to me," he uttered with quiet ferocity.

"Someone you love?" she dared to ask.

"Very much so," he hissed through his teeth.

A tremor moved down her spine. What would it be like to be loved by such a man? Overwhelming, she suspected, in a wonderful sort of way. At the same time, she feared for the man he sought. She'd seen Cormack nearly destroy a man tonight, all in defense of a stranger—her. He didn't even love her.

"After what occurred tonight," he added, "I don't know how I will find him again. Likely anyone who could tell me was carried off by the authorities."

She glanced up to the window overhead, and stopped. "This is the window."

"Then this is good night and good-bye." He shifted his stance. They stared through the darkness at one another, he sullen faced and she suddenly and overwhelmingly morose.

"I'm glad I was there," he said.

"So am I." She wanted desperately to help him somehow, as thanks for saving her. As thanks for behaving like a gentleman when he could have been a lecher or a murderer—or worse. He'd returned her home in one healthy piece, and she couldn't be more grateful. "Cormack, I—perhaps I can help you."

Shadows carved hollows beneath his cheekbones. "How?"

"That man on the stage tonight, his name is Mr. Bynum.

I'm not certain, but I believe he is the proprietor of the Blue Swan, because he's the man responsible for collecting my father's debt."

"Tell me more."

"He escaped tonight."

"How do you know?"

"After the authorities burst inside, like everyone else, I ran. I had a hackney waiting outside, you see, that I'd paid to wait for me just around the corner. Mr. Bynum pushed me aside and took it from me, him and two of his girls."

Cormack straightened, a dangerous heat forming behind his eyes. "I see. And that's when the other man dragged you off into the alley."

"Yes."

Cormack's eyes went flat, and almost black. When she reached a hand to touch his arm—to try and bring him back to the present, he flinched. "I'm listening."

"He seemed to know all the regular patrons at the Blue Swan. He told me tonight that he keeps an office above the tobacco warehouses on Rosemary Lane."

"Why did he tell you that?" he asked in a quiet voice.

"He said for me to come there if I wished to discuss my options for paying off the debt more quickly."

He exhaled sharply. "You know what he means by that."

"Of course. I just wanted you to know where to find him. Perhaps, if given some incentive, he could help you find the man for whom you search."

Cormack moved closer, and his shadow enveloped her. He raised his hand to touch her cheek, to smooth his palm against her skin. She closed her eyes, in ecstasy at his touch.

"Kate..."

"Good-bye, Cormack." She laughed, drawing away. "I mean it this time."

But behind her smile, the mere speaking of the words sent her spiraling into remorse. To think that she would never see him again. That she would never kiss those lips again.

With a shove, he opened the window, and muttered, "I don't know how you would have managed even this part of the night without me. You can't even reach the ledge."

"The window didn't look so high from inside. Good thing I found a tall man to bring me home," she teased.

He braced his hands on her waist, and lifted her to the ledge—

Only to drag her off again, and pin her against the wall, his mouth crashing onto her lips.

She moaned and sighed, consumed by wanting him. By wanting this. By wanting more.

"You're so lovely, Kate," he breathed reverently, his lips moving to her cheeks. "Whoever he is, he doesn't deserve you."

Her arms went round his neck, claiming him as her own for one perfect moment. His mouth found hers again, his tongue moving over her bottom lip to explore the inside her mouth. She savored the taste of him. Touched his hair and the warm skin of his neck, determined to remember the textures, and this moment, forever.

Then he was gone from her arms. The night spun round her, as with a sudden jolt of movement, she found herself on the ledge again, legs dangling down. His hands encircled her ankles, and boldly smoothed over her calves, as if he, too, sought to memorize her.

Gray eyes stared up, burning in the night. "I'll find this Mr. Bynum and I'll pay your debt."

Her pulsed leapt. "Cormack, *no*."

"It is done, Kate," he hissed. "Just promise me you'll never step foot in the Blue Swan or another place like it again for as long as you live. Stay here, where it is safe, and live your life well."

The words he spoke stole her breath, but still she managed somehow to speak.

"Yes," she whispered. "I will."

In a blink, he was gone, only to emerge moments later from the shadows at the edge of the house. Daphne closed the window and watched until he arrived at his carriage, climbing atop to take a seat beside Jackson, where he seized the reins from the other man's hands. The horses started in their harnesses and the vehicle disappeared down the lane.

Daphne maneuvered the dark corridor and the stairs to her room, managing to avoid notice. Distant voices sounded from the vestibule, two night footmen talking about new boots and blisters.

Only after Daphne closed the door to her room did she exhale. Never before had she experienced such an overwhelming sensation of relief. She felt giddy with it, as if she'd executed the greatest, most forbidden dare. She threw herself onto her mattress and rolled onto her back to stare at the ceiling. What a terrifying night.

What a magical night.

Cormack. The memory of their kisses and the fervency with which he had insisted on paying her debt—*Kate's debt*—inspired a bittersweet ache deep inside her chest. In the days to come, she would relive her memories of him, a hundred and perhaps a thousand times.

But she would never tell anyone what she had done. Not Kate. Not Sophia and Clarissa. Because if no one else knew, well...

Then it was as if her visit to the Blue Swan had never happened at all.

Chapter Five

Three hours later, and Cormack still hadn't slept a wink. After leaving Kate at Hamilton Place, he'd gone straight to Rosemary Street, fearful the only trail that might lead to the Invisibilis would grow cold. He'd haunted the alleyways until a wagon loaded with chandeliers and chairs had led him here.

Now he and Mr. Bynum sat on opposite sides of an old desk, both wearing the same clothes as they had the night before, sizing one another up through bloodshot eyes.

"You 'eard me." The man's upper lip curled in contempt. He lifted the ledger and snapped the book shut in Cormack's face. Early morning light filtered through threadbare curtains, along with the sounds of bells clanging on the nearby ships moored off the quay. "I prefer to carry Kate Fickett's debt...er, Mr. Fickett's, that is, thank you very much."

Kate Fickett. The name didn't seem to suit her, but he supposed a person, upon being born, did not choose one's own surname nor complain to one's parents about its unsuitability.

Quite on purpose he had brought up the matter of Kate's debt first, wrongly believing that particular matter of business would be quickly and simply settled. He'd thought it was just a simple matter of monies to be paid. Obviously, he'd been wrong.

"I'm afraid I don't understand. I've offered you payment of the amount in full, including the ridiculous amount of interest you just quoted."

Mr. Bynum scratched his cheek. "Sorry. Not interested."

"I can get you cash, instead of a bank cheque," he gritted out from between clenched teeth. "If that is the issue."

"It's not." He flashed a weaselish smile. "Was there anything else? I've got business that needs attending."

Cormack enforced calm over himself. Leaning forward, toward the desk, he crumpled his gloves in his hand. "She's worth more to you on that stage than what she owes. That's it, isn't it?"

Bynum shrugged. "'At's what keeps the customers throngin' through my doors, nubile pieces o' fluff like 'er. Not their posing and prancing, of course, but every man's 'opes of takin' 'em to bed—which often, I can arrange." The man's lips curled into a dirty smile. "I ain't no saint. Never claimed to be. People know when they come to me, I lend generously, but on my terms. 'At girl will pay off 'er father's debt on my stage, even faster if she's willing to lay on her back."

Fury seared Cormack's veins and he lunged from his chair, half over the desk, to seize the man by his collar. The violence of the movement toppled the inkwell. Indigo liquid spilled across the documents beneath them, to drizzle over the edge and drip, drip, drip onto the floor.

Mr. Bynum's chair balanced precariously on its two back legs. Behind him were stacked boxes of liquor, mirrors, and paintings, salvaged fixtures from the Blue Swan.

"Careful, man." He breathed heavily through his nose. "Once my blood's been shed, there's no negotiating terms."

Bynum's words kindled an even hotter fire in his chest, and Cormack seethed, "I'll pay you double what her father owes."

"She's 'at good, is she?" His laughter revealed a row of yellowed and crooked teeth. "No, don't tell me. Think I'd prefer t' find out for m'self."

Five minutes later, Cormack stormed down the alleyway, shaking the pain from his throbbing fist, supremely satisfied at having knocked that bastard Bynum off his block. Better yet, in his pocket he carried one Arthur Fickett's note marked *Paid In Full*. He did not normally resort to violence to settle business disputes, but in just one night it seemed a singularly pretty face had turned him into a Neanderthal. No, not just a pretty face. Kate Fickett, whom he intuitively knew to be so much more, and had known from the first moment he saw her on that stage.

When Bynum had said such filthy things about her, he'd lost his mind. He liked to tell himself it was because of what had happened to Laura, that he'd become a champion of the downtrodden, but he knew his motivations weren't as altruistic as that.

The only problem now was that he'd burned his only known bridge to finding the Invisibilis. Too late, after obtaining Bynum's signature on Kate's note, he'd attempted to extract the answers he needed, but by then heavy boot-steps and male voices sounded on the stairs, and he had decided to make his exit before he found himself outnumbered by Bynum's thugs.

"'Ey, you there. Wait!" called a woman's voice from behind.

He turned to see her running toward him, wearing a cloak with the hood up to conceal her hair.

"Me?"

She peered at him through hard eyes, rimmed with smudged kohl. He caught a glimpse of black hair, and in that moment, his mind said: *Cleopatra*.

"I 'eard what you did in there for 'at gel."

"You know her?"

Her two pale hands held the cloak together at her throat. "Just from talking to her the few minutes before we went on that stage last night. She's...nice. She ought never to 'ave been in a place like that." She bit into her lower lip. "But then, once, we were all nice girls."

Only then did he make out, from inside the shadowed recesses of her cowl, the dark bruise on her cheek.

"Why did you follow me?" he asked.

"I 'eard you ask 'im about something else," she said in a hushed voice, before glancing over her shoulder. "About those men who follow the club, and meet in the back rooms from time to time."

"It's very important that I find them. Do you know something that might help me?"

"Only that last night, after the constables busted in, one of them dropped this as he climbed into his carriage. I hope you find it of some use." She pressed something into his hand, and backed away. Turning, she disappeared into the shadows of the alleyway.

Cormack looked down. She'd given him a handkerchief that bore a large heel print at its center. But then he thought to turn the folded square of linen over, and saw it: a monogram, sewn in gold thread in the shape of a coronet—with the four distinct "pearls" of a marquess and an ornately scrolled letter R beneath.

* * *

"Daphne Bevington! *What have you done?*"

Daphne turned from the window, where she'd been daydreaming over a handsome face and ardent kisses for the past quarter hour, to see Kate marching across the breakfast room, her face pale and drawn above her black lace collar.

Oh, no. The look in her lady's maid's eyes told her that some aspect of last night's secrets weren't secret anymore.

"Shouldn't you be in bed still?" Daphne asked with wide-eyed concern, placing herself behind a chair for protection, and resting her hands on the upper frame. "Last I recall, you were an invalid."

"I felt very much improved this morning, thank you very much." Kate's lips curved into a sudden smile, but her eyes did not follow suit. Instead, they narrowed. Knowing Kate as well as she did, Daphne realized she was angry. "That is, until I saw *this*."

The piece of paper in her hand crackled. Now not even her lips pretended to smile.

"What is that?" Daphne asked, praying she projected innocence, though she could think of only one subject of recent discussion that might require any sort of formal documentation.

Kate threw a glance over her shoulder as if to be certain

no one had entered the room to observe them, and hissed, "It is the note for my father's debt, previously held by the owner of the Blue Swan."

Daphne's heart leapt. "Ah, I see. 'Previously,' you say? Do you have good news to share?"

At that moment, a footman in knee breeches, coat, and white gloves brought in a large covered chafing dish with steam frilling out at the edges, which he deposited on the sideboard. Kate stood woodenly, the paper clasped in her hands. As soon as he'd gone, Daphne reached for a plate.

"These eggs smell delicious." She heaped a pile on her plate, hoping the smell forced the still-recovering Kate to keep her distance, or even better yet—go back to her room. She didn't want to have to answer any questions. "My, I'm starving. Are you? Or is your stomach still unsteady? You do look dreadfully piqued. Don't worry about me, you go and rest."

"Daphne."

"I swear, Fickett," she blurted in a breathless rush, "I've never seen that paper before."

She snapped her mouth shut. Even to her own ears she sounded guilty of something. Because, of course, she was very guilty, and not good at hiding secrets, so why had she thought she'd suddenly developed a talent for subterfuge? Certainly Kate saw straight through her.

"Well, have a good look at it," Kate said, raising the page by its two top corners, where Daphne could not help but see the lines of its bold black print. "Because it says here 'paid in full.' Can you read it? Yes, I know it's difficult to make out for the *blood that has been splattered on the page*."

Cormack had spilled more blood so that she—or rather,

Kate—could be free! Was it wrong that everything inside her went happy and warm?

She glanced at the page. "There's just a tiny bit there at the bottom edge, from what I can see. Aren't you happy? We ought to celebrate. Your family has been released from its obligation, and you'll never have to go back to that place again."

Kate folded the paper and thrust it into her apron pocket. "It is *blood*, Daphne. I fear it was shed on my behalf."

Anxiety knotted her insides. "I wouldn't know."

She didn't know, not for sure. She didn't know anything. She prayed the blood wasn't Cormack's.

Kate came very close, her brown eyes earnestly pleading. "You know something about this. I know you know, because you're the only soul I told about this debt. And you're the only one I told about my agreement with Mr. Bynum."

Daphne experienced a wave of nerve-shattering alarm. Had Cormack come here looking for her? How else would Kate have come into possession of the document?

Attempting nonchalance, she asked, "Tell me, how did you receive that document?"

"It was delivered this morning by a fellow by the name of Jackson. He asked to see me, but being that I'd been ill, the housekeeper told him I wasn't available to take callers."

Jackson hadn't seen Kate. The real Kate. Daphne breathed out a sigh of relief. "That's all very interesting."

"Daphne, who is Jackson?"

Blessedly, just then, a figure breezed through the door: Clarissa, fresh faced and smiling, followed by Lady Margaretta.

"Miss Fickett, what a relief to see you up and about,"

declared Lady Harwick. "Though I must say you don't look fully recovered."

Clarissa lifted a plate from the sideboard. "I agree, Fickett. You're quite red in the face, which is the opposite of how you looked yesterday, when you were so pale. Are you certain you don't have a fever now?"

"I think I very well might." Kate expelled the words between clenched teeth, with an all-too-obvious accusatory look to Daphne. "In my brain. It feels near ready to explode."

Daphne pursed her lips, and leveled a rebuking glare toward her lady's maid. That was all she needed—Clarissa and her mother asking questions.

Clarissa's eyes widened. "Should we summon the doctor to return?"

Daphne announced, "Of course not. She's being facetious."

"Oh?" The viscountess smiled, spooning a golden scoop of eggs onto her plate. "Facetiousness is not a quality I normally associate with Miss Fickett."

"You don't know her as well as I do," Daphne replied drily.

"I rather like facetiousness." Clarissa laughed. "I wish Miss Randolph would develop such a trait. She's always so dour, with not a bit of humor in her."

Daphne followed along behind them, filling her plate. She truly was ravenous, and her mood increasingly light. Kate's debt had been resolved! Such an enormous debt, and paid, she knew, on her behalf. While she would be eternally grateful to Cormack, he could now fade into her past as a happy and treasured memory. Yes, truly and fondly treasured.

"How was the Heseldon ball?" she asked, eager to turn the bent of the conversation away from herself and Kate. "You must tell me every detail."

"Wild fun." Clarissa's eyes shone at the memory. The youngest of the Bevington sisters was such a social creature. She never tired of activity or making new acquaintances. "So many people have only just arrived in town. Now the fun shall truly begin! And if you can believe it, Kincraig actually behaved himself. He even danced with me, though he has much to learn about footwork. Everyone wanted to know where you were, and thought you quite the dear heart to have stayed home to take care of everyone."

"Is that what you did?" muttered Kate beneath her breath.

Daphne pressed her foot down on top of Kate's toe. "Of course it is. You just don't remember because you were insensible."

Kate turned toward her, so that only Daphne could see her face and hear her whispered words. "I suppose that's true. If I were called before a court of law, or say, *your mother*, to vouch for your whereabouts last nights, I wouldn't be able to do so."

"What are you two whispering about over there?" Lady Harwick inquired.

"Kate's being sweet enough to accomplish a few errands for me this morning." Daphne lowered her plate to the table. "Kate, just one more thing—oh, why don't I just walk you out?"

In the corridor, they waited until the footman traveled past, this time with a silver tea pot.

Her voice still low, Daphne touched Kate's arm and squeezed. "Fickett, I don't mean to be elusive, but please trust me, it's better that you don't know. All that's important now is that you and your family are safe, and won't be turned out from your home."

Emotion glimmered in Kate's eyes. She inhaled, and bit her lower lip, which trembled. "Thank you, Daphne. Really. *Thank you.* Whatever you did. But it was so much money, and I worry that somehow you placed yourself in a harrowing situation, or...or compromised your reputation, by attempting to deal with Mr. Bynum yourself. You mustn't ever do that for me. I'd never forgive myself."

Kate looked so tormented. Daphne couldn't keep the truth from her a moment more. "I did go there...to the Blue Swan—"

"Oh, my God, I knew it." Kate's eyes widened, and flooded with tears.

"But I met the most wonderful man, and Kate, don't despise me, but I told him my name was Kate, because I was frightened and I didn't know what else to do, but he...he made everything right."

"Oh, dear. I can see your admiration for him written all over your face. You're glowing. Look at your cheeks. Did you...did he—?" Kate demanded fervently.

"A kiss. Well, perhaps five or six, but they were magical." And wildly passionate, such as she'd never forget.

"I'm going to be sick." Kate put her hands on her waist, and bent forward.

Daphne raised her back up. "Don't be. He was a gentleman. A complete and utter gentleman. And I'll never see him again. Truly, I know nothing but his first name, and he understands that he should never try to see me...or you, I suppose, again. He will forevermore be an exciting and happy memory."

Kate covered her eyes. "You shouldn't have done it."

Daphne pulled her hand away. "You'd do the same for me."

"Of course I would, but, *Daphne*, it's different for me—"

"No it isn't—at least, it shouldn't be."

"But it is. You have a future. I know you say you don't intend to marry, but what if someone found out? The scandal would be enormous—"

She lifted a silencing hand, and smiled. "Pah, I can't hear you. Besides, Mother will come out looking for me in a moment. Just go, sweet friend, and pay a visit to your family to share the news, and don't worry another moment more."

Returned to the table, she took a bite of her fried potatoes. Her adventure the night before—and more so, her intense relief that it was all over—had made her ravenous. In a blink, she cleared her plate. She considered going for another, but her mother folded her napkin and stood.

"It's nearly ten. Mrs. Brightmore will be expecting us for our review of the account books." Her mother, of late, had insisted on both girls accompanying her on her daily visits with the housekeeper, as they would both soon have households of their own to manage. Daphne humored her, and went along.

Clarissa stood and pulled a piece of paper from her pocket. "I've prepared another list of questions."

"Very good." Lady Harwick nodded, pleased. "Daphne, what about you?"

"Ah...no, I thought I'd just ask whatever questions come to mind." Or let Clarissa ask all the questions. Even better. Nothing put her to sleep faster than an account book being opened.

"Very well."

They followed Lady Margaretta into the corridor. However, a flurry of activity at the front of the house drew their attention. One of the footmen held an enormous arrangement of brilliant coral roses.

"I knew it!" Clarissa exclaimed, clasping her hands together. Her smile transformed her face. "I think I even know who sent them. Oh, Daphne, wait until you meet him."

How romantic! Despite Clarissa's fickle taste in suitors, Daphne sincerely hoped she would find someone wonderful and fall in love. Perhaps last night it had happened. In that moment she remembered Cormack as he'd stood in the alley, his face and clothing slick with rainwater, his hand extended to her. A sudden longing struck her, deep inside her chest, such as she had never experienced before.

"Don't assume, dear," Lady Margaretta chided softly. "They may very well be for your sister. Mr. Ollister, could you please carry the flowers into the green sitting room?"

They followed the footman inside the high-ceilinged room, where hand-painted green paper covered the walls, the perfect color for spring. Ollister placed the flowers on a table beside the window.

Clarissa pulled her by the wrist. "Oh, Daphne, this is just the beginning of our wonderful season. Let's open the card together."

Daphne didn't want to look. She had a sneaking suspicion the flowers might be from Lord Rackmorton, the scoundrel she'd seen the night before at the Blue Swan. He'd been so overly attentive yesterday afternoon at Lady Buckinghamshire's Venetian breakfast, and he had scowled so terribly when she'd had to leave, insisting on escorting her all the way to the carriage. Everyone considered him such a gentleman, and she'd have such a time explaining why she felt compelled to dump the entire arrangement out the window. She wondered what had become of him in the moments after the constables arrived, but didn't concern herself overly much. She knew full well that men with names like Rackmorton rarely had to answer for their actions.

"That's all right," she said to Clarissa. "I'm certain they're for you. You open the card."

Clarissa slipped the little envelope from the center of the arrangement, and lifted the flap. "Oh."

Her countenance reflected surprise.

"What does it say, dear?" Lady Harwick hovered close. "Are they for you or for Daphne?"

"Neither of us." She gave a little nervous laugh.

"Oh." Her mother blushed. "They are for me?"

"Not you, either," her sister declared. "Though I wouldn't at all be surprised."

"What does that mean, that you wouldn't be surprised?" Daphne inquired, dismayed and a little unsettled. Both her sister and her mother had new suitors? "What happened last night?"

Clarissa threw her a sly look. "Mother has a friend. His name is Mr.—"

"I do *not* have a *friend*!" Lady Margaretta exclaimed, her face even redder now.

"—Birch! And he is smitten."

The viscountess raised a hand to the tendril of hair that slipped from her nape. "I don't even know what you're talking about."

"Tell me!" wailed Daphne.

Clarissa winked. "I'll tell you later."

"There's nothing to tell," Lady Harwick assured, but the brightness in her eyes told another story.

"The card, Clarissa," Daphne urged, feeling a bit dismayed over talk of her mother and any man but her father, though she knew she ought not to be. "What does it say?"

"It's for Miss Fickett."

Kate? Kate didn't have any suitors that she knew of—

Oh, no. Daphne swallowed down a gasp, as anxiety flooded her stomach.

"Miss Fickett?" Lady Margaretta repeated, her smile taking on a curious slant. "I wasn't aware she had a suitor. Daphne, what do you know of this?"

"Ah...no." Daphne's voice sounded hollow. "I wasn't aware, either."

Clarissa examined the white card stock again. "There isn't a name, just an initial, the letter *C*. Clearly a man's handwriting." She turned the card for the benefit of their mutual examination, her eyebrows raised above sparkling eyes. "So masculine."

Daphne's gaze fixed on the solitary letter, emblazoned in thick black ink, and a whisper of pleasure swept through her, weakening her knees.

Her mother turned to the footman. "Mr. Ollister, could you please summon Miss Fickett? Hopefully we'll catch her before she leaves the premises on Miss Bevington's errands."

Daphne knew for a certainty Kate hadn't gone anywhere, because there weren't any errands, and if her maid was going to visit her family, she'd wait until the morning rush at the shop was over. But that didn't mean she was going to wait here for her web of well-intentioned deceit to unravel on the drawing room floor.

Daphne reached for the vase. "You know Miss Fickett, she's very private. I can take the roses upstairs to her."

She would take them into a closet, or outside and throw them over the back wall. Anywhere that Kate wouldn't see them, and be more concerned than she already was.

"No, no. I want to see her face," said Clarissa, eyes sparkling with glee. "A suitor. How exciting."

"The flowers are indeed beautiful, and such uncommon blooms came at no small expense," the viscountess observed, touching the luscious petals. "I'd hate for the household to lose Miss Fickett, but the idea of a romance is thrilling, is it not? As long as the gentleman's intentions are honorable."

Daphne bit her lower lip. Things would only get more awkward once Kate appeared.

At that moment, Kate entered the room and curtsied to the viscountess. "I was told I'd been summoned?"

Daphne exhaled through her teeth. Oh, fig. What a tangle.

"Miss Fickett," Clarissa sang like a happy little bird. She waved the card in the air like a prize won in a party game. "Look what's arrived for you. Forgive me, I opened the card thinking the flowers were intended for either myself or Daphne. How conceited of me. Surprise, they are for you!"

Kate's eyes widened. "That can't be."

She blinked rapidly, and her cheeks bloomed a deep crimson.

"See for yourself, here's the card. Oh, dear. You appear discomposed." Clarissa touched Kate's arm and, moving even closer, gave a comforting rub. "Do you even know who this Mister C is?"

"I...believe so." She blinked, staring down at the card. "And I'm not upset, this is just...very unexpected."

Bless her! Kate did not so much as glance in her direction. Daphne moved to stand beside the vase, and smelled one of the blooms. Beautiful. So fragrant and lovely.

"Does he have honorable intentions, my dear?" asked Her Ladyship.

Clarissa placed an arm around Kate's shoulders. "You know we consider you as dear as family, and won't suffer any man treating you with anything less than the respect you deserve. Just say the word, and I'll have Mr. Ollister take them to the rubbish heap."

"Oh, no. Don't do that," Kate gasped, raising a hand to her cheek. "He is someone I met only briefly, but is...very much a gentleman, in manner and deed."

"You intend to see him again, then?" Clarissa's demeanor softened.

"No, it's not like that at all," Kate answered. "Indeed, I believe the flowers were simply intended as a very kind gesture of farewell." She looked at Daphne and offered a gentle smile.

Daphne nodded. Yes, that was it. A kind farewell.

Her chest tightened with a surge of the most exquisite tangle of emotions. Admiration. Longing. Relief. Cormack had proven himself to be nothing less than a hero, and an impeccable gentleman. He had done exactly as he promised, and asked for nothing in return.

How utterly tragic—and somehow *perfect*—that she would never, ever see him again.

Chapter Six

That's the last of it, then?" Cormack inquired, from his place in the tub. He dropped the newspaper he'd been reading, now folded, to the floor. Hugin and Munin dozed nearby, having already gone for an early morning run in the park that ran adjacent to the hotel.

Bergamot-scented steam rose up around him, compliments of the doe-eyed maid with strong shoulders who'd poured the buckets of water just moments before. She'd offered to massage his shoulders, a service he'd politely declined, despite his muscles being a tangle of tension. Two days before, when he'd accepted the same offer, things had quickly gotten out of hand.

Jackson, who over the past two years had acted as his driver, his valet, and his man of all business, replied, "We didn't have much to begin with, my lord, but yes, everything's been packed. So...a house, you say?"

They waited for the girl to go, before continuing.

"She's a pretty girl," Jackson observed, once she had gone.

"I had not noticed. You ought not to, either."

"Hmm." His manservant rolled his eyes.

Jackson often called him a prude, but he'd never been one to avail himself of such a la carte services. While he could be just as randy as any other hot-blooded man, he preferred his liaisons to be of a certain quality, with women of passion, motivated by mutual attraction rather than monetary need. If such opportunities came less frequently, so be it. He found them infinitely more satisfying than those requiring an obligatory coin and the further exploitation of a girl in unfortunate circumstances. She could tidy the room, or shine his boots, and he'd compensate her just as generously and hold his conscience clear.

Along those lines, he hoped to meet someone soon. Widows were always the obvious choice. A love affair, he feared, was the only way to blot out Kate's memory, which against all reason lingered vividly in the back of his mind even now.

"Not just a house. I want a palace, at least in London terms. See what you can find, somewhere in Mayfair. I liked what I saw of the area last night."

Jackson grinned. "Expensive."

"All for a necessary cause."

Money. Lord knew he still had plenty of that. He'd spent only a fraction of his Bengal fortune since returning to England two years ago. The resurrection of Bellefrost Manor to her former shine and glory had been no great expense, since she had not been overly grand to begin with. Yet to him and his family, she was priceless and they had continued to live there despite now being in possession of the much grander Champdeer estates, which earned enough in tenant rents to wholly support themselves.

Originally, he'd thought to bring his mother and father to town, along with little Michael, but he feared that in some way, his parents' spirit had been forever broken by Laura's death. The mother he'd once known would have grown giddy at the thought of suddenly becoming a countess, and of going to town for her first London season, and his father, while never impressed by a title, would have enjoyed days filled with scientific exhibitions and lectures. But they had declined, preferring to remain at Bellefrost with Michael, in the insulated world he had created for them. They were reasonably happy, of course. They did not live each day immersed in misery. Michael was a delight, for all of them, but at the same time a reminder of the injustice done to Laura. A grievous injustice that had yet to be set right.

His parents had long ago begged him not to seek revenge. Not because they'd forgiven whoever had dishonored Laura, nor forgotten. But because they feared losing him, too, perhaps to a duel or to some other violence or misfortune. Also, who would be there for Michael once they were gone? It had to be him.

So he hadn't told them of his true intentions in coming here, and he'd promised not to stay long, saying that he intended only to take in a few weeks of the customary festivities. The opera. A gallery viewing. An agricultural lecture or two, but nothing else. After all, it wasn't as if he was looking for a wife, because Sir Snaith had undergone a change of heart about the return of their lands. He was more than willing to overlook a little scandal in the Northmore family's recent past, in exchange for a gentleman's agreement that his young daughter would one day be betrothed to an earl, the earl of course being himself. Cormack was fully at peace with that future because by marrying the girl he would bring about the return of their ancestral properties and bring his world one step closer to being whole again, leaving only the mystery and injustice of Laura's death to be resolved.

This new endeavor of taking a house in London would require that he write his parents a letter to advise them he intended to extend his stay. He would of course again invite them to join him. After all, whatever revenge he exacted would be of a private nature, so as not to distress them more. What he intended, even he did not know, but the man responsible would answer for what he had done. Cormack had committed murder in his mind a thousand times over, but would he kill the man who had shamed his sister if given the chance? He didn't like to think about it. He only knew he wasn't walking away.

"So, somewhere near Hamilton Place, you say?" Jackson grinned slyly, naming the square where Kate lived. He spread a piece of linen and laid out a shaving blade and leather strop.

He hadn't said Hamilton Place, but Jackson knew him better than anyone else.

He shrugged and rubbed a cloth heated by the water over his face. "I liked the feel of it last night. It's close to Hyde Park, where the Four-in-Hand Club gathers to show off to one another on Sundays, and there's a few gentlemen in that club I'd like to meet."

The Four-in-Hand Club boasted within its membership some of the most powerful titled men in England. They were competitive, and gamblers by nature. It only made sense that there might be members of the Invisibilis among them.

"Grosvenor Square is closer to Hyde Park. So is Berkeley Square, for that matter."

"I don't care for those areas quite so much." It was not that he wanted to pursue a relationship with Kate. She'd made clear that couldn't happen.

"No, I didn't think you would." In a circular motion, his manservant frothed the shaving lather in an earthenware mug. "While I'm off looking for a house, what do you intend to do?"

He set down the cup and lifted the blade, which he drew across the well-worn strop.

"Go to Savile Row, for bespoke clothes, then Tattersalls, where I'm going to purchase the most ridiculously priced horseflesh I can find."

"Ah, a horse. After all, it is the attention of their lordships you wish to attract. Not the ladies."

Or a lady's maid, for that matter. He had done his duty to Kate, and sent her some lovely flowers, in what he hoped would be perceived as a fond gesture of good-bye. Now he must focus on the reason he was here, once and for all. Still, the idea of catching a glimpse of Kate walking in the park with her mistress would be immensely satisfying. He'd like to know she was happy, or at least safe and content.

He rested his head back against the heated metal. "That newspaper says the Marquess of Rackmorton rides in the park each afternoon at six o'clock sharp. He's the only Marquess of R-dom whom I can discern is aged in his early thirties." He eased lower into the tub.

Jackson approached with the mug of shaving lather and chuckled. "Then I feel sorry for him."

* * *

Two days later, Daphne sat in Lady Harwick's new canary yellow barouche, with her mother and sister, as they entered the gates at Hyde Park Corner. Already a haze of dust hung over the park, with hundreds of carriages crowding the lane. As they traveled past, excitement rippled through the fashionable pedestrian crowd that lined the central thoroughfare, in the form of raised voices and movement. Faces turned and stylishly clad bodies—most of them fellow members of the *ton*—surged toward their vehicle, with all eyes greedily seeking them out with more than customary interest.

But as all ladies of their class would certainly do, the three of them maintained blasé expressions and pretended not to notice.

Yet Clarissa said between her teeth, with only the barest movement of her lips, "Why is everyone looking at us?"

Lady Margaretta tilted her parasol just enough to obscure her face from curious eyes, and with a tilt of her head inquired, "Neither of you have done anything that requires a confession to your mother, have you?"

I have, Daphne mentally confessed, and prayed the interest of the crowd had nothing to do with her dancing on a stage made from shipping crates, or traipsing about London with a handsome saltpeter merchant.

"There's Havering," murmured Daphne. "Ask him if my petticoat is caught on the outside of the door."

Indeed, Lord Havering appeared on horseback to ride alongside the carriage.

"Ladies." He tilted his hat, revealing a glimpse of ash-blond hair. They acknowledged him fondly, with Daphne reaching both of her gloved hands for his, which he gallantly turned, and pressed upon them an affectionate kiss.

"Hello, my dear," he said to her.

"Hello, *my* dear!" she exclaimed.

"And good morning to my other dear," he said to Clarissa with a bow of his head.

"And to you, Fox!" she replied.

The crowding on the road forced their driver to slow their barouche to a stop, and their handsome escort followed suit. Havering, or "Fox" as they called him, had been their neighbor growing up. Having long ago repudiated all ties to his scandalous scoundrel of a father, for reasons that were only ever whispered about, he had been unofficially adopted into the family.

All her friends asked why one of the Bevington daughters hadn't snatched up the handsome Corinthian as a husband, but he was more like a brother to them all. Except for Sophia, perhaps? They had been closer than the rest, likely because of their proximity of ages, but Sophia had married the Duke of Claxton instead. Sophia had once confided to her sisters, under the strictest of confidences, that despite Wolverton's affection for the young man, he had long ago warned Havering against making designs on any of his granddaughters. Sophia didn't know the circumstances of the prohibition, and none of them had ever pried for more answers.

They'd come to a consensus that perhaps it had something to do with Havering's mother, who, according to the village gossips, had gone quite mad when he'd been just a boy, and died in an asylum within months of having been committed there. It was a sad and terrible story, and they supposed that because madness often repeated itself in families, their patriarch simply sought to protect his own. Whatever the case, Havering had never seemed anything but admiring of the old man, and the old man of him, and that was all that seemed to matter.

"Daphne," Havering said. "Please tell me again on what night your debut ball will take place."

Daphne straightened the seams of her glove, hoping her downward glance concealed her frown, and the faint shadows under her eyes. Her ball. She hardly looked forward to it, knowing that the most exciting man in London wouldn't be there. No offense to Havering.

Cormack. She sighed inwardly, trying to ignore the sudden surge of longing that had only intensified in the days since they'd said farewell. In her mind he had come to represent a fascinating world of adventure, one that existed far and away from wallpapered drawing rooms, museums, and manicured parks and gardens. A place where young ladies such as she weren't ever supposed to go.

For three nights she'd suffered the most intriguing and torturous dreams of him, and as a result hardly got any rest at all. The night before, for instance, she'd awakened just after midnight from the most sensual of fantasies, where they'd both been completely naked and making love in a field of flowers. Even now, their heady fragrance teased along the edges of her mind, along with the memory of the way he'd teased her breasts with their petals, before sucking all traces of the syrupy nectar from her aroused tips.

At one point, as she'd boldly stroked his male sex to attention, he'd been wearing a helmet like the Achilles statue, which she had found odd . . . but strangely titillating. Once awake, she'd been unable to return to sleep. She'd spent the rest of the night at her window, staring out over the city and wondering where he was, and hoping he was thinking of her. And replaying, again and again, every moment of the dream in her head. Just remembering brought heat to her cheeks, and a shameful wish to see him again.

"Daphne?" Havering was still there, waiting for his answer. "Are you all right? You look a bit feverish."

"Two Thursdays hence," she blurted.

"Invitations go out Tuesday," added her mother.

Daphne remembered something just then that she'd intended to ask him. "Please tell me you intend to be my first dance. With Wolverton unable, and father and Vinson gone, I can think of no one else I'd rather it be."

Cormack, her heart sighed. She wished it could be Cormack.

"To be honest, Wolverton had already spoken to me about it." He reached to cover her hand with his own. "I'd be honored. You know you are like a sister to me."

"Then it's settled," said Lady Harwick, who watched, misty eyed.

"About the invitations..." He leaned toward them and rested his forearm on the pommel of his saddle. "I've had three acquaintances in the last hour press upon me to use my influence to see that they are included on the guest list."

Her mother smiled. "What a compliment!"

"And what a relief." Clarissa relaxed into the seat. "For a moment after entering the park, we were concerned that we'd committed some dreadful faux pas, the way everyone went to chattering and staring. It is good to know we are still in good standing."

Havering repositioned himself upon his saddle, unaware of the two Aimsley sisters, who at that very moment passed behind him in their carriage, gazing at him with the most fervent admiration—until their keen-eyed aunt leaned forward and, with her folded fan, smacked them both on the knee, to which they responded with squeals of outrage.

"Oh, Havering," snorted Daphne, watching with unconcealed amusement over his shoulder. "I know who else will expect a dance with you. In fact, I must be on my guard that I am not shoved out of the way."

Clarissa grinned. "Just think of the spectacle when he's forced to dance with them both at once. I know for a fact that neither one is willing to settle for being second."

"They're behind me right now, aren't they? The Aimsley sisters?" He grinned wickedly, and his eyebrows crept up. "You've invited them to your ball just to torment me."

"Mother insisted," Daphne confided playfully.

"I did nothing of the sort—at least not for that reason." Lady Harwick smiled serenely, but her eyes sparkled with humor. "They are both delightful girls, just a bit overly enthusiastic in their admiration of you. How can I fault them for that?"

Their driver lowered his cane, and the barouche again moved forward.

Havering gathered his reins, and rode along beside them. "It has been lovely speaking to you ladies, but I have an appointment, and must take my leave of you. Oh, but one final thing. You mentioned the reaction of the gallery when you rode into the park today. Perhaps you haven't heard, but word on the vine has it your daughters have been declared, by those revered authorities who do all the declaring, to be the season's Incomparables. Note the plural." He grinned. "Two sisters. When has that ever happened before? I say congratulations, to the three of you, and to Wolverton."

Daphne glanced toward Clarissa, who raised her eyebrows and shrugged.

With a touch of his finger to his hat, and a kick of his heels, Fox cantered ahead.

"What wonderful news," declared the viscountess with an exuberant smile—one that instantly tilted into a frown. "What *terrible* news. While the distinction of being an Incomparable is indeed an honor, I had hoped this would be an enjoyable season for you both. Now everyone will scrutinize our every movement and word, down to your choices of dance partners. The smallest misstep will be spun into scandal. You know the *ton*. They thrive on spectacle, even if manufactured and untrue." She sighed, closing her eyes. "Lord, I pray Mr. Kincraig does not humiliate us with any future drunken antics."

The most recent, of course, had been two nights before when he'd been found in the fountain at Buckingham Palace, utterly sotted and wearing only a ballerina's tutu. Or so she and Clarissa had overheard from the top of the staircase when the King's Guards had delivered him to their home, with sworn promises of discretion. He'd been taken to one of the downstairs guest rooms to sleep his liquor off, but when Wolverton's valet sought to attend to him early the next morning, he'd already taken his leave of the house. The whole incident had been such a disappointment to them all, when just the day before, according to her mother and sister, he had behaved so charmingly at the Heseldon ball.

"Ah, Mr. Kincraig. Well, then," Clarissa murmured in a wan voice. "Consider me worried."

"And I as well," Daphne said softly, fretting silently over the word her mother had just said: *scandal*.

But not because of Mr. Kincraig.

What she, Daphne Bevington, had done three nights before had been more than just a small misstep. Yes, she'd gone to the Blue Swan for Kate, but hadn't she owed as much loyalty to her own sister, whom she held so dear? If word of her appearance on the stage of the Blue Swan became public knowledge, it would utterly destroy her younger sister's chance for a respectable match. No venerable family would ever welcome her into their ranks.

Why hadn't Clarissa been more foremost in her mind that night, balanced with her concern for Kate? She just hadn't been thinking and now, in retrospect, she suffered beneath the weight of a crushing guilt. She had the sudden urge to throw her arms around her sister, and press a kiss to her cheek and tell her a thousand times that she loved her. But then she'd have to explain her sudden outburst of emotion, not just to Clarissa but to their mother, and she just couldn't. Not yet. Perhaps years from now, when everything had turned out well after all, and they could both laugh about it.

But for now, Daphne's secret had driven an invisible and regrettable wedge between them, even if Clarissa didn't realize. They'd always told each other everything. But though the words had been on Daphne's tongue a thousand times in the three days since, she couldn't reveal to Clarissa what she'd done. She refused to place that burden on her sister's shoulders.

Just then, a horse caught her attention—a magnificent animal! A bay mare with black legs, unparalleled by any other creature on the path. She'd always loved horses, though she did not ride anymore, not since that day four years ago when her father had died.

Clarissa touched her arm, and stared in the same direction. "Daphne, just look at that gentleman. Isn't he magnificent? Who is he?"

She pointed, of course, in the same direction as the horse Daphne had just been admiring.

Her gaze swept upward to deduce the identity of its rider, who sat tall and broad shouldered in the saddle, impeccably dressed in a dark blue riding coat and fawn breeches. The direction of the sun shone at such a slant as to hide the upper half of his face in the deep shadow created by his hat brim, but his mouth and chin—

That mouth and chin.

She turned her head sharply, concealing her face with the brim of her hat.

She'd recognize those lips anywhere. They'd kissed her. Turned her world upside down, and left her dangerously dissatisfied with the path her life was destined to take. Only a moment ago, she'd been aching to see him, but she'd never truly anticipated that she would.

Cormack. *Here?*

Of course he was. Hyde Park was public. Anyone could ride there. Oh, she couldn't let him see her. If he recognized her and endeavored to speak with her, there would be a mountain of questions. Questions from Cormack and her mother and her sister, none of which she could answer.

She held her rigid pose several seconds more, fixing her gaze on the pleated blue ribbon at the edge of her hat brim, hearing her mother and Clarissa's voices, but not comprehending a single word they said. One second, two seconds, three. There came no shout of *Kate!* nor the clip-clop of horses' hooves beside the carriage. He *hadn't* seen her, and he'd ridden past without stopping. She let out the breath she'd been holding and, with all discretion, glanced over her shoulder—

To see his horse still traveling away, but Cormack half-turned in his saddle, *his gaze fixed piercingly on her*.

He did not smile, or tilt his head in acknowledgment. Instead, his nostrils flared and his eyes flashed with obvious temper.

Then... *he winked*.

Daphne jerked round, sinking against the seat cushion. Her lungs shriveled into currants, and she could not breathe. If only she could disappear.

"Daphne, are you all right?" asked Clarissa. "You didn't have the sausages this morning, did you? After what happened three days ago, I just don't trust them, and neither should you."

The viscountess reached to press a gloved hand over hers. "It's all that silly talk about being an Incomparable, isn't it? I shouldn't have made such a fuss. Please don't give it another thought."

"I'm... fine." But she wasn't, oh, she wasn't. She wanted to retch. He was there, somewhere behind her. Perhaps watching, even now.

Ladies' maids often went riding with their mistresses, but she feared she'd dressed too fashionably to be believed as being in service. Her frilly parasol and a hat from London's finest milliner certainly gave her away. It was just as her older brother, Vinson, had once teasingly foretold—her weakness for frippery would be her undoing.

Yet the park was enormous and packed full of riders, carriages, and pedestrians. Certainly they wouldn't cross paths again. She could hardly sit still in the carriage, because she felt so trapped. But if she got out, how would she explain running away?

At the same time...the most exquisite excitement thrummed in her veins. She'd never expected to see him again, and there, like a vision, he'd suddenly been.

Oh, yes. *Yes. Yes!* Her heart rejoiced.

Oh, no, no, no.

At that moment they passed Lady Castlereagh's barouche, which had stopped near a small cluster of elms. Her Ladyship's two bull mastiffs stood on the bench seats and woofed at passersby. The more thickly wooded Kensington Gardens stood in the distance, across the shimmering blue surface of the Serpentine. The lady stood in her carriage and called to them. "There you are, Lady Harwick. And the Miss Bevingtons! Oh, do please stop and visit."

Daphne glanced around to be certain Cormack wasn't two feet away, observing her real name being declared for all the world to hear. He wasn't, but who knew where he was? Though the excitement of seeing him again thrilled her to her core, she had to make sure they did not cross paths again. Perhaps he waited near the gates, knowing they would eventually pass through to depart, and the longer they remained inside, lost in the throng, the sooner he would lose interest and leave.

"Yes, Mother," she blurted, hoping her expression gave away none of her desperation. "Let's do stop."

Her Ladyship directed their driver to pull their conveyance to the side of the path. There, numerous others had parked, and their occupants meandered across the grass, conversing and laughing, an impromptu party. She even spied the Duke of Wellington speaking to Fox. Stepping down, Daphne breathed a sigh of relief.

While her grandfather and parents had never made a practice of snobbishness, as some members of the *ton* did, she could not deny being a member of a very small and elite group. She'd grown up attending their children's balls and Christmas parties, and now as a young lady, she'd become a full-fledged member of their ranks. They all knew her name as she knew all of theirs.

She delved into their midst, knowing Cormack, being a tradesman and without a title, wasn't one of them, and couldn't breach their circle of exclusivity. Here, she'd be protected from crossing paths with him. After speaking briefly with Lady Castlereagh, she laughed with friends, compared parasols with the Aimsley sisters (who she knew full well only pretended to be friendly so they could get closer to Fox), and smelled Mrs. Danville's purple hybrid roses, which she wore pinned in a fetching corsage high on her shoulder—

Before seeing him through the trees.

He stood tall and beautiful, like something out of a romantic novel, the reins of his mount clasped in one gloved hand. His eyes pierced her through, like a blade.

* * *

The most mortifying thing was that the moment Cormack had seen her in that fine carriage, as beautiful and splendorous as a queen, his heart leapt like a smitten boy, even as his rational mind realized her wicked deception.

I am a maid…

No *maid* wore a bonnet like that, an extravagant creation of flowers and ribbons.

…paying off a debt…

Her parasol alone, trimmed thick with ruched, variegated lace, had certainly cost more than a cow.

...my father borrowed money...

All bloody false untruths. The truth was: she was one of *them*, a member of the same exclusive society that had for two years protected his sister's seducer.

And yet she had allowed him to rush off into the night like a heartsick suitor to slay what he now suspected had been an imaginary dragon, and spend a minor fortune in the process. And perhaps even laughed in delight as he had done it.

No, he had not been completely honest with her, having assumed his more recent past as a saltpeter merchant like an old suit, but because he hadn't wished to frighten her any more than she already had been.

The moment he had seen her, everything had changed. He no longer felt one shred of anything noble.

* * *

His lips mouthed two words.

Come here.

Though quite impossible, given the distance, Daphne felt certain she heard his voice thunder inside her head, dangerous and commanding, even above the drumroll of her pulse. She glanced away, pretending not to see him. Rejecting him outright. Heat rose to her cheeks, and she inhaled and exhaled, trying to calm herself, trying to ease the dizziness that made the world spin around her.

She looked again, praying he'd gone. But he was still there. His mouth moved once more.

Now.

She thought her legs would collapse. They didn't, but they shook instead and it took every bit of her self-control not to fall to pieces in front of everyone else. Her breath came in shallow bursts at the back of her throat as she frantically pondered what to do.

Oh, but there was nothing to do but comply! His eyes boldly promised that if she did not do as he commanded, then he would most certainly come to her. She could not have that. He was a stranger, with no connections or formal introductions. No one knew him. Everyone would see and have questions and then the gossip would begin and she couldn't shame her family like that, especially Clarissa, who had such a bright future.

Cormack had to be placated, and the damage contained. Which meant talking to him. As discreetly as possible she withdrew from her circle of friends and made her way behind the trees, forcing her feet to carry her across grass and a faintly worn footpath until she stood four feet in front of him, which seemed to be a safe distance but wasn't, because his gaze incinerated her on the spot.

"It seems I've been played for a fool." He looked at her everywhere, his gray eyes raking over her stylish hat and fashion-plate perfect spring dress, with their gleaming ribbons and expensive lace, with such heat she feared they would burn right off her body.

"No," she answered, gripping her parasol in both hands, wishing she could use it to shield herself from his anger. But she wouldn't hide from Cormack. "That's not true."

"Obviously the other night was just some game to you? A spoiled girl out for a wild adventure on the wrong side of London, perhaps on a dare from one of your equally vapid friends, to pretend to be someone you aren't?"

"Cormack, please listen—"

"Don't say my name like that, as if we know one another. Do you know what could have happened?" His gloved hands became fists. "Do you know what that man could have done to you if I hadn't been there to stop him?"

Wanting nothing but to make the coldness in his eyes disappear, she took two steps closer. "Yes, and I—"

"You, or Kate Fickett?" He spat the words. "Do you even know anyone by that name, or did Bynum just run with the information I provided to him and play me for a bigger fool?" He blinked, smiling, but the smile wasn't the same as before. This one was sharp as a knife and frightening. "Or perhaps you were in on it with him. Yes, perhaps that's it. You got yourself in trouble borrowing money from a dangerous man to buy some bauble in a Bond Street shop that your grandpapa refused you, and had to lure in some gullible fool to cover for it?"

"No," she gasped, horrified by his accusations. "None of that is true, you must know it is not, but, Cormack, I'm sorry."

"I don't believe you."

His rejection stung, like a slap to the face. "Then don't believe me. I can't force you to listen."

"What is your name?" he growled, his teeth clenched, taking one step toward her. "Your *real* name?"

Who was this man, saying such cruel things to her? Not the man who had saved her life, and kissed her so sweetly.

"Why ask?" she exclaimed, bristling. "Do you propose now to actually allow me to answer one of your questions?"

"Bloody hell, *tell me*," he demanded, storming toward her.

Her mouth opened, and her lips worked, but she...*couldn't*...

"Don't deny me, else I'll go ask one of them." He jerked his head in the direction of the carriages.

"Daphne Bevington," she blurted, forcing herself to remain rooted to the spot.

His face went blank for a moment, and he searched the grass, as if trying to remember something. "The Earl of Wolverton's granddaughter. The papers this morning declared you the season's Incomparable, along with your younger sister."

"So I've been told," she said coldly.

He remained quiet for a long moment. "So it seems I've the power to destroy you."

"You wouldn't," she insisted.

"I might."

"For what reason?" she cried, hating him in this moment, and wishing more than anything she had never met him at all.

"Miss Bevington?" called a male voice, one she recognized. "Is everything all right?"

Cormack said nothing, his eyes staring back at her like smoked glass.

"Don't," she whispered. His gaze shifted to a place beyond her shoulder. *"Please."*

She turned to find Havering crossing the grass on long athletic legs, accompanied by Lord Rackmorton, who stared at Cormack with burning black eyes. To make matters worse, her cousin, Mr. Kincraig, followed behind, his eyes tellingly bleary and his cravat a painfully jumbled affair.

She threw a pleading glance to Cormack. His gray eyes,

shielded by the brim of his hat and unseen by anyone else in that moment, held hers with heart-stopping intensity. In that moment Daphne could only hear the sound of her blood pulsing inside her head, fueled by the understanding that he could shatter her future, and her family's future, with just a few explosive words.

"All is well," she answered in a light tone. "I lost my parasol to the wind, and this gentleman was kind enough to capture it for me."

"Indeed, the wind is frightful today," Fox answered, pointedly glancing toward the trees, whose leaves were utterly still, because of course, there was no wind. Beneath the brim of his hat, she saw one of his eyebrows arch up.

Rackmorton came to stand beside her. "I believe your sister is looking for you." He scrutinized Cormack, his expression haughty and dismissive. "And I'm sorry, but I don't believe I know you. Miss Bevington, could you do me the honor of introducing us?"

"We...barely had time to speak two words to one another. I'm afraid I've not been properly introduced, either," Daphne answered without inflection. "He is...a stranger to me. I'm afraid I don't even know his name."

Cormack's gaze, which remained fixed on hers, went flat.

"Ah," said Rackmorton, his eyes narrowing on the outsider in their midst, one who stood a head taller than he. "But I *do* recognize you from somewhere."

"Oh?" answered Cormack, his tone cool.

He did not appear the least bit intimidated. Indeed, he mirrored Rackmorton's arrogant stance, and matched the sharpness of his gaze unblinkingly.

Rackmorton crossed his arms over his chest, and

planted the heels of his glossy leather shoes far apart. "From Tattersalls. Two days ago, you purchased that beautiful animal right out from under me."

Cormack tilted his head, a wicked glint in his eye. "Did I? I hope there are no hard feelings."

"Well, of course there are." Rackmorton laughed, but there was still a distinct undercurrent of tension in his voice and manner.

Fox smiled, peering between the two of them as if amused. "A handsome animal."

"Indeed," agreed Kincraig blandly, looking bored to death.

"I take my stable very seriously, but so must you," said Rackmorton, his gaze settling on the gelding with unabashed longing. "May I . . . have another look at him?"

"Certainly."

And just like that, the men converged, thick as thieves in their fine top hats and great coats, to stand in the shadow of Cormack's magnificent bay. Forgotten, Daphne backed away, the sound of their introductions filling her ears.

"—Rackmorton, of Cornwall. Did we go to school together?"

"I'm certain we did not," said Cormack.

Of course not. Because he wasn't one of them, as they'd soon discover. While he might be wealthy, and the perfect man with whom to discuss horse pedigrees, as a merchant tradesman rather than a titled gentleman he wasn't someone they'd invite into their libraries for port and cigars. That was rather a closed club. She sighed miserably, her heart bruised and her romantic feelings for Cormack destroyed. He'd reacted so unfairly, and with such disdain.

But that wasn't completely true. She'd glimpsed something in his eyes, hidden behind that frightful hardness, that confessed her deception had hurt him.

"...and this deuced ugly fellow is Havering..."

"And I am Mr. Kincraig, Miss Bevington's cousin, the young lady whose parasol you so gallantly rescued from this afternoon's terrifying windstorm."

Mr. Kincraig! Her throat closed on a furious scream. At least Fox hadn't called her out for her untruth.

Just then, two dark streaks dashed past her, Lady Castlereagh's mastiffs, trailing their leashes.

"Oh!" she cried, filled with a sudden terror that the bay would startle and rear up—

But a sharp command from Cormack slowed them in their tracks, until they crouched low to the grass and approached him, their canine mouths grinning wide, for a pat on the head. Daphne exhaled shakily, relieved. Taking up their leashes he walked the dogs toward her, and held out the leads.

Her heart jumped at his nearness. She examined his face, searching for some sign that the ice inside him had melted, but his gaze remained cold.

"Would you mind, Miss Bevington?" he said with an edge of dismissiveness. "You were leaving anyway, were you not?"

She glared back at him and snatched the two leashes, having been effectively dismissed. But she didn't want to leave. She didn't trust him alone with them. His shoulders blocked the gentlemen's view of her.

Beneath her breath she demanded of him, "What are you going to do? What are you going to say?"

"Don't expect me to settle your mind or your conscience," he murmured. "I'm not inclined to do either just yet."

Had those same lips once kissed her? She could hardly believe it, when now, they only spilled the vilest of words.

He turned on his heel. "Gentlemen, I believe our introductions were interrupted before they were finished."

Daphne turned from them and allowed the dogs to tug her away by their leashes. Cormack had the power to destroy her. But would he do so? She wanted to believe she knew him, and that even after the ugly exchange that had just occurred between them, she could trust that he would not. Perhaps, even if he chose to expose her secret, they wouldn't believe him anyway, and it would go no further.

He was, after all, a saltpeter tradesman.

And if he dared claim to have seen Daphne Bevington running wild on the seedy side of town?

She exhaled a sigh of cautious release. Even she had to say such a claim would sound far-fetched, and something that clearly fit an instance of mistaken identity. He wasn't a member of the *ton*, and as such, his allegation would be met with immediate suspicion.

"I am Lord Raikes," she heard Cormack say. "How pleased I am to make all of your acquaintances."

* * *

Hours later, when the house was dark and quiet, Daphne sat beside Kate in her grandfather's study, a lantern set on the table between them.

"He told me he was a saltpeter merchant, but you can see the truth right there in black and white."

Kate lowered the latest copy of *Debrett's Peerage* to her lap. "He is an earl! What a charade the two of you have put on for one another. It is like something out of one of those romantic novels."

"Only it isn't romantic," Daphne said morosely. "Or funny. Really, Kate, how can you smile at a time like this?"

Kate patted her arm. "I wasn't smiling because I thought it was funny, but because I wanted make you feel better."

"I know you were, and I'm sorry for being snappish." Daphne sighed. "It's just that after everything that happened, I took great comfort in believing our paths would never cross again."

"You are certain he's the only other person that knows about the Blue Swan?"

"I think so." Daphne pressed her hands to her eyes. "If only it was just *my* reputation in peril! But my family's good name and Clarissa's future hang in the balance."

"You always worry about everyone but yourself. I think...I think you are still trying to—"

"Don't say it."

"You don't even know what I was going to say."

"You were going to say I'm still trying to make up for that day in the country, when my father died."

Kate peered at her, and softly said, "Aren't you?"

"I suppose." She closed her eyes against a sudden rush of tears. "Shouldn't I? It was my fault."

"No, it wasn't," Kate assured her, as she had done countless times before.

"Go on and tell me the reasons why, just like everyone else does." Memories crowded her mind, painful and sweet. "'Animals are unpredictable. No one could have known your horse would startle and rear up like that.' But,

Kate, if I hadn't acted like a spoiled child and refused to ride in, if I hadn't been showing off, my father wouldn't have had to come to get me."

She had taken her father away from all those who loved him, and she would spend the rest of her life trying to atone for having done so.

Kate sighed. "Another day, another moment, and things would have turned out differently. You can't blame yourself."

But she did. And now she had failed them again. It was too much, given all that had occurred over the past several days, and this afternoon's confrontation with Cormack. "Let's not talk about it anymore."

Kate studied her. "Very well. But you know if you ever would like to talk, I am here."

"You know how much my family means to me," she said. "Lord Raikes has the power to destroy it all. Haven't I caused them enough pain for one lifetime? I feel so guilty for exposing them to possible scandal. Not just a scandal. It would be the scandal of the decade."

"I am just as responsible. You were there at the Blue Swan to help me."

"No, Kate, it was all my own doing—"

Kate shook her head. "But even if he's angry, I can't believe that he would ever hurt you."

"You act as if you know him."

A little smile curved her lips. "Well, he did send me some very nice roses."

Daphne scowled at her. "You're trying to make me laugh again, but it's not going to work."

"I thought you said you loved my facetiousness." She reached to squeeze her hand. "Poor Daphne."

"You should have seen him. He was so angry with me. The nerve of him, when I have every right to be just as angry with him."

"Unfortunately, no one cares if an earl goes to the Blue Swan."

"I thought you were trying to make me feel better."

"I'm sorry, Daphne." Kate stood from her chair, and slid the volume into its place on the bookcase. "It's very late. Why don't we get you into bed? You'll feel better in the morning, I vow."

"You go on. I'm going to stay here and read for a little while."

"Are you certain?"

"I am. I'll see you in the morning."

"Very well," Kate said reluctantly, moving toward the door. "Good night, then."

After she was gone, Daphne dimmed the lantern and went to the window, finding it difficult to believe what had taken place below it just three nights before. She'd thought the moment was so magical. That she'd carry those memories with her forever. Now she wanted nothing more than to forget them.

So why did she stare into the night, wishing he would appear?

And then, quite suddenly, he did.

* * *

Like a vision, she stood at the window, just as he'd hoped she would—as if he'd conjured her from a fantasy, her hair in loose waves to her shoulders, her throat and arms bare, in a simple, cap-sleeved gown of white muslin. Only he had to keep reminding himself he couldn't think of her like that anymore.

He waited, as she pushed open the frame.

"How did you know I'd be here?" she asked in a quiet voice.

"I took a chance, and look, there you are."

"Here I am."

The night sounds of the city rose up about them. Wheels and horses on the nearby street, and from somewhere, the lively strains of a violin.

"Just so you know, I didn't tell them anything," he said.

He heard her exhale…in relief?

"I suppose I should thank you, but forgive me if I don't," she said harshly.

Clearly, she wasn't the least bit grateful, a response he hadn't expected and that caused him to bristle.

He'd come here intending to speak in a more conciliatory fashion, but instead found himself responding in like manner. "Forgive *you*? I hadn't intended to, but why?"

God, she provoked him, so much he almost forgot how sweet her kisses had been. Almost.

"You told me you were a saltpeter merchant," she accused.

"I used to be one," he countered. "I'm quite certain you've never been a lady's maid."

"That's not the point," she snapped. "You lied about your identity and led me to believe you were someone you weren't, so how dare you threaten me for doing the same?"

"I never threatened, I only made an observation—"

"An observation that you had the power to destroy me?"

"I never said I would actually wreak the destruction of which I was capable."

"The intent was there," she said into the silence.

"Don't suppose to know what I intend. Then, or now."

She crossed her arms over her chest, and huffed, "Why did you come here? What do you want?"

He wanted things to be different between them, for them to stand eye to eye, rather than her being perched up there like a goddamn unattainable golden-haired Rapunzel and him on the ground, a worshipful pauper. The comparison only confirmed what he knew: that she was one of them and that he, despite his new title and fine address, would always be beneath them, figuratively ankle deep in dirt.

"Being that we are such dear friends," he said in a dry tone. "I need a favor."

"A favor?" She snorted unkindly. "And you think to have one from me?"

"Consider it more of a demand, if you wish."

"I knew it," she hissed, recoiling like an angry cat. "Blackmailer!"

He chuckled darkly, knowing he shouldn't feel so amused. "Would you mind so terribly including me on the invitation list for your debut ball?"

"My ball. Why?" She gripped either side of the window frame. Bathed by shadows, she looked so beautiful, he felt it in his heart, an ache that hadn't left him since seeing her on the stage that night. It made him angry to feel any emotion at all, but all he could think in the next moment was how the moonlight painted her hair an almost magical hue.

"Because I'm asking so nicely."

"You said it was a demand. What are you, Cormack? Gentleman or villain? I'd really like to know."

"May I get back to you regarding that? I haven't quite decided myself."

To his surprise, she softened at that bit of humor, her shoulders releasing their rigidity. "I'm supposing this has something to do with the man for whom you were searching at the Blue Swan. Do you believe he will be at my debut ball?"

"Perhaps." It was easy to tell from the newspaper society page who ran with whom, and the Bevington name was never far from Rackmorton's and his circle. "You know how it is with the *ton*. A title is only the first qualification. Admission requires formal introductions, and I have no connections of which to speak. There are thousands here in London for the season. I am concerned with only a few. To speak plainly, I need an 'in,' and I don't have forever to wait for the right people to invite me to the right party."

"The right party. Again, you believe he will be there at mine."

"It is only a hunch."

"Cormack, what did he do to you? The other night you told me he hurt someone you loved."

"We aren't on confiding terms, Daphne. Not anymore."

"That much is true." She straightened again. "Still, I won't have you murdering someone at my ball. Mother would be scandalized."

"As well she should be. Very well, then. In exchange for the invitation, and out of respect for your dear mother, against whom I hold no particular grudge, I promise that if I murder someone, I will do it somewhere else."

"You're generosity astounds, Lord Raikes," she answered, heavy on the sarcasm. "But I fail to see why you need me at all. You took right up with the gentlemen this afternoon, without any difficulty at all."

"Men rarely give a thought as to who is on an invitation list. They leave those details to their discerning wives, mothers, and daughters. I don't have time or the inclination to charm all the ladies in town."

Now that he was here in London, all he wanted to do was return to Bellefrost. He missed the quiet of the country, and little Michael. The season ran all the way to August. God help him if he had to stay here that long. For a time, the prospect of taking part had intrigued, and even dazzled. But everything had changed the moment he saw Daphne in Hyde Park. Her duplicity had only proven everything he despised about the upper classes, and the artificiality that tainted them all.

She half-sat on the sill. "Speaking of mothers, mine doesn't know you, and when she sees your name on my list, she'll have questions."

"Make something up."

"I'm not promising anything," she answered cooly. "I'll see what I can do."

Her dismissive tone riled him, and he responded in kind. "Don't play coy, Miss Bevington. I'll expect an invitation, delivered the same day as the others."

He provided his address.

"Now you're just playing games," she said, leaning out from the window, no doubt oblivious to the alluring crush of her breasts against her bodice. "That address is just on the other side of those mews, and I know for a fact it belongs to his Grace, the Duke of Durden—"

"Who is spending the summer at his estate in Northumbria, and so I have taken the lease."

For a moment he thought she might actually topple off the sill.

"Oh, you!" she accused, in obvious exasperation. "Have you made it your sole purpose in life to torment me?"

After seeing her in that carriage in Hyde Park this afternoon, the picture of cool and utterly controlled female perfection, he could only chuckle at having discomposed her so greatly. "I know it's difficult for you to believe, but none of this has anything to do with you."

It was a lie, of course, one exacted to preserve his pride. Even now, despite everything, he wanted to pull her down from her high perch, and into his arms and kiss her the way he had before.

"I'm going to close the window now," she said in a surly tone.

"Good night, then."

"I don't wish the same for you." She pulled at the window.

"Daphne." He grinned, knowing a smile would ruffle her. If he couldn't kiss her, then he would settle for the satisfaction of getting under her feathers.

She stopped. "What is it?"

"I might need you to introduce me to some people as well."

At that, the window slammed shut.

Chapter Seven

In the end, his entrée into society hadn't required Daphne Bevington's assistance at all.

His original plan had worked magnificently. He'd invested in a horse that cost more than all of Bellefrost Manor on its finest day, taken that fine animal for a trot round the park, dressed like the earl he now was, with all care to keep his nose high in the air. Just like that, His Lordship had come a-calling.

Apparently the Marquess of Rackmorton had been so impressed by him, or perhaps only his horse, that he'd received a couriered invitation to the dowager Marchioness of Rackmorton's Monday night musicale.

The marquess presently stood on the opposite side of a cavernous, candlelit study, pouring him a brandy. Pressing Daphne for an invitation to her ball had been wholly unnecessary. Now he wished he wouldn't have. Indeed, he hoped he never saw her again. She would only muddy his thoughts and distract him from his course.

The guests were still arriving and the performance would not begin for another half hour. As soon as Cormack had crossed the threshold, he'd been swept away into his host's private domain, a breathtaking, cavernous room with walls covered floor to ceiling with dramatic oils of land-scapes, portraits of men long dead, and dogs.

"So truly, you're completely fresh to London?" said the marquess, as he approached a cabinet cluttered with bottles of port and brandy. "You don't know anyone, and haven't ever passed a season in town?"

"I was not raised into this life."

"Ah, a rarity among my circle, a man untried and inex-perienced at these endless social requirements the rest of us find so dreadfully rote. You're rather like a virgin, I'd say." Rackmorton grinned, selecting a bottle. "Mind you, I adore virgins, but the female sort—but not the sort who frequent my mother's parties. I warn you now, my friend, dally care-fully with these or not at all, else you'll find yourself wed."

Cormack flinched inwardly at Rackmorton's crass talk, but maintained a relaxed outward façade. While the hand-kerchief the cat-eyed girl had given him outside Bynum's office had proved Rackmorton to be a member of the In-visibilis, he had no evidence the marquess, in particular, was the member of the Invisibilis who had dishonored his sister. Neither had he proven the man innocent. He had to start discounting suspects somewhere. Why not start here? Besides, befriending one of the members would eventually lead him to the others.

He turned to the window, through which guests could be seen mingling in an already crowded drawing room. "I have heard that Catalani will sing tonight. I've never before had the pleasure of hearing Madame."

He'd made no mention of his time spent in Bengal, preferring to reveal as few details about himself as possible. People who were friends shared about their lives—about their family, their experiences, and travails. He already knew from their brief time together that he would never choose this man to be his friend.

Rackmorton, looking every bit the self-assured aristocrat, with his aquiline features and elegant carriage, crossed the carpet and handed him a glass. "Perhaps, then, this evening will hold some charm for you, as it's intended to do. As for me, I'm afraid these events get rather stale. And God help you if everyone finds you intriguing—you'll be invited to everything, and you'll never have a moment's rest."

"I, myself, prefer the quiet of the country. Fresh air. Green fields." His gaze narrowed on his host. "Or perhaps a good hunt, with friends."

He waited, muscles tensed. Would Rackmorton bite?

Rackmorton half-sat on the edge of the desk and nodded. "But something brought you to London."

Curses. He did not.

"Mhm," he murmured in response.

"We are of a similar age. Am I wrong to presume that your family is, of late, pressuring you to marry, so as to provide the necessary heir?"

From the other side of the closed oaken door came the sounds of laughter. More guests having arrived for the musicale.

"Actually, no," Cormack responded. "That's all been arranged already, as part of a land agreement between families."

"We English do prize our property. My cousin fell prey

to a similar agreement." Rackmorton winced, and gave a lopsided smile.

"He is married to the homeliest bumpkin but"—he shrugged—"they do have three fine, strong-boned sons."

"There is that, at least," Cormack answered.

"I don't know what you're in for, Raikes, but I have more refined tastes than that." His host's gaze narrowed upon him, as if scrutinizing his worthiness in some way. With a jerk of his head, he indicated a narrow corridor that enjoined the inner corner of the study. "I've got just enough time to show you something. Come have a look."

Cormack followed him, curious to observe his host pull a key from his pocket. The corridor appeared to join the study with His Lordship's sleeping chambers. Midway between, Rackmorton stopped outside a narrow door. With the turn of a key, they entered. His lordship quickly lit a lamp, and—oddly—secured the door behind them.

The duke lifted the lamp so that the light illuminated the walls. "What do you think?" He let out a low chuckle. "Aren't they splendid?"

Paintings, lithographs, and sketches covered the walls, each portraying beautiful nude women in wanton poses, mostly alone, but some in the arms of male partners.

Cormack blinked, startled. "What an...extensive collection."

Rackmorton reached to straighten a frame. "I've collected them since university. Some are very expensive and considered art because of the artist who painted them, while others are complete trash."

Cormack loved the nude female form as much as the next man, but there was something about this place that made his skin crawl. He wanted nothing more than for

Lord Rackmorton to again produce his little key and unlock the door, so they could return to the company of others. Hoping to hurry that moment along, he continued along the line of pictures, pausing to view each one, under the pretense of being interested, so that once he'd seen them all, they could call it an evening and leave.

Yet in the farthest recesses of the room, a curtain had been drawn across the wall.

"What's behind there?" Cormack asked, not because he wanted to see, but because instinct told him he must.

Rackmorton shrugged. "Naughtier stuff. It's not for everyone."

"May I?" Cormack forced himself to say.

"Certainly." Rackmorton winked. "Don't say I didn't warn you."

He pushed past the curtain to find more paintings, but as he'd been warned, these canvases featured women bound or shackled at the wrists and ankles, with sashes or ropes across their mouths. Their faces expressed excitement and ecstasy, but in several, he thought he also glimpsed fear.

Heat and blackness gathered behind his eyes and his hand tightened on the glass.

"Sometimes I almost prefer them to real women," Rackmorton murmured. "They don't ever complain." He caressed a fingertip over the hip of a reclining blonde.

A blonde, yes. It was then Cormack realized—and a glance backward confirmed it—that all the women portrayed in Rackmorton's illicit private collection were blonde.

"You've a preference for fair-haired ladies, that much is apparent." Laura, of course, had been a brunette.

NEVER ENTICE AN EARL   155

"Always and only, I'm afraid," Rackmorton said. "Anything else holds no attraction for me."

How was it that he could be so crushingly disappointed, and relieved, all at once? Just imagining this man touching his sister sickened him, as did the idea that he might have been Michael's father.

The duke shrugged. "Strange, I know. I think it all goes back to my nursemaid, Cleotilde, a very loving woman who—" He chuckled, a dirty sound, from deep in his throat. "Ah, but that's a story for another time. I don't know you well enough, I'm afraid."

Cormack felt certain they would never know one another well enough for that particular level of sharing. Well, that was that. His hand itched to look at his watch. Wasn't it time to go?

"Say, Raikes," said Rackmorton. "You aren't offended by this, are you?"

Yet if Rackmorton was a member of the Invisibilis, he was still of use in that he could lead Cormack to the others, and for that reason, he kept the revulsion from his face and extended the conversation with the first blather that came to mind.

"Not at all," he forced himself to say. "Bondage, when enjoyed by both partners, can be very...exciting." God, he sounded like an idiot. What else was he to say? "Er...I can only assume your new bride, by necessity, must be blonde?"

He pitied the poor girl, whoever she might turn out to be, who would no doubt enter her marriage an innocent, only to be shocked by her husband's very noninnocent habits.

Rackmorton reached to straighten one of the frames.

"Funny you should ask that. Here, let me show you my newest acquisition, but you must vow on your gentleman's honor not to tell anyone what you've seen." He grinned wickedly. A paper-wrapped frame leaned against the wall. Setting the lamp on a small table—beside a leather-bound copy of the Marquis de Sade's *Justine*—he tore the paper away with great flair and anticipation, as if revealing a masterpiece. "I had it commissioned last month, and have not yet had a chance to hang it."

Cormack looked at the picture, painted in a florid slathering of oils.

He cleared his throat, and . . . cleared it again.

Yet from deep inside his chest, anger ruptured up, so hot and untempered he feared it would spew out of his eyes in streams of fire, revealing his emotional weakness toward the subject, one that he hadn't realized until now that he had.

"Do you recognize her?" Rackmorton prodded in a sly tone.

It took every bit of his strength to speak without inflection. "She looks like the young lady I met two days ago in the park." He wouldn't, couldn't, say her name—not here, in this place, while looking at that damned picture, in which she'd been contorted and tied.

"Yes, the beauty with the parasol. Daphne Bevington." From a small desk drawer, the marquess produced a hammer and nail. In that moment, Cormack's glance happened down. Inside the same drawer lay a small leather notebook with Medusa imprinted on its cover—

The sound of hammering jerked him back to the present.

"What do you think?" Rackmorton's eyes glowed in appreciation, as he affixed the canvas to the wall. "Her sister,

Clarissa, is also a beauty, but Daphne…Daphne's got a certain spark in her eye—an adventurous spirit—that I find very alluring. I wouldn't spring all this on her immediately, of course, but I think after a few months of marriage she might take instruction well and, eventually of course, perhaps even come to enjoy herself."

Snap. Glass shattered.

"Good God, man, are you all right?" Rackmorton exclaimed, staring at Cormack's hand.

The crystal rummer lay in shards at his feet.

"Forgive me—" His open palm revealed a narrow gash. "I don't know what happened."

"No, forgive me." His host offered a handkerchief, one that, yes, now no surprise, bore the same embroidered monogram as the one the girl in the alley had given him.

"I've my own, thank you." He pulled one from his pocket and held it to the wound. "I wouldn't want to stain yours." He didn't want to accept anything from this bastard.

"A defect in the crystal, no doubt. They are purchased by my mother from one of those massive warehouse shops. Who can vouch for their quality? I shall have the remainder inspected."

A sudden rapping came upon the study door, and the muted burble of a female voice.

"Damn it, that's her now," he muttered, before shouting, sounding very much like a peevish boy called in from play, "I will be there momentarily."

For one fleeting moment, Cormack considered knocking Rackmorton out cold and taking the notebook from the drawer, but numerous people had seen him enter the study in the company of His Lordship, and would certainly observe his exit.

"Just leave the glass for now. The girl will clean it later." Rackmorton returned the hammer and closed the drawer. With the lamp, he returned to the door. "Ladies. Until next time."

Cormack followed him to the study and watched him return the key to the desk. Together they returned to the drawing room, where in the time they'd been gone, a rather large company had gathered. The dowager marchioness latched on to him, and the next quarter hour passed in a blur of faces and introductions and invitations—

But everything stopped when he heard her voice behind him.

Like magic, with her arrival the room brightened and crackled with electricity. Faces turned, and gazes sought her out—but he did not move. He simply closed his eyes, savoring the sound as she greeted other guests and responded to compliments, conveying charm with every syllable.

She moved nearer...

Her presence teased the back of his neck and down his spine, as tantalizing as a courtesan's feather, tempting him to turn.

Which of course, unable to resist her, he did.

* * *

As soon as she entered the room, she sensed he was there. Her heartbeat increased in tempo, racing toward an exhilaration she knew she ought not to feel. Her ears pricked, listening for his voice, and she searched a sea of faces, careful to keep her expression blank.

He was nowhere. She'd been wrong. Disappointment

crashed through her, and she wondered how long they would have to stay before they could politely return home.

"—and this is my middle daughter, Daphne."

Hearing her mother's voice, she turned to find the gray-haired Sir Keyes, leaning on his cane, and the elegant Lady Dundalk, in one of her signature velvet turbans, standing beside her mother. Both in their seventies, they had been dear friends of the family for as long as Daphne could remember.

But there was also another man, slim and attractive, with streaks of gray at his temples, in what was otherwise a head of dark hair.

Her mother gestured toward him. "Daphne, this is Mr. Birch, to whom your sister and I were introduced at the Heseldon ball."

Mr. Birch. Of course! The man her mother had blushed over so furiously when Clarissa had mentioned his name.

"My nephew." Lady Dundalk beamed.

"Miss Bevington, how do you do?" Mr. Birch smiled warmly at Daphne and momentarily bent his head over her hand.

Yet his attention immediately abandoned her for Lady Margaretta, who peered back at him, her cheeks noticeably bright. Daphne's heart turned over just then. It had been one thing to hear her mother might have an admirer, but quite another to see the besotted fellow firsthand. She felt unsteady, and not altogether as happy as she should—

"Daphne," Clarissa whispered, leaning close. "There is the man we saw in Hyde Park yesterday afternoon."

"What man—" But she already knew. At seeing Cormack, the words evaporated from her lips.

He stood in the midst of a group of gentlemen, dressed

impeccably in evening clothes, looking very much like the earl that he was.

Her sister leaned near her ear and said, "I do believe he's looking at you."

He *was* looking at her. *Piercingly.* For someone who had complained of not having the right connections, he'd certainly had no difficulty obtaining an invitation to the most exclusive gathering in town. But their last conversation remained fresh in her mind, the one where he'd all but threatened to expose her. With him standing before her, and her mother's and Mr. Birch's laughter sounding from behind, she suddenly felt confined on all sides.

She back stepped. "I'll rejoin you momentarily."

She just needed a moment to gather her thoughts.

"Daphne?" Clarissa said, reaching for her arm.

But she twisted away, smiling as if nothing were wrong. "Truly, I'll be but a moment."

Daphne retreated out the doorway, avoiding eye contact with the other guests who might seek to ensnare her in conversation, and found the short hallway that led her to Kate, who, as was customary, had accompanied the ladies of her household to assist in them in whatever way might be required throughout the evening.

There were several other abigails in the room, sitting in small groups gossiping, while some, like Kate, read books. They all looked up when Daphne entered, and Kate stood with a mild look of surprise. "Miss Bevington? I hadn't thought to see you again so soon. Is something amiss?"

She touched the cluster of curls behind her ear. "I believe the pins in my hair have loosened, the ones on this side. Would you mind checking them?"

They hadn't, of course. Kate was a veritable master at

hairpins, and hers never loosened, not without hours of dancing and activity.

"Of course," Kate said, agreeably, though her eyes already asked questions.

Seated in the same chair from which Kate had just stood, she submitted to an entirely unnecessary inspection.

"Are the flowers very lovely tonight?" Kate asked.

"White roses and gardenias. Very pretty and they smell divine." Daphne adjusted her evening glove at her elbow.

"I do hope we can hear the music from here."

"I'm sure you will. Catalani has astounding range."

"He's out there, isn't he?" Kate murmured, suddenly near her ear.

Daphne froze, remembering the way he had looked, staring at her across the drawing room. Arrogant and self-assured. The moment had thrilled her, more than she would ever confess.

"He who?" she replied in a cool voice.

"Don't pretend you don't know who I'm talking about." Kate went through the motions, adjusting pins and arranging curls. "Lord Raikes."

Daphne tapped her finger on the armrest of the chair. "Of course he's out there. All it took was a fine horse from Tattersalls, and it's as if he never belonged anywhere else."

"Is that what bothers you? That he isn't an outsider, as you first believed?"

"No, Kate." She straightened in her seat. "What bothers me is that he has so much as threatened to expose me if I do not assist him with the proper introductions about town, but not only that, to include him on the invitation list to my ball."

"But why? Because he wants social connections, or is there something else?"

"He's trying to find someone. A man whom he believes moves in these circles. Don't you see, it is the worst sort of betrayal? He is nothing but a rogue! He kissed me in a way I don't think I'll ever forget, but all he wants now is to use me to satisfy some quest for revenge against a mysterious villain he refuses to name."

"It would certainly liven up the evening, having him there. Or are you concerned he will murder someone on the way to get a sandwich from the sideboard?"

Daphne bit into her bottom lip. "He promised not to."

"I say invite him." Kate smiled broadly.

"Did you not hear everything I just said? Fig! It is vexingly hot in here." Daphne fanned herself, and restlessly readjusted her bodice, which felt unbearably close against her skin. "Someone should open a window. You must all be very uncomfortable."

She glanced about at the other girls. No one nodded or voiced agreement for a good five seconds, then everyone's heads went to bobbing.

"Oh, yes, Miss."

"—terribly warm."

One of them jumped up. "I'll open the window."

"You're the only one who's suffering," Kate whispered under her breath. "Don't think I don't know why." She let out a delighted giggle. "You're intrigued and despite everything, you like him."

Daphne turned her head to the side. "I can see I will receive no sympathy or comfort from you."

"You reap what you've sown," she chided, but in a teasing tone. "Regardless of your motivations, a young lady like you, with your name and your good breeding, should not have gone off like that, unaccompanied, and pretended to be someone you weren't. Every time I think of what could have happened—" Now her face grew serious, and her hand tightened on the comb. "If he had not saved you, I'd have never forgiven myself for my part in your coming to harm. No matter what you say, I'm forever indebted to him, obviously, in more ways than one."

Daphne rolled her eyes. This had to be at least the thirtieth time she'd been submitted to the same speech over the last twenty-four hours, with Cormack always the celebrated savior and she the impetuous fool.

"Very well, I shall just leave, then," Daphne sniffed, and half-rose from the chair.

"Oh, sit down, Daphne." Kate's hands pushed her back down.

At hearing that sharp command, spoken so familiarly by a maid to her lady, several of the girls nearby stared at them in wide-eyed dismay. Daphne, and Kate as well, smiled sweetly until attentions were diverted elsewhere.

Daphne whispered, "To think I came here to feel safe, and all you've done is ridicule me and make me feel worse."

"Lord Raikes isn't going to hurt or embarrass you."

Daphne stared at her, eyes wide and accusing. "You make him out to be some sort of angel, but Kate, he is badness personified. I don't understand why you persist in defending him."

"He saved my dearest friend and paid my father's debt. I simply can't believe he is a devil as you have made him out to be. I think if the two of you just talked—"

"Well, that's not going to happen. I don't wish to speak to him ever again."

A resonant *bong* sounded, filling the room with its deep baritone.

Daphne stood from the chair. "Ah, well, that's the first gong. The musicale is about to start. I suppose I must rejoin the others or they will come looking for me."

Her cheeks flooded with heat, she knowing it was only moments until she'd see him again. She'd only just passed into the corridor—

When a hand closed on her wrist, and she felt herself firmly pulled into the shadowed alcove of a nearby doorway. However, shadows didn't conceal the identity of the broad-shouldered man who handled her so assertively. Her heart pounded in her throat. "Cormack, what are y—"

He dipped, his head and shoulder blocking all light, to smother her words with his mouth. Daphne's resistance fell away to an overwhelming rush of desire.

Chapter Eight

*H*is hand, warm and long fingered, came beneath her chin. Another laid claim to her waist, then sensuously slid over her dress to seize the curve of her hip. Her body went hot there...*everywhere*...and her heartbeat came alive.

The night after they'd escaped the Blue Swan, he'd smelled of rainwater and soap. Tonight he smelled expensive, like crisp linen and whatever tonic his valet had used when shaving him. She had feared they'd never touch again, but he had come to find her for this. She inhaled, greedy and wanting more. More kissing, more knowledge of his fascinating male body, more Cormack. They twisted, melting into each other, his hands sliding up her torso to graze, ever so teasingly, the undersides of her corseted breasts.

But then—

"Oh, you." She pushed at his chest, outraged, but only managing to wedge herself more deeply into the wood-paneled corner, because pushing against him was like pushing against a stone wall. "I am angry with you."

"You shouldn't have lied to me," he uttered quietly, bracing her chin between his fingers and thumb. "And I concede I shouldn't have lied to you. But I believed you when you told me you were a maid. I didn't want to make you feel any more uncomfortable than you already were."

"As if now is the time for explanations, when you have made it more than clear that you refuse to hear mine. Truly, Cormack, how dare you kiss me!"

"I was under the impression you liked kissing me," he said in an almost playful tone.

Oh, she did like kissing him. Terribly much, and that was the problem. So much that she wanted to forget every ugly thing he'd said to her yesterday afternoon in Hyde Park and again last night outside Wolverton's library window, and just stay here forever in his arms.

But she had more pride than that.

"Well, I don't like kissing you, so don't expect any more of it." She exacted a glare upon him, and gave another push against his stonelike chest—

He only looked amused by her failed efforts to move him, lingering there, scandalously close. As if to prove his physical superiority, he easily planted a kiss on the tip of her nose. "There you go. That's what I think of 'no more kisses.'"

Everything inside her warmed at his easy little gesture of affection, which sent her spirits crashing beneath a landslide of shame. She shook her head vehemently, and swiped her nose with her hand.

"The nerve of you, after—"

"By the way, I can't help but notice Lord Rackmorton has taken an interest in you."

"And?"

"I don't wish to go into explanations—"

"No, you wouldn't, being that you're so dead set against facts and rational information."

"Don't entertain him as a suitor." His gaze went oddly dark.

She drew back, shocked. "I'm afraid you've no say."

"He is no gentleman. No matter what else is said between you and I, you must remember that."

"As if you are!" she replied. "You've said far too many terrible things to me and threatened me with public humiliation. Never once have you allowed me to explain my side of the story, of why I came to be at the Blue Swan that night."

"It doesn't matter anymore." His lips bent into a satisfied smile. He backed away, to rest casually against the opposite wall, appearing in complete control of himself and the situation at hand. His gaze drifted admiringly over her neck and shoulders. "All that matters is that you were there. And that you have placed me on your invitation list as I asked."

"I haven't." She tossed her head defiantly. "Yet."

"But you will."

"You were invited tonight, with no help from me—"

"Simply because Rackmorton wanted to show off." He shrugged. At speaking those words, his jaw tightened and his eyes darkened. "I've no guarantees of additional invitations."

"How can you be so sure?"

"Are you declining to do this favor for me?" he teased. Or did he?

"What if I am?" She wanted him to say the words. To

threaten her. Because he hadn't outright ever done so, he'd only ever implied, and she couldn't fully despise him until he did. Against all rationality, her heart still argued on behalf of the man she'd once believed him to be.

"Why don't you find out?"

She glared at him.

"That's what I thought." He crossed his arms over his chest. "I believe I could come to embrace this new role as a blackmailer."

"I'm not at all surprised. It should come quite naturally to you, being that you are also a complete and utter blackguard!" She jabbed an angry finger in his direction. "Not only that, but you have a black heart, and a black soul—"

He chuckled, his eyes crinkling at the edges, appearing nothing less than delighted.

At that moment, Kate entered the corridor. "I thought that was your voice I heard."

Only then, she saw Cormack, and her eyes widened.

"Hello," he said, one eyebrow raising up.

"How do you do?" she answered, blushing, and throwing a look of alarm to Daphne.

"I have certainly been better," he answered smoothly. "I have just been called a veritable library of hateful names. What is yours?"

"Kate Fickett, sir, and you..." She glanced to Daphne, then to Cormack again. "Why...you must be Lord Raikes."

"I'm flattered that you would know."

She pressed her fingertips to her lips, and curtsied. "Oh, my lord, thank you for what you did. For saving my dear Miss Bevington, and for...for..." Her voice thickened, and tears came into her eyes. Daphne wrapped an arm around her shoulders. Only then did Kate push out the words: "—for settling my father's debt."

Daphne saw it. The ice in Cormack's eyes melted a fraction, and his smile lost its dangerous edge.

"You are very welcome," he answered quietly.

"I must repay you."

"I wouldn't hear of it," he responded with a tilt of his chin. "It's only money, and fortunately I have plenty. I'm pleased to have put it to good use."

"Even so, sir, I'm so sorry you were drawn into such an unpleasant situation."

"No apologies are necessary," he assured, his gaze unwavering. His lips tightened into a thin smile. "Not from you."

His gaze shifted obviously to Daphne, and he nodded curtly. "Good evening to you both."

He pivoted on his heel and strode away. She and Kate stood for a few moments in silence.

"*Oh, my*," whispered Kate.

"Yes," Daphne said curtly. "I know."

*   *   *

Cormack hadn't intended to kiss her, just to talk—because to be honest, after seeing her in the drawing room, he could not stay away. Then, she had looked so lovely when she'd emerged from the cloakroom, a goddess in white silk, caught somewhere between light and half-light. There was something about Daphne Bevington in shadows, with her skin so golden and eyes so brilliant and blue...one glance, and he'd lost control of himself all over again. He'd thought if they talked he could instill some distance between them, at least on his part, but with each interaction his feelings for her grew that much more tangled.

He returned to the drawing room, now filled wall to wall with guests. Ladies in ball gowns and gentlemen in trousers and dark coats. Everyone made their way to sit in the orderly rows of chairs that had been placed around the room. His new friend, the duchess, situated herself in the front row, closest to the piano. Cormack could not help but notice the way Rackmorton hovered along the edge of the crowd, directing others to their seats, as if he oversaw the activity himself. That is, until he saw Daphne, who moments later appeared flushed and smiling, as if nothing at all had just occurred.

The muscles along Cormack's shoulder's clenched.

Rackmorton moved quickly, claiming her, leading her toward the front row as well to sit two chairs away from his mother. Her own mother, Lady Harwick, and younger sister—whose appearance was charmingly similar to Daphne's—sat just behind, solemnly watching their approach. He did not miss the look of concern that passed between them. Above the heads of the seated guests, Daphne looked back to where he stood, pinning him for a moment...then she smiled at Rackmorton, gaily tossed her head and, with his hand on her back, lowered herself into the chair. Rackmorton, of course, took the one beside her.

That look she'd thrown him—

God, he felt incinerated, from the inside out. It told him exactly what she felt, that he had no say in her life. He didn't, of course. She was right. All efforts to blackmail her aside, their dalliance had taken place in shadows and could never emerge into the light, could never become anything more. He certainly couldn't marry her, as he was obligated elsewhere. Marrying the Snaith girl when she became of age was his only chance of putting the Northmore legacy back together again.

Rackmorton, on the other hand, could marry Daphne, and if that was what Daphne wanted, it was her decision. Why the temptation to meddle in her private affairs?

Besides, if he interceded, who was to say she might not be married off to some other lecher a thousand times worse? *Ton* marriages were rarely undertaken for anything as gauche as love or affection or the prospect of happiness, but to create dynasties powerful enough to sustain future generations.

Though he needed her to penetrate the closed doors of the *ton*, in all other aspects he had to let her go.

Everyone grew silent as a slender woman in a silver gown took the floor, stood beside the pianist, and began to sing. Such a voice. Beautiful and rich, with a range that filled the room. She held everyone's rapt attention. Which was what he'd hoped for. He moved along the shadows at the back of the room to slip out the door and returned to Rackmorton's study. The small lamp they'd used before had burned out, leaving the room in darkness, with only the light through the window to see. Moving quickly, he took the key from the drawer, and hurried to the corridor, and the locked door. With a turn of the key, the lock clicked, and he entered the room, leaving the door open so that he could see. He avoided looking at the pictures on the walls, feeling as if he'd entered a gaol full of wrongly imprisoned women and yet was unable to set them free.

Most especially the picture of Daphne. He wanted to destroy it. Burn it. Blot it from his memory, but most of all from Rackmorton's. But if the painting were to go missing, Rackmorton would know he'd taken it. He couldn't chance being called out by one of the *ton*'s most influential lords and being locked out before he found the man who was responsible for Laura's ruination.

At the desk, he removed the notebook. As with the painting, he considered taking it and immediately leaving, but how soon before Rackmorton would notice it gone? Would he be immediately determined to be the culprit, or would someone like the innocent housemaid stand accused? He didn't feel comfortable taking that chance, because he didn't really know what he was dealing with in Rackmorton, whether he was truly dangerous or simply vulgar. Squinting, he found a match in his pocket and after a few attempts, struck light against the table. Opening the cover he examined the first page, slightly yellowed with age. Bloody hell, the bastard had horrible handwriting, and from the looks of things, the first page had been written by an adolescent boy. Legibility only slightly improved as he continued through the pages, but even when he could make out the letters, there was very little he understood. Everything appeared to have been written in coded jibberish, and even the names listed, which he assumed to be members of the Invisibilis, were clearly not real ones. Scrofulous Seymour and Blight Wither? Still, he read each name, doing his best to commit them to memory, noting that several had been marked through with thick black lines of ink, as if they no longer existed.

He struck another match. Silence pressed thick into his ears, making each turn of the page sound thunderous. Instinct told Cormack it was time to leave, and time to leave now. Yes, the musicale would remain underway for another hour at least, but go, yes, go he must, before he was discovered creeping about like a thief.

Taking one final glance through the pages of words that made no real sense, he closed the leather cover and returned the notebook to the drawer, and for a moment stared into the flat, dead eyes of the Medusa. He shunned the portrait of Daphne, vowing to return at some point and see it removed from Rackmorton's wall, and destroyed. A moment later, and he'd turned the key in the lock and made his way toward the marquess's desk. He'd only just returned it to its place, and shut the drawer, when the door opened. His heart nearly leapt from his throat as Rackmorton appeared.

"What are you doing in here?" said Rackmorton, his expression blank.

"Ah...well, I hope you don't mind, but I bloody well needed a smoke, and I didn't know where else to go without appearing rude." Cormack produced a cigarette from his pocket, the French sort that he'd taken such a liking to in Bengal. "I was hoping to find matches. I forgot mine."

Rackmorton grinned. "Things started to feel close in there for you, did they? I feel the same. Do you have another one of those?"

"Of course. Do you mind if I open your window?"

"It sticks, so allow me."

Beside the open window, they lit the cigarettes and smoked together in silence for a few moments. The sound of music came through the open door, and through the glass he could just make out Daphne's face.

"So some of the others and I are going out after tonight. Care to come along?"

It only made sense that Rackmorton's set would be

made up, at least in part, of members of the Invisibilis. This might be his chance to find out who might have visited the Duke of Rathcrispin's hunting lodge three years before. "Yes, I would. Thank you for the invitation."

"Be prepared to lose lots of money. We're all very competitive."

"All the better. Who doesn't like a sharp-edged game, with potentially disastrous chances?"

Rackmorton nodded. "We'll take my carriage. Send yours home for the night if you like."

* * *

It was nearly two o'clock when Daphne and her mother and sister returned to Wolverton's house in Hamilton Place. After kissing Wolverton good night, she and Clarissa went upstairs.

"What a fun night," declared Clarissa.

"Yes, it was very nice," Daphne replied without enthusiasm. She couldn't help it. She felt so dissatisfied. She'd allowed Rackmorton to lead her about as if she belonged to him, just to nettle Cormack for telling her she shouldn't, and now she feared she'd encouraged the man. Why had she done that? But she knew the answer: to make Cormack jealous. It had all been for naught, because by the end of the evening when she had left, the two men appeared to be fast friends, which was strange being that Cormack had warned her to stay away from the marquess.

"Soooo. What do you think about Mother and Mr. Birch?"

Daphne looked at her in surprise. "He...seems very nice."

"They sat together all night. They talked and laughed together. Isn't it wonderful?"

"What are you saying?"

"What if Mother gets married again?"

"Sometimes you are the silliest flibbertigibbet. She laughs and talks with lots of people, some of them gentlemen. That doesn't mean she's going to marry them all."

Clarissa looked at her with sudden seriousness. "Would you be upset if she did remarry?"

She closed her eyes, and in her mind saw her father's smiling face, which made her heart hurt, but she knew the right thing to say. "Of course not. She's still young and beautiful and I'd want her to be happy. I just wouldn't want to encourage her into something when she wasn't at all ready, by proposing love matches where there are none."

"Yes, of course you're right. Well, I suppose we'd best both get straight to sleep. Tomorrow will be a late night! The Vauxhall Gala! I can't wait." Clarissa removed her gloves, and ascended the staircase a few steps ahead of her.

"Neither can I," Daphne declared.

She'd never gone to a gala, and everyone talked about what fun they were, if a bit wild at times. Kincraig had already lined up a cadre of young gentlemen to escort them and, yes, to keep them safe. Havering would also be there. She would go and have such a fine time she'd forget all about Cormack.

As soon as Clarissa disappeared into her room, Daphne hesitated outside hers. Returning back down the stairs, she entered the conservatory, where all the invitations to her ball sat carefully organized in boxes. Moonlight streamed through the windows, reflecting off wide palm fronds and the pale, round faces of night flowers. Their fragrance weighted the air, intoxicating and lush, making her feel like doing something reckless.

Half of the envelopes had already been sealed by the footmen, but everything past the *M*s were still open to be completed tomorrow. Part of her wanted to challenge him, to call his bluff and see what he would do if she refused to carry through with his demands.

Still, she wrote the necessary address and enclosure card and inserted the envelope into the *R*s. Tomorrow, Cormack, Lord Raikes, would receive his invitation.

Whether he attended was completely up to him.

* * *

A crash of thunder awakened Cormack from a dead sleep. He lay tangled in sheets, and stared at the Venetian plasterwork medallion at the center of his robin's-egg-blue ceiling, attempting to command focus in a damnably blurry world.

Sunlight streamed through the parted curtains, along with the sound of birdsong and horses clopping by.

Another crash rippled through his head, accompanied by a dagger blade of pain, straight through his left eye. He groaned. "Oh, no."

Lord, he shouldn't have drunk so much, but the night had dragged on and he'd needed drink just to survive the company of his companions, a vapid lot of thirty-something-year-old *children* concerned only with gambling away their fortunes and indulging the next piece of willing female fluff—of which there had been endless supply, as long as coins flashed. He'd done his best to focus on the cards, blocking out the sights and sounds of libertines plundering a constant flow of purchased pleasure.

The night had left him more certain than ever his nephew, Michael, was the result of force, and no love affair, because he could not imagine Laura ever falling in love, even fleetingly, with any one of those lechers, at least two more of whom he had successfully identified as members of the Invisibilis, Dump Dump Dinglemore and Charlie Churlish, who when he'd inquired about their nicknames for each other had drunkenly flashed identical medallions to the one he carried in his pocket.

That is, until Rackmorton threw them a blistering glare. It had taken him several painful hours of carefully constructed conversation to deduce that neither had ever been to Rathcrispin's hunting lodge, and thus would never have crossed paths with his sister.

He'd returned home, mortifyingly sotted and frustrated almost beyond bearing.

"You're awake, I take it?"

Cormack started at the voice, and turned his head, which sent the world spinning again, but somehow at the center of the vortex he perceived a man sitting in the chair by the window, with long legs crossed at the ankles, his Hessians polished and gleaming. A raised newspaper obscured his identity.

"Unfortunately," he croaked.

Lowered, the paper revealed a familiar face. "Good afternoon, then."

"Havering," he said. "To what do I owe this pleasure?"

Fox chuckled. "You look terrible."

Cormack closed his eyes. "I feel terrible."

Havering, for his part, did not look terrible but annoyingly sober and clear-eyed. "It's no surprise, when you run with that set."

He wished he could say he had learned his lesson, but he would continue to do whatever it took to break into the social circles that protected the man he sought from discovery. He had to remain patient and trust his instincts that if he kept his eyes wide and his ears open, he would deduce the identity of Laura's seducer.

"I hope you don't mind me letting myself in. No one answered the door. Nice house, but you need some servants." He folded the newspaper, in the most practiced and efficient manner, and set it aside on the barrel-shaped table at his elbow, beside his top hat.

"I have servants . . . er . . . a *servant*."

"Might it be that naked man or that naked woman sleeping under the table in the drawing room?"

"Damn it, Jackson." He raised up onto one elbow and squinted at Havering. He'd done as Rackmorton suggested last night and dismissed Jackson for the evening. Clearly Jackson had found his own entertainment.

"Oh, I see. The fellow. I don't believe he'll be providing valet services this morning, judging from the number of bottles littered about the floor. First off you need a good butler, and he'll set up all the rest. Would you like me to make inquiries?"

"I'd be grateful, thank you." He ran a hand through his hair, exerting the pressure of his fingertips along the top of his skull, and in that small way, assuaging some of the pain. "But certainly the proper staffing of my house is not why you're here."

"Lord no. I've come to enlist your help. Everyone else I can call on has other obligations." Havering stood and moved to stand beside the window, where he leaned his shoulder against the frame and looked down to the street. "You're my only hope."

"What can I do for you?"

"I, along with their so-called cousin, Mr. Kincraig, have been tasked with chaperoning the Bevington girls and a cadre of their declared suitors on an outing this afternoon. They've invited three gentlemen each, their mother's idea. Between you and me, Daphne has long insisted that she will not marry, and Her Ladyship thought this might be a way to encourage time with some suitable young gentlemen without being overly pushy in trying to change her mind."

Daphne? Not marry? He couldn't imagine that her passionate nature would ever allow her to live her life alone, without someone to love.

"If you have Mr. Kincraig's assistance, why do you need me?"

"Kincraig is…undependable at best. Not to mention only ever one step ahead of the most salacious imbroglios. You name the scandal, and he's likely had a hand in it."

"Duels?"

"Of course."

"Gambling?"

"He's lost his fortune, several times over." He smiled. "But he's got a golden touch, it seems, in that he always wins it back."

"No doubt he's a seducer as well."

"Hmmm, yes. The latest scandal involving some governess, I hear."

Cormack lay on his back, staring at the ceiling. But at hearing the words *scandal* and *governess* from Havering's lips, he mentally stood at attention.

"Most gentlemen of my acquaintance consider governesses forbidden quarry."

"Let's just say that from what I hear, while a guest at a northern hunting estate, our Mr. Kincraig was rumored to have been hunting more than the deer."

Cormack tensed, his blood turning to ice. Could it be possible that the man responsible for his sister's destruction existed in closer proximity to Daphne than he could have believed? That he was indeed a relative?

"Seems like I may have heard something about that. On whose estate did this take place?" He waited . . . waited to hear more.

"I don't know anymore, thankfully. Only that Wolverton was furious and summoned him for a lecture."

"Damn," he growled, sinking again into his pillow.

"What did you say?"

"That damn, my head hurts. You called him a 'so-called cousin.' Why?"

Havering chuckled. "I just know I don't trust him. There's just something about the way he appeared out of nowhere, presented by His Lordship's investigators as a distant relation and likely heir, when no one ever knew of his existence before. But if Wolverton is satisfied, it's not my place to demand details. I suppose it will all be sorted out and verified before any letters patent is granted allowing him to assume the earldom. Still, that doesn't make him a suitable chaperone for the girls. You, I have much better feeling about, despite your grievous lapse in judgment in going with Rackmorton last night."

"Haven't you ever suffered a lapse in judgment?"

"You aren't supposed to ask about that." He grinned. "It also helps that you are already betrothed. Won't you let me formally introduce you to the Earl of Wolverton and Lady Harwick? It should be an entertaining afternoon. Have you ever been to the Monument?"

Cormack blinked, his mind registering what Havering had just said, that he was betrothed.

"Amazing. I—I only shared the details of my situation with one person." Rackmorton.

"That's how things work here. You whisper something to one person, and before you blink, the rest of the world knows." Havering chuckled. "The sooner you learn, the better. It wasn't a secret, was it?"

Chapter Nine

No, of course not." Still, in that moment his head ached more intensely.

Had Daphne heard? It was all he could think, but why should he care if she had? Because he didn't want her to think him a lout for kissing her when he knew full well he could never, ever marry her because of the land agreement with Sir Snaith. Still, he would have liked to have explained that to her himself. Inwardly, he battled with his conscience, knowing he ought to stay away from her.

But...Mr. Kincraig would be there, and he needed to investigate him further.

"The fact that you're not in the market for a wife and that I can vouch for your honor—"

He held silent, not splitting hairs with Havering. No, he wasn't formally betrothed, but he might as well be, because one day he would indeed marry the Snaith girl, and in doing so, complete his intended destiny. His loyalty must be to his family, and as part of that, he would have a closer look at Mr. Kincraig. This afternoon, in fact. He knew better than to condemn the man on the spot, but this was precisely the sort of information he'd hoped his efforts would provide. Was Kincraig a member of the In-visibilis? And had he ever visited the hunting lodge of the Duke of Rathcrispin? Those were the questions he had to answer before deciding his next course of action.

"Can you vouch for my honor?" With a groan, he rolled from the bed, taking the sheet with him, for modesty's sake. The world tipped and swayed, but he held himself steady, and after everything righted itself, he padded across the carpet to the washbasin.

"I've got good instincts," Fox assured, raising a finger-tip. "I know you'd make a suitable and, most important, a *formidable* chaperone, to assist me in keeping the overea-ger bucks, fortune hunters, and scoundrels in line—and they are myriad, my fellow, converging at any given mo-ment like hungry hounds. I can't claim to understand the workings of a woman's mind. By my observation they seem to lose all sensibility over the most black-hearted fel-low, the one who will, in turn, break their heart. But these two angels—both of whom are far too trusting of the male gender—are my girls and I'll do whatever necessary to protect them."

Cormack glanced at his visitor in the mirror. "What makes you a suitable chaperone? Are you married or spo-ken for?"

"No, not yet."

Cormack fixed the sheet at his waist. "Then why don't you marry them? Or, er . . . one of them."

He bent over the basin to splash water on his face.

"Heavens no, that would be like marrying a sister. A little bratty sister whom you adore to pieces, but…no. Not marriage."

Cormack reached for the towel. "How did you come to be so tight with the family?"

"We grew up in the country together, as neighbors." He chuckled. "Their older brother, Vinson, was my best friend." His voice lowered as he said this.

"Was?" With a linen towel, he blotted the moisture from his face.

A shadow moved over Havering's face. "You wouldn't know that story, would you, being so new to these circles. It was in all the papers. He died. Drowned, four years ago, while we were on an expedition to New Guinea. He was always interested in plants and bugs and scenery and the people of the world. He wanted to see all these things, not just read about them in books, and I'd agreed to go with him." He broke off. "But that's a story for another time."

A moment of silence passed between them, then Cormack said quietly, "Again, your marrying into the family would seem the obvious choice."

He might be able to abide that, Daphne marrying Havering.

"To be blatantly honest, I did once have quite a *tendre* for the eldest, Sophia." He smiled over steepled fingers. "But she is most happily married now, and a duchess, and I am proud to call His Grace a friend. We shall see what else life throws at me."

There was something rueful and restless about Havering, as if he were a man who hadn't yet found his place.

"As for this outing today…Rackmorton, is he one of

the Bevington suitors?" Cormack asked, in all nonchalance.

Fox's eyebrows went up. "He has certainly made his interest in Daphne known, but I do not believe she shares the sentiment. I think she has good instincts."

"After what I witnessed last night, I am relieved to hear that. I feared that you and he were close friends."

"It's a dreadfully small world that converges every year for the season. For the most part, we all know each other, but I wouldn't call Rackmorton and me close, or even friends." He pulled his watch from his pocket. "Come along now, we've only just enough time."

* * *

Clarissa tied the wide pink ribbon of her hat under her chin. "So we've decided on the Monument, then?"

They made their way from their rooms to the staircase.

"Mother says the view of London is magnificent—if you can make it to the top."

"You didn't invite Rackmorton, did you?" Clarissa's voice dipped low.

"Of course not."

"Good, because last night he acted as if the two of you already had an understanding."

"Which is precisely why I didn't invite him." Nothing about her season thus far had changed her mind. She wasn't marrying anyone, most especially him. There was also the small detail that she'd seen him in London's seediest gaming hall, in the company of two prostitutes. Unlike Cormack, who had been at the Blue Swan searching for someone, the marquess most assuredly hadn't been there looking for anything but women and spirits and a table at which to gamble. She remembered his predatory smile, and the way he had lustily reached for those women. She couldn't share that detail with her sister—or with anyone, for that matter—but she'd never forget. How could she admire or respect a man, after having seen him revel in such depraved environs?

Her sister drew on her gloves. "It's as Sophia said, there's something about the eyes.... On the other hand, it would have been nice to invite that dashing Lord Raikes. His eyes are nothing short of heaven."

At hearing Cormack's name from her sister's lips, Daphne feigned insouciance. "Why didn't you, then?"

"It wasn't me he was looking at so intently last night. But didn't you hear?" She tilted her head. "Oh, perhaps not. I think you were chatting with Kate this morning when Mother told me. I was trying to decide which three gentlemen to invite on this afternoon's excursion, and of course, the earl came instantly to mind—but she told me Lord Raikes is betrothed. All the ladies are devastated."

Daphne gripped the banister, frozen between steps. Betrothed. Cormack...? For a moment, everything went black. She couldn't see or breathe.

"You're certain?" she asked, through lips numb with shock.

What sort of man went around kissing young ladies when he was already betrothed? Only the most dastardly of men, that's who.

"Quite. You know how things are. The moment he walked into the room last night, there were those who made it their business to know." She gave a rueful snort. "Lucky girl! She's from the country, I hear, someone he knows from his family's seat. Daphne, are you coming?"

"Yes...of course."

Clarissa continued to the drawing room, where her mother and grandfather could be seen and heard speaking with Havering and Kincraig, who at Her Ladyship's request were to chaperone them on their afternoon excursion.

Daphne, however, hurried in the opposite direction, toward the conservatory—desperate now to reclaim the invitation she'd written out the night before. She would not invite Lord Raikes to her ball. Oh! She would blackmail him in return with a threat to tell everyone he had deceived and kissed her. No London ballroom would ever welcome him then.

Only she'd never actually tell anyone, because it would be too embarrassing a truth. Yet upon entering the conservatory, the sight of an empty table met her.

"Mr. Ollister is delivering your invitations at this very moment," said the housekeeper, breezing in behind her, returning a cloisonné vase to a cabinet in the corner of the room. "You must be so excited, Miss Bevington! Two weeks from now, and the house will be transformed, all in celebration of you."

"Yes," she answered weakly. "I'm very...excited. Thank you, Mrs. Brightmore."

Not wanting Mrs. Brightmore to see the expression on her face, which would certainly tell the opposite story, she approached the birdcage and trailed her finger along the wire frame. Inside, the little creatures sidled along their perch, eyeing her and each other.

She had kissed the fiancé of another woman. The

knowledge devastated her. She could not help but feel doubly duped by Lord Raikes, and betrayed.

Mrs. Brightmore quit the room, but someone else entered. She stifled the urge to cry out to the intruder that she needed a moment alone.

"You sent him an invitation to your ball, didn't you?" Kate asked.

Daphne closed her eyes. How could she have been such a fool? "I'm sure I don't know who you mean."

"Don't be coy. Lord Raikes!"

"The footman has already taken them." Daphne laughed in an attempt to sound lighthearted, but the sound came out thick and rueful. "So it appears I have."

Kate drew closer. "How thrilling. He really is the most impressive gentleman. I had such a strong feeling about him. I like him, Daphne. I can't help but hope he's the one to convince you to marry."

"He is betrothed to someone else."

Kate gripped her arm, her expression furious. "Daphne, *no*. The way he looked at you last night, why, I felt certain he had intentions. And he...why, he kissed you last night as well! Didn't he?"

"No," Daphne denied emphatically, with a shake of her head. "He did not."

"He *did*!" her friend exclaimed. "Your face confesses everything."

"Oh, very well! He *did*," Daphne confirmed.

"How could I have been so deceived? He is a rake of the lowest sort!"

Daphne grabbed both of Kate's hands in hers. "You mustn't tell anyone, most especially Mother. There'd be a terrible fuss."

Kate stared into her eyes. "I won't," she whispered, the rigid line of her shoulders easing a degree. "Of course I won't. Just don't be alone with him ever again. You must promise me."

"You don't have to coax an agreement from me."

Steps sounded at the door, and once again Mrs. Brightmore entered. "Miss Bevington, your guests have arrived, along with the carriages. Everyone's waiting in the vestibule."

"You must go and have a wonderful time," Kate urged. "It's the most certain way to forget him."

"You are right, of course. It really doesn't matter that the invitation went out. Even if he does attend, I'll be so busy enjoying myself, I'll never see him."

"And isn't that for the best?"

"It is. Lord Raikes who?" Daphne exclaimed.

"Perfect! Now tell me, who did you invite this afternoon?" Kate's demeanor brightened. "That handsome Sir Whinton, or perhaps the dashing Lord Batley? They both sent you the most beautiful arrangements with the most charming sentiments written on their cards."

"I didn't invite either of them." Daphne put several steps between them.

Kate tilted her head in question. "Then who? Daphne, please tell me you invited someone you actually like. As in for a possible future husband."

The sound of male laughter echoed from the direction of the house entrance, along with her sister's delighted giggle.

"Oh, fig. There's no time, I'll tell you later. Everyone's waiting on me."

Parting ways with Kate, she neared the vestibule. Kate

was right. She must simply do as she'd always planned. She must throw herself into the gaiety of the season. Once it was over, she'd have such happy memories to cherish in those ensuing years when she fully intended to devote herself to her family.

Pushing her shoulders back, she took a deep breath and pushed into the room and—

The breath died her lungs.

Cormack! He stood beside Havering, staring at her with smoke-and-cinder eyes.

Well, *of course he did*, because she couldn't imagine anything worse than seeing him now with her nerves all in tatters, and today was apparently her day to suffer a thousand torments as atonement for the sins of her past.

Well, she wasn't going to run. She was going to have a splendid afternoon with her three "suitors," who in truth were just three dear friends, none of whom had any true aspirations to wed her.

"Miss Daphne," said Havering. "You remember Lord Raikes? I've recruited him to assist me and Kincraig in chaperoning today's affair."

Daphne pushed out a smile, one she hoped appeared radiant and blasé. "Lord Raikes, you say? Oh, yes. Now I remember. From the park. You weren't at the musicale last night. Oh, you were? I must not have seen you."

Fox's eyes narrowed. Cormack stepped smoothly forward and extended his hand. She stared at it, at his long fingers with their squarish knuckles, plainly discernible through his fitted gloves. He had such masculine hands. Those hands had touched her. Sweetly in the past, but far more intimately in her dreams. Those dreams crowded her mind, making her blush.

Everyone watched and waited. Breathing through her nose, she lowered her hand into his.

Even through two layers of leather, the contact *shocked*, moving through her palm and up her arm to spiral in glorious, dazzling circles through both of her breasts, which was the oddest thing, because he hadn't even touched her there. *Though last night, for the briefest moment, she'd wanted him to. She remembered the dream, and what he'd done with the flowers, and his mouth—*

He hesitated, glancing darkly into her eyes, then bowed, lightly pressing his lips...to her knuckles.

Her legs weakened—

She swayed, nearly toppling, but Kincraig, of all people, caught her by the arm and waist. Her mother called her name. Cormack reached as well but stopped short of touching her. Other male figures crowded about, all inquiring over her well-being.

"Daphne," he urged. "Let me lead you to a chair."

"No, please." She sank against him, but just as quickly pushed away. "I'm not dizzy. I did not faint. Nothing like that! I—I simply lost my balance. It's these mules. They are new and the soles polished, and we are on marble. I slipped. I'm so sorry to have concerned everyone, but you are all...overreacting." She forced a laugh, her cheeks burning.

"You didn't eat breakfast," the earl scolded in a quiet voice.

Lady Harwick touched her face, as if to gauge her temperature. "You always get faint when you don't eat."

"No, Mother, that's me," Clarissa said from behind her. "I get faint when I don't eat." She bestowed a smile on the gentleman beside her. "I'm delicate like that, you see.

But my dear older sister could go days without eating and would still be as strong as an ox."

"Perhaps we shouldn't go to the tower?" Havering said quietly. "It's quite the strenuous climb."

"She said she is well," her sister said.

"I am well."

"I do, at times, have that effect on the ladies," said Cormack, grinning. All the gentlemen laughed.

"You had nothing to do with it, I assure you," Daphne snapped. "And I am going to the Monument, if I have to go alone."

Her mother shot her a sharp glance. "Gentlemen, please watch her today on the stairs."

They all assured her, in a rumbling of voices, that they would.

Daphne twisted away from them. "Please, let's just forget about it and begin our afternoon." Somehow, in trying to avoid Cormack, she came face-to-face with him.

"Well...Miss Bevington." A small smile lifted one corner of his lips. "Before you arrived, we were acquainting ourselves with...ah...the gentlemen." He glanced over his shoulder.

"Yes, the gentlemen," repeated Havering, with a too-bright smile.

Everyone else—her mother and sister and grandfather and Havering—all looked at her with expressions of thinly veiled dismay, which she ignored, preferring instead to greet her companions for the afternoon.

"Sir Tarte," she said. "How happy I am that you could accept my invitation."

She extended a hand to George, Sir Tarte, whom she'd known for forever and a day. An excellent conversationalist and dancer, he was also quite the dandy, but not the ridiculous sort—at least she didn't think so. His striped scarlet-and-gold coat, ruffled cravat, and bright green leather shoes that boasted three-inch heels looked very fine...on him. She could always depend on him to make her laugh until she cried, and they always had a wonderful time in each other's company.

"I'm thrilled to have received your invitation, darling girl." With one hand raised behind him, high in the air, he bent over her hand and pressed a kiss to her glove, before glancing up from under a perfect tumble of blond curls. "Mother, as you can imagine, is beside herself with joy."

His mother—a close friend of Lady Harwick's—had never been reticent in expressing her hope that one of the Bevington girls would marry her son. But of course, just as Clarissa had, Daphne had invited not one but three gentlemen with whom to share the afternoon.

She avoided Cormack, who stood just two feet away, his arms crossed over his chest, watching with rapt interest, and searched out the next.

"Bamble, I see you over there," she called. "Come say hello to me."

Lord Bamble sat on the bench in the corner, chewing his thumbnail and staring into a well-worn book. At hearing his name, the dark-haired, dark-eyed young man started and looked about, a flush rising to his pale cheeks. For as long as she'd known him, which was since they'd been about nine, he always seemed to have a book in hand. He stood and thrust the slender volume into his pocket, and rushed forward. "Miss Bevington, I was so very surprised to receive your invitation."

"Surprised!" She beamed up at him. "Bamble, you are always so charmingly modest."

She could think of no one more sincere or gentle among her circle of acquaintances, and his shabby appearance, inspired by intellectual distraction rather than lack of appropriate funds, only added to the endearing nature of his character.

He blushed an even deeper shade. "Thank you for saying so."

And it really didn't matter so much that he hadn't noticed at all when she'd nearly fallen and come running like the others. In fact, perhaps she liked him better because of it.

At that moment, a shoulder eclipsed Bamble, and Neville Sheridan's deeply tanned face came into view.

"Oh, and me. Don't forget me." He laughed, his eyes crinkling around the edges, and beamed at Daphne. He clapped Bamble on the back, as if they were old friends, because Captain Sheridan of the Royal Navy did seem to be old friends with every member of the *ton*, and their servants, and every person he met on the streets.

She smiled. "How could I forget you, Captain Sheridan? Perhaps you are last in this moment, but never least."

Though older than Tarte and Bamble by at least two decades, the captain cut a dashing figure and exuded confidence in every action and word. On those rare occasions when he was in London and not sailing off to some obscure corner of the world, he could be found at the carriage races, horse auctions, or pugilism matches (or so Daphne had heard), entertaining anyone who would listen with his stories of high-seas adventure.

She then briefly greeted the three gentlemen her sister

had invited, all of them young and distinguished fellows she recognized from the blur of parties they'd attended since the onset of the season. As for Cormack, from that moment on she intended to ignore him. *Completely.* To her, he did not exist!

She stole one quick glance, but she immediately diverted her gaze, so he wouldn't see, only to slide another look—

He smiled at her, lips pursed as if fighting a smile, but discreetly looked away.

Her blood surged and her cheeks went hot. He had never looked more handsome than today. His cheeks bore the faintest bit of shadow, which only made him look dangerous. She wanted to touch his face. She wanted to slap his face. He'd been betrothed all along! Why, if his fiancée only knew what he'd been up to.

She marched straight past him. "Havering, come with me, won't you? Lord Raikes can escort Clarissa and her company." She twined her arm through Fox's and led him toward the door.

"Whatever pleases you," he answered indulgently.

Her mother called after them, "Please return no later than four. We've the gala tonight."

Fox raised his hat in acknowledgement. "Yes, my lady."

A gentleman passed them, coming up the walk just then. Mr. Birch! Tall, and wearing a top hat, he nodded graciously and continued to the door. Daphne turned to see her mother greet him, bright-cheeked and wide-eyed.

Oh, but Cormack eclipsed her view of them. Daphne cast what she hoped was a searing glance at him, but he wasn't even looking at her. Instead, he gave his full attention to Clarissa while she chattered up at him, already attached to his elbow.

Daphne had never felt so angry or betrayed, but—
his poor fiancée! In truth, Cormack was no better than
Rackmorton, visiting bagnios and pretending to be a
well-mannered gallant by the light of day. Who was to
say that he wouldn't have visited the Blue Swan that
night with or without a quest for vengeance? Now, given
the benefit of retrospect, she could clearly see that she
had been the one to assign heroic qualities to him. Obviously she'd been wrong.

Inside the carriage, Daphne arranged her skirts so that
the fine muslin wouldn't crush, and she exhaled in relief,
grateful to be away from Cormack, if only for a short time
in which she could devote her full attention to her friends.

A man she assumed was Fox took the seat beside her.
Only then she recognized the muscled thigh beside hers as
belonging to someone else. Not Fox's, but Cormack's.

Chapter Ten

"Oh!" she exclaimed, peering up into gray eyes smoldering with sensuality and mischief and even, perhaps, a glint of anger, which only heightened the tension between them.

"How foolish I am," Cormack drawled, turning his head to address the other three gentlemen. He sat with his hat on his knee, and his leather gloves draped across one thigh. "Somehow I've managed to climb into the wrong carriage—"

Fox hovered in the doorway, the toe of one boot already inside. He laughed and waved a hand. "No trouble. I'll join Clarissa's group."

"Wait, Havering...no!" Daphne called, but he disappeared and the door shut. With Cormack staring down at her, she slowly eased back into her place trying not to look as discomposed as she felt.

"Get out," she hissed.

"I will not." He murmured near her cheek, peering past her toward the window. "Look, the other carriage has already left. Now most especially, I can't shirk my duty and leave you alone unsupervised with your *suitors*, any one of whom could secretly be a black-hearted libertine bent on taking your virtue."

"The only libertine in the carriage is you."

For a long moment, he studied the other three gentlemen in the carriage. Grinning, he leaned even closer. "I'm quite certain you're right."

With a jerk, the vehicle began its movement and traveled out onto the street. Cormack sat beside her, immense and magnetic, his long legs bent at the knees. The fabric of her skirt being so delicate, she felt the sinewy hardness of his leg where his thigh touched hers. Her body reacted, as if hungry for him. Her mouth went dry, and her breasts felt as if they'd swelled to twice their normal size, crushing against her stays. Even the rhythm of the carriage as it traveled over the street pavers added a sensual thrill to a moment she couldn't claim to understand.

"Let's all get to know one another better, shall we?" Cormack said smoothly, like a medieval torturer, eager to inflict his particular version of pain.

"We all know each other quite well," Daphne snapped, annoyed that Cormack sounded so at ease while she felt like jumping out of her skin, all because of his uninvited presence. She bestowed a gracious smile on the three other gentlemen, one intended to dazzle—only Bamble didn't see, because he was already peeking into his book. "I've known each of these fine gentlemen for years."

Whereas she'd spent only a few extended moments in time with Cormack. And yet despite that truth, Daphne couldn't deny the feeling of intimacy between them, even here under these awkward circumstances. His every glance teasingly said, *Stop being so ridiculous. I know you.* And she feared he did. Her body and her soul seemed to recognize this. It took all her effort to resist the temptation of easing against his solid warmth, and to deny herself the pleasure of twining her arm through his.

"Well, I haven't, and I'm always eager to make new acquaintances." With a shift of his legs, he aligned his boot alongside her slipper, a scandalous liberty that no one in the carriage seemed to notice. She exhaled softly, and jerked her foot away.

Sir Tarte leaned forward, resting both hands on the pommel of his walking stick. His eyes glowed with interest at the stranger in their midst. "I heard you say you were at the musicale last night, Lord Raikes? Yes! I thought I recognized you, but I've never met you before. Tell us, how are you acquainted with Miss Bevington?"

Daphne turned her face to stare out the window at the London street passing by, an attempt to conceal the magnitude of anxiety racing through her. Would he embarrass her in front of her companions, by revealing some detail about her forbidden venture into the Blue Swan? Before, she would have thought never. But this morning she'd discovered she didn't really know him at all. Her heart raced at the possibility.

"Hmmm. How did we meet?" The silk-over-steel tone of his voice *teased* her, and implied the most wicked threats.

Oh, she couldn't bear it. She turned to Cormack, eyes wide and alarmed.

"By complete chance in the park." Cormack flashed a smile at her, one that stunned her to her core with a pleasure so perfect and pure, she wanted to cry from it. "It was all very improper, without the necessary introductions, necessitated by an escaped parasol, tumbling across the grass."

She exhaled, relieved and, yes—begrudgingly grateful. Cormack nodded, as if to say, *What did you expect?*

Improper, yes. Everything between them was improper, including the way she felt now, with her heart racing and wanting to reach out and touch him, even with the knowledge that he belonged to someone else. She hated him for making her feel this way.

"Sail caught wind and got away from you, did it?" chuckled the captain. "Happens to the best of us."

"Indeed," answered Daphne.

"How very heroic of you," exuded Sir Tarte, his gaze warm with admiration.

"It was only a parasol," Daphne muttered, perplexed by the fervency of Tarte's response.

Captain Sheridan peered over Bamble's shoulder, to the book he held. "A naval adventure? Why, Bamble, are you interested in naval history?"

His lordship half closed the book, and answered, "It was my greatest wish to serve His Majesty on the seas. Indeed, the physicians say ocean climes are best for my convulsive asthma, but you see I've a very inconvenient fear of drowning. I can barely suffer taking a bath."

"My!" exclaimed Tarte, with a mortified chuckle. "How peculiar."

"And *confining*," added Cormack.

Daphne sighed.

"It's true." Bamble nodded, looking faintly morose. "So any shipboard adventures for me must come from the pages of a novel."

Captain Sheridan grinned at Bamble. "I served with the fellow who wrote that book." His grin widened. "I'm told he based the heroic character, Captain Laramore, on myself."

"You don't say," Bamble said. He shifted in his seat, his eyes widening. "That scene, with the pirates dressed as Bahamian strumpets—"

"All true," Sheridan said. "In fact, there's even more to that story, that I . . . er, can't share in the presence of a lady." He glanced pointedly toward Daphne. "But there are many stories I can tell."

The conversation went on until at last the carriage trundled to a stop and the footman opened the door.

Bamble, Tarte, and the captain all exited, leaving her momentarily with Cormack.

He turned to her suddenly, and said, "Bloody hell, Daphne, these aren't suitors. I don't know what they are, or what you were thinking when you invited them."

Outraged, she answered, "Who are you to say what I need?"

"You need a *man*."

She scowled at him. "What is that supposed to mean?"

"Truly? You don't know? All right, then, just watch."

He climbed out to join the rest, and stood to the side as the captain assisted her down.

"Thank you, Captain Sheridan," Daphne said.

In the distance, with the tower behind her, Clarissa waved. "We'll see you upstairs, on the observation gallery."

Daphne smiled. Now that she'd escaped Cormack in close confines, she was determined to enjoy herself, or at least appear as if she were doing so. Bamble stood on the pavement just a few feet away, his book still clasped in his hand. Moving toward him, she extended a hand. "Dearest Bamble, will you see me up?"

"Me?" Peering up at the towering façade, his face paled. "Oh heavens, no. Three hundred and eleven steps? I'm afraid my asthma precludes such exertion, as well as my outright terror of heights." He let out a shrill chuckle. "I shall wait for you here at the bottom, and you can tell me all about it."

Cormack turned to her and mouthed the words, *What a surprise!*

Her face grew heated. How dare he! But he dared even more, passing close beside her to growl, "One down. Two to go."

Daphne did her best not to reveal her exasperation. "There is a bench just over there where you can...read." She looked to Captain Sheridan and, with renewed enthusiasm, announced, "As for myself, I can't wait to see the view of the city from such a height. Captain?"

The captain came to stand beside Lord Bamble, nodded, and raised a hand. "Do forgive me the delay, dear, but I'll join you all in just a moment." His expression flushed, he sidled closer to the gentleman who stood beside him. "So, Bamble, what I was going to tell you about those strumpets—"

A glance to Cormack found him winking ridiculously, and holding up two fingers.

Daphne swallowed her dismay. Her suitors were not behaving as suitors at all. Not that she had wanted them to, but she hadn't expected them to ignore her and find each other so fascinating. Abandoned by Lord Bamble and Captain Sheridan, she sought out her only remaining hope, Sir

Tarte, whom she knew with a certainty would not disappoint her.

But Tarte wasn't even looking at her. Instead he looked toward the sky, worry knitting his brow. "Say, Raikes, just look at the clouds."

Cormack glanced above. "There may be rain."

Tarte's gloved hand fluttered over the ruffles at his throat, and then up to his hair. "I do believe I'll retrieve an umbrella from the carriage." The footman, anticipating his need, handed one to him.

"Well, then. Let us begin our climb." Cormack's eyes pierced into hers, as if issuing a private challenge.

Sir Tarte came from behind to lower a gloved hand onto his shoulder. "What do you say, Raikes? Last one to the top buys pineapple ices afterward at Berkley Square?"

Why had she never seen it before? In his heeled shoes, skinny trousers, and superfluous cravat, Sir Tarte did indeed appear the ridiculous dandy. Next to Cormack, tall and elegant in his simple, but perfectly bespoke dark coat and fawn breeches, Tarte looked like a clown.

"I accept your wager," said the earl. "Prepare to pay."

"I'm already assured of losing this particular contest." Tarte chuckled. "Oh, to be blessed with such athleticism. Such muscular legs. And those shoulders! Say, are you a member of one of the pugilism clubs?"

"No, but I've considered joining. Which, in your opinion, is the best?"

Daphne's temper flared. Obviously they'd all forgotten her, finding each other infinitely more interesting. She ought to climb back into the carriage and order the driver to return her immediately to Hamilton Place—only, they likely wouldn't even notice!

"Miss Bevington," Cormack called after her.

"What?" she answered sharply, glaring in his direction.

"Go on ahead without us. We'll follow just behind, and rejoin you before you can count one, two—"

She clasped her hands onto her ears, but she still heard him say, "—*three*!"

With the sound of his laughter in her ears, Daphne spun on her heel and flounced to the stairs.

* * *

As Sir Tarte blah-blah-blahed in his ear, Cormack watched her go. The chit had the most mesmerizing swing to her skirts, one that awakened every male hunger inside him. As a combustive heat built in his chest, sparking and churning more ferociously the farther she moved away from him, he felt more certain than ever that Daphne Bevington would be the death of him—or at least his ruination. Now that she was clearly very angry with him, he wanted nothing more than to remind her of the attraction between them.

Out of politeness, he allowed Tarte to climb the stairs first, but the man's absurd shoes slowed him down so that he wobbled side to side, and had to reach for either the railing or the wall to steady himself.

Ahead of them, Daphne ascended the spiral staircase. Light filtered through narrow window openings just enough to provide him with glimpses of her golden hair and her pale shoulders. Her skirts were fashioned of some gauzy, delicate cloth, and sometimes, the perfect slant of sunshine revealed the outline of her legs and the mesmerizing shape of her buttocks.

Tarte let out an exclamation, half falling up the stairs.

"Sorry there, Sir Tarte, I didn't mean to run you down."

"It's not your fault, I stopped suddenly." Tarte looked up, his face red, and sweat shining on his brow. "It seems I've turned my ankle."

"What a shame." Cormack caught the umbrella in his hand. "Try to make your way back to the carriage. I'll ensure Miss Bevington comes to no harm."

He hastened his pace, at one turn catching a glimpse of Daphne's pale face as she peered over her shoulder, and the next, only a tantalizing flash of her skirt. At last, he broke free onto the observation platform, which lay wide and square around the circular tower. The scene that awaited him at the top of the stairs momentarily stunned him. He had seen beautiful mountain scenery in Bengal, but he had never, in his life, stood suspended so high in the sky as now. The view of the city from this vantage point took his breath away—almost as much as Daphne Bevington did, each time he looked into her blue eyes.

"It's something else, isn't it?" said a voice beside him. "This view."

Cormack turned his head to find Mr. Kincraig standing beside him. Every muscle, every molecule went on guard.

"Indeed it is," he answered.

"Do you know I used to be scared of heights when I was young? I didn't even like to climb trees."

"What a shame." He scrutinized the man's features, searching for any similarities to Michael's. He perceived none, but the boy was so young, and his appearance still that of a babe's.

"Life has a way of changing people, though, doesn't it?" Mr. Kincraig leaned against the railing, looking out over the city like a pirate on the bow of his ship. "Can't say I'm afraid of anything anymore."

"So you are Miss Bevington's cousin?"

He shrugged. "So some say."

"What an odd thing *to* say."

"I'm certainly not the only one saying it." He chuckled, and rubbed a hand to his forehead, looking put out. "God, I wish I had a smoke. These sorts of obligatory outings drive me absolutely mad. Aren't you Daphne's chaperone? Lord knows it's not me. Hadn't you best go and find her?"

For a moment, he hovered, caught between duty and desire to find her.

"You are right, of course."

Cormack paused only a moment more to take in the sight of the buildings, spires, and roadways, and the carriages, wagons, and pedestrians that scuttled between them like beetles. The Thames, which abutted the city to the south, glimmered a dull greenish-gray.

He backed away from the edge and moved alongside the railing, searching, but she was nowhere to be seen. Clarissa and her three suitors took turns peering through a looking glass out over the city. Fox stood several feet away, looking off into another direction.

"Look," Clarissa said, "I can see all the way to the river. How impressive. Why have I never come here before?"

The gentlemen vied for her attention, each striving to point out the most interesting landmark.

But Daphne. Where was she? His heart still beat heavily from the climb, and it sent an exhilarating rush coursing through his blood. He felt like a stalking animal, consumed by mindless craving, an all-consuming need. He scanned the platform. The wind gusted, not severely but enough to lift his hat, which he removed as he strode along the parapet. He rounded the bend, to find her standing back to the rail, the city of London spread out behind her—a sensual fantasy, suspended in the clouds.

"You think you're a man because you're the only one to make it to the top?" she asked, her eyes sparking fire. "Well, you are wrong."

He shook his head slowly. "You know I'm right. They are wrong for you."

"Who are you to decide? Why did you come this afternoon? You are my blackmailer, not my friend. You've ruined everything!"

"Havering invited me—"

"You should have declined."

"I wanted to talk to you."

"Whatever you have to say, I don't want to hear."

"Listen—" He stepped closer.

She backed away. "Leave me alone."

"Don't you understand, I *can't*?" Only once he'd said the words did he realize the truth of them.

"You are *betrothed*," she accused, her cheeks flushed and eyes bright. "You are betrothed to another woman and you kissed me. Now stop interfering in my life, when you have absolutely no right to do so."

He turned from her, rubbing a hand across his face, in an effort to force away the frustration, the need for her. He should walk away. Join the other group, or go to the carriage and wait. But once again he faced her. God, what was he doing? He couldn't walk away.

"Could you not plainly see that all of your family and friends are dismayed? Truly, Daphne, those three fops are your choices?" he remarked bitterly. He gripped the umbrella in his hands.

"They are all three fine gentlemen, which is more than I can say for you. Bamble is sweet natured and—"

"A complete ninny," he interrupted, moving to stand close beside her, his palm skimming flat over the top of the railing to rest adjacent to hers. "He would never pay you a moment's notice, because he's too besotted by his books. *And* his perceived infirmities."

She snatched her hand away, and stepped back.

"Captain Sheridan—"

"—will be gone in two months' time," he interrupted, pivoting sharply, and closing the distance between them. "Returned to the far side of the earth, for God knows how long. Because he is more in love with the ocean and the camaraderie of the service than he could ever be with you."

Without realizing it, she'd backed herself into a corner, and could go no farther. She bumped against the rail, and her eyes widened in alarm—and fury.

"Perhaps so, but Sir Tarte is a delightful fellow—" she blustered, her cheeks filled with high color.

Cormack lowered his face so they were nose to nose. "Sir Tarte is wearing rouge."

"I—I hadn't noticed." She blinked rapidly, her voice distinctly cool.

"The rouge? Or that he is clearly more interested in me than you?"

Her eyes flew open in outrage. "How dare you imply—"

"All I've implied is that he has exquisite taste," he teased, before growing instantly serious. "Daphne, why would you choose any one of those three earwigs when you could have any eligible man you wanted at a snap of your fingers? It's as if you don't want a man who will satisfy you—"

"If you must know, I don't intend to marry. Ever. It was decided long ago."

Yes, he recalled Havering saying the same. He frowned, catching her chin in his hand, and gently urging her to look into his eyes. "Decided by whom?"

She turned her face, and sidestepped, escaping him.

"By me." She whirled and backed away, her gloved hand on the railing. "Because it's my choice. Everyone in my family knows, but Mother, being a mother, hopes I will change my mind, and so she had this idea for an afternoon out with several suitors, where there wouldn't be any pressure to favor any one person over the other. I confess, I humored her. I invited three gentlemen who are long-time friends, because I thought we'd all have a lovely afternoon together, and that would be all. But of course *you* came."

With a glance over his shoulder to confirm no one observed them, he again closed the distance between them.

"Stop doing this," she said. "It is wrong for you to pursue me when—"

"I'm not pursuing you."

"Then what are you doing?" She stared up at him, her eyes unwavering.

"I hate things the way they are between us," he said through gritted teeth.

"You made them that way," she accused.

He looked to the sky, and gave a low, rueful laugh.

"If only you did not provoke and madden me so." He closed his eyes, and breathed. "I am *not* betrothed," he growled, moving so close he smelled her fragrance, so close he could kiss her if he so chose. "I would not have kissed you if—"

"You are lying to me, and I don't believe you."

"Daphne."

Her gaze darted over his shoulder because obviously she had no wish to be observed, or overheard, either. The wind caught her curls and plastered the gauzy fabric of her dress against her body, revealing every delectable curve and valley to his hungry eyes, and eliciting a needful response. For a moment, a forbidden fantasy invaded his thoughts, of pressing her to the wall behind them, and kissing her until she melted, of tugging her dress from her shoulders and kissing her bared breasts as the city bustled below, unseeing and unaware of the passion raging between them, high above.

He moved closer, scandalously so, so that his chest brushed against her breasts. Every time he allowed himself to get this close, his thoughts went heady and he could only react with touch. This time was no different. His hand covered hers on the rail, wrapping round it tight.

Her eyes went smoky. He bent to kiss her.

Her eyes flew open wide, and she swung sideways, her bodice tightening against her bosoms to form a tantalizing cradle. "Don't."

Just then, Clarissa and her troupe rounded the corner, with her chattering at the center.

Daphne stormed away, to stare out over the city. She looked so angry and distant and unobtainable. He could think of nothing else but to change that.

"Where are the others?" Havering inquired.

"Bamble has asthma, and a fear of heights," responded

Daphne, over her shoulder. "Captain Sheridan was kind enough to stay below to entertain him with tales of the high seas."

"What about Sir Tarte?" asked Clarissa.

Cormack provided that answer. "He has turned his ankle."

That brought chuckles from at least two of the gentleman, and a sharp glance from Clarissa. She reached for the arm of the third. "You said we could see Buckingham from this perspective?"

The young man led her away, and the others followed.

In that moment, rain pattered down all around. Daphne whirled round, looking up to the sky as if it betrayed her. Cormack opened the umbrella and held it between them, extending the offering of shelter to her, yet she only stared at him, refusing to budge.

"Don't be ridiculous." He strode forward, covering her. Raindrops glistened on her skin. "Come out of the rain."

"I can't be close to you." She stepped out from beneath.

He grasped her wrist and—

"Unhand me." She jerked in an attempt to free herself.

Havering turned back toward them. Cormack instantly released her, and they mutually pretended to admire the view.

"If it gets much worse, we'll have to go back down," Havering called.

"It's only a sprinkle," Cormack said. "Let's give it a few moments."

Fox nodded, and rejoined the others, who had all opened umbrellas and now looked like a cluster of mushrooms.

"Listen to me," he uttered quietly.

"There is nothing you can say—" Daphne broke free, shunning the shelter of the umbrella as if to follow the others.

He ought to let her go. He ought to set her free. But he had never seen any woman more beautiful than Daphne in this moment, walking away. His heart exploded and the resulting reverberations soundly overrode all common sense. He caught her by the arm and pulled her back, lowering the umbrella to shield them from view.

"Lord Raikes!" she cried, but a gust of wind carried her voice toward the city.

"Don't call me that." He seized her against his chest. She closed her eyes, as if in pain. He pressed his mouth fervently to hers. "Not you, Daphne. I am Cormack. You know me."

The sound of Clarissa's voice, cooing at the pigeons, came from not ten feet away.

"No." She turned her face. "I don't. I thought I did but then you changed, and you threatened to blackmail me."

"Just words. Do you believe I could ever hurt you?" he demanded.

"Then why did you say them?"

"Because the moment I saw you in the park in that carriage, everything in the world turned upside down. That first night, after the Blue Swan, I felt like a hero in your eyes. But when I realized who you really were, I became just another admirer, eager for your glance."

"Stop, Cormack."

But he caught her chin, and kissed her.

"She is twelve," he murmured raggedly against her lips. Daphne blinked dazedly. "Twelve...?"

A glance behind the umbrella proved they were alone

again, their company having moved round the corner to the next viewpoint.

"Ernestine Snaith is twelve years old. While it is true I have entered into an understanding with her father that we will marry when she is nineteen, in order for my family to regain lands that have been in our possession since shortly after the Conquest, we are not formally betrothed, and will not be for some seven years."

He bent to kiss her again. "I wouldn't have kissed you otherwise."

"Cormack," she whispered, softening against him.

He deepened the kiss, his tongue darting urgently between her lips and over her tongue and teeth, desperate to claim her more completely. He inhaled and savored her lemon-and-mint-sweet breath. She moaned, tilting her head up and spreading her hands at the front of his coat.

The fantasy returned, and in his mind he was already lifting her skirts and raising her bare bottom against the stones—

Daphne twisted away, installing several feet between them, and raised her fingertips to her lips. Eyes glazed, she stared at him in silence, as drops glistened on her cheeks and hair and like diamonds against her skin.

"What?" he growled in frustration, and once again came to stand beside her, shielding her from the rain, his blood simmering with frustration. "It's true, I can never marry you."

"Why would you even feel the need to say that?" Her eyes flared wide. "I've already said I've no intentions of marrying you or anyone else."

"Then what?"

"I'm afraid."

"Why?"

"Because when the time came, I might not be able to let go."

At that moment, Clarissa again came round the corner again between two of her suitors, her arms tucked into theirs. The third followed behind, his face a scowl, holding two open umbrellas, one which he held over Clarissa and his competitors. Havering, for his part, chuckled behind them.

"It's getting far too damp!" she called. "We're returning to the carriages!"

"Where is Kincraig?" Cormack asked, trying not to sound overly interested.

"Downstairs already," Fox answered.

"Go on," Daphne replied. "We will be right down, after one last look."

When alone again, neither of them moved.

He turned toward her, bracketing her against him, his arm at her waist. "A man disgraced my sister, Laura, and now she is dead. It's why I came to London. That is the man for whom I search. I would never disgrace you the way he did her. I would never hurt you."

"I know that. Somehow I always have."

"Then let me kiss you again." He bent toward her face. "Let me touch you. Let me take you somewhere that we can be alone—"

She pressed her fingertips against his mouth. "I can't."

He exhaled, holding her tighter.

She pressed against his arm. "Let me go, Cormack."

"I don't know if I can."

"Then you must try harder."

With that admonition, she twisted free of him and ran through the rain to disappear down the stairwell.

Chapter Eleven

There is nothing quite like a Vauxhall Gala night." Fox grinned at him from the opposite bench.

Cormack peered out the window. "Just look at all those lights."

He could not help but think of Laura in that moment, and how much she would have enjoyed such a magical sight. A thousand variegated lanterns shone in the darkness, revealing in golden cast throngs of guests moving through the trees. Daphne would be here, and he had no doubt whatsoever that they would cross paths. He would show her they could still be friends. That he could stand aside while she found happiness, and be the first to wish her well.

Now, with the benefit of being separated from her for several hours, he had talked sense into himself. Where, after all, had he thought all that marvelous kissing would lead?

Thankfully, Daphne had thrust the necessary boundaries

between them. Which was one reason he'd accepted Fox's invitation to the Vauxhall Gala tonight. With Havering's help, he'd simply recalled the Duke of Durden's impeccable staff to man the house and stable, as he ought to have arranged from the start. To anyone else he looked like the perfect gentleman. By God, it was time he started acting that way.

Besides, he couldn't stay away if he wanted to. The man he still pursued socialized in these circles. Was it Mr. Kincraig? Whatever the case, he was more determined than ever to find out, and knowing the man would be here tonight, as well as Rackmorton and countless other members of the Invisibilis, filled him with the compulsion to end this thing once and for all, tonight if possible.

Moments later, Jackson let them out from the carriage, amidst a sea of other carriages and arriving guests.

"Be on your guard," the young man warned, securing the door, and scanning the crowd. "While all of the *ton* may well be here tonight, there is always a dangerous element lurking about, eager to lighten your purse or steal your boots, sometime at the expense of one's life. We'll wait over there, in the field for you, with the other conveyances. Just whistle, and we'll come." He climbed onto the rear perch, and the new driver snapped the reins. Jackson saluted as they rolled into the shadows to join what appeared from this distance to be scores of other carriages.

Cormack joined Havering on the pavement, and together they entered the gate, showing tokens to the private gala at the Pavilion. "Your man is right. The gardens can be dangerous."

Cormack listened, but felt no qualms about delving into the darkness and jostling elbow to elbow with strangers.

When had he ever not been on guard? Having lived six years in the wilds of Bengal, under no one's protection but his own, he'd learned to exist in a constant state of vigilance, one he'd been unable to put to rest even upon returning to England.

"Who brought Lady Harwick and the young ladies tonight?" he inquired.

Fox responded with a wink. "Mr. Kincraig, who is still a bit rough around the edges, but at least he is making more efforts to be part of the family than before. He actually insisted on bringing them tonight, without having to be summoned by Wolverton."

Good. He would make every effort to befriend the man, as he had done with Rackmorton, and extract whatever answers he could.

They moved in and out of the light, along the colonnade. Everywhere, people laughed and danced and played. The music grew louder, and at last he saw the orchestra stand, constructed of several ornately colored floors, and housing the musicians whose skilled efforts set the tone for the night. Here, beneath enormous hanging flower bouquets and Turkish chandeliers, danced the *ton*, markedly different in appearance from the common people crowding the rest of the park. The ladies wore silk dresses and sparkling jewels, and the gentlemen dark evening clothes.

He searched the colorful tumult for Mr. Kincraig, but when his gaze instead found Daphne, it felt like a sudden and forceful kick to his gut. She danced with a handsome dark-haired fellow who smiled down at her in obvious enchantment. She smiled back at him, too, but in keeping with the steps of the dance, she twirled free and joined with the next partner, who appeared as equally besotted as the first. Clarissa danced in the same grouping, along with a number of other stylish young people.

Lady Harwick warmly smiled at them on their approach. She reached for and squeezed his hand. "Welcome, Lord Raikes. Havering tells me you were the most devoted chaperone to Daphne this afternoon. Thank you for giving your time. We are all most appreciative."

"I was happy to do it." He ought to feel guilty, accepting such praise. After all, he'd been wholeheartedly in favor of seducing her daughter just hours before. But his and Daphne's flirtation or dalliance or whatever they'd shared was now ended. It felt very nice to stand here beside Lady Harwick and to be considered to be one of her friends.

A taller, mature fellow stood beside her, his expression attentive, and his gaze clearly adoring on Her Ladyship.

"Hello," Cormack said.

"Forgive me," said Lady Harwick. "This is Mr. Birch."

They all three chatted for a moment, before Mr. Birch went in search of lemonade for the marchioness.

Together they watched the dance, Cormack finding it harder to watch Daphne in the arms of other men, dancing and laughing so gaily, than he had expected. He had bared his soul to her that afternoon and felt she had done the same. Despite their having made peace, he felt completely adrift.

Her Ladyship sighed. "Thank heavens she is spending time tonight with other gentlemen and not Sir Tarte, or Captain Sheridan or Lord Bamble." She laughed anxiously. "Each of whom I find an admirable fellow in his own right but do not perceive as a suitable match for my daughter."

"I do believe she came to the same understanding this afternoon."

Lady Harwick's expression brightened and she rested her hand on his arm. "You don't know how relieved I am to hear you say that. You are the most delightful man. My husband used to do the same thing, sense my fears and know just how to soothe them. That's how I know you will one day make a very good husband for your betrothed. I only wish my Daphne could find someone like you."

Cormack pressed his lips together, wondering if it would be better to remain silent. But he could not. "Miss Bevington told me this afternoon that it has long been her intention never to marry."

"Indeed, what she says is true." Her Ladyship sighed. "And I hope I do not press her too much in my hopes that she will reconsider. I truly do respect her choice. However I fear that same choice is grounded in the misguided belief that she bears the blame for her father's death. You see, she was riding the horse that reared up and struck him. But there was a lightning strike, and the animal startled. There was nothing anyone could have done." Her voice softened to nothing, and her eyes misted over.

"How terrible. I'm very sorry you suffered such a tragedy."

"Thank you." She touched a hand to his arm. "But I fear Daphne has always believed she must pay some sort of penance, by selflessly devoting her life to me and her grandfather and her sisters at the expense of denying her own dreams."

It hadn't made sense to him that such a lovely young woman as Daphne wouldn't want to find love, or marry. Now he understood completely. The danger she'd faced to help Miss Fickett. Her devotion to her family. She placed everyone's cares above her own.

Mr. Birch reappeared from the shadows. "I have returned with lemonade for all." He balanced three cups of the stuff, which they all quickly dispatched.

The song ended and the dancers moved across the wooden floor, some remaining for the next set, while others abandoned their places to find friends in the adjacent supper boxes or to make merry under the canopy of the trees.

Her Ladyship still stood between them, silent and pensive, watching Daphne, worrying about her daughter's future happiness, he knew—and, he suspected, wanting to join in the fun.

It seemed the perfect moment for Mr. Birch to ask Her Ladyship to dance, but the fellow remained silent.

At that very moment, he saw Mr. Kincraig on the far side of the dance floor, speaking to several men. His curiosity piqued, he glanced down to Lady Harwick.

"Would you...like to dance, my lady?" he asked her.

Her eyes widened with surprise. "Why...yes, I would love to."

Cormack did not miss Mr. Birch's momentary expression, one of abject failure, with his eyes closed and his mouth a tight line. Maybe the fellow was shy or simply did not know how to dance. Well, perhaps he could help Mr. Birch get over his fears. He knew better than anyone that there was nothing like seeing the woman one adored in the company of another man, to compel one to action. Every time he saw Daphne whirl past in the arms of another man, he had to prohibit himself from doing the same.

Whatever the case, he led her to the floor. As they took their places, he happened to see Daphne staring at him from across the clearing. She was lovely, every moment of every day, but there was something about the light from the lanterns, playing with the shadows on her skin and the high flush on her cheeks, that made her even more bewitching—especially when she smiled at him, as she did now.

In a night painted in shadows, she stood out like a brilliant jewel. She wore an azure gown, trimmed with gold, and crystals shimmered in her upswept hair. His gut twisted with desire, and for a moment, he savored the sensation, but he closed his eyes and after a moment, the music started, a lively country dance.

The next moments passed in a blur of music and movement. He guided Lady Harwick to the right, to the left, and they parted to circle round the next person in line, to join hands again. Faces flashed by, smiling and laughing. Kincraig, he observed, spoke with Rackmorton and that fellow from the night of the musicale . . . Dump Dump Dinglemore. Ah, yes, and there was Charlie Churlish as well, with several others. He would endeavor to join them as soon as the dance was done. It wasn't, after all, as if he'd come here to dance.

Even so, Lady Harwick shouted above the din, "You are such a good dancer!"

Of course he was. Laura had needed a practice partner all those years ago, when she was learning her steps, and dreaming of growing up into a young lady to experience nights like this. Strange that in this moment, when he was surrounded by a heaving mass of people, he should miss her so much. Knowing that the man who had ruined her might be here tonight, laughing and carrying on as if she had never existed, only renewed his hatred.

They repeated the same steps, traveling down the line, crowded on all sides by other dancers, who at times broke through. Rather than break the rhythm of the dance, it only added to the Bacchanalian revelry of the night

Then, when it was time to change partners, Lady Harwick twirled off into the arms of another man, a tall fellow with a mustache . . . and Daphne was suddenly in his.

* * *

"I think you went in the wrong direction," he said. Shadows revealed the hollows beneath his cheekbones, and lips that did not precisely smile. His heart beat strong and sure beneath her palm, which rested at the center of his chest. "I'm supposed to be paired with that dear lady over there."

He indicated a gray-haired matron who wandered unpartnered, her gloved arms held aloft, only to be swept away into the dance by Havering.

"Perhaps I did go the wrong direction, but quite on purpose and for good reason." She half-turned within the circle of his arms to find two dancers—her mother and Mr. Birch. "That dear man wanted so badly to dance with Mama, but did you know he has a war wound? I didn't either. He conceals the limp very well."

Despite everything, she liked Mr. Birch very much, though she hadn't wanted to. He wasn't her father; no one ever could be. But she realized things couldn't stay the same. She wanted her mother to find happiness, and, yes—Clarissa as well. Still, she felt as though everything she knew was slipping from her grasp, and she needed something to hold on to. In this moment that thing was Cormack.

"And you encouraged him?" He spun her around, and around again, with such skill she could only close her eyes and savor the pleasure of being in his arms. There was something about the night, and the sparkling lanterns and the music, that made her feel reckless and daring.

"Of course I did. Why wouldn't I? He's just a bit self-conscious on the dance floor, and doesn't believe himself to be very nimble."

Another couple collided into Cormack's back. With a faint look of irritation, he sheltered her from the blow.

"Apologies!" the man shouted, and they spiraled away.

The corner of Cormack's lips hitched upward into a smile. "I don't believe 'nimble' even signifies on a night like this."

"Just look at my mother's smile. She likes him, I think. I'm sorry, Cormack, you are left to dance with me."

She smiled up into his face, wanting the night to never end. She wanted to flirt. She wanted to played with fire. It was easy to do here in the gardens, where magic danced among the trees and worry and regret seemed so far away.

Her heart soared when he pulled her close, into an embrace, and murmured against her temple, "You won't ever hear me complain."

* * *

He could do this. He could dance with her. Touch her even, and then walk away. He would prove it to himself, and to her.

The music trilled and dipped, and they circled one another, hands sliding, however briefly, over one another's skin and clothing, her gaze never leaving his. But then, as all country dances required, they spun in opposite directions to claim the next partner. He watched her go, and saw her smile fall when she met the arms of the next man—Rackmorton, who peered back at him, grinning like a hyena, with bared teeth, and in a whirl, he lost sight of them.

The woman in his arms gazed up. A beauty, she had blonde hair and bosoms that strained at the silk of her gown. "Lord Raikes, I am told?"

"That would be me, and you are?" he inquired politely.

"Lady Bunhill," she replied, suggestively trailing her fingertip across his chest as the crowd converged about them. Despite the lanterns in the trees, and the blaze of light cast out from the Pavilion, shadows settled everywhere, and there were many in the crowd behaving in ways that they might not in the more mannered walls of a Mayfair ballroom. "I'm so glad to meet you. Rackmorton says you're great fun."

"Rackmorton?"

"Yes, he's a friend. I am a widow, always looking for new friends."

He did not misunderstand the invitation she extended. But while he had no intention of accepting what she offered, he did not immediately rebuff her. She was flirtatious and lovely, and he needed distraction, however temporary, so that he might forget the beauty on the other end of the floor. When they had danced, Daphne had looked at him with far too much warmth, a contradiction to her earlier edict that they remain apart. Now it was time for him to be strong. Perhaps if she observed him in the company of another, she would know it was all right for her to do the same. For her to forget him, as she should. She was right. He had to let her go.

So he allowed it when Lady Bunhill wrapped her arms around him and led him toward the refreshment table, where she poured them both glasses of burned wine, insisting on lifting her cup to his lips, and then her own.

"Mmmm, intoxicating. Rather like I imagine your kiss would be," she flirted. "Walk with me?"

She led him toward one of the many walkways that broke off from the clearing. He hesitated, but told himself it was only a walk.

"You seem to know your way around."

"That I do," she responded, with a teasing lilt to her voice.

She led him down a narrow path, into an alcove, where . . . strangely, he made out the vague outlines of some ten to twelve men, whose faces remained concealed by shadow. His pulse increased, and every cell of his being became alert. Someone else approached from behind; he heard their footsteps. Glancing back, he saw another blonde woman, cajoling a man along the path, drawing his arm over her shoulders. The woman, from this distance, looked to be a near mirror image of Lady Bunhill.

"There you are." Another figure emerged from the shadows, straightening the eye holes of his hood. "That didn't take much effort to get you here, but Bunhill is quite the temptress."

It was Rackmorton. The voice left Cormack with not a smidgeon of doubt.

Lady Bunhill pulled away from him, and walked toward Rackmorton—as did the second woman, who had escorted the gentleman behind him.

"Thank you for the compliment, my lord," Lady Bunhill purred, draping herself against him.

"You can reward me later," murmured the second, planting a kiss on his silken cheek.

He shrugged them both off, and urged them away. "Now, go along. The both of you. Leave the men to their talk."

Cormack's first concern was where Daphne had gone, but he could only assume she now danced with another partner, or had returned to the protection of her family. His next thought was that he was most certainly standing in the company of the Invisibilis. "Raikes, I believe you already know Mr. Kincraig."

He glanced back at Kincraig, whose longish hair brushed his bearded jawline, which made him look like a swashbuckler with the glaze of drink in his eyes. Had this man seduced his sister? He was certainly handsome and always quick with a word of dry, sardonic humor, but there was something in his manner that to Cormack spoke of self-loathing. Which usually meant a person suffered some sort of regret.

"Indeed I do," said Cormack.

"Hello there, Raikes," Mr. Kincraig answered. "Are you as confused as I am? Are they *both* Lady Bunhills?" Glancing to the men in the shadows, his eyes narrowed, but his smile conveyed a keen interest in the present situation. "Is that a real name, or something they've made up?"

So...Kincraig wasn't a member of the Invisibilis. Or was he?

Rackmorton circled in front of them, pausing dramatically. "We've been watching you gentlemen for some time, and we like what we see. You're rich, you love beautiful women, and you like to have a damned good time—as do we."

Cormack hadn't expected this. He'd rather thought they were going to try to beat him up or something juvenile like that. Now he sensed what was coming, and he didn't like it. He only wanted to kill one of them—one who very likely stood, at this moment, just feet away. Kincraig, perhaps? Or someone else who stood in the shadows, his identity hidden from view. But he didn't want to have to become one of them in order to do it.

"We are members of a rather ancient society." Rackmorton's voice grew hushed and reverent. "The name of which I can't speak to anyone who isn't a member—which we are now inviting you to become." He lifted and spread his arms magnanimously. "I don't have to tell you, it's quite the honor. Only the most select are welcomed into our midst as brothers."

"How inclusive of you," declared Kincraig, moving more in line with Cormack's position. "To invite this fellow and I into your very special club. I like clubs. I go to them all the time, but usually we all aren't standing in the dark where I can't see anyone's faces. I like faces, too, for the record."

Cormack remained silent and watchful. It would serve him no purpose to anger or offend.

Rackmorton's chin snapped up. "You'll see our faces once you agree to join us. When we are brothers, in truth."

"I never had a brother." Kincraig looked at Cormack. "What about you?"

"No. I had a sister." No one else could know how speaking those words hurt him, to his core.

Mr. Kincraig nodded, unfazed, and returned his attention to Rackmorton. "What will joining your club get us? Are there meetings, and are we obligated to attend them?"

"Of course there are meetings. All clubs have them."

"You should know now, then, that I don't like meetings that last any longer than five minutes. What benefits are there to joining your group, and suffering through these meetings?"

"For one, there are opportunities to make more money." Rackmorton laughed. "We know all the right people. Hell, we *are* all the right people."

Chuckles came from the darkness.

Kincraig shrugged, and shook his head. "But you see, I make plenty of money on my own. People are always wanting me to invest, and promising me, sometimes even in writing, beneficial returns. Will you do that?"

"In writing, you say?" His Lordship snapped. "Of course not. Did you not hear the word 'secret'?"

Cormack laughed at the ridiculousness of the conversation. He simply couldn't help himself.

"Ah." Kincraig nodded. "Then I remain unimpressed. What about you, Raikes?"

Cormack offered a noncommittal response. "I am still on the fence."

Looking to Rackmorton's blank face, he inquired, "What else do you have to offer?"

"There are also women." Rackmorton strode toward them. "Lots of beautiful women like the ladies Bunhill, and wild private parties. Sometimes we all get together and—"

"What? Make love like a bunch of wild monkeys?" Kincraig crossed his arms, rubbing his chin, and rocked back on his heels. "An interesting endeavor, to be sure, but not particularly to my taste. Besides, I get plenty of women on my own. Raikes, you're dreadfully handsome, I'm certain you do as well."

Cormack shrugged. "Could it be that they believe *their* women are better? If so, perhaps they could please explain how."

Rackmorton sneered. "We're inviting you to join a most exclusive club. Hardly anyone is ever invited to join. Are you interested or not?"

"Do we have to join together, or not at all?" said Kincraig.

The marquess clasped his hands to either side of his head and groaned.

"Oh, good God," he shouted, turning to stride toward the trees. "I have never suffered so many damn questions in my life."

"It's entirely an individual choice," said one of the other masked figures.

"May we give you our decision, say, next week? I'd like to think about it before committing." He turned to Cormack, eyebrows raised. "Raikes, why don't you and I pick a day—say, Tuesday—and submit our answers together, with no pressure whatsoever that they should be the same. Perhaps written in blood? Not mine of course, because I don't like to bleed, but we could prick *your* finger. What do you say?"

Cormack stared at Kincraig, torn. If he threw his lot in with Kincraig, so as to investigate his possible connection to Laura further, he would sacrifice this opportunity to infiltrate the Invisibilis. Was he certain enough?

"Wait a minute here." Rackmorton wedged between them, arms raised. Glaring at Kincraig, he said, "Consider yourself, Mr. Kincraig, disinvited. Obviously we were wrong about you. Rathcrispin was right. You could never be one of us."

Recognition of the name shot through Cormack like a blast from a blunderbuss. There could be no mistaking: he referred to the Duke of Rathcrispin, who had allowed the Invisibilis the use of his hunting lodge that neighbored the Deavall estate.

"What a fickle bunch you are," Kincraig drawled. "Why me, but not him? Do you have a secret signal that I missed, where you all just agreed to blackball me? I am wounded." He clasped a hand to his heart, a portrait of mock Shakespearean tragedy. "I think I might even cry. After that unforgettable week we all spent together in the country. After all the fun we've had together."

A loud blast sounded from the direction of the dance.

"What was that?" said Cormack, half-turning.

*   *   *

Daphne searched for Cormack in the crowd. She knew she shouldn't. That she was just courting trouble by wanting another dance with him, as an excuse to be in his arms, but he had looked so handsome under the lantern light and the night seemed nothing less than a fantasy.

The dance floor was so crowded, she skimmed along its edge—

And that's when she saw him, with a voluptuous blonde attached to his side. The woman smiled up at him and laughingly drew him into the shadows. Cormack didn't hesitate, but followed her down the narrow footpath.

Daphne's heart stopped beating. Where was he going with her? She took several steps in that direction, only to retreat and turn back toward the tangle of dancers crowding the floor. Tears filled her eyes. How it hurt. Her heart.

But she had no right to complain, when she'd insisted that afternoon that he let her go.

Suddenly, she didn't feel like dancing anymore. She wanted her mother. She continued on the circular path, weaving in and out of revelers. Clarissa danced by in the arms of another handsome partner. At last she spied Lady Margaretta in the deeper shadows along the edge of the trees with Mr. Birch.

"Hello!" she called, raising her hand and walking toward them.

But they didn't hear her above the din. As she grew closer she could only watch, stunned, as the two embraced and Mr. Birch bent...to kiss her mother.

It was as if the earth moved beneath her feet, and she stumbled. Her future shattered before her eyes, and rearranged like a puzzle with its pieces in all the wrong places. Her mother and Mr. Birch. Of course she'd known they'd quickly come to be friends, and that they enjoyed one another's company, but this? So quickly?

She'd been so worried that her mother would be left alone, that she would be the one to provide the widowed viscountess with companionship so she would never be lonely.

But what if Lady Harwick married again? No doubt Clarissa would as well. Soon, none of them would need her.

What if *she* would be the one left all alone?

Wouldn't that be a suitable punishment for what she had done?

"Daphne?" Her mother had seen her and now walked toward her, Mr. Birch following behind. Lady Margaretta looked so *concerned*, and he...*apologetic*.

"Don't mind me!" Daphne called, forcing gaiety into her voice, as if she hadn't seen their embrace. "I'm looking for Clarissa. I'll find you later."

She rushed away, the lanterns and faces around her now blurred by tears.

Only it wasn't Clarissa for whom she searched, but Cormack. And she wouldn't find him because he was with someone else.

* * *

"There, I heard it again," said Cormack, infinitely more concerned now than before.

"Likely just the fireworks," another of the Invisibilis said from the shadows.

"You all agree, don't you, that we don't want Kincraig anymore?" Rackmorton glanced around. The silent figures in the shadows shrugged and grunted.

A tangle of screams and shouts sounded from behind them.

"Those aren't fireworks," Cormack insisted darkly. "Those are people screaming."

Peering down the shadowed walk, Cormack could just barely make out a portion of the clearing, where the crowd pushed like a school of fish from one side toward the other.

"You're right. Something's going on back there," said Kincraig.

"We're almost finished here," Rackmorton hissed. "You, Raikes. Don't let that fool sway you with his ridiculous talk. Join us."

A blast sounded—clearly a *gunshot*. There were hundreds of people attending the festivities at the orchestra stand, but all he could think of was Daphne, and whether she had been shot. The blood drained from his face, and from his limbs, and his heart seized in his chest.

Forgetting all else, he ran toward the crowd.

A wall of people met him, all running and trying, it appeared, to escape. Women screamed and fell, only to be lifted up by those trying not to trample them. He searched the faces, searching for her, or any member of her family. He had to ensure they were all safe. Another shot sounded, and the crowd's panic intensified.

Havering hurtled out of the shadows. Cormack caught him by the arm.

"What has happened?"

"Raikes. Oh, thank God." The crowd jostled them from all sides, shoving them together. Fox looked at him only briefly, before his eyes returned to search the crowd. "From what I observed, a large mob broke through the boundaries and someone shot a gun in the air. They are just ruffians, I think, intent on petty thievery and wreaking havoc, but everyone panicked and scattered. I can't find the ladies. They aren't with Kincraig. He was off in the shadows with some strumpet when all this took place."

"I know," Cormack shouted above the din. "I was with him."

"What?" Fox's eyes darkened.

"I'll explain later. Do you think the ladies were together?"

"I fear not. They were all at different corners of the dance floor when the melee broke out."

"If you find Her Ladyship or the girls, take them to the base of the large tree near the Pavilion entrance. I'll do the same. We'll meet there and escort them out."

Not waiting a moment more, they both returned to the fray.

Just knowing Daphne was lost in the churning tumult struck panic into Cormack's heart. She could already have been trampled, assaulted, or worse. Far worse. He couldn't think about it. He just had to find her. He plowed into the crowd, pushing and shoving through, searching every face and shadow. He scooped up an older woman from where she'd fallen, and a moment later planted his fist in the face of a brute who ripped an old soldier's medals from his chest. Then, amidst all the shouts and pleas for calm, he heard a shrill scream. His blood went cold, because without a doubt he recognized her voice. He dove toward the trees, praying his ears and sense of direction did not betray him.

He found her there, surrounded by four toughs, three men and a woman. She wielded a small tree branch in her hand, and swung it fiercely each time one of them lunged close. He rushed toward them.

"Stay away!" she warned. Her hair had fallen free of its pins, and her silk gown sagged off one shoulder, in tatters. Rage blurred his vision. What had they done to her, to put her in such a state? Her hair and neck still sparkled with jewels—likely only paste, but no doubt that was what her attackers were after.

"We can take y' down hard or easy, my lady," threatened one of the men. "Yer choice."

"Come near me, and you'll be the one going down." She tightened her grip on the branch. "And you won't be coming up again!"

"I want 'er dress," the woman shouted. "Don't tear it any more than it already is."

Just as Cormack grew near enough to attack, one of the men lunged, shoving her from behind. With a cry, she spun round, swinging the branch and clocking the fellow on the side of his head. Yet in a flash, the harpy attacked her from behind. The two others followed.

The same blackness he'd experienced in the alleyway the first night he'd met her threatened to overtake him again. He leapt onto the attackers, who were so intent on tearing the jewels from her hair and neck they didn't see him. With a shout, he wrenched them off her. Fists flew and met flesh, and when it was all done, he triumphantly carried her out from the trees.

"I'm so glad you are here." She clung to him, pressing her face to his neck. "Did you see me hit that big one with the stick?"

"I did," he murmured, his lips against her temple, letting the scent of her fill his nostrils. "I am so very proud of you."

She stiffened in his arms. "My mother, and my sister— where are they, do you know?"

"Havering's looking for them. I'm certain they're safe."

"You're bleeding, but I can't tell from where." Her hand touched his face. "Does anything hurt?"

He carried her to the base of the tree, where he and Fox had agreed to meet. Scores rushed past them toward the gate, certainly intent on escaping the garden for the night. Several park wardens rushed in, blowing their whistles and bellowing for order.

Cormack exhaled roughly. "You're bruised, on your cheek."

"I'm safe, because of you." Her hand curled inside his. "It's all that matters."

"Are you hurt? Anywhere that I can't see? Did they touch you?" His gaze and his hands moved over her, searching for any other injury or sign of trespass.

She allowed his inspection. "They only dragged me into the trees, and that awful woman pulled my hair, I suppose trying to get at these worthless crystals."

Damn him to hell, he couldn't stop looking at Daphne with her torn silk dress and a bruise on her cheek, safe and in his arms. He'd never been more enraged or relieved, and couldn't imagine ever releasing her from his arms again, so intense was his desire to protect her.

After a moment, Havering appeared, gasping for breath. "You found her! Is she harmed?"

"Stop talking about me like I'm unconscious," Daphne insisted. "Do you see my eyes open?"

Despite everything, Havering flashed a grin. "And for that I am relieved. Take her, Raikes, and get her far from here."

"Do you think the river would be faster?" Cormack asked.

"I fear any departing boat will be so overcrowded it might overturn. No, take the carriage. We'll all meet at Wolverton's."

"But my mother, and Clarissa," cried Daphne, her hands fisting in Cormack's shirt. He soothed her with a whisper, and a gentle stroke to her hair.

Fox replied, "Kincraig found them, just moments ago. He's taken them to his carriage and will see them home."

"What about you?" asked Daphne.

Gunfire sounded again, and they all ducked.

"Bloody hell!" Cormack swore, doing his best to shelter her with his body.

Havering backed away. "I'm going in with the wardens to show them where that idiot with the gun has holed himself away. He thinks he's hidden, but I saw the muzzle flash. Don't worry about me. I'll find a ride and rejoin you later. Go, now, get her to safety."

As soon as they emerged from the gate, a familiar whistle rent the air, the one that only he and Jackson used. Carriages cluttered the road, with the ladies and gentlemen of the *ton* crowded inside them, some even hanging off the sides. Again, he swept Daphne into his arms and carried her to the steps where Jackson waited at the door, slamming it behind them, and scrambling back on top.

Inside, he exhaled in relief, with Daphne still held fast in his arms, her arms wrapped just as tightly around his neck and shoulders. The carriage veered and tilted. Apparently his new driver had exceedingly good driving skills, because a glance out the window showed them plowing half onto the pedestrian pavement to pass the outer row of waiting carriages, which greatly advanced their position on the crowded road. He only hoped the man didn't get them killed.

Still, they would be going nowhere fast, which put him in a torturous predicament, being that Daphne Bevington, his greatest mortal weakness, presently plastered herself against him so tightly he could feel the delicious swell of her breasts through his shirt. He closed his eyes, and did his best to calm his rapidly beating heart, and the agitated arousal that coursed through his blood, certainly a result of the fear and excitement they'd just experienced.

"You are safe now." He released his hold on her and made a gentle attempt to pry her free.

She allowed the separation, but made no move to increase it. Half draped across him, she peered up at him like a sleepy-eyed mermaid and said nothing. Light from the carriage lamps shone through the window, revealing the curve of her bare shoulder, and the pale upper half moons of her breasts.

"You should go and sit over there. On the other bench." Thank goodness the carriage shop had returned the bench completely refurbished and in proper working order so they could each have their own comfortable seat.

"I don't want to," she answered in a hushed voice.

"Daphne, this afternoon at the Monument you made a very smart decision, and I'm trying my damnedest to do the right thing by you—"

Her hands came up beneath his jaw, and she silenced him with a kiss, her eyes open and staring straight into his.

He held himself rigid, fighting the urge to touch her, to twist his hands into her hair and to push her down onto the cushion where he could spread his body atop hers.

She blinked, and breathed against his mouth, slowly sliding the tip of her tongue across his lower lip, before sucking it into her mouth and giving it a little bite.

He groaned. She sighed, tilting her head and kissing him more deeply, her hands moving up into his hair. His cock stirred. Then, more than stirred.

When was the last time he got hard just from a kiss? Oh, hell.

Chapter Twelve

Daphne. I'm serious now. Go sit on the other bench."

"It's just a kiss," Daphne whispered.

He smelled so good. She had never smelled anything so divine. She wanted to inhale him, and taste him. Yet she'd known he would protest. Indeed, she would have been disappointed if he hadn't.

"I thought we had decided not to do any more of this kissing." He peered at her intently. "Remember?"

"I do remember," she said, her voice thick with emotion. "Oh, but Cormack. You just saved my life for the second time. I can't help it. I want to kiss you. Won't you just please stop throwing my own words at me and...kiss me back?"

She heard the sound of his breath catch in his throat, as instantly, he pressed his mouth to hers. Pleasure coursed through her in warm, joyful waves of bliss.

He had always initiated the kissing before, letting her know that he found her desirable. This time, she wanted to be the one to communicate the same.

"Thank you."

"For what?" he asked raggedly, against her lips.

"For being you. A hero. Not just to me. To Kate, to my mother. To your dear sister."

She held his face in her hands, and pressed butterfly-soft kisses across his nose and cheeks and eyelids, as he whispered her name. His hands gripped her arms, as if he intended to stop her...but he didn't.

* * *

With a sigh, she explored lower, parting the linen at his throat, and pressing a trail of kisses down the center of his chest. An odd, strangled sound burst from deep in his throat, one that pleased her.

"Daphne, no." His entire body quaked. "You're confused. You just survived a terrifying ordeal."

"It's just kissing—"

"No, it's *not* just kissing." He gripped her by the arms, and gave her a solid shake, his gaze burning into hers. He was trying to be noble, which only made her want him more. "You are innocent, and you can't know what you do to me with just a kiss. A look. With just a toss of your hair."

"Cormack, I know what I said at the Monument this afternoon, that I couldn't go any further, because I wouldn't be able to let you go when the time came. But tonight, out there under the lanterns, under the stars, I realized that neither can I let you go now."

"I can't marry you, and if I can't marry you, *this* will not occur." He shook her again.

"I don't want you to marry me. I just want to be close to you, whatever that means, even if it's just for tonight."

"What are you saying?" His gaze flared with heat.

"That I want you, Cormack," she said unsteadily, terrified of speaking the words aloud, yet knowing they had to be said. "That I want *us*, right now. I know what I mean by that. I may be inexperienced, but I'm not misinformed."

Suddenly he was gone from her arms, and she was left with an empty bench. She twisted round to find him in the distant corner, arms outstretched along the walls and his long legs bent at the knees, staring at her through glassy eyes. "Don't do this to me."

He looked so tall, and handsome and tortured, that she almost laughed.

"I made the decision never to marry, Cormack. That doesn't mean I intended to die a virgin."

He closed his eyes and cursed. "You don't know what you are saying."

"I know exactly what I'm saying." She crossed the space between them, sinking between his knees, and closing her hands over his. "One day I fully intend to be everyone's favorite old maiden aunt, one with a beautiful secret." She smiled, her countenance flushed and bright. "Please give me this memory. I want it to be you."

"Old maiden aunt, my eye," he answered vehemently, his gaze moving over her face, then lower to her breasts, which rested between his open thighs. Fully aware that her torn gown gaped, she held still, allowing him to take his fill of the view. "You ought to find someone special and marry. This memory you ask for should belong to him."

"There's not going to be a husband. I belong only to me," she answered fiercely, squeezing his hands. "And I want to share this with you."

"I've no right —"

"But *I* have every right," she whispered, running her hands up the tops of his muscled thighs...over his pelvis...and up his rigid stomach, allowing her curiosity to lead her. Feeling the powerful flex and seize of his muscles beneath her palms, her mouth went dry with what she knew to be desire.

His hands came to either side of her face, suddenly and fiercely, his expression a portrait of torment. "Daphne."

She leapt against him, crying out in pleasure as his arms closed around her. She couldn't get close enough, and as if he couldn't, either, he shoved her skirts up to her hips and brought her legs, bent at the knees, around his waist. With one hand at the center of her buttocks, and the other splayed wide at her back, he seized her against him, and thrust his hips upward and off the seat so fiercely, his cheek turned against her breasts, that she felt the sudden invasion of his arousal into the swollen place between her legs. She moaned, as the most wonderful, but elusive, sensation fluttered through her legs, and up her spine. *There*, everything went hot and damp and needful. Instinctively she tilted her hips, wanting more. As if in answer, he moved, the heels of his boots sliding heavily against the floor of the carriage, replicating the same sensation as before, only this time deeper and more satisfying.

"Daphne," he repeated raggedly, still clenching her against him as if they were in a raging flood and she, at any moment, might be torn from his grasp. And yet she sensed the tremble in his arms, and the control that held him rigidly taut.

"You're hesitating," she murmured, bending...twisting...to kiss his lips. "Don't. I won't change my mind."

The carriage lurched to a halt, but started again, rocking

them against one another, but he held her so tight she did not fear toppling to the floor.

"You foolish girl." He exhaled, and for a moment he did not move, but then his face turned, so that his nose and mouth found the channel between her breasts, and he groaned against her skin. "What man could refuse you?"

"I don't care," Daphne whispered. "I only want you."

He cursed. "I have, from the first moment, and every moment on, wanted you."

Strong hands pressed up her back, their fingertips firm against her skin, one moving higher to twist in her hair. Slowly... gently, he pulled, tilting her head back, exposing her neck and the upper swells of her breasts to his mouth. Daphne closed her eyes, abandoning herself to a thousand unfamiliar sensations, all pleasurable, and waiting in a half-delirious state for whatever would come next.

At first his lips only teased the sensitive skin at the crook of her neck, while the fingertips of his other hand tested the tops of her breasts. But with a sudden jerk to her bodice and her stays beneath, her breasts sprang free into the cool night air, and with a guttural sound, his mouth closed on her nipple.

"Cormack!" she cried, squeezing her thighs and pressing against him, a movement that caused the satin thread of pleasure that ran along the center of her body to pull exquisitely tight and dangerously close to breaking.

He hissed. "You can't know what that does to me."

Voices shouted outside the carriage, but faded quickly with the clatter of horses' hooves. The knowledge that others passed so close by, without knowing the goings-on inside Cormack's carriage, only heightened Daphne's excitement in the moment.

"Then show me," she dared to whisper.

His white collar framed his tanned throat, just below his handsome face. He gripped her arms just below the shoulders and she allowed him complete control, looking down into the shadows between them to watch as his tongue laved her sensitive peak, his tongue making circles until at last he sucked the rigid tip, grunting hoarsely before paying the same courtesy to the other. She writhed, but he held her in place, while her hips instinctively moved against the growing ridge in his trousers, bringing her a more profound satisfaction.

"*Minx*," he growled, his voice thick with desire.

Reality fell way, leaving only a frenzy of touch and sensation. His mouth on hers. The feel of his skin and hair beneath her fingertips. And pleasure. One kiss wasn't enough. She could barely inhale for breath before demanding another.

Her passion flamed higher with each slant of his lips, each touch of his hand, until with a sudden movement, he twisted, and she found herself on her back staring up at the painted ceiling of the coach and Cormack's face, him sprawled above her. Gray eyes flashed into hers before moving hungrily over breasts still bared for his view. "You are a fantasy come to life."

Daphne could not remember a time when she had ever felt more beautiful. Propped on one elbow, he raked her skirts up her thighs.

Cool night air bathed her bare skin and her passion-drenched flesh. Staring down at her, his eyes went to blazes, and his cheeks went ruddy.

"You're beautiful," he said reverently.

"*You* are beautiful," she replied.

He groaned, spreading over her, kissing her, pressing his hands along the length of her bare thighs.

Suddenly, he lifted his head and turned it as if listening. Twisting to sit, he seized her up from the bench.

"We're just going to stop?" she asked, bewildered and dazed. "Just like that?"

He tugged up her corset and straightened her skirts.

"Yes, just like that, unless you want an audience. Jackson knocked, didn't you hear?"

No, she hadn't. Only then did she realize the carriage had completely stopped, and that she no longer heard the sounds of horses and other carriages on the road around them.

Oh no. Her hair was everywhere. She set about doing her best to straighten its pins. Her mother or even George the groom might very well be standing right outside the door.

Tilting the bench cushion, Cormack produced a folded wool blanket, which he hastily shook out.

"Put this around your shoulders and try not to look as if you've been ravished." His lips set forth a strained laugh.

Only then did he hurl himself onto the opposite bench, and let out an uneasy breath.

A rap came upon the door, a second before it swung open.

* * *

To Cormack's surprise, he looked out at his own terrace house. "Jackson, why are we stopped here when I specified Wolverton's residence?"

He had actually hoped they would be returned to the

earl's residence, so that Daphne would be forced to sleep another night on her decision.

"One of the horses has gone lame. We simply couldn't push him any further."

Cormack moved to the front of the carriage to inspect the injured animal, and gave instructions to the driver.

"The earl's residence is just two streets over. I will walk Miss Bevington home."

"I'd take the footpath, sir, so as not to risk being trampled by some drunken driver."

Just over his shoulder, the street remained jammed with carriages, a common sight when the season was in full swing, but even more so tonight with the flux of revelers simultaneously returning from Vauxhall.

"Thank you, Jackson." Daphne emerged from the interior, Cormack's carriage blanket arranged like an elegant hood over her hair and body. Nothing about her demeanor suggested the scandalous activities in which they'd indulged just moments before.

Once she stood beside him, the carriage departed in the direction of the mews, minus one horse from its harnesses, while Jackson followed, gently leading the lame animal in the same direction.

"Very nice," Daphne said, gazing at the front of the house.

"Would you like to . . . see the inside?" He stared at her, knowing she saw the fire in his eyes.

"I would." A flush rose into her cheeks.

"Then we had best make haste, before anyone sees."

Together they rushed down the walkway and up the stairs. With a turn of the key in the lock, he pushed the door open. A vestibule cloaked in shadows welcomed them, as

well as two mastiffs who excitedly circled them, panting
and growling happy greetings low in their throats.

"Their names?" She rubbed their heads, which elicited
their immediate adoration.

"Hugin and Munin."

"They are very handsome, and I like them very much.
But no butler, or footman?" She moved through the cavernous entrance hall.

"It's just me here, and I require very little attention. I
told them not to wait up."

"Where are your chambers?" Daphne inquired in a
hushed voice, already ascending the marble stairway.

Anticipation quickened his breath. "Why don't you find
them? I will follow."

He quickly guided the dogs by their collars into a side
room and closed the door, leaving them to whine from the
other side.

She released the blanket from her shoulders, discarding
it to the stairs, and half-turned to smile at him. Moonlight
bathed her gown, defining every rise and swell of her body
for his hungry gaze. He followed her the rest of the way up,
admiring the gentle sway of her hips as she climbed.

When he reached the landing, she was already halfway
down the corridor. He followed slowly, watching as she
pushed open a door.

"Are these rooms your chambers?" she asked, her voice
a soft, velvet tease. "No, I think not. The furnishings aren't
fine enough for an earl." She proceeded to the next. "What
about...this one? No again. I can't see you sleeping in a
room done up in lilac and pink."

He overtook her suddenly, unable to contain his passion
a moment more. He caught her from behind, pressing her

to the wall, his mouth against her neck. Her back arched in ecstasy and her hands spread wide against the scarlet wallpaper as his hands descended the length of her body, caressing her breasts until she moaned, then moving lower, across her belly.

"I want you here," he rasped against her neck. "But I won't make love to you for the first time against a wall."

In one swift move he lifted her into his arms and carried her to the end of the hall. "It's not too late to turn back. Tell me now, and I'll take you home."

She encircled her arms round him and pressed her face to his neck. "I don't want to go home."

With a thrust of his boot, the doors swung open to reveal an enormous state bed, draped in curtains and tassels, illuminated in the moonlight coming in through the window. "What do you think?"

"I think it's perfectly pretentious," she murmured, as he crossed the floor. "Just right for an earl."

An earl. He still had trouble thinking of himself in that way. The title remained simply a means by which to advance his search for Laura's seducer, and when alone he tended not even to think of it, or how the inheritance would affect his future. One day, he supposed, he would be a marquess and his eldest son, should he be so blessed with one, would be the earl—

But he didn't want to think of that faraway future now, not here alone in the shadows with Daphne, when that future could not include her.

He fell over her, onto a silken paradise, kissing her face, neck, and shoulders, and heard her slippers fall, *thud...thunk...* to the floor.

But something whispered in his mind that he could not

ignore. "Something changed your mind tonight, something that upset you, and I want to know what it is."

"The riot—" she murmured dreamily, reaching for his shirt and tugging it free of his breeches. "You saved me. I want to be with you."

"Not that." He kissed her eyelids, and her cheeks. She sighed and embraced him, raising her arms to encircle his neck. "Something else."

"I saw you go with that woman into the forest, and it made me realize—"

"You aren't the jealous sort. That isn't why you are here with me tonight." He stared down at her face, that looked just like Daphne...but so like someone else, a fantasy painted in shadows, lush and eager to share his bed.

She remained silent for a long while. "Tell me."

"I saw my mother kissing Mr. Birch."

He smoothed a tendril of her goddess-hair from where it had caught between her shoulder and the coverlet. "How did that make you feel?"

"I don't want to talk about it. Not now."

"Which is why you should."

"It made me feel happy for her."

"And?"

"Sad for me." Her eyes closed.

He lowered to kiss them again, and like magic, they fluttered open. "You've sworn that you won't marry."

"I won't. Even if...she and Mr. Birch...marry, but I realize I want something for myself. This. You." Her voice thickened. With a sudden frown, she shoved him off her, and rolled away from him, onto her stomach. "You've ruined things now by being so serious. On purpose, I think, so you wouldn't have to make love to me."

Cormack smiled, staring at her rounded buttocks beneath the blue silk. "On the contrary." He touched her ankle, which was covered in the sheerest silken stocking, and traced his finger...up..."If you don't allow me to make love to you, I'll tell everyone I saw Daphne Bevington—"

...up her calf...and circled his thumb behind her knee.

She shifted and sighed and, reaching for the pillow, gave up a little gasp. "What?"

"—dancing on the stage of the Blue Swan."

She rolled again, smiling, and threw the pillow at his face. "Scoundrel! So you think to resume your blackmail of me, do you?"

"I do indeed." He climbed over her, straddling her waist, easily pinning her by the wrists so she could not move, something she allowed without struggle.

Bending low, he caught the upper edge of her bodice with his teeth and dragged the silk low. Still finding her completely concealed by her corset, he growled in complaint and did the same with her corset, managing to reveal, with some effort, one perfectly round breast.

The moment his mouth closed on her nipple, she arched and twisted, breaking free of his grasp, only to hold his face, and rake her fingers through his hair. "Oh...Cormack."

He lifted himself off her enough to pull her skirts up over her thighs.

"Wait!" she said.

Wait, she said. But her eyes did not say *stop*. She stared up at him, her breast exposed, and the smooth skin of her thigh gleaming in the moonlight.

"Yes?"

"If you wish to make love to me—" She pushed him onto his back, and half-rolled to splay atop him, her breast puddled against his chest and her thigh across his hips, as if she instinctively knew how to torture him. But her expression was one of innocence, her first time playing this game. "You must tell me a secret that I may hold in confidence against you."

The front of his breeches caught her eye, and the swollen ridge that had become apparent there. She rested her hand on his hip, just inches beside him.

"May I?" she said in a soft voice.

"Of course." He held rigid.

She hesitated, but for only a moment, before smoothing her hand over him. At feeling her inexperienced touch, everything hard went harder. She gasped. "It moved."

But she smiled, above widened eyes.

"Yes, it does that," he answered thickly.

Swallowing hard, she worked the fastening of his breeches, pulling down the center placket until his stomach and cock were laid bare.

She whispered, "It's very...turgid."

"What an interesting word to use," he answered raggedly.

"And bigger than I expected."

"It gets...bigger."

"Oh yes?" She met his gaze. "How?"

"Ah...well..."

"Like this?" She touched him softly, at the crown, and slowly drew her fingertip down his length.

"That works remarkably well."

"And this." Her hand closed around him and tested his girth.

"Yes. Oh, hell. Not too tight—"

"I'm hurting you?" She froze, her hand still gripped there.

He covered her hand with his own. "No, that is not the problem at all."

"Then show me."

Slowly, he guided her hand into a rhythm, which as a student she took to very well, so well—

"Oh, my," she breathed.

He removed her hand and pushed her shoulders...

"I can't...let you anymore...I'll explode."

...until she lay on the bed. His heartbeat raced, and everything blurred into a haze of desire. He did not undress her. He could not survive the wait. Pushing her skirts high, he crouched over her and stroked her stomach, the delicate skin at the tops of her stockings, and the place between her thighs, which he found slick and ready. She writhed, luxuriating like a cat at his touch.

"I can't wait." He *couldn't* wait.

"I don't want you to."

Parting her thighs he positioned himself, as she grasped his shoulders tight. "*Wait.*"

He laughed, a desperate sound. "I just told you I can't, Daphne. I want you too much."

She grabbed the front of his shirt and, smiling playfully, her eyes glazed with desire, she demanded, "Your secret. I would have it before we go further."

His breath rasped in his throat, as her body cradled his sex between her thighs, tormenting him with the promise of splendor.

"I wish...it could be you..."

Did she understand? *Forever.* He wished it could be her.

She released him, and lay back on the bed, her eyes shining. "Yes. Cormack. Make love to me now, hurry."

Gripping her hips, he thrust, entering her body a few inches before she arched and twisted, her head falling back against the coverlet. He tugged her bodice, freeing her other breast, and moved his hand over them both in solemn appreciation.

"I wish it could be you," he repeated.

"Yes," she whispered, choking on a sob of passion.

Harder, and more desperate now, he thrust again, breaking the last wall between them.

Daphne cried his name and held him tightly, wishing she could hold him like this forever, joined with her, not only body but heart and soul. For a long moment, neither of them moved. Her body protested, claiming reckless abuse.

"Is that it? Are we finished?" she asked softly, dismayed.

His shoulders, and the muscles of his back, bunched powerfully beneath her palms.

"Not yet. Just give me a moment…please, to assert some control —oh, hell, I don't have any, darling, I'm sorry—"

He moved suddenly, thrusting even deeper inside her body, spreading her, filling her more completely than she had ever imagined possible.

"I want to see," she gasped.

He jerked, but lifted, and she peered between them, at their bodies joined in the moonlight. "I'm yours. Part of me forever, but all of me tonight. And you are mine."

"I fear forever," he said, lowering again to kiss to her temple.

"No…"

His hips moved again…and again…taking up a rhythm that both pained and pleased her…. The quiet of the room, broken by their gasps and moans, until there was only…pleasure, which she felt suddenly desperate to intensify, to perfect.

He guided her into a new and faster tempo. The mattress bounced beneath her hips as he pumped faster and faster, while guiding her hips upward to meet him.

A euphoric pleasure sluiced down her spine, to center between her legs. She cried out, unable to contain the sudden and unexpected power of her passion. He cursed hoarsely, and whispered her name, and suddenly—

An explosion of stars, of unimagined pleasure—inside her head—inside her body, so deep she wanted to cry from the beauty of it. She arched, feeling the strong pulse of his sex inside her womb. He stretched out over her, seizing her into his arms, crushing the breath from her, which only made her smile.

A moment later, and he had pulled the bed linens and coverlet over them.

"That was…the most marvelous thing I have ever experienced," he murmured against her neck, before burying his face between her breasts. "I should have been stronger, but I can't resist you."

"I have no regrets. Please, don't you have them, either."

"You might regret this tomorrow."

"I don't see how, when all I can think of is when we can do it again."

He laughed, emitting a delightful rumbling sound from deep inside his chest. "You are incorrigible."

Suddenly, the sound of dogs barking and men's voices echoed up through the house. Cormack froze.

"Who is that?" gasped Daphne, her eyes widening. She clasped the sheet against her breasts.

"I don't know," he growled, raising up.

Boots thumped on the stairs. Lots of them. From below-stairs, Hugin and Munin howled.

"I've got to hide." She made as if to leap from the bed.

The rapid advance of footsteps thudded in the corridor, accompanied by raucous laughter and the emission of a shrill whistle. *Jackson.*

He seized her arm and pulled her back. "There's no time."

Chapter Thirteen

At the very same moment the door flew open, he dragged the sheet over her head and shoved her down. Jackson burst through first, his arms outstretched, trying to hold back the others.

"Now see here, His Lordship isn't accepting callers at the moment. Won't you fine gentlemen return tomorrow?"

He wore a good-natured smile, but threw a look of utter panic over his shoulder toward Cormack.

Realizing the identities of the men who pushed aside his manservant, Cormack secured the sheet even more securely over Daphne, and urged her with his open hands against her shoulders to remain concealed.

"He'll see us, boy," announced Rackmorton. At the sound of his voice, Daphne plastered herself against him. "Now run along. Or don't." He laughed. "The more the merrier."

His glazed eyes fixed on the bed. "My, my, my, what have we here?"

His Lordship was drunk, as were the other four with him. More than one bottle passed between them.

Cormack's muscles tightened, but he enforced an easy calm to his features. "As you can see, Rack, I'm entertaining."

Two of the others threw themselves into armchairs before the unlit fireplace. Another adjusted his cravat in the mirror while the fourth threw open the window and unfastened his breeches with the clear intention to urinate.

"How'd you get so lucky, in all that tangle of a mess?" Rackmorton's eyebrows went up. "Is it Bunhill?" He moved closer. "Even better, is it *both* of the Bunhills? If so, I'd be happy to join you."

"It is not the Lady Bunhills. I made a new friend."

"Do I know her?" His gaze raked over the shape under the sheet and his lips spread into a houndish smile. "Who is it?"

If it were even possible, Daphne scooted closer, gouging her fingers into his sides.

Along the far wall, Jackson paced, lifting a hand to rub his face, his expression one of thinly veiled fury. Cormack knew he only had to say the word, and his manservant would intervene and assist.

"A gentleman never tells."

"That's not true. We only say that for appearances." He grinned. "We tell all the time, at least to each other."

"Speak for yourself. I do not."

He came another step closer, touching his gloved hand to the bed. Teasingly, he trailed his fingertip over the linen, veering in a sudden movement to graze the bottom of her foot. Daphne jumped, and drew her legs up. His eyes erupted in flames of interest.

"Don't do that again," Cormack warned.

"No, truly." His lip drew back in a canine leer. "Let me see her."

"*No.*"

"Spoilsport."

"If you don't mind me asking, *why* are you here?"

"Because we're bored. Because we happened to be in the area. Because things ended so abruptly, when those roisters broke into the gala."

"So they did."

Rackmorton dared lean across the bed to prop his elbow on a pillow and rested his head on his palm. "I just wanted to make sure Kincraig and his ridiculous talk didn't taint your opinion about me and my associates."

Cormack remained silent, prepared to intervene if His Lordship made the slightest move to touch Daphne again.

"Bastard." Rackmorton rolled his eyes. "He completely ruined the moment. Whenever new members are inducted, it's important to instill an air of pomp and mystery...it's just always been done that way. You understand the importance of tradition."

"Of course."

"But we are here now. As a show of goodwill, without even wearing our masks. Not all of us, of course, but I feared if we all barged in, we might come off as...intrusive." He crossed his booted feet near the end of the bed, looking like a contented houseguest. "I just wanted you to know, the invitation still stands and we'd be honored if you joined us."

"Point taken." He'd had quite enough. Now it was time for them all to leave. "Thank you for stopping by, but I hope you can understand that at this particular moment

I'd rather be finishing what I started...when you weren't here."

Rackmorton's gaze again dropped to the form beneath the sheet. "I can imagine that you would." He chuckled, low in his throat. "We shall leave you to your endeavors, then."

The others assembled near the door.

Cormack watched in relief as Rackmorton eased up from the mattress—only to swing his open hand round to clamp onto Daphne's behind.

Underneath the sheet, she squealed and bored her head and hands into his chest. Cormack's hand shot to Rackmorton's wrist, exerting such crushing force the man bellowed in pain.

"Ow!"

"Mine," Cormack uttered, clenching him a degree tighter before shoving his hand away. "Don't trespass again."

Rackmorton rolled from the mattress, his face red and rubbing his wrist. "Bloody hell, you take your women seriously. All in jest, and among good friends. By the way, I saw you that night, at the Blue Swan, when you ran out into the lane. As my carriage traveled past. I know...who you are, and what you've been looking for here in London. And I can tell you it's Kincraig. After tonight, we just can't protect him any longer. Consider it a gift, offered in anticipation that you will join us."

He straightened his coat, ran his fingers through his hair, and spun on his heel at the door, where the others stood silent and watching. "We'll talk again soon."

Cormack held Daphne still until they disappeared into the corridor. Jackson followed them. "I am so sorry. They were in the house before I realized."

"Lock the door after them, and let the dogs out from where I shut them up."

"Yes, my lord." He pulled the doors closed behind him. Cormack slipped from the bed, and latched them in the event anyone decided to make a sudden return. Going back, he found Daphne at the center of the mattress, with the sheets held high as her face, which was white with shock.

"I think I'd like to go home now."

* * *

Once they were dressed, Cormack insisted on summoning the cook from her sleep.

"Isn't it a little late for that?" Daphne asked from the far side of the drawing room. She now wore a green-and-silver-threaded shawl around her shoulders to cover her ruined gown. Cormack had told her he'd purchased the luxurious fringed item days before as a gift for his mother, but that he believed it should serve a more necessary purpose now.

He responded in a hushed voice, "She doesn't have to know we did not just arrive."

He paced, clearly impatient to see her delivered home. She, too, wanted nothing more than to return to the comfort and security of her grandfather's house. The incident with Rackmorton had almost scared the life from her. And yet, she wasn't ready to be separated from Cormack.

"What will you do about Mr. Kincraig?"

"I don't know yet. Go talk to him tomorrow, I suppose, and just ask him outright."

He'd told her everything. About Laura and Michael, and the Invisibilis and his reason for coming to London.

"Promise me you won't kill him. He is the family's only hope for an heir."

"I'm not going to kill anyone," he answered quietly. But she supposed if he intended to, he wouldn't tell her. "I just need to know the truth, then I can decide what must be done."

"When will I see you again?" she asked in a rush, suddenly fearing that he would tell her never. That her relation to Kincraig made any further relationship between them impossible. That the love affair between them was over before it had even begun.

She knew they couldn't last forever, but still, she wasn't ready to say good-bye. The end of summer would come quickly enough, and she suspected he would then return to his home in the country, and she would in turn go to Camellia House in nearby Lacenfleet to stay with Sophia and Claxton, where she would spoil her sister and assist with preparations for the baby's arrival.

"Whenever you wish," he answered steadily, his gaze touching upon her hair and her mouth. "Wherever you wish. I am yours to summon."

The promise in his eyes thrilled her and gave her assurances that he would seek to resolve things with Kincraig in a civilized manner, as gentlemen did even under the most difficult of circumstances.

A small woman with wiry red hair entered the room, bleary eyed and stuffing her curls into a lace cap. She gave a little curtsey to her employer. "I am here, my lord. I hear there is a young lady requiring chaperonage?"

Cormack provided Mrs. Green with a brief explanation of the excitement at Vauxhall that had separated Miss Bevington from her family, and the situation with the roads.

"That, my lord, is what you call a riot, and not the first to have taken place on those grounds. My dear girl, you must have been terrified. It's why I won't spend my shilling to go there. Why, I can have a slice of ham and a jig right here in the kitchen, without all that other trouble, though I do like a display of fireworks from time to time."

"The fireworks. We didn't even get to see them tonight, I'm afraid."

Though the passion that had taken place between herself and Cormack had been much more fiery and explosive than any display of fireworks she had ever seen.

"Thank heavens for honorable men like His Lordship, who will risk his own life to see a young lady of quality to safety."

Cormack's jaw tightened at that pronouncement. "Shall we be off, then?"

The three of them walked along the footpath toward Hamilton Place, with Mrs. Green chattering cheerfully between them. It was then that an unexpected sadness came over her, one she couldn't even explain. Making love with Cormack had been just as wonderful as she'd dreamed, even more so. Perhaps if they'd had more time after to simply hold each other, and talk, before Rackmorton and his cohorts had interrupted them. Her heart felt...slightly dissatisfied. Incomplete.

Daphne looked over Mrs. Green's head, to find Cormack staring at her. He winked at her, and offered a reassuring smile, as if he understood just how she felt.

When they arrived, several carriages crowded the curbstones in front of Wolverton's house. Among them was the one that had delivered her and her mother and sister to Vauxhall earlier that evening, the one belonging to Kincraig. His was not at all as fine as Wolverton's town coach, which, despite the earl's offer to make use of it for the night, he had obstinately refused.

The door swung open. Her heart leapt with joy when her mother's face appeared, and Mr. Birch's beside her. He climbed out, and assisted her mother and sister down. She hadn't yet stepped foot on the pavement to cross the road before her mother and sister were tearing down the walk, their rumpled gowns pale streams of color in the night, crying out relieved greetings, then enveloping her into their arms and leading her to the house.

Daphne explained, "One of the horses went lame, so we've walked just this last bit."

It wasn't a lie, and for that she felt relieved.

"As you can see, we have only just arrived ourselves," announced Clarissa. "What a miserable night this has turned out to be."

Lady Margaretta leaned close, squeezing Daphne around the shoulders. "My dear, I know that you saw Mr. Birch and I—"

"I'm not traumatized, Mother, I just didn't want to intrude."

"You're very certain?"

"I am."

Clarissa winked at her. "Well, I for one am utterly traumatized."

Mr. Birch, oblivious to the true nature of their conversation, followed behind. "But we are all safe, and that's all that matters."

The three ladies burst into giggles.

Her grandfather waited at the door in his bath chair, his valet, O'Connell, standing at his side. A backward glance over her shoulder found Cormack slowly following them, his face drawn, and, it seemed, several shades paler.

Oddly, Kincraig greeted Cormack with a hearty "Well, hello there. Shouldn't we come up with some sort of a secret greeting, or even a handshake?"

To Daphne's relief, Cormack only said, "May I pay a call on you tomorrow? I'd like to talk to you a bit about what happened tonight."

By all appearances, he intended to handle the matter like a civilized gentleman.

They all moved to the drawing room, and Daphne heard Cormack explain, "We actually made it as far as my residence and—" He paused, closing his eyes for a moment. Daphne's face colored. "—waited for things to clear a bit there, before coming on."

Lady Margaretta reached to squeeze his hand, smiling radiantly. "And I see you picked up another traveler along the way."

"Yes, that is Mrs. Green, my cook."

The marchioness looked between them. "Thank you, Mrs. Green. I know you must rather be sleeping, instead of playing chaperone in the middle of the night."

"Oh, no, ma'am. I understand. Thank heavens your daughter found herself under the protection of a gentleman such as His Lordship, who understands the importance of propriety and appearance. The earl even insisted on riding with the driver, so there would be no questions."

As Mr. Birch explained everything that had occurred to Wolverton, Lady Harwick bestowed an adoring glance on Cormack, who looked to Daphne a bit green about the gills. "And there *would* be no questions. We have not known

His Lordship long, but we've no doubt at all about his character, and trust him implicitly. We are so thrilled to have made such a lifelong friend. Girls, upstairs now." Her mother herded them toward the door. More discreetly, and out of the hearing of the gentlemen, she murmured, "Baths await you, and bed."

On the way to the door, Daphne reached to touch Cormack's arm, and he turned from Wolverton and Mr. Birch, with whom he'd been speaking.

"Thank you again, my lord, for seeing me home."

His eyes conveyed a thousand sentiments. *I'll miss you. I hope you are well.* And, she feared, *I ought to have been a stronger man.*

"I'm only glad," he said, "that everything turned out well."

"Everything *did* turn out well," she answered. "Perfectly, in fact. Good night, then."

"Good night, Miss Bevington."

It pained her just to turn her back on him and walk away. Upstairs, a bath did indeed await, before a small fire on the grate. When she entered the room, Kate turned from the cabinet, one of Daphne's sleeping gowns in hand.

"There you are. I saw your arrival from the window and had the water brought up just then, so it should be nice and warm still."

"I'm so glad to be home. I can't wait to crawl into bed."

"Lord Raikes saw you home, then?"

"He did."

"Given the history between you," she said quietly, "I hope you weren't alone with him?"

"Not for long." A confession crowded Daphne's lips. She wanted to tell Kate everything, but couldn't. The loss of her innocence must remain a secret between herself and Cormack.

"Goodness, your hair. Let's get it combed out." Kate helped her undress, pausing at the loose and untied laces of Daphne's corset, but for only a moment. Heat scalded her cheeks, but she said nothing. When she was naked, she stepped into the bath.

A gasp sounded beside her, from Kate, who seemed to be staring wide-eyed at the water. No, not the water, Daphne realized, looking down as well. A faint smear of blood stood out against the pale skin of her inner thigh.

"Oh, Daphne." Her face went as white as the gardenia soap in the dish.

"Now don't get hysterical, Kate."

"It is too late. I already am."

Daphne wasn't going to stand there naked, halfway in the bath, defending what she and Cormack had done. She sank down into the warm, fragrant water, and closed her eyes.

"He must marry you. You must tell your mother, so that she can go to Lord Wolverton."

"Don't be ridiculous. You aren't going to say anything, either. I forbid it. And please, I beg you, don't think badly of Lord Raikes."

"How can I not? How can *you* not?" Kate exclaimed, her hands balling into fists. "Oh, I could murder him. He is betrothed to another."

"Not truly. Not yet. She is twelve years old, Kate, and there is only an understanding in place, so that he can regain possession of family lands. He is an honorable man, trying to put his family and his legacy back together."

"He's filled your head with romantic delusions."

"I'm not deluded in the least." She bit her thumbnail, her heart bursting with emotion. "I love him, Kate, and though I won't force him to say it, I believe he loves me. It's enough for me. I'll remember this night forever and with no regrets."

"You're too foolish and inexperienced to know otherwise."

"You've never been in love, Kate. Once you have, you'll understand that none of the rules the world tries to put in place over us will matter anymore. He will marry another, and I, not at all. The world will go on as intended. Nothing has changed."

"Everything has changed. He has seduced you!"

"No, Kate, quite the opposite. To be completely honest, he tried very valiantly to resist." Daphne sank into the water a few more inches, up to her chin. "You see, it is I who quite intentionally enticed the earl. No one is accountable in this save me."

* * *

At the curb, Cormack waved off his driver. "I prefer to walk tonight, thank you. Please return to the house, and retire for the night, the both of you."

Jackson called from the rear, "My lord—"

"Go."

Craving the solitude of the night shadows, he set off down the road. He wandered. Where and for how long, he did not know, the people and carriages and houses all a dull blur as he moved past. His conscience railed over what he had done, demanding some fraction of logic or reasoning to make what had happened between himself and Daphne right. Yet that reasoning eluded him, and so he kept right on walking.

His motives for agreeing to marry the Snaith girl were pure, were they not? What sort of legacy would he leave for future generations of Northmores if it did not include the land and, indeed, the very *pride* they had owned and defended and died for, not for mere decades, but centuries?

And yet tonight his heart had been rent completely in half, and whether she knew it or not, a half now belonged to a young woman with moonlight-silk hair and blue eyes. Like him she carried inside her soul an unhealed wound, and she sought to heal herself, and perhaps others, in whatever imperfect way her conscience saw fit. By all accounts, she would not agree to marry him even if he were free to offer for her. It had been clear she intended from the start that their night together—and any that followed—would be a secret love affair, the memories of which she would cherish to her dying day.

And yet . . . he had enjoyed his share of love affairs, both secret and not, and knew the difference between *those* and *this*.

God help him, he was in love. Desperately. Wildly. He felt sick with the burden of it, not knowing what to do.

At last, settling upon no clear answer, near dawn he made his way home.

Just then an enormous man—astoundingly tall and thick—approached him on the sidewalk, dressed in the street clothes of a commoner, likely on his way to or from his place of employment.

"Evenin', govna'," he said as he walked past, tipping his hat and offering a jaunty smile. "'Ope y' 'ad a marvelous night."

"Thank you," he answered. "I did indeed."

Because he had enjoyed a marvelous night. The most marvelous and devastating night of his life.

Zounds, but truly, now that they were closer, Cormack could honestly say the fellow was perhaps the largest man he had ever seen.

"Mr. Kincraig sends his regards."

"What did you say?" He pivoted on the heel of his boot, just in time to see the club swing for his face.

Chapter Fourteen

"Daphne, we've the florist coming this afternoon to confirm the flower arrangements for your ball." The marchioness folded her napkin and reached for the newspaper. They sat in the breakfast room, enjoying a late morning meal.

Daphne twirled her fork in a mound of uneaten eggs. "I won't forget."

"Speaking of flowers," said Clarissa, breezing into the room. "There's an arrangement in the drawing room that just arrived for you, Daphne. Very beautiful, even more extravagant than the others, so much so that it made me momentarily jealous." She made a face. "No, wait...wait. I am still utterly jealous."

She laughed, amused by her own drollery.

Daphne's pulse leapt, and she straightened in her seat. Had Cormack sent her flowers? Certainly he wouldn't be so reckless to do so, though knowing his sense of humor, he would use some silly moniker. Only, she didn't see him being silly today, not when he planned to meet with Kincraig to confront him about his sister.

"Who are they from?" asked Lady Margaretta.

"Are you insinuating that I am nosy enough to read sentiments not intended for me?" She closed her eyelids exaggeratedly, in an expression of mock offense. "Well, I'm not. Not *always*." She poured herself a cup of tea.

"Thank you for telling me, Clarissa. I'm on my way upstairs to change, so I'll look at them now."

She went directly there, knowing the flowers likely weren't from Cormack, but now hoping they were. She could not help but worry that he'd spent the entire night regretting what had happened between them. Wasn't that why she loved him?

Her breath caught in her throat. Loved him. She did indeed love him. She had for a while now, and perhaps from the beginning.

A large arrangement of wild roses in reds, blues, and yellows awaited her. Smiling, she plucked the card from their center. For a moment, she closed her eyes, because somehow not knowing...but the wishing and hoping... was the best part.

The envelope was sealed, which they rarely ever were. That made her smile. That was why Clarissa hadn't read the card, because she might tear the envelope and that would be evidence of her nosiness. It was also evidence that whoever wrote the sentiments intended for them to be private, between just the two of them.

She slid her thumb beneath the edge, and carefully beneath the flap, not wanting to tear the paper herself, because if the flowers were from Cormack she intended to keep the card, and a carefully pressed selection of the blooms... well, forever.

Only... upon removing the card, she saw that it had been embossed with a gold Medusa head, one she now knew to represent the Invisibilis. She bit her lower lip and read the message.

She blinked, and blinked again. *No.*

A strangled cry broke from her lips. She closed the card, not wanting to see the words, praying they were a dream. But opening it again, she saw they were real.

Written in block letters, in thick ink, were the words MEET ME OR I TELL EVERYONE. EVERYONE. EVERYONE. Along with a nearby address and the specified time. Below the words had been drawn a swan, and in the curve of its breast, one word had been written: BLUE.

* * *

"Is 'e dead?"

Grass crunched in his ear. Something nudged his shoulder. Something nudged his shoulder, harder. The toe of a boot.

Cormack's eyes flew open.

"Gor! 'E's alive!" The two men who stood on either side of him stumbled back. They looked nearly identical, only one being bent at the shoulders, and wrinkles lining his face. A father and son, he had no doubt.

He pushed up, fighting dizziness. Hell, his head. How it pounded! How it hurt. He touched a hand to his temple, and it came away covered in blood. He remembered the big man. Yes, and the club that had certainly done this damage to his face. Ah, hell. That's what he got for being out on the street so late at night, and alone. He'd been robbed.

"You're not from around 'ere, are y', sir?"

"I don't know." He squinted, looking all around and seeing only farmland, and two massive horses harnessed to a large wagon. "No, I'm not."

He reached inside his coat, to confirm the money he'd carried was gone.

Only it wasn't. He held in his hand a leather purse filled with bills and coins. That didn't make sense.

If he hadn't been robbed, then what?

"Y' got somethin' pinned to yer shirt, there," said the old man.

He glanced down, but the movement made him dizzy. But it was a piece of paper, with something written across it. "What does it say?"

"Don't know," he said.

"We can't read," added the other.

They both chuckled.

He ripped the thing off, and held it before his face.

Stay the HELL away, the note said.

Stay the hell away from what? From Mr. Kincraig, he presumed. That was completely out of the question now. Anger quickly turned to rage. He had to get back to London. Why had he promised Daphne he wouldn't kill Kincraig? It was all he wanted to do right now.

"I'll get the missus," said the older one. "She's got a salve that will fix you up right."

"No, sir," he answered, struggling to his feet. Both reached out to steady him. "I'm sorry, but I don't have the time for that. What I do have is money." He held the purse aloft. "I'll pay one or both of you well to return me to

London. You must understand, it's very important that I return."

* * *

"Daphne, you said we were just going for a walk, but I have a feeling that something else is going on here." Kate moved along beside her on the sidewalk. Carriages rattled by, as did riders on horseback.

"I've agreed to meet someone," she answered. "That's all."

Kate scrutinized her from beneath the brim of her bonnet. "Someone? As in Lord Raikes, I suppose? I told you, I can't agree to be part of that. Yes, we are friends, but your mother and grandfather entrusted me with your reputation, and—"

"No, not Lord Raikes," she answered. How she wished it was. "Someone else."

"Another man?" Kate's eyes widened.

"I'm not even sure." She slowed her pace. "Here we are."

They had arrived at a small parklike area, where there were several benches and numerous fine, tall trees. She turned, looking everywhere, at everyone. She didn't recognize a single face.

"What do you mean you aren't even sure? You don't know if you are meeting a man or a woman?"

"Kate, please, just listen to me. This afternoon I received a message from someone who knows I was at the Blue Swan that night. They threatened that if I did not meet them here now, they would tell everyone. Kate... my family. I can't hurt them with such a scandal."

"Who is it?"

"I'm not certain." Daphne shivered, her hand coming up to loosen the ribbon of her hat beneath her throat. "But I've got to find out what they—or this person, wants."

"What are we going to do?"

"*You* aren't going to do anything."

"But—this is all my fault."

"No, it is not, and neither is it mine. We are simply two friends who would do anything for one another, and we have found ourselves in a predicament."

"Not me, Daphne. *You.* I fear you are in danger."

"I doubt the situation is anything as dramatic as that. But whomever my threatener may be, he or she will be here soon." She looked about, and touched Kate's arm. "Do you see that bench over there, under the tallest tree? I need you to go sit on it, and wait for me."

"I don't like the sound of that." Kate sidled closer, holding her reticule against her stomach. "I think I should remain with you."

"You know I would do anything for you, Kate, and now I beg you to do this for me."

"You're frightening me."

Daphne gently pushed her in the direction of the bench, and watched her until she sat down. With a little wave to reassure her, she turned back toward the street. Several people walked by, but no one alone. Several minutes passed, in which she reassured herself that she must remain calm.

Then a dark carriage came down the thoroughfare, its driver staring straight ahead. The vehicle slowed, and came to a stop.

Daphne stood rigid, staring at the door. When it opened, she peered into the shadowy darkness.

"Oh, no," she whispered. "You!"

A man's voice answered. "Surprised?"

* * *

"Here it is." Cormack pointed. "Yes, here. You can stop."

"Gor!" the younger farmer said. *Gor!* being his favorite expression, and one he had used at least a thousand times on the ride into London. *Gor!* he was driving Cormack mad.

"That would be your house?"

No. It was Kincraig's house, a conservative affair on a lesser street within Mayfair.

The old man peered up at the front façade. He let out a low whistle. "Very fancy."

Cormack did not wait for the wagon to come to a complete halt before leaping down. He had not escaped the ministrations of the resident farmwife. He felt certain she'd wrapped his head in twelve yards of homemade bandaging. Not that those twelve yards prevented the smelly green salve she'd smeared on one-half of his forehead to remain in place. Half the stuff presently slid down his jaw.

"Thank you, gentlemen." He paid them, and without so much as a sentimental good-bye, they were on their way.

The butler opened the door for him, and after he answered that His Lordship was indeed at home and reading the daily papers in his study, Cormack charged inside, the man's voice ringing in his ears.

At seeing him, Mr. Kincraig's eyes flared wide with interest. "Good morning, Raikes. My goodness, don't you look like someone's old moldering mummy."

"Thanks to you," he growled, leaping over the desk and taking the man to the floor.

"Me?" said Mr. Kincraig, staring up in utter calm, his hair in disarray all around him.

Gripping him by the shirt, Cormack gave him a hard shake. "I'm going to kill you, but first, I want to know why."

He wouldn't kill the man, though, because he'd promised Daphne. He would only make the man wish that he was dead.

Kincraig's eyes narrowed, and he simply said, "I'd like to know why as well. Mind the shirt. Don't tear it please."

"She was beautiful, and smart, and everyone loved her. Did you even care about her? Did you even know you'd gotten her with child?" Cormack raised his fist, and slammed it down at the center of Mr. Kincraig's face.

But in a blur, he found himself flat on his back, their positions changed. Now his opponent stared down at him. Cormack blinked, not certain of what had just happened, knowing only that the man must have remarkable physical skills to have achieved the switch.

Kincraig peered down at him, hands pinning his shoulders. "Can you please let me know who we are talking about?"

The confirmation that Laura had been that inconsequential to the man who had dishonored her sent emotion tearing through Cormack's chest, more painful than any physical injury. "My sister, the governess you seduced while staying at the Duke of Rathcrispin's hunting lodge, and left to bear her shame alone. Congratulations, she is dead and you have a two-year-old son."

Mr. Kincraig clearly had certain talents, but he was lithe and lean where Cormack enjoyed the benefit of muscle. Cormack wrenched himself free of the man, and leapt to his feet to circle Kincraig, who did the same.

"I'm afraid that's impossible," he answered, with a shake of his head.

"Don't dare deny your crime." He hurtled himself at the man, slamming him into the bookcases and twisting his hand into his cravat. Several books fell, and the butler rushed in.

"Sir, ought I summon help?"

"No, Mr. Crandall," he said, his chin moving above Cormack's fist. "Please leave us."

The man backed away, leaving them alone.

Kincraig remained unruffled, and entirely passive. "I make it a practice never to deny my crimes. I've been to Rathcrispin's hunting lodge once, and that was two months ago. I admit to a temporary dalliance with a governess while there, but if a fully developed two-year-old son has resulted from the affair, the power of my loins is impressive indeed."

"Rackmorton told me…" Cormack's growl faded. He released Mr. Kincraig, and stepped away. "I knew better than to trust the man, but why would he lie about something like that?"

Kincraig straightened his shirt. "Who did that to your face?"

"The man you sent." But even as he said the words, he knew what Mr. Kincraig would say.

"I don't have a man, I'm afraid. There is only me. I don't wish to cast aspersions, but I think you ought to look toward—"

"Rackmorton," Cormack hissed, a new fear coming to mind.

"You're going there now? I'll go with you." Apparently Kincraig wasn't a man to hold grudges. "I'll just get my coat."

"No. If you wouldn't mind, please go to Wolverton's and ensure that Miss Bevington is all right."

"Which Miss Bevington?" His dark brows rose in question.

"Daphne."

"Do you mind me asking why? Has something happened to raise your concern?"

"Did he ever show you his collection? The paintings he keeps locked in his study?"

Mr. Kincraig's lips twisted. "Those. Yes, some weeks ago. Why?"

"He recently added a new acquisition to his collection, one inspired by her. I believe he may have some sort of fixation with her. Given what happened to me last night, and the fact that he purposefully led me to believe you knew Laura, I find myself increasingly concerned for her safety."

Mr. Kincraig crossed his arms over his chest and bit his bottom lip. "There's something here that doesn't make sense."

"I don't know what you mean." Cormack made his way to the front door.

His companion followed. "Rackmorton's angry with you because you were snooping around about the Invisibilis, isn't that right? Trying to find the man responsible for what happened to your sister?"

"Yes."

"I understand that you say he has a portrait of Daphne,

which is concerning in nature, but I don't understand why that has anything at all to do with your being beat up by his toughs and a sudden concern for her safety, unless…"

He pulled the handle, opening the door, but Mr. Kincraig pushed it shut.

"Unless what?" Cormack scowled.

"You and Daphne."

"That's right." He met his gaze steadily. "Me and Daphne. I will speak to Wolverton when the time is right. Once all this is settled."

"That's all I needed to hear." Mr. Kincraig pulled the door open. "I'll go to Wolverton's now. Join us there, when you're through."

Cormack departed Mr. Kincraig's residence, and made a stop at his own. It would take him only a moment to wash and change, which would give him time to calm himself before confronting Rackmorton. He would need all his patience and wits about him, to extract the answers he sought before decimating the man. The marquess had thrown the blame of what occurred to Laura on Mr. Kincraig, but why? He could only presume he was trying to protect someone else.

Upon seeing his approach on the walk, his footman's eyes widened, and he leapt to his feet, opening the door. A glance in the vestibule mirror proved he looked like a ghoul, with one green, slimy half of his dead face still sliding off. "Heavens."

He turned with the intention of going to the stairs, but Kate Fickett stood at the center of the marble floor.

Seeing him, she screamed.

"No, please don't," he said, attempting to reassure her.

"Your face!"

"It is only medicine. I've been injured and a very nice woman from a farm applied...this awful salve. Kate, why are you here?"

Just then Jackson entered the room. "Oh, my heavens. Do you need a physician?"

"All I need is a washbasin, a towel, and a set of clean clothes."

Despite his reassurances, Kate still looked very afraid. "Lord Raikes, I came to you because I did not know where else to go. It's Daphne—"

"She's all right, isn't she?" he demanded, moving closer.

"I don't know." Tears spilled onto her cheeks.

Her emotional response struck panic through his heart. "What do you mean you don't know?"

"Someone sent her a message this morning, saying they knew about her being at the Blue Swan." She wheezed through a nose that had grown puffy with her tears. "They said if she didn't meet them today, that they'd tell everyone."

"Who?"

"That's just it, I don't know. They came in a carriage I didn't recognize, and with no distinguishable markings. One moment she was standing on the pavement, and then she was gone."

"Rackmorton," he growled. Rackmorton had been at the Blue Swan that night, and like a snake he had waited for the most opportunistic moment to bite.

"I don't think she would have gotten into a carriage with Rackmorton. She rather abhors and mistrusts him."

He could not imagine that Daphne's abductor would be anyone else. Again, the memories of the paintings he had seen in Rackmorton's secret room filled his mind.

Rackmorton's secret room.

He swore. "If he has harmed her, I will kill him."

"I pray you will!" she exclaimed. "What if he forces her to elope? To marry him? She cannot marry anyone else. She can only marry you."

"Please know I have already come to the same understanding. Miss Fickett, please listen to me. Wait here for me to return, in the drawing room. Do you understand?"

If the girl returned to Wolverton's home in her present state, she would only inspire panic in the household, and he had every intention of sparing them that experience.

She nodded. "Where are you going?"

"To find Daphne, of course."

Once they parted ways, he raced upstairs, changing so quickly from his mud- and blood-covered clothing that he was still lacing his breeches when he exited the house.

Jackson waited in the street, mounted on one horse and holding the reins to another.

"You don't have to do this with me," Cormack said, swinging into the saddle.

"And yet here I am. Don't deny me the pleasure."

A short time later, they arrived at the same house where he'd attempted, like a fool, to tell Daphne good-bye. After knocking on the door, and being told Rackmorton was not receiving guests, Cormack barged past the footmen, with Jackson following behind, and headed straight for the study. As he reached for the door, he heard a muffled scream. He attempted to turn the handle, but the door was locked.

Had that been Daphne's voice? He couldn't tell, the sound had been too muffled.

He kicked the door, which produced no result. He kicked it again—

Beside him, Jackson pointed a gun and shot, blasting the handle to bits.

Cormack glanced at him. "I knew I kept you around for something."

"I'm happy to be of assistance," he answered cooly, blowing the smoke from the barrel.

Inside the study, Rackmorton was nowhere to be seen. Cormack heard a man's voice from inside the secret room.

"Come now, darling. Don't make me force you."

He strode furiously to the door. This one, too, was locked.

"Gun." Cormack extended his hand.

Jackson gave him the weapon, handle first.

Blast. And the doorknob was gone, obliterated to bits scattered across the floor. He and Jackson burst into the room. In the corner, Rackmorton's butler stood, his pantaloons around his ankles. A blonde servant girl stood with her arms upraised, still holding a silver tray, which she had clearly been using to fend him off.

With him distracted, she ran for the door.

"What are you doing in here?" demanded Cormack.

"I have privileges," he snarled.

"Where is he?"

He whirled, cursing at them. "How dare you discharge a weapon in Lord Rackmorton's home, and destroy his property."

"I said, where is he?" Cormack advanced, forcing the man into the corner.

"You have no right to do this. When he finds out you've done this—"

Cormack grabbed him by the neck. "Tell me where he is. Somewhere here in the house?"

The man wheezed. "I don't know where he is, but he left hours ago."

"My Lord, I do believe he's telling the truth," said Jackson.

Cormack let go of him, and the man collapsed, holding his neck with both hands. Had he just wasted valuable time coming here, when he ought to be on a different trail? How could that be? Even so, he wasn't done here. Striding to the far corner of the room, he wrenched the nude portrait of Daphne from the wall, and kicked his boot through. Tearing the canvas with his hands, he did not relent until the thing was in ribbons.

On the way out of the study door, he passed the dowager.

"What has happened here?" she demanded.

Cormack bowed curtly at the waist. "My lady, your son has quite the private art collection in there, which your butler is presently admiring. But then, I'm certain you've seen it."

"Art collection?" Her eyebrows raised in interest. "Why, no, I'm sure I don't know what you mean."

"Just there. Do you see that smallish door?"

"Just a storage room, but it's been years since I..." She frowned, and paused, before entering the door.

He continued on, but paused a moment on the threshold, until as he expected, the dowager screamed.

Hopeful that there had been some misunderstanding, and that Daphne now waited safely at home, Cormack sent Jackson to escort Miss Fickett to the Wolverton residence, but he rode directly there and found the family, along with Mr. Kincraig, gathered in the drawing room in a quiet uproar, having only just discovered Daphne's absence. Havering was there, and by chance, the Duke and Duchess of Claxton had just returned from their country estate. Mr. Kincraig pulled him aside to quietly explain. It seemed a florist had arrived for a scheduled appointment her mother felt she would never miss.

It was then, they all realized he was there. Everyone exclaimed about his bruised and swollen face.

Forced to provide some explanation, he answered, "I was attacked on the street last night after delivering Mrs. Bevington home, and dumped in the country."

Clarissa cried, "But who would do that, and why?"

He was on the verge of confessing everything about the Blue Swan and the Invisibilis, just so the sharing of that knowledge would help in whatever way to find her, but at that moment a man arrived to deliver a note, with the announcement it had come from Miss Bevington.

Her mother grappled with the envelope, as the rest of them gathered closely around.

"Indeed, the missive is written in her handwriting," she announced, her expression dismayed. "It says...oh, my heavens. It says that she has eloped."

Just then, Miss Fickett entered the room, followed by Jackson.

"Eloped?" she cried, her eyes wide and frantic. "With whom?"

"It doesn't say," replied Lady Margaretta, the note trembling in her hand, and tears in her eyes. "Only that we shouldn't come after them. That she knows they will be very happy."

Wolverton thundered, "I wasn't even aware she had developed an affection for anyone."

"She hadn't." Clarissa took the note, and read the words herself. "I don't believe it. I would have known. She would have told me." Strangely, she looked directly at Cormack just then and whispered, "I thought perhaps it would be *you*. Was I wrong?"

"She has been abducted," said Kate, tears threatening against her lashes. "I am certain of it. She has been taken against her will. We must find her."

She quickly conveyed what she had seen, with the carriage rolling up the curb, and Daphne disappearing immediately after. Kate, God bless her, left out all the rest.

"I think it is Rackmorton!" growled Havering.

"Yes!" Clarissa said, nodding.

"I was just at his residence," said Cormack.

Everyone turned to look at him.

He gritted his teeth. "I went there to confront him, believing him to be the one responsible for what happened to me last night—"

Havering demanded, "And was he there?"

"No, and neither was Daphne. There's only one route I can imagine them taking," he said, already racing toward the door. The other gentlemen followed on his heels.

"The road to Gretna Green," the duke muttered.

Already, Cormack's footsteps carried him to the door. "I only pray we can overtake them in time."

Chapter Fifteen

"Don't you dare," Lord Bamble shouted, leaping across the carriage at her, but too late. Daphne threw the pages she had ripped from his book out the window, and they caught in the wind, scattering in a glorious display.

"You horrid little witch," he bellowed. "I had not even read those pages yet."

"Well, I have, and guess what? The hero, Captain Johnson, catches fever on page four hundred thirty-two, and he dies. How do you like that?"

"Arg!" he cried, clapping his hands to his ears. "How dare you ruin the ending for me!" He leapt upon her. "You have left me with no choice." He produced a thick cord, and grabbed for her hands.

While at first she'd been terrified after he had unexpectedly dragged her into the carriage and subdued her until they were underway, Daphne had come to the realization he wasn't going to murder her under any circumstance, so she didn't hold back one bit. She kicked at him with all the power within her, and shoved and slapped his hands away. But to her surprise, Bamble was actually quite agile. After pursuing her about the carriage some twenty times, he managed to wedge her face into the corner long enough to tie her wrists, after which time he flung himself, wheezing, onto the opposite bench.

He stared at her from across the bench, breathing heavily. "Do you see what you have done?" He wheezed. "Now I am suffering an attack."

"Dearest Bamble, I think I am at last halfway to despising you." She gasped for breath, exhausted now. "Which is very sad, because I actually liked you. Very much so, and I always had, since childhood. Please, you must tell me why you have done this when we have always been such good friends."

He shook his head vehemently, pulling another book from the satchel under the seat. "I don't want to talk about it. Just be quiet. We're almost there."

"Tell me!" she exclaimed.

He blurted, "Because I owe a very large amount of money."

She saw the glimmer of regret in his eyes, but at the same time, fear. No doubt he had kidnapped her only under duress, and at the order of someone else. But who, and why? By now, the florist would have arrived at the house, and her mother would be aware of her absence. She prayed for a swift rescue, but what would Kate tell them, and how would they know where to look? Her only hope, she feared, was finding out who had forced Bamble to do this, and why. In understanding the reason, perhaps she would save herself.

"I've only ever seen you reading books," she said. "How could you have gotten into that sort of trouble?"

"There's a lot you don't know about me. I like to gamble."

"And that is how you came to be at the Blue Swan."

"Not exactly."

Her eyes widened at the moment of realization, and she exclaimed, "You're one of them, aren't you? The men Lord Raikes is looking for. A member of the—"

"Don't speak it. The name is only for members to ever say. When I saw you there on the stage . . . why, I couldn't believe my eyes. At the time, I just wanted to be certain you didn't see me. I'm not exactly proud to say I patronize such establishments. The knowledge would kill my mother. Only later did I realize the gift that had fallen into my hands."

At that moment, the carriage slowed.

"What do you mean?" she demanded. "What gift? Bamble, do you intend to marry me?"

"Heavens, no." He avoided her gaze. "You're far too much trouble for me."

The wheels slowed to a stop, and within moments the door opened. A glance outside revealed a nondescript field, with no landmarks of which to speak.

"Good-bye, Daphne," Bamble said, gathering his belongings.

"Where are you going?"

"Back to London. I hope you understand, I *am* sorry about all this. Truly sorry, but it was the only way I could get him to forgive my debt."

"Who?"

Bamble scrambled down the stairs and Rackmorton appeared to take his place.

"Hello, my dear." He climbed the stairs and joined her inside. "Are you ready to become my marchioness?"

"You!"

His hungry gaze devoured her, and a tremor of fear raced down her spine. If he was capable of scheming to this degree, and of kidnapping, of what else might he be capable? What did he intend? Behind her back she worked at the cord Bamble had tied on her wrists, stretching and tugging so as to loosen it.

"I know. It's a surprise. I apologize for the dramatics, but I feared you would never get into a carriage with me, let alone agree to wed. And I've ensured your . . . unfortunate distraction will not interfere. Raikes, yes, I know all about him, and the little dalliance you've shared. I saw your . . . dress there on the floor beside the bed, you see, just the merest glimpse of it, but it was such a distinctive color of blue. It took every ounce of my control not to kill him then, knowing it was you there with him under that sheet, but the others would have seen."

His eyes glinted with such fury, her fear only increased, but now for Cormack. Worry crashed through her belly, almost sickening her.

"What have you done to Lord Raikes?" she demanded.

He shrugged. "Don't worry your pretty head over it. I only acted to guard what has been mine all along. And he deserved it after all, regardless even of you. At first we didn't realize who he was. But, after he started snooping around, Bamble pulled out one of his books, a volume of *Debrett's*, and that answered quite a few questions. He was that fellow, years ago, badgering his bettors and causing problems. The Duke of Rathcrispin was so furious with us all, for bringing down question upon his good name. Tragic thing about his sister. Honestly, I don't know who was responsible for that particular scandal, but it wasn't me or anyone else of whom I'm aware. Still, you might as well forget about Lord Raikes. He and his revenge plot are dead in a ditch somewhere in the country, far, far away."

No. She couldn't live...she couldn't exist if something had happened to Cormack.

She fought off grief and calmed herself. She had to believe Cormack was still alive. At last, she worked her hands free of their bindings.

She quietly suggested, "Very well, if marriage is what you want, let us return to London and announce our engagement to the papers in the typical way. We can plan a wedding. Please don't deprive my mother—or yours—of that joy."

"Oh, God, no. Your family wouldn't allow it, I have no doubt. I've seen the way they look at me, with dislike and, yes, even revulsion. I don't know why, considering all I have to offer. Nonetheless, your protectors would step in. It's what compelled me to arrange for this whole elopement. Given the circumstances, I knew Raikes would cause problems. He forced my hand, and I had to act."

Daphne, filled with fury, seized up her reticule from the bench beside her and, swinging it hard, struck him against the side of the head. "You will let me go."

He fell to the side, clasping a hand to his face.

"Now that's enough!" he shouted, reaching for her, lunging, his arms and legs securing her against the bench. "I had hoped to be a gentleman about this, but it appears I shall have to take you now, to ensure your compliance."

He grabbed at her skirts, and yanked them high—

Just then, something darted into view outside the window. A rider on a horse? Daphne turned, losing sight of them.

But Rackmorton plastered himself beside the open window, extending his head all the way out to see.

"Damn it all to hell," he bellowed.

The rider—no, riders—appeared again. She recognized Cormack, his hair flying back from his battered face. He was alive. She had never been more relieved. And there, racing behind him, were Claxton and Havering as well! A flash of movement drew her attention to the opposite window, where Kincraig appeared on horseback.

Suddenly, Rackmorton produced a pistol.

"Careful!" she screamed, but Havering rode past, disappearing from his saddle with all the skill of a circus performer, to climb onto the driver's roost.

Twisting, Rackmorton pummeled the carriage roof, shouting. "Faster! Don't slow down."

Daphne struck him with her reticule again, doing her best to knock the firearm from his grasp, but he shoved her back.

In that moment, Cormack hurtled through the window, only half of him making it through. Rackmorton aimed, but she kicked at his hand and the gun went flying. The marquess didn't hesitate, but did some kicking of his own, thrusting his heel against Cormack's shoulders.

Daphne screamed, terrified he would fall out and be trampled or run over by the carriage wheels, but with a powerful flex of his arms he dragged himself through—

Rackmorton shoved at him, trying to force him back out. Cormack's fist came round, finding satisfaction at the center of the marquess's face, and his legs went sprawling. Daphne, remembering his crude threat, kicked him in the groin, and he screamed, rolling to his side on the bench, and falling in a ball to the floor. The carriage rolled to a sudden stop.

Cormack slid all the way through the window to sit upright across from her, and demanded, "Are you all right? Did he hurt you? Did he—"

"I am unhurt!" she cried. "How did you find me?"

"We just followed the trail of destroyed books, and once we found Bamble, he spilled everything." With a growl, he dragged Rackmorton through the door and down the stairs, to discard him on the grass at the side of the road. Havering had control of the horses' harnesses, while Kincraig climbed down, dragging the driver behind him, and Claxton dismounted. Soon, they had all gathered around the man who had put into action a plan to abduct her.

Cormack! She could not contain her joy at seeing him. Daphne descended the steps, and running across the grass, threw herself into his arms, pressing kisses onto his bruised face. "Your face. What happened? Oh, my darling—"

He stiffened, and she realized the mistake of what she had done.

"Interesting," muttered Kincraig.

She released Cormack immediately, and stepped back, looking between Claxton and Havering, who stared at her in wide-eyed dismay. "And you—Havering!" They all stood there, staring at her in silence. Knowing not else what to do, she flung herself into Fox's arms.

"*My darling Havering.* You saved me as well." He stood unmoving in her arms. Peering up, she saw that he stared thunderously at Cormack.

"Claxton? Kincraig?" she said weakly. "Thank you all."

Cheeks burning, she climbed back into the carriage and closed the door.

But already day turned to night, and Claxton made the decision that they would send word to London that they had recovered Daphne unharmed, but out of concerns for safety and the dangers of traveling the road in the dark, that they would pass the night at the nearby inn. They supped in absolute silence, with Rackmorton fuming alone on the far side of the room, his back to them all. Daphne hadn't known if words on Cormack's behalf would help or hinder their situation. But each time she'd tried, he had silenced her with a glance.

Eventually, the fire on the hearth grew dim, and Claxton quietly, but firmly, suggested she retire.

"This way, miss," the innkeeper's wife instructed, leading Daphne toward her room. Rackmorton had been committed to a windowless room beneath the stairs, the door of which was just a few feet away, and he could not effect an escape without their knowing.

Halfway up the stairs, Daphne turned to glance over her shoulder just in time to see Claxton level his gaze upon Cormack. "I believe you and I have something to discuss in private."

Havering muttered, "Damn you, Raikes."

Cormack nodded solemnly. "Yes. Yes, indeed we do."

Daphne burst out, her hands gripping the banister, "Did you ever stop to think that perhaps Lord Raikes is blameless, and that this is all my doing? That I seduced him?"

"Quiet," barked the duke, his eyes flashing fire. "Go to your room, and do not come through the door until morning."

She did not budge, but remained in that spot, defiant and mutinous.

Cormack said to her in a quiet voice, "Daphne, you must do as Claxton says. Everything will be all right."

"But this is all my fault."

"Please," he said.

With a groan of frustration, she did as she was told.

* * *

Only when she was gone did any of them speak again.

The duke turned his attention fully on Cormack. "Obviously a matter has arisen that requires immediate resolution. Do you dare deny that you have been intimate with my unwed sister-in-law?"

Cormack closed his eyes and shook his head.

Havering cursed. He stood against the wall, his arms crossed over his chest, his jaw tight and furious. "I'd never have expected it of you, Cormack. To think I entrusted her to you. Implicitly. God, wasn't I a fool? If her brother Vinson was here, he would drag you out into the yard and shoot you dead for dishonoring her so. So help me, I am tempted to do the same."

"I understand your anger."

He hated feeling as if he had disappointed these men, both of whom he held in the highest respect, but his foremost concern at the moment was Daphne, and that she not be hurt in any of this.

"Correct me if I'm wrong," said Claxton, with a lowering glare, "but I thought you were betrothed."

"Which makes this all the more sordid," Fox growled. He broke away from the wall, to pace the length of the floor.

Cormack chose his response carefully. "There is no formal betrothal, but rather an agreement that was intended to bring about the return of my family's ancestral lands. The girl in question is but twelve years old. It is her father with whom I will have to contend, and I will do so."

The duke's nostrils flared in displeasure. "Indeed you will. You will break this agreement, as discreetly as is allowed. Although it riles me beyond bearing that Daphne should marry a libertine who cared so little for her so as to seduce her. Your unforgiveable actions have left us no other choice."

How true the words were. Daphne was his choice. Even before he'd discovered her abduction, he'd known he couldn't live his life without her. Hell, thinking back now, he'd known since the moment he'd first laid eyes on her. All this had been inevitable, and he could not find it in his heart to regret the result, though he abhorred the circumstance. He would marry her. He would give his life to keep and protect her. He just wished he could protect her now from even a modicum of shame. There was also the very real concern that she might not wish to marry him. She had always been so emphatic in that regard. Once they were alone, he would do anything in his power to persuade her.

But in this moment, he had to persuade the two men who cared so deeply for her happiness.

He said, "I would have married her regardless of your discovering our affair, once I persuaded her to agree. Make no mistake, *I love her*," said Cormack emphatically. "And I know that she loves me as well, though she has not confessed it back. But I fear she will resist."

His Grace's eyes narrowed. "If she loves you as well, then why would she?"

"She has vowed not to marry, I am certain as some self-imposed penance for her father's death."

"He is right, Claxton," said Havering. "She has sworn it time and time again, that she has no wish to wed." More softly, he added, "I think Raikes is right about the reason as well."

"She is stubborn and strong willed." Cormack looked toward the stairs. "Mark my words. She will refuse me."

"She will not have that choice." The duke exhaled through his nose. "You will undertake to obtain a special license tomorrow, as soon as we return to London. Do you understand? We will speak to Wolverton and Lady Harwick as soon as we return. You will accept full responsibility for all of this."

"I do," he answered resolutely. "And I will."

* * *

Daphne lay wide awake, listening to the silence of the inn, and wondering what had happened downstairs. In a rush of emotion, she had given them away. Now the duke would attempt to make Cormack marry her, in some misguided attempt to preserve her honor.

A quiet tapping came at her window. Pushing up, she rushed to the glass to see Cormack's face in the dark.

"Cormack," Daphne said, pushing the frame open to find him perched on a ladder. "I am so very sorry. To the bottom of my heart. I have ruined everything."

"No, you haven't." He reached inside and, with a warm smile that instantly calmed her racing heartbeat, took her hand. "The duke forbade you from passing through that door, but he didn't say anything about the window. Come down, and take a walk with me. I'll help you down."

When they had reached the bottom, he took her hand and led her toward the distant field.

"Where are we going?"

"Just over there, on that hillside. I want to watch the stars with you."

She allowed him to lead her there, knowing that once there everything weighing on her heart could be said. Already from his demeanor, she knew what he would say. That he had agreed to marry her, as a consequence of their secret affair being discovered. But she wasn't about to allow him to sacrifice himself and betray his duty to his family. Not for her, when she did not deserve such sacrifice.

On the hillside, he spread his coat on a space of grass and, sitting pulled her down beside him, where they sat for a long moment in silence.

In the darkness she could just make out the pale outline of wildflowers, and for a moment, she closed her eyes and remembered the dream where they'd made love in a field of blooms. But this wasn't a dream, and she couldn't imagine that he was anything but angry at her now for bringing this calamity upon them both.

"Daphne, we're going to be married."

She'd expected the words, but they still struck pain through her heart.

"No." She shook her head emphatically. "I refuse. You have an agreement to marry the girl so that you can obtain the lands your family lost."

"I'm afraid it's too late for that."

"We were just supposed to have an affair! It wasn't supposed to be like this."

"I'm sorry about the way it all came about, but I'm not sorry it's happened."

"I am. I have destroyed your dreams and broken my vow to myself. Don't you understand, I don't deserve you, I don't deserve a happily-ever-after?"

"Why not, Daphne?" he said. "Please help me understand."

"I caused my father's death with my selfishness, and I vowed that night never to fall in love. Never to marry. What point are vows, if they are not kept?"

"What I don't understand is how such a vow honors your father. How does that bring him back?"

"It doesn't, but, Cormack, my mother and father were so in love. More so after years of marriage than on the day they first wed. Not only did I shatter her happily-ever-after, I deprived my grandfather of his son and his heir, and my two sisters of their father. I owe my life to them. That sort of debt is never fully repaid."

He reached out and covered her hand with his own, twining his fingers between hers, and clasping it tight. "Your family does not expect that from you."

His gentle manner elicited the deepest feelings inside her, feelings she couldn't even define. She desperately wanted him to hold her, but could see no alternative but to push him away.

"Of course they don't, but I made the promise *to myself*...because...because it was the only way I could live with myself." She dashed away the tears from her eyes, but still, they flowed, over her lashes and down her cheeks. "What good are promises to those you love, unless they are kept? You made a promise to your family as well—"

"Then let us make new promises. Better ones, that honor

those that we love." Suddenly he seized her against him and pressed her back onto the soft ground. The fragrance of flowers filled her nose. His lips kissed the tears from her skin. "If your father was alive, I would ask him, no beg him, to allow me to marry you. But he is not, and so I ask you."

"Cormack, don't," she warned thickly.

He kissed her hard, the power of his passion stealing her breath and her resistance.

"Lands. Honor. Family. They are nothing without you."

His lips grazed over her cheeks, her eyelids and mouth in a pleasurable assault she found herself helpless to resist. She softened beneath him and wrapped her arms around his waist, wanting nothing more than to make love to him, here under the stars. But though her body surrendered, her heart still resisted.

"Accept me," he murmured against her skin. "Be my wife."

Yes. The word hovered on her tongue, but she refused her mouth permission to say it. She did not deserve this sort of happiness, not tonight, and certainly not forever.

His hands touched her calves, her thighs, as he raised her skirts. Her body reacted, going liquid with desire, aching with a need so powerful she could only touch him as well, pushing his shirt up to smooth her hands greedily over her stomach and chest.

"Say it," he urged, lifting away to unfasten his breeches, and lowering again to kiss her. She kissed him back, moaning as he lowered himself between her thighs, hot and thick, where suddenly he stopped and rested his forehead to hers. "Please, Daphne, please..."

"My love," she whispered, though the word was barely

a breath, moving beneath him, begging with her body that he make her complete.

"You are *my* love, but that's not good enough. I deserve more, as do you." He breathed raggedly, touching her hair. "You demanded a secret of me, when I took you in my bed."

She stilled, listening not only with her ears, but with her heart.

"Do you remember, I told you I wished it could be you?"

"I remember."

"It wasn't a secret, not really." He nuzzled her cheek, and her neck. "But more like a dream."

"Cormack."

"You make my dreams come true." He shifted, gripping her hips, and in one thrust entered her.

She cried out, stunned by pleasure.

"Say it, that you'll marry me." He moved his hips, kissing her more deeply, more fervently with each thrust, claiming the deepest part of her, to her soul. "Please." He wrapped his arms beneath her, seizing her to him so tightly she had to gasp to breathe. "Say you will marry me, that I can love you not just now, but forever."

At hearing his plea, at last the walls around her heart collapsed, setting her free to love him. New tears filled her eyes, this time formed of joy instead of pain.

"Yes," she whispered, twining his arms around his neck. "I will marry you. I love you, Cormack."

He laughed, a joyous sound from deep in his throat. Lowering to press a hot kiss on her mouth, he rolled, bringing her atop him. There, below a canopy of stars, she lowered to press her lips to his mouth, to his throat, until he pushed her back, guiding her with his hands and his body, to take up the same rhythm as his. "Yes, like that. You can't know...how good this feels."

She arched, her head falling back as she found a deeper pleasure. "I do," she whispered. "Oh, Cormack, I do."

*   *   *

The next morning, after what had been a completely sleepless night for Cormack—and, he knew for a fact, for Daphne as well—the gentlemen gathered outside, while the innkeeper's son harnessed the horses. Rackmorton had already been dispatched to London on the back of a braying, bucking donkey they had secured for the sole purpose of humiliating him on his long ride back to town. Kincraig had volunteered, quite readily, to follow a short distance behind to ensure the marquess's course remained true.

Havering looked at Cormack. "One day we'll all look back at this, and it will be the most entertaining story."

Claxton glowered darkly. "We aren't at that point yet. I do not look forward to explaining this turn of events to Wolverton and the marchioness, not to mention my wife."

Hearing footsteps, Cormack turned to the door of the inn and watched as Daphne approached. Instantly forgetting the duke and Havering, he strode forward and reached for her hand. She appeared so small, and so pale and terrified, so different from the temptress of the night before. Wanting to reassure her, he pulled her his arms and kissed her ardently.

He murmured against her temple, "Darling, I can't wait to marry you or to introduce you to my family. Don't look so anxious. All will be well."

She clung to him, and at last a smile overtook her lips. "Let us go. Oh, Cormack, take me to Bellefrost. Take me to meet them all."

The four of them made use of Rackmorton's carriage, riding in comfort, but also in relative silence, for the next hour. Cormack never once released Daphne's hand. At last they turned down the long drive.

"Here we are. This is Bellefrost." Pulling her into the circle of his arms, he watched her face as they drew nearer to the place he called home.

Her cheeks warmed, and she smiled. "It's beautiful. I see why you love it here."

When the carriage stopped, they disembarked, but something stopped Cormack from leading them directly to the stairs.

"A moment, if you will," he said to Claxton and Havering.

Tucking Daphne's hand into his elbow, he took her round the side of the house, and down the pebbled lane to the family cemetery. From the gate, she led him, easily finding the pink marble tombstone that bore his sister's name.

"I'm so sorry, Cormack. That you lost her. That you still don't have the answers you tried so hard to find."

"Don't be. Today is not a day for regrets. I hope I've made clear to you I have none. I just wanted to bring you here, because she was so special to me."

"I wish I could have met her. I wish that she could have been here, to greet you on your return home. She must have been so proud to call you brother."

She slipped her hand into his, but the gesture turned into a full embrace, and he kissed her. "I'm so happy that you're here."

Footsteps sounded behind them. Tiny ones, running along the path. Cormack turned to see Michael bounding toward him as fast as his short little legs would carry him, followed by his father, Lord Champdeer. At the house, a curtain moved in a window, and there his mother's smiling face appeared.

Daphne quickly released him and stepped back, as he lunged forward to sweep the little boy up into his arms, and high over his head. The child squealed with delight.

Being reunited with the family he adored so completely brought a sudden surge of emotion into his throat, so fast and immense that he could not trust himself to speak. He loved Daphne, and he knew they would love her, too. But that did not mean he did not worry about how best to say the words he must say. The beginning of a new dream, as wonderful as it might be, meant the end of another.

* * *

He brought the child to settle in his arms, but the boy wiggled, demanding to be released, and barreled straight toward Daphne, where he grabbed a fistful of her skirts and stared up at her with wide-eyed curiosity.

Lord Champdeer, gray haired and dressed in a neat black suit, smiled faintly, his gaze moving with unconcealed interest to Daphne.

"Michael saw you from the window, and he was off like a shot." He chuckled. "But I see you have brought guests. Please come. Let's invite everyone inside."

* * *

"—and we are going to be married," said Cormack, his throat growing distinctively husky on the last word.

Silence owned the moment. As if he sensed the gravity of the moment, even little Michael did not make a sound.

Cormack lifted a hand to her back to steady her. Only then did she realize she'd swayed. She had been nervous on the ride to Bellefrost, but now she could scarcely breathe. That Lord and Lady Champdeer loved their son was obvious. How would they react to her?

Lady Champdeer, Cormack's mother, looked back at her with tear-filled eyes. "Oh, my dear girl—" She rushed forward to enfold Daphne in her arms.

Relief washed over Daphne, and she exhaled, pressing her cheek against that of the woman whom she fully believed would become a second mother to her. Across the room, Fox and Claxton observed quietly, with Fox throwing her a reassuring wink and a smile.

Still holding Daphne tightly, Lady Champdeer said to her son, "I'm so glad you've come home. The both of you."

And yet, his father, the marquess, stood silent and unmoving behind her.

Michael slipped off his stool, book in hand, to reach for Daphne. "No cry, lady. Noooo."

She picked him up, unable to resist the promise of his snuggly warmth, and lifted him to perch between herself and the countess. "I'm not crying because I'm sad. I'm crying because I'm so very happy to meet everyone, but most especially you." He kissed her on the cheek with a wet open mouth, causing her and his grandmother both to laugh in delight. And to cry more tears.

Lady Champdeer reached into her pocket for a

handkerchief—not one, but two. "One for myself, and one for you as well."

She handed it over to Daphne, and before releasing her from their close embrace, she affectionately squeezed her hand tight.

"What an unexpected but welcome surprise." The marquess's countenance broke, no longer inscrutable, but infused with warmth and emotion, and he strode toward Cormack to pull him into an embrace. They stood there a long moment in silence, until Cormack broke away.

"Father, I know this changes everything for us."

"You refer of course to the agreement with Sir Snaith." The older man shook his head. "How can I have allowed you to take on such a burden? A burden that should have been mine alone." He looked at Daphne. "He has told you the truth, I hope, that I am to blame for the loss of the lands that surround this home. I have always had what his mother calls a fanciful mind. I take keen interest in science, and experimentation of nature, and of late, with the conduction of electricity. But my interests and hopes for the future led me to make several unwise investments. My son . . . my capable and prideful son, tried to repair the mess I had made."

"We are family," Cormack uttered in a thick voice. "It is what family does. And I regret deeply that I cannot follow through in bringing about their return, but I've been unable to arrive at any alternative."

"Oh, my son!" Lady Champdeer exclaimed. "There is nothing to regret. Your face confesses everything. You love her."

"I do."

"Then I do as well! Your happiness is far more important to us than any patch of dirt."

Cormack's father smiled, looking between them both, his eyes aglow. "So release yourself from this obligation, one that ought never to have been placed upon you. Marry this young lady. Love her. Give me more grandchildren, because—" He chuckled. "Heaven knows this one needs distraction."

At that moment, Jessup the butler, the sparkly-eyed old fellow Daphne had been introduced to moments before, lumbered in carrying a tray of glasses and a crystal decanter. "My lord, I thought a celebratory toast might be in order."

"Indeed!" exclaimed the marquess. "Gather around, and I shall pour."

Glasses were passed out to everyone, including Jessup. There was also a miniature tin cup for Michael filled with milk. Everyone save for Fox, who remained behind as Claxton crossed the room.

Cormack called out to him. "Havering, are you coming?"

Yet Havering stared transfixed at the portrait of a young woman on the wall. A woman Daphne could only assume to be Cormack's sister, Laura.

"Fox . . . what are you doing?" she said.

Fox turned from the portrait, his face ashen. "I . . . I know this young lady. Her name is Miss Picard."

Lady Champdeer lifted a hand to her lips. "Picard was my maiden name. My daughter used it in her employment." She looked between her son and her husband.

Cormack straightened, and took several steps toward him. "Havering? How did you know my sister?"

Havering's gaze, hazed by a sudden wash of tears, settled on the child. "And that is her . . . son?" He came forward to peer at the child, still in Daphne's arms, gently lifting the boy's face to peer into his.

"It is." Everything about Cormack's demeanor changed. His jaw grew rigid, and his spine appeared to bristle.

"My God. I have made a terrible mistake. I should have searched longer. Been more diligent in carrying through. It's just that when I found out she'd died—"

"Havering," Cormack said softly. "Are you a member of the Invisibilis?"

"No," Havering said, meeting his gaze directly.

"Then what, Fox?" Daphne asked in a whisper.

"But at one time I was. It all started when we were just boys in school. Everyone was in some sort of club. Invisibilis was ours."

Lady Champdeer gasped, and her husband gripped her shoulder. Claxton's scowl deepened to black.

Cormack glanced to Daphne, thunder rising to his eyes.

"Let him explain," she whispered. "Please, Cormack."

Cormack confronted Fox. "Tell me now, are you the father of my sister's child?"

Silence held the room, as everyone waited for his response.

"Daphne, look at the boy," Havering answered. "Is there any question to whom he belongs?"

Daphne stared down at the little child clinging to her skirts, raising his book high in his hand. At the large, dark eyes, and raven's-wing hair. She had seen portraits of a similar boy, only her mind had not recognized the similarities until now, with Fox's gentle encouragement.

"Vinson," she whispered, her eyes welling with tears. "This little boy is my brother's child."

Just then, they heard the sound of footsteps in the corridor. Lady Harwick entered, along with Clarissa and Mr. Birch.

She offered no greeting. Instead she stood very still, the

blood draining from her face, and she swayed. Mr. Birch stepped forward to steady her. But she gently pushed free of him and entered the room, one slow step at a time, as tears gathered in her eyes.

"Oh, Daphne. Fox. Is it true?"

She stood in front of Michael, who stood pressed into Lady Champdeer's skirts, and her mouth took on a tentative smile.

"May I see him?"

"Of course."

She lifted him into her arms and stared into his eyes. "Of course he is Vinson's. He is the most beautiful child. Havering, please explain how this came to be." A tear fell down her cheek. "How we did not know. But first, Daphne, please tell me you are unharmed. I simply could not wait in town, and the innkeeper directed us here."

"I am not."

"Thank heavens. How did you come to be here? The butler explained this is the home of Lord Raikes."

"Mother, I am betrothed to Lord Raikes."

"Lord Raikes?" Her mother clasped the child against her breast. "If I do not sit, I think I would faint."

Mr. Birch stepped forward to support her with his gloved hand. "Why don't you sit. This has all come as a shock."

Daphne stood, touching a hand to the top of Michael's head. "Fox, you must explain how this came to be. Laura and my brother?"

"Vinson and I were inducted into the Invisibilis when we were boys, away at university. But after school, some of us grew up. Some did not. Our interests changed. Still, he and I agreed to attend a so-called Gathering of the Ages at the hunting lodge of the Duke of Rathcrispin, largely for old time's sake. Rathcrispin's sons were members. Once there, we wished we weren't. The other members were still just the same way they had always been, concerned only with indulging in any form of debauchery. Vinson and I entertained ourselves actually hunting, if you can imagine that. It was then we met your sister, where the duke's property joined that of the Deavalls'. She had three little boys with her, and one of their kites had got stuck in a tree, which resulted in Miss Picard becoming stuck in the tree. Your brother climbed up, and managed to safely carry her down."

"And then Vinson seduced her," growled Cormack.

Lady Margaretta's head dipped, and Daphne bit her lower lip to keep from crying out. "My brother *would not have* ... he was the most honorable man."

"That's such an ugly word," Havering answered softly. "And I know you are angry, and hurting, but I won't let you disparage the memory of the man who was, and who will always be, my best friend. He and your sister fell in love. Much like you and Miss Bevington have done."

Cormack's gaze flashed. "If he loved her, he would have married her, and this child would not be without a proper name."

"That's just the thing, Raikes. He did marry her."

Lady Champdeer rushed to her husband's side, and he wrapped a protective arm around her.

"No," interjected Lord Champdeer. "She would have told us. She said nothing of a husband."

"I think, sadly, because after his death, she could not produce the necessary proof." Havering withdrew a leather case from his chest pocket, and sorted through the contents a moment before withdrawing a folded piece of parchment.

"But here it is. Vinson carried it with him every moment on the voyage, you see. The night before he died, he revealed to me that he had married Miss Picard. I was so shocked. We did not keep secrets from each other, but then again, neither of us had ever been in love before, and I think...well, I think they both wished to keep it a private matter until they could do things right, and inform the families together."

Lady Champdeer cried into her handkerchief quietly. Lady Margaretta covered her mouth with her gloved hand.

"Upon his return, he intended to do everything correctly, as he put it, and meet her family, and gift her with a proper wedding day. But that night, as if he foretold his own death, he told me if anything should happen to him I should deliver this to his wife, so she could go to his family, and they would know her as his wife and embrace her as a member of their family."

"What happened then?" Cormack demanded hoarsely.

"He died, of course," Fox answered in a quiet voice. "And when I found this among his belongings the document had been half destroyed by dampness, with all the details blurred beyond legibility. The moment I disembarked after returning home, I journeyed to the church where they had married, thinking to restore the necessary portions of the document and deliver the terrible news to Miss Picard—a woman I knew in truth to be Mrs. Bevington, the wife of my dearest friend."

Cormack's mother and father clasped hands, she sighing heavily.

"Go on, young man," urged His Lordship.

"However, while at the church, the young woman there told me her father, the parson, had recently succumbed to the curse of dementia. Given his habit for performing secret and sometimes unadvisable marriages, and her father writing in his own peculiar shorthand, this had caused her some difficulty in later producing accurate records and verifying details. She also told me that months before, a young woman she recognized as Miss Picard arrived at the parsonage, asking to see one of the ledgers. The young lady was visibly distraught, having learned from a newspaper of the drowning of her husband. The daughter, wishing to give her privacy in her moment of grief, left the parsonage to do a bit of shopping, and returned only to see the young lady leave again in tears. Only months later, when she realized her father was suffering periods of confusion and increasingly telling parishoners he had no recollection of them, did she realize what might have transpired. Only when she went to the Deavall estate to inquire about Miss Picard, she was told the young lady had left their employ and subsequently died. After she repaired the document that I presented to her, I...traveled there myself and they confirmed the tragic news."

"Why did you never tell the families?" asked Lady Margaretta, her eyes wide and pleading.

"You were already so consumed by your grief, as I assumed Miss Picard's family to be grieving as well. I made the decision not to increase the tragedy tenfold by revealing such sad details. Only now I am so sorry. I had no idea there was a child. I shall forever try to make it up to little Michael. I made a grievous mistake."

Daphne looked at Cormack, who stared at his sister's portrait. She could not discern what emotions he felt, which was strange, being that from the first moment it seemed she'd been able to read him like a book.

"No, Havering," Cormack answered softly. "As much as I would have liked things to turn out differently, I can find no fault or malice in your actions. At last, you have put Laura's spirit to rest."

"Yes," cried Lady Champdeer. "You can't know how much hearing this account means to us. My dear daughter. How I would have wished to have known Vinson. She loved him that much, I believe, that she would hold her silence rather than cast aspersions on his name after his death. Now, at last, you have given Michael his proper name."

"And, Havering, you have given me the greatest gift." Lady Margaretta kissed the now-sleeping boy in her arms. "A piece of my son, and his dear father through him, that lives on."

"Grandfather will be beside himself with joy," cried Clarissa, rushing forward to embrace her mother and the child. "Mr. Kincraig? Perhaps not so much."

Havering exhaled with relief, his cheeks flushed. "Actually, I think he will be...relieved."

Daphne's mother stood, passing the child to his other grandmother. "And now instead of a debut ball, we shall surprise everyone with a wedding celebration. Lord Raikes." She extended her arms to him. "I am shocked, of course, but could not be more pleased. I can think of no gentleman whom I would rather embrace as a son."

"Ahem," interrupted Claxton.

"Except for Claxton," she exuded, "who has made my dear Sophia the happiest expectant mother on earth."

"What is this about a wedding?" said a voice from the door.

Yet another visitor appeared. A short and rather portly fellow stood at the door, walking stick in hand. His sharp gaze immediately found Cormack, who pulled Daphne into his arms. "I was out for my morning walk and saw all the carriages."

"Sir Snaith," said Lord Champdeer, both of his eyebrows raising up his forehead. "I do believe you and I have some business to discuss."

"My lord," said the Duke of Claxton, before looking to Cormack. "If there is no objection, I would like to sit in on the discussions. I have negotiated treaties between the world's empires. Perhaps I can be of some use here?"

Cormack left Daphne's side, pressing a kiss to her temple. "This should be interesting."

Daphne, left alone, immediately snared her sister to the side and in a quiet voice asked, "How serious are things between Mr. Birch and our mother?" She laughed happily. "Should I be concerned that she will be wed even before me?"

Clarissa grasped her by the shoulders, and smiled. "My dear sister, I would not be surprised. They are quite serious, I believe. He dotes on her, and she on him. You should have seen them in the carriage ride all the way here. Mother would have been hysterical, but for him calming her and entertaining the both of us with the most charming stories."

Hearing this, Daphne felt compelled to cross the room to where her mother still sat, cradling Michael. She wrapped her arms around Lady Margaretta's shoulders, careful not to disturb the boy. "I am so happy."

"I am so happy for you, my dear."

"I am so happy for *you*."

"Truly? You like Mr. Birch?"

"I do. Very much so."

"That is very good to hear." Her mother's eyes glazed

with tears and she smiled. "Because I do believe I love him."

"Mother!" She pressed a kiss to her cheek, and whispered against her skin. "That's wonderful."

Margaretta murmured, "I'll always love your father."

"I know you will. But you have such a big heart, there is just as much room in it for Mr. Birch. And in mine as well. I'm going to go give him a kiss."

"Daphne!" her mother exclaimed, beaming. "He would be so delighted, I think."

In that moment, a beautiful warmth slipped over her shoulders and down her arms. Something like peace. Something like...forgiveness.

* * *

An hour later, the men emerged. To Daphne's great relief, everyone wore smiles. Sir Snaith joined the others for tea, and soon everyone sat around the enormous fireplace, on chairs and big comfortable pillows, for conversation.

Eventually, though, Cormack drew her away to the privacy of the nearby corridor, the look of love so strong in his eyes she could hardly bear not to push him onto the carpet so that she could cover him with kisses from head to toe.

"Tell me what was said."

"The Northmore lands will be returned to their rightful owners—"

"Cormack! That's wonderful." She threw her arms around his neck.

"—in exchange for a ridiculous amount of money, which is of no consequence to me." He bent to passionately kiss her mouth. "I am forever in Claxton's debt. He has additionally obligated himself and the duchess to give little Ernestine, when she turns seventeen, the season of any girl's dreams. As you can imagine, the sponsorship of a duke and duchess is of no small consequence."

"That will be no great hardship. My sister loves to plan such occasions."

His face grew suddenly serious. "You don't mind marrying by special license? Because I can't wait a day more than necessary."

"Wait for what?" she giggled.

His eyebrow arched up. "You know what."

Daphne's hand found his, and drew it between them to press a kiss to his knuckles. "I would marry you now, in this moment, if I could. My darling, I don't believe we shall ever see such a day like this again, ever in our lives. I felt nothing but despair this morning, but now I am the happiest woman alive."

"I vow now, in this moment, to make sure that smile stays there for the rest of your life."

"You are the most unselfish man I have ever known."

"I'm purely selfish," he murmured. "You have a beautiful smile." He grew serious and pulled her closer. "Never doubt that I loved you from the first moment I saw you."

She kissed him, raising her hands to frame his face. "Never doubt that I will love you forever."

Epilogue

"Just look, Sir Keyes. The flowers. The candles. Everything is beautiful. Just beautiful!" exclaimed Lady Dundalk, peering over Daphne's shoulder into the ballroom.
"Your dear mother always puts on the best parties."

Daphne stood between her mother and grandfather in
the reception line, welcoming guests to her debut ball.
She could barely contain her happiness. Surrounded by her
family and friends, there was nowhere else on earth that
she would rather be.

Sir Keyes leaned forward on his cane. "I hadn't noticed
any of that because of the pretty young lady standing here
in front of me," he said, his eyes twinkling.

"You always know just the thing to say," she said, and
kissed them both affectionately before they moved on
down the reception line.

She turned to welcome the next guest in line. Her favorite guest of the evening. The one she'd been waiting for,

with breathless anticipation, to arrive. She got light-headed
and fairly trembled, lowering her hand into his.

"Hello there, Miss Bevington," Cormack said in an
intimate voice, offering a smile that made her toes curl
with pleasure inside their beaded satin slippers. He bent
to kiss her gloved hand. "Thank you for the invitation.
I hadn't expected one, you see, being so new as I am to
town."

"Oh, you," she said, giggling. How fun. She rarely *giggled*, except with her sisters. But having him here...look-
ing at her that way...

She giggled again.

"Harrumpf!" said her grandfather, who glowered up
from his chair—but the smallest smile turned the corner of
his lips, and his eyes twinkled. All was well.

"I see that you are not wearing flowers," the earl said.

"I am not." Apparently the florist had forgotten them,
but her mother decided not to make a fuss.

"Then I hope you might consider wearing these." With
gentlemanly flair, he produced a small box from behind his
back, which he deftly opened and removed an artful cluster
of flowers, ivory and the palest yellow, with ribbons shining throughout. They complemented her gown perfectly.
She glanced at her mother, but her mother was smiling at
Cormack.

The florist forgot. What a story. They had plotted the
flowers, and nothing could please her more.

"They are lovely," Daphne said, beaming adoringly at
Cormack.

"May I?" He raised the corsage toward her bosom.

"No you may not," interjected Lady Margaretta with a
good-humored glare. Taking the flowers, she pinned them

at Daphne's shoulder. Beneath her breath, she murmured, "Everyone is already staring."

A glance down the line of waiting guests proved that to be true. A host of wide eyes peered at them with interest.

"I hope you'll save a dance for me tonight?" said Cormack.

"The two of you are holding up the reception line," her mother warned softly, reaching a hand for Cormack and gently guiding him through.

"I can't make promises," Daphne called after him. "My dance card is very full."

His gaze remained fixed on Daphne until he arrived in front of Sophia and Claxton, who also stood greeting guests in the line, at which time the duchess raised a hand and, with a fingertip to his jaw, redirected his face toward her.

"Good evening, Lord Raikes," she said, with an amused smile. The duke rolled his eyes.

A half hour and a score of guests later, and Daphne, Sophia and Clarissa entered the ballroom, an entrance the small orchestra announced with a majestic flourish of music. They passed Mr. Kincraig along the way, observing from the stairs. Since Michael's arrival into the family, he had remained friendly but held himself somewhat distant. Kate was there as well, as Daphne's special guest, dressed in a lovely gown a shade darker than Daphne's. Her mother waited there, having already joined Mr. Birch, and she reached for Daphne's hands and drew her to her side, while Havering pushed Wolverton's chair to the center of the floor.

The room grew silent as Wolverton stood, with Havering's assistance. Leaning on the young lord's arm for support, he straightened his shoulders proudly. Light from the chandeliers shimmered off the medals on his chest, awarded in his younger days for valiant acts of bravery in the service of England.

"Thank you all for coming," he announced. "As you know, we are all here to celebrate the debut of my granddaughter, Miss Daphne Bevington. However, I want you all to know Miss Bevington is unable to be here tonight."

His gaze met hers, his aged countenance a portrait of pride and love.

A murmur rippled through the room, and two hundred curious glances came her way. In that moment, Daphne's eyes filled with tears of happiness.

After a long pause, Wolverton continued, "That is because the woman you see before you tonight is now the Countess of Raikes." The volume of voices arose in the room, exclamations of surprise and congratulation. "I'd like to introduce you to her now, as well as to her new husband, Lord Raikes, whom she married this morning."

Suddenly, Cormack was there at her side. Lord and Lady Champdeer appeared nearby, their faces flushed and beaming.

Daphne's husband tucked her hand into the crook of his elbow and led her forward to join Wolverton and Fox. As they walked, he peered down at her with such bold and unconcealed admiration that Daphne could only blush from the intensity of it.

As they grew closer, Havering smiled and murmured to Cormack, "You know this dance was supposed to be mine. But I suppose I can't call you out over it now that you've married her. Congratulations to you both."

Daphne kissed Wolverton's cheek. "Thank you, Grandfather."

He nodded. "He loves you. That much is clear. Be happy, my dear. Your father would be so pleased."

He gestured to the orchestra, who launched into an elegant but lively waltz.

Cormack drew her into his arms, and smoothly guided her into the first turn. "I feel as if I'm dreaming."

"As do I," said Daphne. The room whirled about her, a magical night filled with family and friends. "But all this is real. You are my husband, and I am your wife. Which makes our lives, and our future together, better than any dream."

**This season takes its most scandalous
turn yet when Miss Clarissa Bevington
has a salacious secret all her own...**

Please turn this page
for a preview of

*Never Surrender
to a Scoundrel.*

Available in Winter 2015

Chapter One

"I can't remember ever being so happy," Clarissa Bevington exclaimed, looking about in flush-faced wonderment. Truly, she had never seen her grandfather's ballroom look more beautiful, nor felt any more special. She inhaled deeply, delighting in the heady scent of roses and delphinium.

At the far end of the ballroom, the head footman, Mr. Ollister, carefully lowered an enormous crystal punch bowl onto the tea board. The housekeeper, Mrs. Brightmore, perched at the top of a ladder, steadied by two housemaids, certain she'd glimpsed a sneaky bit of dust atop an archway that none of the rest of them had been able to see. The room had been thickly festooned in garlands, and profuse arrangements of pink and ivory flowers overflowed urns that had been placed before each of the massive Corinthian columns that lined the marble floor. Cook's voice could be heard shouting orders, all the way from the kitchens.

Clarissa Bevington grabbed Daphne, her older sister, by

the hands and together they spun in wide circles across the ballroom floor, blonde curls and skirts flying. At the ages of twenty and twenty-one, respectively, and a shade older than most London debutantes, they still sometimes delighted in being utterly silly.

"Just like when we were little girls," said Daphne, laughing. "Wishing we could go to one of mother's parties."

"Only now, we are without a doubt *mature ladies*, and won't be sent off to bed with our governess before the guests start to arrive."

Of course, it had already been a season to remember, with Daphne recently wed in a surprise turn of events to the dashing Earl of Raikes.

But tonight belonged to Clarissa, and the occasion of her debut ball. All her friends and family would be in attendance including her grandfather, the Duke of Wolverton, and her widowed mother, Lady Margaretta, who would be escorted by her new beau, Mr. Birch, whom they had all come to love. And of course there were her sisters: Sophia the Duchess of Claxton and her husband, His Grace, the duke, who excitedly awaited the birth of their first child. And Daphne and Lord Raikes, who had insisted on delaying their honeymoon until after tonight's grand event.

Her family, after years devastated by the deaths of her brother, Vinson, and then her father, had at last remembered how to be joyful again. Much of that had to do with the discovery of little Michael—Vinson's young son and now Wolverton's declared heir, who, without a living mother or father, had been welcomed into the family with boundless love and endless kisses.

His sudden appearance in their lives had been especially welcome in light of last month's disheartening disqualification of Mr. Kincraig as Wolverton's successor. Until then, Mr. Kincraig had been the earl's only hope for continuing his line, but the earl's investigators—the very same investigators who had presented Mr. Kincraig as a potential heir—had at last made sense of the reckless gambler's tangled lineage enough to prove he wasn't a relation after all. No one had seemed more relieved than Mr. Kincraig, which she supposed proved him to be no imposter or scoundrel. He had announced his intention to depart England by the end of the month to seek—and likely lose—his next great fortune (or two, or three!) abroad.

Daphne led her toward the stairs. "We'd best get upstairs to prepare, else our mother will come looking for us."

"You only want to see Cormack again."

"That too." She laughed, blushing. "But you know how Mother gets when we are late."

"Girls!" Clarissa mimicked, with her hands on her hips. "I know very well that you both have perfectly accurate timepieces—"

"—because Aunt Vivian gave each of you one for your last birthday," concluded Daphne, in the same familiar voice.

Mrs. Brightmore, having descended the ladder, cast them a gently reproving look.

Daphne laughed, and set off toward the doors.

Yet for a moment, Clarissa could only stand motionless, savoring the bittersweet immensity of the moment.

Daphne, her dear sister. Clarissa's heart squeezed tight with affection.

And their mother. How glad she was that Her Ladyship

had found a happy and welcome companion in Mr. Birch. *Her grandfather.* He doted on them all so much, and never once had she doubted his love. She would miss living here and seeing them every day.

Her life as she had come to know it would change very soon...though no one could know that. Not yet. That was because she carried a secret, close to her heart. The most *wonderful* secret. One she shared with the most eligible bachelor in London. Two weeks ago, Lord Devonby had asked her that most important question—and she deliriously and most happily had said yes. But he had wanted everything to be perfect for her and insisted that they wait until tonight at her ball, where he would very properly request an audience with her grandfather, and ask for her hand.

While at first she'd believed Devonby to be just another handsome face, consumed by the same youthful and sometimes empty pursuits as all young gentlemen of the *ton*, he'd revealed to her the sincere, magnanimous, and honorable man beneath. Once she knew the truth, there'd been no holding her heart back.

They'd kept their romance a secret, wanting to savor the unfolding feelings between them away from the curious eyes of the society and its gossips, but also for the simple romantic fun of doing so. How glad she was to have found someone with whom she could have fun. She was almost sorry to see their game end, one in which they'd stolen away for every secret moment and exchanged clandestine notes of the most intimate kind, but for a couple as deeply in love as they were, certainly all that would continue even after they were wed.

She and Daphne parted ways in the upstairs corridor,

with Daphne continuing on toward the chambers she shared with her new husband—only to rush back and throw her arms around Clarissa in a sisterly embrace.

"I'm so very proud to have you as my sister," she murmured. A moment later, she smiled radiantly, as she had done almost constantly since marrying Lord Raikes. Clarissa could only interpret her happiness as a sound endorsement of that venerable state. "It's your turn, my dear sister. Next time I see you, you'll be making your entrance on that grand staircase, just as you always dreamed when you were a girl."

One last squeeze, and she was gone—which was all for the best. Clarissa had never been very good at keeping secrets, and a moment more would have seen her blurting out the news of her impending engagement.

She had no wish to ruin tonight's wonderful surprise.

*   *   *

"I shall see you at Miss Bevington's ball tonight, then, Mr. Kincraig?" said his companion, Lord Havering, as they exited the doors of White's Club.

He flashed a rakish grin. "Any chance to reacquaint myself with Wolverton's liquor cabinet is a welcome opportunity indeed."

Fox studied him, as he drew on his gloves, one by one. "I suspect there's more to it than that."

Like him, "Fox," as he was called by those who knew him best, had no discernible family of his own, and had been thrown by circumstance into the midst of Wolverton's welcoming brood. After a period of understandable suspicion over whether he was plotting some sort of trickery against the earl and his family, Havering had warmed to him, and he to Havering.

"Perhaps so." He looked out over the busy street, crowded with carriages and hackneys, uncomfortable with revealing anything more. After all, it had taken him years to perfect the obscurement of his true thoughts and feelings. He wasn't about to start emoting now, here on the pavement, in front of God and Fox and everyone. He kept his manner and tone cool. "Whatever the case, I wouldn't miss it."

He wouldn't miss it. Though it would take a team of horses to pry the sentiment from his tongue, he'd grown fond of the old earl's family, even though he found the whole idea of a debut ball frivolous and silly. Soon, he would be gone from their lives, and he would likely never see any one of them again. Most especially Clarissa, whom one didn't have to be an intelligence agent in service of the Crown to observe that she had fallen head over heels in love with the annoyingly charming and well-connected Lord Devonby.

God, how he despised the fellow, and all his glorious noble perfection, for no good reason other than Clarissa adored him. No. Of course he *himself* did not love her, it's just that she could provoke him like no other by constantly fussing over him, and complaining of the way he tied his cravat, and by always looking at him so directly with her perceptive blue eyes--

What did it matter? He was leaving in a matter of days. Perhaps even tomorrow.

Damn it.

How thankful he was that it was time to say his good-byes.

With that, Dominick Arden Blackmer, who for the time being answered to the name of Mr. Kincraig, climbed into his carriage and settled back for what would be a brief ride to what had been his abode for the last year, where his scant belongings were packed and the house had been shut up and made ready for his departure.

Because it was time to leave. One did not become attached. Life only ever made sense when he was alone.

Where would tomorrow take him? Perhaps he would learn the answer tonight.

Just then, his carriage passed a chapel where a small group crowded the pavement, throwing rose petals high over the heads of a newly wedded couple. The sight momentarily transported him back in time, to another wedding. His own. But Tryphena was dead, for three years now. Even though he walked and lived and breathed, sometimes he believed he was as well.

The sight of a familiar face jerked him back to present. He flicked the curtain aside and peered out the window, instantly recognizing the groom as Lord Devonby, hand in hand with a slender, dark-haired young woman who held a bouquet. If there was any doubt in his mind what he observed in that moment, Devonby put it to rest by pressing an enthusiastic kiss upon his bride's lips.

His carriage moved on until he could see no more.

How...regretful. Did Miss Bevington know? Certainly not. It had been only yesterday afternoon when he'd observed that flirtatious glance between them, and the furtive touch of their hands behind the garden column.

No doubt the news would devastate her, and would douse the enchanting light that always seemed to reside in her lovely eyes. Because of that, he could take no pleasure, no satisfaction in what he'd seen. His fingers curled into his palms and he resisted the urge to order his driver to turn around so that he might confront the bastard directly, in front of his new bride and their families. Everyone. But it was not his place. He would be gone from all their lives— from *her* life—in a blink. So instead he held silent, and simmered.

In the confines of his temporary home, he shaved and dressed. He paced and waited. Though he was to have an audience with Wolverton this evening before the ball got underway, he had no wish to arrive too early. He didn't want to cross paths with Clarissa, because once she looked at him with her expressive blue eyes he'd be compelled to tell her what he had seen. Certainly she deserved to know, but telling her wasn't his place. He and Clarissa were not on those sort of terms, not like she and Havering, who was more like a brother to her.

Havering. There was his answer. Knowing Clarissa as long as he had, Fox would know how to best break the unfortunate news. Fox could comfort her, after Dominick was long gone. Calling the carriage around once again, he traveled directly to Wolverton's house, whereupon entering he observed from a distance a small army of confectioner's assistants in the ballroom setting up some sort of display of little cakes or meringues on a table, while at the center of the house workmen finished the installation of a god-awful pink carpet onto the grand staircase, pink being Clarissa's favorite color, and one that he had to concede always looked very pretty on her. The scent of flowers hung everywhere, so strong he fought the urge to sneeze.

Ah, there—Havering stood just around the corner,

speaking to the Duke of Claxton. He moved toward them, only to be intercepted by Mrs. Brightmore, who discreetly lifted a hand toward Wolverton's chambers.

"Ah." He paused midstep. "Now?"

"Indeed."

"It's early yet."

She winked. "Some of us have other duties to perform this evening, other than to saunter about in fancy clothes, drinking lemonade from a little crystal cup."

His gaze returned to Havering, but in the end he changed direction, taking the corridor to Wolverton's chambers, as he had so often done over the past year under the guise of being summoned, or more often *commanded* by the earl to do so. His role, after all, had been to play a gambler and a drunk. Someone consumed by his own addictions, but more importantly, inattentive to his surroundings. Though he'd played double duty as a bodyguard to Wolverton, his primary assignment had been to lure into the open the man or men who wanted Lord Wolverton, and his every living heir, dead. Lady Harwick and the young ladies hadn't been told, because the earl had no wish to frighten them, or burden them with as of yet unsubstantiated explanations of past tragedies.

Entering the anteroom, he joined his team. O'Connell, His Lordship's valet. Mr. Ollister, the first footman. And Mrs. Brightmore, the housekeeper, who stepped through a small doorway on the opposite side of the room, because it wouldn't have done for her to be seen walking down the corridor in his company.

"Reports?" asked Mrs. Brightmore, who briskly circled round to collect a sealed envelope from them each, which she quickly secured at the center of her corset. He had written out his final report the night before, having been made aware his next assignment could come any day.

"How is Wolverton today?" he asked O'Connell.

"Very well. He wishes to see you when we are through here."

Mr. Ollister straightened. "Let us finish our business, so we can all return to our posts." He looked to Dominick.

"As we all suspected, the Home Office has seen fit to revise the scope of our mission. Now that the earl has a true heir, your role, Blackmer, has been substantially compromised in that you are no longer the assassin's lure you were intended to be. Even though no attempts have been made against Wolverton's life, we will continue to secure the premises, and now also devote ourselves to protecting the child. Blackmer, while you could certainly remain on indefinitely as security, no one believes you would look very convincing in a nanny's cap—"

Everyone chuckled.

"As such, Home Office has seen fit to assign another agent to fulfill the nanny role, while you have received new orders." Bending, he extracted a folded square of parchment from his boot, which he handed over to Dominick.

Mrs. Brightmore said quietly, "I hope it's what you want."

"Indeed," murmured O'Connell.

They all knew his situation and that this small-scale assignment, for him, had been intended as punishment. As professional exile. Perhaps at last his superiors had forgiven him for Tryphena's death, though he would never forgive himself.

Breaking the seal, he opened his orders and read. A smile broke across his face, and he exhaled in happiness and relief. At last, the Home Office had seen fit to return him to international service.

"Very good." Mrs. Brightmore clasped her hands in front of her apron. "I'm so happy for you, Blackmer."

As required, he tossed his orders into the fire.

"As are we all," said Mr. Ollister, grinning. "But there is little time for celebration. Let us all return to our duties—that is, except for you, Blackmer. Enjoy your last evening in London before you are returned to the jaws of danger."

"Which, as we all know, is precisely where you wish to be," said O'Connell. "The earl is waiting."

After confirming his orders had burned to nothing, he continued on into the earl's private chambers.

Wolverton sat in his wheeled bath chair beside the window, dressed in his finest for the party. Below, carriages crowded the street and finely dressed guests lined the pavement, waiting their turn to enter the house.

"And so, it is time for us to say good-bye," he said.

Dominick approached the earl, and bowed. "Yes, my lord. I leave tomorrow."

"Very good, then." The old man smiled up at him, his eyes warm with admiration. "I know this assignment was not your first choice, and that you are eager to return to the more exciting realm of international espionage."

He nodded. "Spy games have always been my true calling."

"There was a time when I played a few of those games myself."

"So I have been told. You are quite the legend."

The earl chuckled, clearly delighted by the compliment. "Thank you. My only regret is if my actions somehow placed my family in any sort of danger."

"Yes, my lord, but we don't know that."

He nodded. "I just want you to know how very much I have appreciated your devotion to myself and my family. I thank the Lord every day your particular skills were not needed, but I must admit I slept more peacefully at night knowing you, along with O'Connell and Mr. Ollister, were there to protect us."

"Thank you for saying so, my lord."

"Godspeed."

* * *

"Stay just there, out of sight!" said Sophia, looking out over the gathered crowd of guests. "Mother will give the signal."

Clarissa stood at the top of the staircase, with her sisters and eight of her dearest friends, each of whom held wreaths covered in flowers. Well, six of her dearest friends, and two Aimsley sisters because her mother had quite insisted. They all clustered about her, in a happy crush.

"Everything is so lovely, Clarissa."

"We're having such a wonderful time."

"I can't wait until the dancing starts."

Daphne gestured. "Ladies, it's time."

Sophia quickly lined them up into the order they'd agreed upon. In the ballroom, the orchestra began to play. Each of the young ladies held her wreath and made her way toward the stairs, smiling down over an admiring crowd gone suddenly silent. The first two began their descent.

Clarissa asked Sophia, "Do you think the wreaths and the procession are too much?"

"Don't be silly. It's your night. Besides, I had twelve

attendants, in case you've forgotten, and they were all wearing those ridiculous ostrich plumes." She winked.

Clarissa moved to take her place on the landing, and the crowd murmured in admiration. Her mother and grandfather waited at the bottom of the stairs. There was His Grace, the Duke of Claxton, standing with Lord Raikes, and Mr. Kincraig. Oh, and Havering. But...

"I don't see Devonby," she murmured. She couldn't very well descend the stairs if her fiancé-to-be was not even in the room to see her. But her sisters urged her to follow her attendants down the steps and she complied. Again, her gaze swept the room. Had he been delayed? Why wasn't he here?

"Who did you say you were looking for?" said Daphne, from where she followed just behind.

"Did you say Lord Devonby?" said the eldest Aimsley sister, glancing over her shoulder. "Well, he won't be here, of course."

"Why not?" asked Clarissa.

The younger Aimsley turned and said, "He married Emily FitzKnightley this afternoon and they are already off on their honeymoon."

Clarissa's heart seized.

"That can't be true," she said, through numb lips. Her blood pounded in her ears, so hard she could hardly see or hear. "Wouldn't we all have known about it?"

"It came as a surprise to everyone, and they married by special license. We ought to know; we are her cousins and served as her bridesmaids."

"Clarissa, stop whispering. Straighten up and smile," Sophia murmured.

Clarissa did stop whispering. Indeed, she stopped everything, as a rush of dizziness swept over her. Devonby, married? The chandelier above the staircase seemed to twist and spin on its chain.

"I'm so sorry, I—" she murmured.

"Clarissa?" inquired Daphne.

The world pitched, turning upside down in a blur of muslin, feminine squeals of surprise, and pink.

* * *

Dominick read the Aimsley girl's lips, and saw Clarissa's face go white. Damn it. That she should find out the news of Devonby there on the stairs in front of everyone.

He watched, helpless and separated by a sea of people as Clarissa wavered. Then went limp.

He didn't think twice; he just moved, pushing through the crowd to where she lay amidst a tangle of flowers and feminine limbs. Gathering her up in his arms, he lifted her, sweeping her away, down the hall.

Lady Margaretta followed. "Clarissa!"

"Tell her...I'm fine," Clarissa pleaded against his neck, her voice thick and her words barely discernible.

"She is well, I believe," he called back. "She only fainted for a moment. From the excitement, I'm sure."

Her Ladyship nodded, and paused midstep with her hands raised. "I shall come straightaway after seeing to the other girls and ensuring that no one has been injured!"

He carried her into a small sitting room, where he deposited her—or attempted to deposit her—on a settee.

"Let go, Clarissa."

"No," she retorted.

She held even tighter to his neck, and sobbed into his

shirt. Knowing not what else to do, he simply sat with her there clinging to him. Trying very hard not to notice how soft and warm and perfect she felt, because that would serve absolutely no useful purpose.

Fox rushed in. "Is she all right?"

Thank God. He had no intention of being Clarissa's hero. That honor ought to belong to someone else. Someone permanent in her life.

"Take her please?" he asked, hands raised imploringly behind her back.

Fox took one step toward them, but just then Clarissa's sisters and their husbands arrived, instantly distracting him, and he drifted off to the side.

"Oh, Clarissa!" exclaimed Daphne, rushing toward them. "I'm so sorry."

Sophia did as well, touching a gentle hand to her sister's head. "Did you slip? Or did you faint?"

"Is she hurt?" inquired Claxton from the door.

"No, no, no," she cried, toward the wall, over his shoulder, refusing still to look at anyone. "I'm fine. Only embarrassed. I'm so stupid. How could I have been so stupid?"

"You're not stupid," assured Sophia. "And you mustn't be embarrassed. You're not the first debutante to faint at the moment of her debut. Remember Elizabeth Malloy? At least you didn't expose your bare bottom to two hundred people the way she did."

Lord Raikes murmured, "I must say, I'm sorry to have missed that."

Fox burst out in laughter, but clasped a hand over his mouth.

"Gentlemen!" Daphne rebuked.

Clarissa seized Dominick's neck tighter, and cried harder. "I am mortified! I just want to be alone."

Lady Margaretta entered the room and, after quickly assessing the situation, said, "I think what would be best is if everyone gave Clarissa a moment alone and returned to the ballroom. You can all help her by telling everyone she is well, that she only fainted and that she'll be returning to the party as soon as she is recovered."

Everyone left the room, her sisters throwing glances of concern over their shoulders on the way out.

"Are you all right here, Mr. Kincraig?" Her Ladyship asked, touching a comforting hand to Clarissa's back, who still snuffled against the front of his shirt. God, she'd made a handkerchief of him. No doubt his shirt was a mess, and he'd have to go immediately home after.

"I'm certain she would rather be with her mother."

"No." Clarissa shook her head vehemently, pressing her face to his neck. "Not yet. I have disappointed you, Mother, and everyone else!"

"Of course you haven't." Lady Margaretta bit her bottom lip and patted Clarissa's shoulder. She sighed and glanced toward the door. "I really must go and see about Wolverton. He must be very concerned."

He nodded. "And so I will…stay with Clarissa. If you promise to return. Quickly."

It seemed the appropriate thing to do.

"I'm afraid you don't have any other choice," she winked, despite still looking worried.

And in the next moment, they were alone.

"Oh, Mr. Kincraig, I'm so humiliated."

"It was that horrible pink carpet, wasn't it? You slipped on it, didn't you?"

"Oh, you horrible man." She shook her head, and drew away enough to glare at him through tearstained eyes. "You don't understand!"

"I think I do."

"You can't," she declared. "It's not just that I've fallen down a staircase in front of the whole of society, it's...it's..." A surge of new tears flooded her eyes.

He swallowed hard, feeling ill prepared to cope with such an intense display of female emotion. Forthrightness seemed the only way forward. "I know about Devonby getting married, and I know how you felt about him."

"How *could* you know? We never told anyone."

"The attraction between two people is not difficult to perceive, if one pays attention." He would leave it at that.

Her stared back at him. "You were paying attention?"

"Not on purpose."

Her eyes narrowed just a bit. There. When she looked at him like that, he felt like she saw straight through him.

"*Devonby.* The bastard!" he blurted, in an effort to throw her off. "He is a scoundrel of the lowest form," he declared, hoping to make her feel better. "Would you like me to call him out for a duel? You know how fond I am of spectacles, and I'd be happy to make one for you, on my way out of town."

"No!" she cried. "You can't tell anyone. *Anyone.*"

"He should be made to reckon—"

"*Swear it*, Mr. Kincraig," she insisted, twisting her hands in the front of his coat, her eyes suddenly wild. "You will tell no one."

Her vehemence startled him. "Your secret is safe with me."

"Good," she whispered, her shoulders suddenly slumping. "Because I must share another. If I don't, I fear I will explode."

Another secret? He did not like the sound of that. He half raised off the settee. "Perhaps I should get your mother? Or one of your sisters—"

She yanked him back down into place beside her.

"It must be you," she insisted, half choking on her words. "Someone who doesn't care a whit about me. Someone who can give me advice without the complication of a heart."

How she misjudged him. He almost felt stung. Oddly, he wasn't.

He could only suppose she'd written some letters to Devonby and now wanted them back or some other such nonsense. "What is it, Clarissa? What is this secret you have to tell me? Whatever it is, we can talk it out, and we can—"

He didn't get a chance to finish his sentence before she threw herself into his arms. "I'm pregnant, Mr. Kincraig. *Pregnant.* What do you suppose *we* shall do about that?"

He choked out a curse. Not because of what she'd told him, which indeed would be shocking enough—but because at that very moment he saw her mother standing in the door, white-faced with shock, having just pushed Wolverton inside.

"Clarissa? Mr . . . Kincraig?"

Clarissa twisted, still half sprawled on his lap, her arms a circle around his neck. "Oh, no." In the next moment, she scrambled closer to him, as if she could somehow disappear into him. Which only made the situation look worse.

Wolverton wrested control of the chair, turning the wheels so that he positioned himself just two feet away. Glaring at Dominick, he thundered, "I trusted you with my life. All of our lives. But clearly, I ought not to have trusted you with *her*."

Lady Sophia has long been estranged
from her husband, Vane Barwick,
Duke of Claxton.

Yet a shocking encounter with him—
and a single touch—is all it takes to
reawaken her passion for him…

Please turn this page
for a preview of

Never Desire a Duke,

the first in Lily Dalton's
One Scandalous Season series.

Available now.

Chapter One

"The scent of gingerbread in the air!" exclaimed Sir Keyes, his aged blue eyes sparkling with mischief. Winter wind swept through open doors behind him, carrying the sound of carriages from the street. "And there's mistletoe to be had from the peddler's stall on the corner."

Though his pantaloons drooped off his slight frame to an almost comical degree, the military orders and decorations emblazoned across his chest attested to a life of valor years before. Leaning heavily on his cane, the old man produced a knotty green cluster from behind his back, strung from a red ribbon, and held it aloft between himself and Sophia.

"Such happy delights can mean only one thing." He grinned roguishly—or as roguishly as a man of his advanced years could manage. "It is once again the most magical time of year."

He tapped his gloved finger against his rosy cheek with expectant delight.

"Indeed!" The diminutive Dowager Countess of Dundalk stepped between them, smiling up from beneath a fur-trimmed turban. She swatted the mistletoe, sending the sphere swinging to and fro. "The time of year when old men resort to silly provincial traditions to coax kisses from ladies young enough to be their granddaughters."

At the side of her turban a diamond aigrette held several large purple feathers. The plumes bobbed wildly as she spoke. "Well, it *is* almost Christmastide." Sophia winked at Sir Keyes, and with a gentle hand to his shoulder, she warmly bussed his cheek. "I'm so glad you've come."

A widower of two years, he had recently begun accompanying Lady Dundalk about town, something that made Sophia exceedingly happy, since both had long been dear to her heart.

Sir Keyes plucked a white berry from the cluster, glowing with satisfaction at having claimed his holiday kiss.

"I see that only a handful remain," Sophia observed. "Best use them wisely."

His eyebrows rose up on his forehead, as white and unruly as uncombed wool. "I shall have to find your sisters, then, and posthaste."

"Libertine!" muttered the dowager countess, with a fond roll of her eyes.

Behind them, two footmen with holly sprigs adorning their coat buttonholes secured the doors. Another presented a silver tray to Sir Keyes, upon which he deposited the price of Sophia's kiss and proceeded toward the ballroom, the mistletoe cluster swinging from the lions' head handle of his cane. Together, Sophia and the dowager countess followed arm in arm, through columns entwined in greenery, toward the sounds of music and voices raised in jollity.

With Parliament having recessed mid-December for Christmas, the districts of St. James's, Mayfair, and Piccadilly were largely deserted by that fashionable portion of London's population oft defined as the *ton*. Like most of their peers, Sophia's family's Christmases were usually spent in the country, but her grandfather's recent frailties had precluded any travel. So his immediate family, consisting of a devoted daughter-in-law and three granddaughters, had resolved to spend the season in London.

But today was Lord Wolverton's eighty-seventh birthday, and by Sophia's tally, no fewer than two hundred of the elusive *ton* had crept out from the proverbial winter woodwork to wish her grandfather well. By all accounts, the party was a success.

In the ballroom, candlelight reflected off the crystal teardrops of chandeliers high above their heads, as well as the numerous candelabras and lusters positioned about the room, creating beauty in everything its golden glow touched. The fragrance of fresh-cut laurel and fir, brought in from the country just that afternoon, mingled pleasantly with the perfume of the hothouse gardenias, tuberose, and stephanotis arranged in Chinese vases about the room.

Though there would be no dancing tonight, a piano quintet provided an elegant musical accompaniment to the hum of laughter and conversation.

"Lovely!" declared Lady Dundalk. "Your mother told me you planned everything, to the last detail."

"I'm pleased by how splendidly everything has turned out." The dowager countess slipped an arm around Sophia's shoulders and squeezed with affection. "The only thing missing, of course, is the Duke of Claxton."

The warm smile on Sophia's lips froze like ice, and it

felt as if the walls of the room suddenly converged at the mere mention of her husband. It didn't seem to matter how long he had been away; her emotions were still so raw.

Lady Dundalk peered up at her, concern in her eyes. "I know you wish the duke could be here tonight, and certainly for Christmas. No word on when our esteemed diplomat will return to England?"

Sophia shook her head, hoping the woman would perceive none of the heartache she feared was written all over her face. "Perhaps in the spring."

A vague response at best, but the truth was she did not know when Claxton would return. His infrequent, impersonal correspondence made no such predictions, and she had not lowered herself to ask.

They came to stand near the fire, where a delicious heat warmed the air.

"Eighty-seven years old?" bellowed Sir Keyes. "Upon my word, Wolverton, you can't be a day over seventy, else that would make me—" Lifting a hand, he counted through its knobby fingers, grinning. "Older than dirt!"

"We *are* older than dirt, and thankful to be so." Her grandfather beamed up from where he sat in his bath chair, his cheeks pink from excitement. His party had been a surprise for the most part, with him believing until just an hour ago the event would be only a small family affair. He appeared truly astounded and deeply touched. "Thank you all for coming."

Small, gaily beribboned parcels of Virginian tobacco, chocolate, and his favorite souchong tea lay upon his lap. Sophia gathered them and placed them beneath the lowest boughs of the potted tabletop yew behind them, one that would remain unadorned until Christmas Eve, when the

NEVER DESIRE A DUKE   351

family would gather to decorate the tree in the custom of her late grandmother's German forebears.

Her family. Their worried glances and gentle questions let her know they were aware that her marriage had become strained. But she loved them so much! Which was why she'd shielded them from the full magnitude of the truth—the truth being that when Claxton had accepted his foreign appointment in May, he had all but abandoned her and their marriage. The man she'd once loved to distraction had become nothing more than a cold and distant stranger.

But for Sophia, Christmas had always been a time of self-contemplation, and the New Year, a time for renewal. Like so many others, she made a habit of making resolutions. By nature, she craved happiness, and if she could not have happiness with Claxton, she would have it some other way.

She had given herself until the New Year to suitably resolve her marital difficulties. The day after Christmas she would go to Camellia House, located just across the Thames in the small village of Lacenfleet, and sequester herself away from curious eyes and the opinions of her family, so that she alone could pen the necessary letter.

She was going to ask Claxton for a legal separation. Then he could go on living his life just as he pleased, with all the freedoms and indulgences he clearly desired. But she wanted something in return—a baby—and even if that meant joining him for a time in Vienna, she intended to have her way.

Just the thought of seeing Claxton again sent her spiraling into an exquisitely painful sort of misery. She had no wish to see him—and yet he never left her thoughts.

No doubt her presence would throw the private life His

Grace had been living into chaos, and she would find herself an unwanted outsider. No doubt he had a mistress—or two—as so many husbands abroad did. Even now, the merest fleeting thought of him in the arms of another woman made her stomach clench. He had betrayed her so appallingly that she could hardly imagine allowing him to touch her again. But a temporary return to intimacies with her estranged husband was the only way she could have the child she so desperately wanted.

Sophia bent to adjust the green tartan blanket over Wolverton's legs, ensuring that His Lordship would be protected not only from any chill but also the bump and jostle of the throng gathered about him.

"May I bring you something, Grandfather? Perhaps some punch?"

His blue eyes brightened.

"Yes, dear." He winked and gestured for her to come closer. When she complied, he lowered his voice. "With a dash of my favorite maraschino added, if you please, in honor of the occasion. Only don't tell your mother. You know just as well as I that she and my physician are in collusion to deprive me of all the joys of life."

Sophia knew he didn't believe any such thing, but still, it was great fun to continue the conspiratorial banter between them. Each moment with him, she knew, was precious. His joy this evening would be a memory she would always treasure.

"I'd be honored to keep your secret, my lord," Sophia said, pressing a kiss to his cheek.

"What secret?" Lady Harwick, Sophia's dark-haired mother, approached from behind.

A picture of well-bred elegance, Margaretta conveyed

warmth and good humor in every glance and gesture. Tonight she wore violet silk, one of the few colors she had allowed into her wardrobe since the tragic loss of her son, Vinson, at sea four years ago—followed all too soon by the death of Sophia's father, the direct heir to the Wolverton title.

"If we told you, then it wouldn't be a secret," Sophia answered jovially, sidestepping her. "His lordship has requested a glass of punch, and since I'm his undisputed favorite, at least for this evening, I will fetch it for him."

Wolverton winked at Sophia. "I shall have the secret pried out of him before you return." With that, Margaretta bent to straighten the same portion of Lord Wolverton's blanket her daughter had straightened only moments before.

Still a beautiful, vibrant woman, Margaretta drew the gazes of a number of the more mature gentlemen in the room. Not for the first time, Sophia wondered if her mother might entertain the idea of marrying again.

Sophia crossed the floor to the punch bowl, pausing several times to speak to friends and acquaintances along the way. Though most of the guests were older friends of Lord Wolverton, the presence of Sophia's pretty younger sisters, Daphne and Clarissa, had assured the attendance of numerous ladies and gentlemen from the younger set. Her fair-haired siblings, born just a year apart and assumed by many to be twins, would make their debut in the upcoming season. That is, if favored suitors did not snatch them off the market before Easter.

At the punch bowl, Sophia dipped the ladle and filled a crystal cup. With the ladle's return to the bowl, another hand retrieved it—a gloved hand upon which glimmered an enormous sapphire ring.

"Your Grace?" a woman's voice inquired.

Sophia looked up into a beautiful, heart-shaped face, framed by stylish blonde curls, one she instantly recognized but did not recall greeting in the reception line. The gown worn by the young woman, fashioned of luxurious peacock-blue silk and trimmed with gold and scarlet cording, displayed her generous décolletage to a degree one would not normally choose for the occasion of an off-season birthday party for an eighty-seven-year-old lord.

"Good evening, Lady..."

"Meltenbourne," the young woman supplied, with a delicate laugh. "You might recall me as Annabelle Ellesmere? We debuted the same season."

Yes, of course. Annabelle, Lady Meltenbourne, née Ellesmere. Voluptuous, lush, and ambitious, she had once carried quite the flaming torch for Claxton, and upon learning of the duke's betrothal to Sophia, she had not been shy about expressing her displeasure to the entire *ton* over not being chosen as his duchess. Not long after, Annabelle had married a very rich but very old earl.

"Such a lovely party." The countess sidled around the table to stand beside her, so close Sophia could smell her exotic perfume, a distinctive fragrance of ripe fruit and oriental spice. "Your grandfather must be a wonderful man to be so resoundingly adored."

"Thank you, Lady Meltenbourne. Indeed, he is."

Good breeding prevented Sophia from asking Annabelle why she was present at the party at all. She had addressed each invitation herself, and without a doubt, Lord and Lady Meltenbourne had not been on the guest list.

"I don't believe I've been introduced to Lord Melten-

NEVER DESIRE A DUKE 355

bourne." Sophia perused the room, but saw no more unfamiliar faces.

"Perhaps another time," the countess answered vaguely, offering nothing more but a shrug. Plucking a red sugar drop from a candy dish, she gazed adoringly upon the confection and giggled. "I shouldn't give in to such temptations, but I admit to being a shamefully impulsive woman." She pushed the sweet into her mouth and reacted with an almost sensual ecstasy, closing her eyes and smiling. "Mmmmm."

Meanwhile, a gentleman had approached to refill his punch glass and gaped at the countess as she savored the sugar drop, and in doing so, he missed his cup altogether. Punch splashed over his hand and onto the table. Lady Meltenbourne selected another sweet from the dish, oblivious to his response. Or perhaps not. Within moments, servants appeared to tidy the mess and the red-faced fellow rushed away.

Sophia let out a slow, calming breath and smothered her first instinct, which was to order the countess to *spit out the sugar drop* and immediately quit the party. After all, time had passed. They had all matured. Christmas was a time for forgiveness. For bygones to be bygones.

Besides, London in winter could be rather dreary. This one in particular had been uncommonly foggy and cold. Perhaps Annabelle simply sought human companionship and had come along with another guest. Sophia certainly understood loneliness. Whatever the reason for the woman's attendance, her presence was of no real concern. Lady Meltenbourne and her now candy-sugared lips were just as welcome tonight as anyone else. The party would be over soon, and Sophia wished to spend the remainder with her grandfather.

"Well, it was lovely seeing you again, but I've promised this glass of punch to our guest of honor. Enjoy your evening."

Sophia turned, but a sudden hand to her arm stayed her.

"What of Claxton?" the countess blurted.

The punch sloshed. Instinctively Sophia extended the glass far from her body, to prevent the liquid from spilling down her skirts, but inside her head, the intimate familiarity with which Lady Annabelle spoke her husband's name tolled like an inharmonious bell.

"Pardon me?" She glanced sharply at the hand on her arm. "What did you say?"

Annabelle, wide-eyed and smiling, snatched her hand away, clasping it against the pale globe of her breast. "Will His Grace make an appearance here tonight?"

Sophia had suffered much during her marriage, but this affront—at her grandfather's party—was too much.

Good breeding tempered her response. She'd been raised a lady. As a girl, she'd learned her lessons and conducted herself with perfect grace and honor. As a young woman, she'd maneuvered the dangerous waters of her first season, where a single misstep could ruin her prospects of a respectable future. She had made her family and herself proud.

Sophia refused to succumb to the impulse of rage. Instead she summoned every bit of her self-control and, with the greatest of efforts, forbade herself from flinging the glass and its scarlet contents against the front of the woman's gown.

With her gaze fixed directly on Lady Meltenbourne, she answered calmly. "I would assume not."

The countess's smile transformed into what was most

certainly a false moue of sympathy. "Oh, dear. You *do* know he's in town, don't you, Your Grace?"

Sophia's vision went black. Claxton in London? Could that be true? If he had returned without even the courtesy of sending word—

A tremor of anger shot down her spine, but with great effort she maintained her outward calm. However, that calm withered in the face of Lady Meltenbourne's blatant satisfaction. Her bright eyes and parted, half-smiling lips proclaimed the malicious intent behind her words, negating any obligation by Sophia for a decorous response. Yet before she could present the countess with a dismissive view of her train, the woman, in a hiss of silk, flounced into the crowd.

Only to be replaced by Sophia's sisters, who fell upon her like street thieves, spiriting her into the deeper shadows of a nearby corner. Unlike Sophia, who could wear the more dramatically hued Geneva velvet as a married woman, Daphne and Clarissa wore diaphanous, long-sleeved white muslin trimmed with lace and ribbon.

"Who invited that woman?" Daphne, the eldest of the two, demanded.

Sophia answered, "She wasn't invited."

"Did you see her *bosoms*?" Clarissa marveled.

"How could you not?" Daphne said. "They are enormous, like cannonballs. It's indecent. Everyone is staring, even Clarissa and I. We simply couldn't help ourselves."

"That dress! It's beyond fashion," Clarissa gritted. "It's the dead of winter. Isn't she cold? She might as well have worn nothing at all."

"*Daphne*," Sophia warned. "*Clarissa*."

Daphne's eyes narrowed. "What exactly did she say to you?"

Sophia banished all emotion from her voice. "Nothing of import."

"That's not true," Clarissa retorted. She leaned close and hissed, "She asked you if Claxton would be in attendance tonight."

Stung at hearing her latest shame spoken aloud, Sophia responded more sharply than intended. "If you heard her ask me about Claxton, then why did you ask me what she said?"

Her hands trembled so greatly that she could no longer hold the punch glass without fear of spilling its contents. She deposited the glass on the nearby butler's tray. Within seconds, a servant appeared and whisked it away.

Clarissa's nostrils flared. "I didn't hear her. Not exactly. It's just that she's—"

"Clarissa!" Daphne interjected sharply, silencing whatever revelation her sister had intended to share.

"No, you must tell me," Sophia demanded. "Lady Meltenbourne has what?"

Clarissa glared at Daphne. "She deserves to know."

Daphne, clearly miserable, nodded in assent. "Very well."

Clarissa uttered, "She's already asked the question of nearly everyone else in the room."

Despite the chill in the air, heat rose into Sophia's cheeks, along with a dizzying pressure inside her head. The conversation between herself and Lady Meltenbourne had been shocking enough. With Clarissa's revelation, Sophia was left nothing short of humiliated. She'd tried so desperately to keep rumors of Claxton's indiscretions from her family so as not to complicate any possible future reconciliation, but now her secrets were spilling out on the ballroom floor for anyone's ears to hear.

"Trollop," whispered Daphne. "It's none of her concern where Claxton is. It is only your concern, Sophia. And *our* concern as well, of course, because we are your sisters. Someone should tell her so." Though her sister had been blessed with the face of an angel, a distinctly devilish glint gleamed in her blue eyes. "Do you wish for me to be the one to say it? Please say yes, because I'm aching to—"

"Erase that smug look from her face," interjected Clarissa, fists clenched at her sides, looking very much the female pugilist.

"You'll do nothing of the sort," Sophia answered vehemently. "You'll conduct yourselves as ladies, not as ruffians off the street. This is my private affair. Mine and Claxton's. Do you understand? Do not mention any of what has occurred to Mother, and especially not to our grandfather. I won't have you ruining his birthday or Christmas."

"Understood," they answered in unison. Her sisters' dual gazes offered sympathy, and worse—pity.

Though Sophia would readily offer the same to any woman in her circumstances, she had no wish to be the recipient of such unfortunate sentiments. The whole ugly incident further proved the insupportability of her marriage and her husband's tendency to stray. Though Lady Meltenbourne's presence stung, it made Sophia only more certain that Claxton would agree to her terms. Certainly he would prefer to have his freedom—and he would have it, just as soon as he gave her a child. Seventeen months ago when she spoke her vows, she'd been naïve. She'd had such big dreams of a life with Claxton and had given her heart completely, only to have it thrown back in her face when she needed him the most. Claxton would never be a husband in the loyal, devoted sense of the word. He would never love her completely, the way she needed to be loved.

Admittedly, in the beginning, that aloofness—his very mysteriousness—had captivated her. The year of her debut, the duke had appeared in London out of nowhere, newly possessed of an ancient title. His rare appearances at balls were cause for delirium among the ranks of the hopeful young misses and their mammas.

Then—oh, then—she'd craved his brooding silences, believing with a certainty that once they married, Claxton would give her his trust. He would give her his heart.

For a time, she'd believed that he had. She closed her eyes against a dizzying rush of memories. *His smile. His laughter. Skin. Mouths. Heat. Completion.*

It had been enough. At least she thought it had been.

"Well?" said Daphne.

"Well, what?"

"Will Claxton make an appearance tonight?"

"I don't know," whispered Sophia.

Clarissa sighed. "Lord Tunsley told me he saw Claxton at White's this afternoon, with Lord Haden and Mr. Grisham."

Sophia nodded mutely. So it was confirmed. After seven months abroad, her husband had returned to London, and everyone seemed to know but her. The revelation left her numb and sadder than she expected. She ought to be angry—*no!*—furious at being treated with such disregard. Either that or she ought to do like so many other wives of the *ton* and forget the injustice of it all in the arms of a lover. She'd certainly had the opportunity.

Just then her gaze met that of a tall gentleman who stood

near the fireplace, staring at her intently over the heads of the three animatedly gesturing Aimsley sisters. Lord Havering, or "Fox" as he had been known in the informal environs of their country childhood, always teased that she ought to have waited for him—and more than once had implied that he still waited for her.

With a tilt of his blond head, he mouthed: *Are you well?*

Of course, Lady Meltenbourne's indiscreet inquiries about Claxton would not have escaped Fox's hearing. No doubt the gossipy Aimsley sisters were dissecting the particulars at this very moment. Sophia flushed in mortification, but at the same time was exceedingly grateful Fox cared for her feelings at all. It was more than she could say for her own husband.

Yet she had no heart for adultery. To Fox she responded with a nod and a polite smile, and returned her attention to her sisters. While she held no illusions about the pleasure-seeking society in which she lived, she'd grown up in the household of happily married parents who loved each other deeply. Magnificently. Had she been wrong to believe she deserved nothing short of the same?

Clarissa touched her arm and inquired softly, "Is it true, Sophia, what everyone is saying, that you and Claxton are officially estranged?"

In that moment, the candlelight flickered. A rush of frigid air pushed through the room, as if the front doors of the house had been thrown open. The chill assaulted her bare skin, and the hairs on the back of her neck stood on end. All conversation in the ballroom grew hushed, but a silent, indefinable energy exploded exponentially. Both pairs of her sisters' eyes fixed at the same point over her shoulders.

"Oh, my," whispered Daphne.

Clarissa's face lost its color. "Sophia—"

She looked over her shoulder. In that moment, her gaze locked with the bold, blue-eyed stare of a darkly handsome stranger.

Only, of course, he wasn't a stranger, not in the truest sense of the world. But he might as well have been. It was Claxton.

Her heart swelled with a thousand memories of him, only to subside, just as quickly, into frigid calm. Without hesitation, she responded as her good breeding required. She crossed the marble floor, aware that all eyes in the room were trained on her, and with a kiss welcomed her faithless husband home.

THE DISH

Where Authors Give You the Inside Scoop

♥ ♥ ♥ ♥ ♥ ♥ ♥ ♥ ♥ ♥ ♥ ♥ ♥ ♥ ♥

From the desk of Lily Dalton

Dear Reader,

Some people are heroic by nature. They act to help others without thinking. Sometimes at the expense of their own safety. Sometimes without ever considering the consequences. That's just who they are. Especially when it's a friend in need.

We associate these traits with soldiers who risk their lives on a dangerous battlefield to save a fallen comrade. Not because it's their job, but because it's their brother. Or a parent who runs into a busy street to save a child who's wandered into the path of an oncoming car. Or an ocean life activist who places himself in a tiny boat between a whale and the harpoons of a whaling ship.

Is it so hard to believe that Daphne Bevington, a London debutante and the earl of Wolverton's granddaughter, could be such a hero? When her dearest friend, Kate, needs her help, she does what's necessary to save her. In her mind, no other choice will do. After all, she knows without a doubt that Kate would do the same for her if she needed help. It doesn't matter one fig to her that their circumstances are disparate, that Kate is her lady's maid.

But Daphne finds herself in over her head. In a moment, everything falls apart, throwing not only her reputation and her future into doubt, but her life into danger. Yet in that moment when all seems hopelessly lost...another hero comes out of nowhere and saves her. A mysterious stranger who acts without thinking, at the expense of his own safety, without considering the consequences. A hero on a quest of his own. A man she will never see again...

Only, of course...she does. And he's not at all the hero she remembers him to be.

Or is he? I hope you will enjoy reading NEVER ENTICE AN EARL and finding out.

Best wishes, and happy reading!

Lily Dalton

LilyDalton.com
Twitter @LilyDalton
Facebook.com/LilyDaltonAuthor

♥   ♥   ♥   ♥

From the desk of Shelley Coriell

Dear Reader,

Story ideas come from everywhere. Snippets of conversation. Dreams. The hunky guy at the office supply store with eyes the color of faded denim. THE BROKEN, the first book in my new romantic suspense series, The Apostles, was born and bred as I sat at the bedside of my dying father.

In 2007 my dad, who lived on a mountain in northern Nevada, checked himself into his small town's hospital after having what appeared to be a stroke. "A mild one," he assured the family. "Nothing to get worked up about." That afternoon, this independent, strong-willed man (aka stubborn and borderline cantankerous) checked himself out of the hospital. The next day he hopped on his quad and accidentally drove off the side of his beloved mountain. The ATV landed on him, crushing his chest, breaking ribs, and collapsing a lung.

The hospital staff told us they could do nothing for him, that he would die. Refusing to accept the prognosis, we had him Life-Flighted to Salt Lake City. After a touch-and-go forty-eight hours, he pulled through, and that's when we learned the full extent of his injuries.

He'd had *multiple* strokes. The not-so-mild kind. The kind that meant he, at age sixty-three, would be forever dependent on others. His spirit was broken.

For the next week, the family gathered at the hospital. My sister, the oldest and the family nurturer, massaged his feet and swabbed his mouth. My brother, Mr. Finance Guy, talked with insurance types and made arrangements for post-release therapy. The quiet, bookish middle child, I had little to offer but prayers. I'd never felt so helpless.

As my dad's health improved, his spirits worsened. He was mad at his body, mad at the world. After a particularly difficult morning, he told us he wished he'd died on that mountain. A horrible, heavy silence followed. Which is when I decided to use the one thing I did have.

I dragged the chair in his hospital room—you know the kind, the heavy, wooden contraption that folds out into a bed—to his bedside and took out the notebook I carry everywhere.

"You know, Dad," I said. "I've been tinkering with this story idea. Can I bounce some stuff off you?"

Silence.

"I have this heroine. A news broadcaster who gets stabbed by a serial killer. She's scarred, physically and emotionally."

More silence.

"And I have a Good Guy. Don't know much about him, but he also has a past that left him scarred. He carries a gun. Maybe an FBI badge." That's it. Two hazy characters hanging out in the back of my brain.

Dad turned toward the window.

"The scarred journalist ends up working as an aide to an old man who lives on a mountain," I continued on the fly. "Oh-oh! The old guy is blind and can't see her scars. His name is...Smokey Joe, and like everyone else in this story, he's a little broken."

Dad glared. I saw it. He wanted me to see it.

"And, you know what, Dad? Smokey Joe can be a real pain in the ass."

My father's lips twitched. He tried not to smile, but I saw that, too.

I opened my notebook. "So tell me about Smokey Joe. Tell me about his mountain. Tell me about his *story*."

For the next two hours, Dad and I talked about an old man on a mountain and brainstormed the book that eventually became THE BROKEN, the story of Kate Johnson, an on-the-run broadcast journalist whose broken past holds the secret to catching a serial killer, and Hayden Reed, the tenacious FBI profiler who sees past her scars and vows to find a way into her head, but to his surprise, heads straight for her heart.

"Hey, Sissy," Dad said as I tucked away my notebook after what became the first of many Apostle brainstorming sessions. "Smokey Joe knows how to use C-4. We need to have a scene where he blows something up."

And "we" did.

So with a boom from old Smokey Joe, I'm thrilled to introduce you to Kate Johnson, Hayden Reed, and the Apostles, an elite group of FBI agents who aren't afraid to work outside the box and, at times, outside the law. FBI legend Parker Lord on his team: "Apostles? There's nothing holy about us. We're a little maverick and a lot broken, but in the end we get justice right."

Joy & Peace!

Shelley Coriell

■ ■ ♥ ♥ ♥ ■ ■   ■   ■   ♥

From the desk of Hope Ramsay

Dear Reader,

Jane Eyre may have been the first romance novel I ever read. I know it made an enormous impression on me when I was in seventh grade and it undoubtedly turned me into an avid reader. I simply got lost in the love story between Jane Eyre and Edward Fairfax Rochester.

In other words, I fell in love with Rochester when I was thirteen, and I've never gotten over it. I re-read *Jane Eyre* every year or so, and I have every screen adaptation ever made of the book. (The BBC version is the best by far, even if they took liberties with the story.)

So it was only a matter of time before I tried to write a hero like Rochester. You know the kind: brooding, passionate, tortured... (sigh). Enter Gabriel Raintree, the hero of INN AT LAST CHANCE. He's got all the classic traits of the gothic hero.

His heroine is Jennifer Carpenter, a plucky and self-reliant former schoolteacher turned innkeeper who is exactly the kind of no-nonsense woman Gabe needs. (Does this sound vaguely familiar?)

In all fairness, I should point out that I substituted the swamps of South Carolina for the moors of England and a bed and breakfast for Thornfield Hall. I also have an inordinate number of busybodies and matchmakers popping in and out for comic relief. But it is fair to say that I borrowed a few things from Charlotte Brontë, and I had such fun doing it.

I hope you enjoy INN AT LAST CHANCE. It's a contemporary, gothic-inspired tale involving a brooding hero, a plucky heroine, a haunted house, and a secret that's been kept for years.

Hope Ramsay

♥ ♥ ♥ ♥ ♥ ♥ ♥ ♥ ♥ ♥ ♥ ♥ ♥ ♥ ♥

From the desk of Molly Cannon

Dear Reader,

Weddings! I love them. The ceremony, the traditions, the romance, the flowers, the music, and of course the food. Face it. I embrace anything when cake is involved. When I got married many moons ago, there was a short ceremony and then cake and punch were served in the next room. That was it. Simple and easy and really lovely. But possibilities for weddings have expanded since then.

In FLIRTING WITH FOREVER, Irene Cornwell decides to become a wedding planner, and she has to meet the challenge of giving brides what they want within their budget. And it can be a challenge! I have planned a couple of weddings, and it was a lot of work, but it was also a whole lot of fun. Finding the venue, booking the caterer, deciding on the decorating theme. It is so satisfying to watch a million details come together to launch the happy couple into their new life together.

In one wedding I planned we opted for using mismatched dishes found at thrift stores on the buffet table. We found a bride selling tablecloths from her wedding and used different swaths of cloth as overlays. We made a canopy for the dance floor using pickle buckets and PFC pipe covered in vines and flowers, and then strung it with lights. We spray-painted cheap glass vases and filled them with flowers to match the color palette. And then, as Irene discovered, the hardest part is cleaning up after the celebration is over. But I wouldn't trade the experience for anything.

Another important theme in FLIRTING WITH FOREVER is second-chance love. My heart gets all aflutter when I think about true love emerging victorious after years of separation, heartbreak, and misunderstanding. Irene and Theo fell in love as teenagers, but it didn't last. Now older and wiser they reunite and fall in love all over again. Sigh.

I hope you'll join Irene and Theo on their journey. I promise it's even better the second time around.

Happy Reading!

Molly Cannon

Mollycannon.com
Twitter @CannonMolly
Facebook.com

♥   ♥   ♥

From the desk of Laura London

Dear Reader,

The spark to write THE WINDFLOWER came when Sharon read a three-hundred-year-old list of pirates who were executed by hanging. The majority of the pirates were teens, some as young as fourteen. Sharon felt so sad about these young lives cut short that it made her want to write a book to give the young pirates a happier ending.

For my part, I had much enjoyed the tales of Robert Lewis Stevenson as a boy. I had spent many happy hours playing the pirate with my cousins using wooden swords, cardboard hats, and rubber band guns.

Sharon and I threw ourselves into writing THE WIND-FLOWER with the full force of our creative absorption. We were young and in love, and existed in our imaginations on a pirate ship. We are proud that we created a novel that is in print on its thirty-year anniversary and has been printed in multiple languages around the world.

Fondly yours,

Sharon
&
Tom Curtis

Writing as Laura London

♥ ♥   ♥ ♥   ♥ ♥   ♥ ♥   ♥ ♥

From the desk of
Sue-Ellen Welfonder

Dear Reader,

At a recent gathering, someone asked about my upcoming releases. I revealed that I'd just launched a new Scottish medieval series, Scandalous Scots, with an e-novella, *Once Upon a Highland Christmas*, and that TO LOVE A HIGHLANDER would soon follow.

As happens so often, this person asked why I set my books in Scotland. My first reaction to this question is always to come back with, "Where else?" To me, there is nowhere else.

Sorley, the hero of TO LOVE A HIGHLANDER, would agree. Where better to celebrate romance than a land famed for men as fierce and wild as the soaring, mist-drenched hills that bred them? A place where the women are prized for their strength and beauty, the fiery passion known to heat a man's blood on cold, dark nights when chill winds raced through the glens? No land is more awe-inspiring, no people more proud. Scots have a powerful bond with their land. Haven't they fought for it for centuries? Kept their heathery hills always in their hearts, yearning for home when exiled, the distance of oceans and time unable to quench the pull to return?

That's a perfect blend for romance.

Sorley has such a bond with his homeland. Since he

was a lad, he's been drawn to the Highlands. Longing for wild places of rugged, wind-blown heights and high moors where the heather rolls on forever, so glorious it hurt the eyes to behold such grandeur. But Sorley's attachment to the Highlands also annoys him and poses one of his greatest problems. He suspects his father might have also been a Highlander—a ruthless, cold-hearted chieftain, to be exact. He doesn't know for sure because he's a bastard, raised at Stirling's glittering royal court.

In TO LOVE A HIGHLANDER, Sorley discovers the truth of his birth. Making Sorley unaware of his birthright as a Highlander was a twist I've always wanted to explore. I'm fascinated by how many people love Scotland and burn to go there, many drawn back because their ancestors were Scottish. I love that centuries and even thousands of miles can't touch the powerful pull Scotland exerts on its own.

Sorley's heritage explains a lot, for he's also a notorious rogue, a master of seduction. His prowess in bed is legend and he ignites passion in all the women he meets. Only one has ever shunned him. She's Mirabelle MacLaren and when she returns to his life, appearing in his bedchamber with an outrageous request, he's torn.

Mirabelle wants him to scandalize her reputation.

He'd love to oblige, especially as doing so will destroy his enemy.

But touching Mirabelle will rip open scars best left alone. Unfortunately, Sorley can't resist Mirabelle. Together, they learn that when the heart warms, all things are possible. Yet there's always a price. Theirs will be surrendering everything they've ever believed in and accepting that true love does indeed heal all wounds.

I hope you enjoy reading TO LOVE A HIGHLANDER!
I know I loved unraveling Sorley and Mirabelle's story.

Highland Blessings!

Sue-Ellen Welfonder

www.welfonder.com